# ASCENSION

## BOOK TWO IN THE DOMINION SERIES

## S. E. LUND

ACADIAN PUBLISHING LIMITED

# S. E. LUND'S NEWSLETTER

Sign up for S. E. Lund's newsletter and gain access to updates on upcoming releases, sales and freebies! She hates spam and so will never share your email!

S. E. LUND NEWSLETTER SIGN UP

# FOREWORD

*You were the model of perfection, full of wisdom and perfect in beauty. You were blameless in your ways from the day you were created till wickedness was found in you . . . Your heart became proud on account of your beauty, and you corrupted your wisdom because of your splendor. So I threw you to the earth.*

Ezekiel 28

And what rough beast, its hour come round at last, slouches towards Bethlehem to be born?

William Butler Yeats

# CHAPTER 1

Alfred Tennyson


"SWEET," A MALE VOICE SAYS. "Michel's little pet. He's not being very careful with you."

I blink, my eyes focusing slowly, pain throbbing in my head. I sit in a chair with my arms bound behind my back. A man in his twenties with reddish blond hair to his shoulders stands directly in front of me.

I glance around, trying to get my bearings. We're in an office in what looks like a warehouse filled with rows and rows of furniture stacked high.

"I'm not his pet."

"Oh, yeah? Then what's up with the bite on your neck? Moles?"

"What bite mark?"

He smiles at me as if I'm a child.

"That one," he says and points.

"It's not a bite," I say but I can't be sure. My hands are tied. Then I remember my dream from last night.

"Sure, sweetheart, and this," he says and points to a wound on his neck, "is just a birthmark. It just so happens to be in the shape of a vampire bite. You know, one of those freaks of nature like Elvis on an English muffin?"

I sit helpless, all my so-called vampire hunter fight skills worthless.

"What are you going to do with me?"

He comes closer and bends down, lifting up a piece of my hair with a dagger.

"I'm not going to do anything with you, but I think my boss has a few ideas and will want to come and have a little visit. If Michel doesn't show up soon, he's going to claim tribute and keep you for himself."

There's nothing I can do or say. I feel helpless at that moment and close to panic. Finally, the man leaves me alone with another bulky guy in leather who smokes a cigarette, flicking the ashes towards me in disdain.

Time passes – I have no idea how long but soon I start to really worry that Michel won't come.

Finally, the first man returns and stands in front of me.

"Time's up, Eve. I guess Michel needs a bit more convincing because he hasn't arrived."

I want to say he's out of town, but don't know if I should so I keep silent. He holds out the dagger and lowers it to my sweater, cutting the buttons so that it opens to reveal my bra.

"Stop," I say, trying to move away but I'm trapped.

He cuts the strap between the cups and my breasts spill out and there's nothing I can do about it. The two men stand and gawk at me and soon, my cheeks are hot and I avert my eyes. Then, the man slides the blade across my left breast above the nipple, drawing blood and I gasp with the pain of the knife blade. He holds a tiny glass vial up to catch some of the blood as it drips off my breast. He puts the stopper on the vial and stands admiring me as I sit there, helpless.

"I should take a picture. Post it on the 'net at one of those vampire fetish websites. Lotta guys would pay good money to watch. Like a piece of art. Hey, Jim, doesn't she look like a piece of art with that line of blood dripping down her tit, her nipples all puckered?"

Another man enters the room and the blond jumps out of the way, and stands to the side, his head down. The strange man is taller than the other two and lean, with long dark hair. I blink away tears and see that he's a vampire from his pale skin.

"Enough fun," he says and holds his hand out. The guard passes him the small vial of my blood. Then, the vampire kneels down in front of me, his gaze fixed on the bleeding cut on my breast, his eyes momentarily reddening. "Boys, didn't I tell you not to play with the pets? You should have taken the blood from her arm, not her breast. Now, Michel will be angry. Leave us."

The two men leave the room and I'm alone with the vampire. He looks really young – early twenties. Maybe even as young as me.

"So you're Michel's new pet," he says, his voice soft, his eyes flicking to my face momentarily before moving back to my wound. "You're pretty, but you've got a lot to learn about what a vampire likes. Your clothes," he says and waves a gloved hand at my sweater and jeans. "Not very flattering. You've got to wear something a bit more revealing. Put your hair up, expose your neck. Show some leg. You look like a college student."

"I am, and I'm not trying to attract a vampire," I say.

"Uh, uh, uh," he says and holds his gloved finger to my lips. "Don't speak until I ask for your opinion. You'll find things are different in my coven. We hold to the old ways."

Of course, I have no idea what 'the old ways' are – I haven't got that far in my reading of vampire history and lore. He stands.

"Elaine!"

A blonde woman dressed in a bustier and leather pants comes into the room on heels that look dangerously high.

"Yes, my Lord?"

"Since that idiot destroyed Eve's sweater and bra, find something appropriate for her to wear. I expect Michel will be by soon to get her back. I want to show him how to keep his possessions safe – and properly dressed."

"I'm not his possession," I say. The woman – Elaine – visibly flinches when I speak.

The vampire leans down, his face level with mine. "And I heard you were so bright. What is it about 'don't speak until I ask for your opinion' didn't you understand?"

I press my lips together and look away. He takes my chin in his hand and turns my face back to his. I keep my eyes shut, not wanting to have to face him.

"Female slaves will keep their eyes on their Master at all times," he says and gives my head a gentle shake until I open my eyes. "You have to anticipate my every need."

"I'm not your slave and I'm not Michel's pet," I say. Then I realize I've spoken without permission and close my eyes, grimacing, waiting for something to happen.

After a pause, the vampire speaks.

"Then what about that bite mark on your neck? Why does he have an operative watching over you like you were a prized possession?"

I don't reply.

"Now, you see, you can't seem to get the hang of this slavery thing," he says. "I asked for your opinion. You're supposed to answer."

I open my eyes and he's back on his haunches, looking directly at me, his arms resting on his knees.

"I don't know anything about operatives."

"You don't know much, do you? Michel just can't commit."

I say nothing and wait.

"Tell me about Eve," he says, standing up and pulling a chair over. "I know you're an Adept. You work for the SCU." He sits on the chair across from me. "I think Michel's in love." He looks me over. "He really has kept you in the dark. Must be guilt." He leans in and runs a gloved finger over my cheek. "Tell you what," he says. "You're not happy with him? You feel unsafe? You just have to call my name and I'll be glad to add you to the harem."

"Harem?"

"Oh, sorry," he says and smiles again. "I forget the politically correct times we're in. I should have said my 'staff'. I suppose I could have called them my 'feedstock', or maybe my 'collection' or maybe my 'donors'. I really just like to call them my slaves."

I look away from him, disgusted with his obvious delight in his power over mortals. He immediately takes hold of my chin and turns my face back so that I have to look at him.

"You're not very quick are you?" he says. "Or are you just impetuous? I like impetuous. One thing I've learned in all my long years of existence is that the hunt and the chase are almost as much fun as the kill. I can see it's going to be a lot of fun to get you broken in if Michel doesn't claim you."

Then, a guard enters the room. "My Lord, he's here."

The vampire stands and faces the door. Several men dressed in dark coats enter the room, all of them with weapons of silver drawn – guns, knives. One even carries a crossbow. They stand in a circle around the vampire as if to protect him.

And then, Michel walks in and my heart jumps – except it's not Michel. It's Julien. He's wearing black leather and black jeans. He glances in my direction quickly and when I'm just about to say something, he gives a quick shake of his head. Then, he stands in front of the other vampire. He had no body armor that I can see or weapons.

"Finally," the vampire says and extends a hand to Julien. They clasp forearms. "I'm surprised Michel sent you. Aren't you two still quarrelling?"

"Luke," Julien says. "Thanks for picking her up when her security detail was taken out."

"Glad to hear Michel was able to get you out of trouble."

Julien nods.

The vampire – Luke – turns to me.

"I thought I was going to have to train her myself. She's a cheeky one, despite the tears. Michel must like them saucy."

"You can leave the training to me," Julien says.

"Oh, that's too bad. You know how I like to break a new slave in, but I have a feeling this one will only top from the bottom," he says, smiling. He pulls up another chair and gestures to it. "Where's Michel?"

"Soren's making Michel stay in Pittsburgh. I'm taking over his territory."

At that, my heart skips a beat. Soren's making Michel stay in Pittsburgh?

"Julien," I say, unable to stop myself. "What do you mean Michel's staying in Pittsburgh?" Tears brim once more in my eyes.

Julien comes to me and stands in front of me.

"Hush," he says and runs the back of his fingers over my cheek, sending some kind of calm chemical through me. "We'll talk later."

"But, Michel..." I start to say but he shakes his head again, and holds his fingers up to my lips.

"Hush."

He returns to his chair and the two vampires sit facing each other, eyeing each other intently.

"How's he taking it? That must be upsetting for him, considering *she's* here."

"He's resigned to it," Julien says. "It was him or her, and there's no way he'd want Soren to have her."

"I figured Michel would pay some price to get you back."

"So are you going to tell me what happened with Eve?"

Luke raises his hands.

"When Jim saw Eve wandering around and Michel's man wasn't in sight, he stepped in and took her off the street. You can't be too careful with the females, I always say. Too valuable. Tell Michel he really must hire better help."

"Point taken."

"And here she is," Luke says, pointing to me. "Only a little worse for wear. Jim was a bit exuberant in retrieving her. She got a bit of a bruise on her forehead when she fell and of course, there's that," he says and points to my breast. "He was a bit too enthusiastic in bringing me a sample of her blood as proof of life but better overkill than underkill."

"Of course," Julien says. "Now, if you don't mind, I think it's time to get back home. I have a long night ahead of me."

Luke smiles. "I'll bet you do. Be my guest," he says and motions to me. "Jim, cut her loose."

Jim goes behind me and removes the ropes binding my hands and I clutch at my breasts, trying to cover up. Julien stands and holds his hand out to Luke, palm up. "If you don't mind?"

"Of course." Luke reaches into a pocket and withdraws the vial of blood, handing it over to Julien. "It was just insurance, you understand. In case one of you didn't show and needed convincing."

"Of *course*." Julien puts the vial into a pocket in his jacket.

Elaine comes in the room with some clothes on hangars.

"My Lord, you asked for these?" She holds them up, one after the other. One is a short black leather dress with a low cut back and the other is a sleeveless black velvet cocktail dress, with a scoop neck, corset bodice and a lace up back.

Luke stands in front of the two dresses and studies each one, a finger at his lips. "I think the velvet is more her style, don't you think Julien?"

Julien nods. "Definitely."

"Good," he says. "Consider this my gift for your new pet." He motions to Elaine. "Take her and help her change."

Elaine tilts her head to me and I look at Julien for some direction. He nods without meeting my eyes and so I follow Elaine into the other room.

"Here, sweetie," she says, her voice soft. "You put this on. I'll see what I can do about your hair."

I undress quickly, not wanting to argue with either Julien or Luke. The dress is a bit loose, but it fits as well as can be expected. Elaine pulls the laces in the back of the dress tightly and it fits more snugly. The bustier pushes my breasts up and the thin cut is still lined with dried blood, but it's no longer bleeding. Then she pulls my hair back, securing it with a series of clips, tendrils falling in long curls around my face. She turns me around.

"You look much better."

She reaches into a wardrobe and pulls out a pair of heels. "I think these will fit you well enough."

I try them on. Sure enough they fit. I look her over. She has several sets of bite marks on her neck and left breast.

"Are you all right?" I ask. "You look like you've lost too much blood."

"It's my week," she says, smiling. "My Lord's very experienced. He knows how much to take. He feeds me a bit of his blood each time so I'll be fine."

"Aren't you afraid you'll die one of these times?"

"Oh, no." She shakes her head. "I'm one of his favorites. He takes good care of us."

I sigh, unable to believe that a woman could be happy as part of a harem, for a vampire or mortal.

"Can I ask what you do when it's not your week?"

"Recover," she says brightly. "Eat really well, rest, sleep. Luke isn't really much for television so we tend to listen to music or I can read if I want to."

"You don't work?"

She laughs. "This is my work," she says and points to her wound.

"You know he called you his slave?"

She leads me out of the room. "I know. I don't really care what he calls me. He's one of the oldest vampires and is very powerful. More powerful than even Michel and Julien."

Than even Michel and Julien? I try to absorb this new information as we return to the room.

"Ah, there she is," Luke says. He stands with his arms crossed and looks me up and down. "Much better. Good enough to eat. I tell you, if you grow tired of her, you can always send her here."

"I'll keep it in mind if she becomes too bothersome." Julien glances at me briefly, but his face is unreadable. Luke goes to the door, one arm draped over Elaine's shoulders. "I'm so glad we had the chance to chat," he says to Julien. "And so glad Michel was able to get you out of your little predicament. Give him my regards."

"Luke," Julien says, bowing slightly. He turns to leave and motions to me with a quick wave of his hand. I follow him. When we get to the door, I frown.

"Wait," I say and it hits me. The sun's still out. "How can you go outside during the day?"

Julien opens the door for me.

"Need to know, Eve." He leads me down the stairs to the loading dock. "Everything's different now."

"What do you mean, everything?"

"I mean everything," he says, taking my arm. "I've been able for years, but I haven't been out, so to speak. This is the price Michel had to pay to resurrect me."

This sends a shock through me. Vampires can daywalk? The questions pour out of me.

"How many of you can do this? How is it possible? Why is Michel staying in Pittsburgh?"

"Not many can daywalk. A handful remain. I was part of a project your mother was involved in. Now leave it at that," Julien says, all matter of fact, like this isn't about the biggest shock of all.

"Wait," I say and grab his arm. "You can't tell me this is related to my mother's work and not explain."

"Why, yes I can."

I clench my fists and follow him outside. A driver opens the door to a limo and Julien motions for me to get in. I shiver in the cool air, too numb to even consider refusing. I sit inside and lean back, enormous fatigue filling me as if I've just escaped a death sentence – which of course I most likely have.

Julien leans over and clips on my seat belt, and I see him eye the cut on my breast. He takes off his coat and covers me with it, and I'm glad to have something against the chill.

"Why is Michel in Pittsburgh," I say again, tears once again blurring my vision. "Can I go to him?"

Julien says nothing while the driver speeds off.

"Julien, please, tell me!"

He turns to me and cups my cheek, frowning. I feel another wave of something sedative flow through me.

"Shh," he says. "Michel's gone and he's not coming back. He had to do this in order to get me back. It was you or him and he would never let Soren have you. You're mine now."

I frown at him, but my ability to argue is fading fast.

"I'm Michel's," I say in weak protest.

"Yes, and he gave you to me so get used to it. You said you'd obey him. Well, this is his order."

"I don't believe you. How do I know you didn't arrange all this just so you could take me?"

He turns back to me and now I see his anger in the thin press of his mouth but I also see pain there, emotion, as if he's almost at the breaking point.

"I *died* for him, Eve. He wouldn't let me go. This is his wish. Now, just obey and honor his order."

"What do you mean, you died for him? Do you mean in return for Marguerite?"

He says nothing and I can only imagine what's going on between these two brothers. I lean my head back against the seat. Despite Julien's efforts to calm me, the pain is deep.

Michel's *gone*.

"I have to go to him," I say, my voice breaking. Then, Julien leans close to me and takes my hand, looking in my eyes and he's so intense that my heart does a flip-flop.

"Eve," he says, his voice soft. "We're at war now. You have to get this obedience thing clear. Soren knows about you and he wanted you in exchange for my resurrection but Michel and I made another deal."

"What deal?"

He sighs. "We have to become everything we've hated the most."

"What do you mean?"

He just shakes his head as if he's unable to speak for a moment.

"Soren gave us a choice and we made it. Michel didn't want you to become Soren's property and neither did I. Both of us know what that would mean. He chose to stay with Soren instead."

"For how long?"

"A quarter century. Maybe more. It means nothing to a vampire, but to a human it's almost half your life. You have to just accept it."

"How can you accept this?" I say, my voice breaking. "We have to fight Soren. I'll *kill* him."

Julien tries to calm me again, but I succeed in pulling my arm away

"Don't!" I say. "I want to feel my emotions." But he grabs my arm again and squeezes.

"Michel wouldn't want you to cry. *I* don't want you to cry." And then my grief fades once more. I just sit there, like an emotionless zombie, staring at Julien as he wipes my tears away. "We can't do anything to change this. Michel knew it would cost us. Eve, Soren isn't just any old vampire. He's an Ancient. They're not of this world. Your vampire hunter skills? Useless."

"Why? Are they faster?"

"They're metamorphs. They can transform at will. You think you've got them? They dematerialize."

"Is that where the vampires turning into fog myth comes from?"

He nods, his face so grim that I'm afraid.

"They have to have a weakness," I say. I dig my nails into my palms, and the pain is short and sharp and I know Julien won't be able to read me as long as the pain lasts. In those brief moments, I make a commitment to myself. I don't care what Michel forbids or what Julien demands. I'll find a way to kill Soren. I'll find a way to kill him and get Michel back.

Julien grabs my hands and pries my fists open. My nails have dug into my palm in three places, drawing blood.

He clucks his tongue. "You won't be able to keep it up forever, Eve. Pain takes a lot of energy and will eventually exhaust you so I'll find out any plans you have in place." He pulls the wound up to his mouth and tongues it and I fight him, trying to jerk my hand away but of course, he's stronger and he does it anyway.

"Don't you do that!' I say, angry that he's doing what Michel did. "Don't try to be Michel. You aren't him."

"I know that only too well," he says and lifts his head from my hand. He has the characteristic red-rimmed eyes and huge pupils of the hunter feeding, his teeth long, his mouth stained with my blood. He licks his lips and just stares at me, not smiling, his face a little terrifying in its feral expression.

"I didn't want this," he says, his face slowly returning to normal. "Michel didn't want this, but we're brothers first. He saved my life many times and I've saved his. He wouldn't want Soren to have you so that he could go free. He *gave* you to me."

"He can't just give me away," I say, horrified. "I'm not a possession you can exchange."

"Yes, you are," Julien says, his brow furrowed. "Get this straight, Eve. We're predators. You're prey. You're an Adept, which makes you valuable. You will be claimed by someone. Better you were claimed by me than Luke. Being my possession saved your life just now."

Then I reach up and touch the mark on my neck. There are two wounds where teeth have penetrated my skin.

"I'm not yours. I'm Michel's.  He came to me in the night. Why didn't I see this when I got ready today?"

He doesn't say anything.

"Michel did come to me in the night." I say again. "If he did, he can come any time."

"Once Soren knew you were alive, one of us had to claim you. Michel wanted to delay claiming you, but he was wrong. It put you more at risk. He didn't come to you, Eve. I did. I had to do it. "

"You *what?*" My blood feels as if it's turned to ice. "Then you raped me because I didn't give you consent."

He shakes his head.

"I didn't. I gave you a nice dream of Michel so you'd be happy. I did it for your protection and it's a good thing, too, considering Luke took you. If you'd been unclaimed, you'd be his now and there'd be nothing I could do about it. Even now, he's stronger than I am."

I look away and close my eyes, the reality that any vampire can just hack into my mind and affect my dreams unsettling.

"I feel like some pawn in this game of power you and Michel are playing."

"Not a pawn, Eve. The queen."

I frown. In chess, the queen is the most powerful piece.

"Eve," he says and leans closer. "This isn't about what you want or what any of us want. This is about what has to be. This was the price we had to pay to keep Soren from claiming you. As soon as he knew Michel had you, he wanted you."

"Why is he doing this to you?"

"You read parts of the manuscript. Michel killed Marguerite. Soren's used that over the years to get much out of us but in truth, the debt will never be repaid. No human life, not even a powerful Adept, can equal that of an Ancient's progeny. Not even my life."

"Why?"

"There's a hierarchy among my kind based on how close you are to the first vampires. Nephilim are at the top, because they're the progeny of fallen angels. Ancients beneath them, then an Ancient's progeny, then the rest of us. Soren enjoys manipulating us, making us do things neither of us would do on our own. He's a monster. But even though he has Michel, and even though he has my compliance, I don't trust him not to come after you as well. I had to claim you. Be thankful it's me and not Luke."

I just sit there, numb, staring into Julien's eyes, Robin's egg blue, fringed with thick black lashes just like Michel's, and I remember my dream and how much I loved it when Michel – when *Julien* bit me.

Unable to argue, drained of all emotion, I close my eyes and turn my head away.

# CHAPTER 2

We drive in silence. Before we've driven very far, I become nause-ated, the headache that's been threatening for the last hour coming into full bloom, blinding in intensity.

"I'm not feeling well," I say, hardly able to hold my head up.

Julien leans over and turns my head towards him, looking in my eyes. I can barely keep them open.

"Stop the car."

Once the car comes to a stop, he unbuckles his seatbelt and moves closer to me, my face in his hands.

"Jesus *Christ*."

"I'm so tired," I manage to say, but the world is spinning, darkness closing in on me. I feel like I'm going to pass out. "Maybe you should take me to the nearest emergency room."

"No need," Julien says, and I pry my eyelids open and watch him. His eyes become bloodshot, his pupils dilated, and he bites his own wrist, twin punctures over his veins. He holds his wrist up to my mouth.

"What are you doing?" I say, horrified that he's trying to feed me his blood.

"You've got a bad concussion," he says. "My blood will heal you. Drink."

Despite my vertigo and weakness, I refuse, pushing his hand away.

"Just take me to a hospital."

"You're not going anywhere in public," he says and forces his wrist to my mouth.

I press my lips together and try to turn my head.

"Don't," I say. "I won't swallow. I won't become your blood slave."

Then he must release some kind of endorphin in my brain that makes me stop resisting and presses me down on the seat. I'm helpless to refuse. He's lying on top of me, and has my nose pinched, his wrist against my mouth, and finally, I have to take a breath. When I open my mouth, he's able to force his wrist to my lips.

I swallow his blood. At first, I'm sick that I'm actually tasting vampire blood, my mind immediately going to the blood whores in Franklin Park and how horrible their lives must be.

"Don't worry, Eve," Julien says, his voice soft. "This little amount won't make you addicted. Although, you may like it so much, you start pestering me for more..." He grins at me while he holds his wrist to my mouth. "If you do, just remember that I expect something in return."

I swallow again, closing my eyes, for it starts to taste unbelievably good, like I need more. I grab hold of his wrist.

"That's just about enough," he says and wrenches his wrist away. I open my eyes and am staring into his and whatever's in vampire blood, it's *good*. Almost too good.

"Oh, *God*," I whisper, closing my eyes, trying to catch my breath from the rush of euphoria.

"Yes, it's good, isn't it?" He leans his face down to mine and kisses my mouth, licking my lips as if to taste his own blood. "I could take you right now," he whispers in my ear, "and you wouldn't fight me, would you?"

He nestles between my thighs, and I just lie there, my eyes closed, riding the wave of bliss, and he's right. He licks my breast, licks the cut, and I arch my back against him it feels so good. He could take me right now and I'd let him, and I know I'd love it, but it's not me. It's not because of how I feel for him. It's because of the blood and the endorphins. If I weren't under its influence, I wouldn't. I'd pull away, I'd fight him and it would be rape.

"I'm not a rapist," Julien says, reading my mind. Instead of trying, he merely exhales heavily, rubbing his nose under my ear, kissing his bite mark. "I'll wait, but one day, Eve, when you realize Michel's not coming back, you'll come to me and ask for it. If you wait too long, I'll make you beg for it on your knees."

"I'll never beg," I say, my eyes still closed. Tears bite at the corners of my eyes, because of what he's said about Michel not coming back.

"You will."

Finally, he sits up and pulls me up as well, fastening my seat belt again and I open my eyes and watch him, and he's so beautiful despite the frown. He runs his fingers through his hair and takes in a deep breath, rolling his neck from side to side as if to ease tension.

"Let's go," he says to the driver and then he turns back to me. "Eve, you should have stayed in the café when you came out of the washroom and Marco wasn't there. You should have gone straight to the car and let the driver know. It was foolish of you to go to the other store on your own. Didn't you stop to wonder where Marco was? Didn't you think of the danger you're in? Michel told you that you needed secure custody."

"I know." I close my eyes, preferring his stern words of reproach to the self-assured tone he used when he was telling me I'd beg him for sex. "This is just all so unreal to me."

"It's real. Don't forget. If you weren't recovering from a head injury, I'd show you just how real this is – I'd spank your little ass."

"You better not try," I say, turning back to him. "Michel showed me how to stake a vampire. I killed him temporarily. Don't think I won't kill you to stop you from hurting me."

"Things are different, Eve," he says and shakes his head. "Don't even think you could beat me now."

"What do you mean?" I frown, but he ignores me and turns to the window, stroking the several-days worth of stubble on his jaw. "Tell me!"

"I'm different. That's all you need to know so get any ideas of staking me out of your pretty little vengeance-filled head."

Finally, I glance out the window at the neighborhood.

"Where are you taking me? Aren't we going back to Michel's place?"

"Can't. Security was compromised. Someone from within betrayed Michel. We're putting in a new security system, renovating the grounds. We're going to my place." He says nothing more and I'm too in shock to argue and just watch out the window, wondering where we're going. We drive towards the docks, to an old warehouse area. The car enters a long alley between red-brick warehouses and stops at a loading dock. Julien helps me out of the limo and takes my hand in his, leading me up the stairs. The warehouse is empty on the main floor. We walk to an old freight elevator and wait for it, taking it to the fifth floor.

The interior is open space with a series of rooms to one side and looks as if construction is still underway. Plastic tarps separate areas that aren't finished from the rest. The whole floor has shiny dark hardwoods and exposed brick and ductwork. Huge multi-paned windows reach to the ceiling in every room, revealing a panoramic view of the city to the north and east.

In one corner of the main room beside the kitchen sits a grand piano with sheet music spread out on the stand. It looks like a brand new Steinway. Beside it is a music stand and a violin case. In the west, walled off by wooden dividers, is an office-like space with desks, computers and a wall of security monitors showing different views of the warehouse exterior.

Julien opens a door and enters a bedroom. Inside is a huge four-poster canopy bed with a lush white silk cover and gauzy white drapes. The windows look out over the river.

"We sleep here." He points to a door. "There's a washroom if you

need it. I'll have a man go to your place and get some clothes for you."
He turns to go. "Now I have work to do."

"You mean *I* sleep here, don't you?"

"I mean *we*, Eve. You're mine. Get used to it."

"You really think I'm just going to hop into bed with you?" I say, frustration filling me. "Just because you look like him doesn't mean I'll want you."

He grabs my hand and pulls me close against his body.

"Michel said you lie to yourself. You've already thought of being with me." His gaze moves over my face and I feel him at the edges of my mind, trying to get in. "This is war, Eve. Now's the time to just obey."

He closes the door, leaving me alone in the huge room. I sit on the bed and just cry.

I go to sleep, lying on my side on the bed, and its only much later that I wake. The sun's down and Julien's under the covers with me, spooned against my body. I gasp when I remember who it is beside me and my body tenses.

Despite my grief, my body betrays me, warming to him immediately and I remember how much lust I felt for him after drinking his blood. I try to block those thoughts out of my head, for I don't want him to read them. I dig my nails into my palms once more.

"I already know," he whispers, and squeezes me. I want to scream at him because I hate how he knows. I hate him and his brother and all vampires. They've ruined my life.

"You were crying in your sleep," he says, his voice soft in my ear. "Now, shh," he says and strokes my hair. "Go to sleep. Don't worry. I said I'm not a rapist and I meant it. I'll wait until you're ready. Your body already is, but your mind isn't. I'll wait until you offer yourself to me. Don't make me wait too long, or I'll make you do it on your hands and knees."

"Don't hold your breath," I say. "I'll never go on my hands and knees to anyone." But then I think, *famous last words, Eve.*

Despite my arousal, I can't keep my eyes open and my body is helpless to fight him. I drift in a drugged-like warmth, my eyelids heavy.


The next time I wake up, I'm alone in the bed and I feel like I have a hangover. I get up, and in the bathroom is a box of my clothes from Michel's house, including a makeup bag with my personal things. I take off the cocktail dress and pull on a clean pair of jeans and a sweater, but I have no bra since I only brought the one I was wearing yesterday. I wash my face and put on a touch of makeup and check out the bite mark on my neck. How come I didn't wake up when he bit me? Did he drug me? How come I didn't see the bite mark in the morning when I looked in the mirror?

Then I sit on the bed with my iPhone and check my mail to see if I have any messages but there's nothing – just the usual spam and news headlines in the feed I subscribe to. In a desperate bid, I send Michel an email, but it bounces back with an error message that says the email is no longer valid. Then, I post a message to the message board where I first contacted Michel.

*"Michel, please come back to me! I can't do this!"* is all it says.

The door opens and Julien comes in, and he seems different, as if he's changed, as if being with Soren has done something to him. He seems harder, no longer playful. He's wearing Army fatigues and a t-shirt that reads Navy SEAL and *I Survived Hell Week.*

"I heard you were up," he says. "Come out and have something to eat."

I don't look him in the eye and follow him out into the main living area, padding behind him in my bare feet.

When we enter the kitchen, wonderful aromas reach my nose. I see an older man fixing something on the stove. He's the one I saw with Michel before.

"Vasily will fix you a plate," Julien says and points to the stool by the island that separates the kitchen from the rest of the living area.

" Hello little Ballerina Girl." Vasily smiles at me. "We finally meet."

"Ballerina Girl?"

"Boss says you were dancer as girl?"

I nod, and check over my shoulder to where Julien is standing, looking out the window.

"I've cooked some good Russian food," Vasily says. "Will make you feel better, give you some meat on bones, you are so tiny like little bird." His voice is deep and he has a very thick Russian accent. He places a plate of food in front of me. It looks like a roast of some kind with gravy, cabbage, and other vegetables.

"Thank you, but I'm a vegetarian."

He frowns. "Eat," he says. "You must regain strength. At least have some bread and gravy."

I sit and take a bite of the vegetables but everything's covered in a meat gravy. Surprisingly, I eat it anyway. It's so good, and I eat happily, not realizing until now how hungry I am and how much the taste of the meat appeals to me. I gaze out the window at the city skyline. To our left is the piano.

"That's a beautiful Steinway," I say, awed at its beauty. "It looks new."

"Brand new," Julien says. He comes to stand in the kitchen beside me, touching my cheek with the backs of his fingers once again. "Delivered yesterday. I got it for you. You should play."

I pull away from his touch, not wanting him to read me. Then he goes to the counter and pours himself a glass of something from a carafe, the liquid thick and crimson.  It must be blood. He tips the glass up and drinks it down without stopping. When he turns to me, his eyes are red-rimmed, his pupils huge.

"That's blood?" I say, a bit shocked. I'd never seen Michel drink any.

He licks his lips and smiles. I can see his canine teeth briefly and they're bloody.

"Good old AB negative. Universal recipient." He smacks his lips. "I shouldn't drink it because it's so rare, but I have a donor on tap." He examines the empty glass. "I don't really like prepared blood. Has an artificial taste due to the anti-clotting chemicals they put it in and the preservatives. My current preference," he says and leans on the countertop, eyeing me, "is for fresh body-temperature B positive with a slightly Northern Ireland flavor, but you take what you can get."

I shiver and make a face, disgusted at the sight of him drinking a glass of blood.

"That was a reference to you, by the way, so don't make a face," he says. "If it keeps me from feeding on you, I'd think you'd be raising a toast to me."

He pours himself some more blood and then shoots it back, making a satisfied sound when he's done as if to irritate me.

"You can tell where my ancestors are from by my blood?"

He smiles. "You drink enough blood, you get to know genotypes. Like good wine."

I push my plate away, leaving the rest of my food unfinished, whatever hunger I had gone. Vasily clucks his tongue and eyes the plate.

"You don't like my cooking?"

"Your cooking's wonderful. I just lost my appetite all of a sudden when I realized I'm food, too."

"We're all food for worms," Vasily says and takes my plate away, scraping the leftovers into a trash bin. He then puts the dishes in a dishwasher and I'm amazed at how domestic he is considering he looks like a Russian Mafioso. "Why don't you play piano," he says, pointing to the Steinway. "Boss said you play. I'd love to hear."

"I'm not in the mood."

He clucks his tongue again. "Boss goes to all this trouble to get it for you and you refuse to play? Maybe you two play duet?"

I turn to Julien. "I saw a violin case. Do you play?"

He shrugs, noncommittal.

"Boss is very good on violin. Plays beautiful Tchaikovsky. Makes old Russian like me cry."

I turn and look at Julien with fresh eyes. He plays violin? I've always thought of him as just a soldier. A knight, maybe, from Occitan nobility, but still a soldier.

I glance at the Steinway. I must admit I'm dying to play it.

"It won't bother you?"

"I'd really like to hear you play," Vasily says. "Boss said you were child prodigy."

"More like child automaton," I say, trying to downplay the prodigy bit because it really means nothing. Child prodigies and normal virtuosos end up at the same point eventually and sometimes, the child prodigies burn out from all the work. Like me.

"Please play," he says. "I never had lessons and have great regret. If you can play, you should. Music has charms," he says and raises his eyebrows, gesturing with his head towards Julien.

I smile at Vasily. He's so sweet, and I'm surprised because it's so at odds with his physical appearance, with his puggish face and short steel-grey brush cut.

I go to the sink and wash my hands first, and go to the Steinway, approaching it like it's a rare animal. It's huge – a concert grand, its ebony exterior shining in the overhead pot light. It must have cost over a hundred grand. I glance through the music on it – it's all mine taken from my apartment. I lay my hands on the keyboard, the keys smooth and cool under my fingertips.

"Any requests?"

Vasily comes over to the piano and stands beside me.

"Play your most favorite piece," he says. "The one that you love the most."

I think for a minute. "I have a new favorite. Chopin. Nocturne in E Minor."

"Why you love?"

"It's Michel's favorite," I say, and glance at Julien. Julien has his back to the room, watching out the windows.

I start to play and glance up to see Julien watching me from the bank of windows, where he stands in the darkness. The piece is very passionate, and I suspect Chopin was struggling with some kind of teenage angst but it just reminds me of how sweet and emotional and passionate Michel is and how he said it made him think of his own heartbreak when he was seventeen. I wonder what price he's paying living with Soren.

The piece ends on a more uplifting note than it starts and I look up at Vasily, who's smiling broadly.

"You got a beautiful touch," he says, standing there beside the piano, his hand resting on the ledge as if he were my teacher.

"She does." Julien says, emerging out of the darkness to stand on the other side of the Steinway. I avoid his eyes, and just sit there, running my fingers over the smooth ebony finish of the keyboard. He searches through the sheet music and selects a piece – *Ballade No. 1* by Chopin.

"Play this. Michel said he wanted you to practice."

I move it out of the way, replacing it with a new piece I was working on before final exams stopped my practice. A Bach prelude.

"No, this one," he says and puts the Chopin back. "He wanted you to learn to play it through."

I can't speak for a moment, a choky feeling in my throat.

"I don't want to play it today."

"Eve," he says. "This isn't about what you want. You said all in to Michel and Michel says you're to obey me as you would him. *I* want." He takes the other music off the stand and replaces it firmly with Chopin. "Think of it as repaying a debt. I did save your life."

"It's because of you that it's in danger."

"Eve. . . " He turns and frowns at me. "You're really pushing me. Vasily was Michel's servant and now he's mine. Even he would never deny me a request and he's a cold-hearted killer. Hey, Vasily!"

Vasily pokes his head around the office divider. "Yes, Boss?"

"Would you ever tell me no if I told you to do something?"

"Never, Boss, unless I wanted to push up daisies."

"Should Eve play the Chopin when I ask her?"

"She should play."

"See?" he says and turns back to me. "Even Vasily's obedient to me. Now, play the piece."

I sit with my hands in my lap. "You can force people to obey. You can't force them to like it."

"Some people actually like to obey orders. It makes them all *breath-*

*less...*" He waves at the keyboard and says nothing more, waiting. "Play," he says and waves me on. "No excuses."

"I'll play more if you play something for me."

Julien frowns. "That's not how this chain of command works Eve. I'm the one who gives the orders. You're the one who obeys."

"Please?" I say, smiling sweetly. "I want to hear you play the piece that made Vasily cry."

Julien shakes his head, smiling back, exhaling in exasperation. Finally, gives in and picks up the violin case. He removes the bow and adjusts it, then he takes out the violin and spends a few moments preparing, tuning the instrument, warming up.

"What will you play?"

He runs the bow over the strings a few times, the instrument resting against his chin and shoulder, his head tilted, his eyes closed.

"Tchaikovsky's Violin Concerto, the Canzonetta Andante in G Minor."

Then he starts to play the theme from the concerto's second movement and he plays so beautifully, the violin's voice so sweet and sad. The piece is familiar – I spent most of my early life in and out of concert halls listening to classical music and he plays very well for an amateur. Very well, and I remember what Michel said about centuries of practice.

I look over at Vasily and see his eyes moist and that brings tears to my own eyes.

As Julien plays, his eyes remain closed, his face impassive as if every ounce of emotion goes into his playing. I wipe my eyes quickly, not wanting him to see my tears. I'm taken aback that he plays, and that he plays so well. He seems like someone with no depth, crass, superficial. Like the world is a big joke and everything in it just toys for his amusement. He finishes and puts the violin down. He turns to me, his face guarded.

"There. Now you play. Don't get used to putting conditions on me or you'll be disappointed. I'm not into obedience."

"That was beautiful," I say, my voice a bit too emotional but he makes no response except to motion to the piano.

I sigh and play the Chopin Ballade but I struggle, paying close attention to each note. I manage to play the first section, and the slow beautiful section, which moves my heart so much, but falter at the coda as usual.

When I'm done, Julien collects up all my music except the Ballade and takes it with him to the office. When he returns, he sits down on the bench beside me. "From now on, the only piece you're allowed to play is this. I don't care if you snivel like a baby while you're doing it. Now," he says and takes my hands, places them on the keyboard. "Play that again. The part you still screw up." He waits, motioning for me to begin when I hesitate. "Chop chop."

I'm so – frustrated. I want to throw something at him.

"Vasily, she's not playing."

"She should be playing, Boss," Vasily yells from the office.

"She isn't. I don't think she has this obedience thing down yet. I'm planning on spanking her little bottom like the bad girl that she is for leaving the coffee shop yesterday without permission and for getting captured," Julien says, that lopsided smirk starting. "Should I spank her twice now?"

"Boss," Vasily says, humor in his voice. "You'll do what you want of course. Who am I to say no? But she did have a very bad day yesterday and is very sad. It might not be good idea to spank her today. Maybe on Tuesday."

I can't stop myself. I cover my eyes and smile, hating him for making me do it.

"Oh, now she's smiling, Vasily," Julien says, his voice playful like the old Julien I remember. "I don't think she believes that I'll spank her on Tuesday."

"She'd be wrong, Boss. If you say you will, you will."

I play the piece again, just to stop him from teasing me. It isn't so bad once I focus. I bite my lip and concentrate, paying close attention, trying to get my fingering just right during the most difficult section. I come to the part that gives me trouble and play slowly, starting and stopping to get it right.

"That's as good as it gets without a lot more work."

"Then work."

I start over, not really upset, for I do love the piece.

"What are you?" I say. "The phantom of the opera?"

He laughs and leaves me at the piano, going to the entrance, then starts carrying in boxes, depositing them in a space by the sitting area. I stop playing and go over to check when I recognize one of my chests. I look inside the boxes – they're from my apartment.

"What are you doing?" He keeps carrying boxes in, ignoring me. "Why are you doing this? That's from my apartment."

"You're not safe there any longer. You'll have to live here now."

"Do you think you might have talked to me about this first?" I grind my nails into my palms. " I have rights. You can't just move me in."

He stops and puts a box down.

"I just did." He stands in front of me. "Eve, you're living in a dream world. Wake up." He snaps his fingers in front of my face. "This is the real world, not the one you wish it would be. People make other people do things against their will all the time. Why," he says, cocking his head to the side. "Weren't you all tied up in Luke's warehouse just yesterday?" He brushes hair off my cheek. "Now go back and play. I like listening while I work."

I close my eyes, trying to control my anger.

"Vasily, she's not obeying me again," he says, his voice all mock-angry. "Do I have to wait until Tuesday?"

"One day has gone since she hurt her head. You might be able on Monday."

I turn on my heels and go back to the piano without another word. I don't want to listen to anymore of Julien and Vasily's teasing repartee. I'm a pre-med student, blood witness with the SCU, dammit. I'm an adult. He's turning me into a dependent.

Of course - I realize it as I start to play Ballade once more. That's his goal. Total control. Me as his prized Adept, the one promised to him when I was just a child, helping him police the treaty. This is what he always wanted. I sigh and decide that I'll comply without saying a word – as if it doesn't matter to me one way or the other.

If I'm going to handle Julien, I'll have to stop letting my emotions get the better of me.

# CHAPTER 3

"*Every* heart sings a song, incomplete, until another heart whispers back. Those who wish to sing always find a song."

Plato

The next day, I go back to the SCU. Julien accompanies me and there's an awkward silence in the car as Vasily drives us over. Julien spends time in the office with Ed while I sit at my little desk by the corner and check over the case file, reviewing the tests that have come back from forensics.

About an hour later, Ed comes out and motions for me to join him.

"I want you to get right back in the saddle again," Ed says as we enter the break room to get a cup of coffee. As Ed picks through the donuts in an open box, he explains. "I thought we might do some biochemical analysis of the vampire blood we have on file. You'll have samples from every vampire in the facility for the last few years. There are tests I want run that we don't have facilities for here."

"Whatever you want. What are you looking for?"

"We're looking for novel proteins, amino acids, seeing if there are any biochemical pathways that might be responsible for vampirism. All this work has been done, but we don't have access to it. It's military. It was mentioned in some of your mother's work. Fill out the requisitions and I'll sign them. The more basic research we do, the bigger our grants."

"It sounds exciting."

"There's nothing new on the case, so you might as well try to get some of your mother's work replicated."

Ed pours us coffee and we go to a small table by the window.

"Why don't you take a trip to the lab in Virginia, see if you can work with one of the Council researchers there? You can cut a lot of corners if you have contacts in the labs. Add a flight and hotel onto that requisition. It'll do you good to get out of Boston for a few days."

I'm not sure I really wanted to go to Virginia, but if it ensures I'm able to work on my mother's research, I'll put extra food in my cats' dishes and pack my bags once more.

"I hear you're going to Virginia," Julien says when he joins me at my desk a little while later.

"To the regional lab in Norfolk," I say, pleased to be doing something real. "There are special tests that can be done there. Ed wants me to meet the Council researcher, start working on my mother's research."

"I don't like it but if Ed wants it, OK." Julien shrugs. "I'll send Vasily with you. I have work to do here and can't go."

Vasily accompanies me on the trip, sitting a few rows over on the plane. I'd like him to sit with me, because he's really sweet and I need someone to make me feel safe, but he says no. It's best for us to be separate for security reasons. I make it through the short flight fine because I'm reading a file Terri gave me that describes the work we'll be doing and it's exciting and way beyond my pay grade, because although I've taken immunology and molecular genetics in my junior year at Boston U, I'm not qualified to work in a real lab.

We get rooms at the Sheraton on Waterside, Vasily next to mine, and I'm surprised Julien let me come here, considering how worried Michel was when I went to Montana. Maybe he feels safer now that he has a deal with Soren. Whatever, it makes me feel somewhat like an adult to be staying by myself.

The Sheraton is close enough to the Virginia Department of Forensic Sciences lab that I can walk if I want to get some exercise, which I do, Vasily trailing behind me in a rental car. I walk, enjoying the smell of the fresh salt air. Gulls wheel in the sky, diving in sequence to pick up bits of my morning bagel as I throw them into the air. In the distance is a large Navy aircraft carrier. I'd like to take a tour of the museum if I have the time.

I sign in at reception and wait for my contact to come and meet me at the security desk.

In about five minutes, a bespectacled man in his early thirties comes out to meet me. Dr. Graydon, head of Biochemistry. He extends a hand and I take it, trying to match the strength and warmth of it.

"Agent Hayden – so nice to meet you. Agent O'Neil sent me an email introducing you and putting a good word in. He and the department head are old friends from college." He wags his brows as if that's a hint that his boss is in the Council as well.

We walk down the hallways leading from the security desk to the administration offices at the north side of the building.

"I'll take you to the lab later, but first I wanted to introduce you to a few of the crew. Insiders."

I smile and shake about a half-dozen hands and am able to make it through the preliminaries. Finally, Graydon takes me through to the lab facilities and we sit down to discuss the work we want done. His office is small and filled with bookshelves, his desk littered with journal articles.

While we're working, I think about Julien's daywalking ability and decide to broach the subject to Graydon.

"Do you know of any research conducted by the military on immune system enhancement in vampirism?" I ask.

Graydon raises his eyebrows and pulls out an address book.

"Immunity? I do toxicology. But I used to study with someone who worked at the Pentagon for a term. She's a civilian researcher now on contract to the Council and might have some idea who you could talk to. I'll give you her name. Don't know if it would be any help, but you could try. Just mention my name and that might break the ice with her."

"Thanks." I take the card on which he's written her name and phone number.

The rest of the morning goes quickly, and after a lunch at a local fish and chips joint with a couple of the researchers, we spend the afternoon processing the shipment of blood samples from the Council prison facilities, filling out lab requisitions, doing various bureaucratic paperwork necessary to get the tests done. This is all new to me, who has only been in university labs and so I'm completely curious and engrossed in the work.

The afternoon flies by and when we're through for the day, I turn down an offer of a ride, preferring to walk back along the waterfront to catch the sunset. I don't see Vasily trailing behind me, but maybe he's farther back, not wanting to bother me.

This is the life I imagined when starting my science degree – doing research, learning more about vampirism, hoping one day to help eradicate the disease that killed so many innocent people over the millennia. The sun finally sets and the reproduction gaslight lamps flicker on, lighting the walkway that skirts the wharf and leads back to Waterside and my hotel. A couple passes me on a stroll, their heads together, laughing over some shared joke.

Seeing them makes my gut knot just a bit, for the only male attention I've received in several years is that of a pair of vampire-killing vampires, neither one of which has any intention of having a normal relationship with me.

What kind of freak am I?

I look up as a man passes. He grabs my arm and shock washes over me as I realize it's Julien. He's dressed in a dark trench, a fedora and scarf.

"Didn't Michel tell you not to walk alone after dark?" he says, his voice rough.

I pull my arm away, anger filling me.

"Are you never going to let me just be?" I struggle with him for a moment, hitting his hand with my fist. "Are you brothers always going to sneak up on me, scare the shit out of me?"

"Hey-hey-hey!" he laughs, easily maintaining his grip. "Take it easy." He manages to pull me closer.

A man walking down the boardwalk calls out from a distance.

"Are you OK, lady?"

I glance up at Julien's face to see the amusement is gone and now, his eyes are hooded. He speaks in a quiet voice, his tone flat. "It's dark out here and I have a switchblade in my pocket and could have him down in three seconds. Do you want this man to pay for your indiscretion?"

I get hold of myself, realize that I'm causing too much of a scene, that he very well could kill whoever comes upon the two of us. Kill me as well for that matter, because he has my hand in his.

"I'm fine," I call to the man, a forced smile on my face. "We're just playing."

"That's a girl," Julien says, putting his arms around me, pulling me closer. "Comply."

The man hesitates, but then moves on. "If you say so."

I stand with Julien's arms around me for a moment until the man's gone and then I try to pull away.

"No, I like this," he says, his voice soft. "Just relax for a minute."

I give up and just stand there as he buries his nose in my hair and neck, inhaling deeply. I'm shaking just a bit, my knees feeling like rubber from the adrenaline. I'm so frustrated that I can't get any time to myself without him intruding, reminding me that he's a killer. I realize that I'm still afraid of him, despite everything – the violin, him feeding me his blood, him biting me to protect me. He's still a vampire and could kill me if he wanted.

"Oh, come on, Eve." Julien pulls back. "You mean to tell me you're still afraid of me?"

I say nothing, just cover my face with my hands, not wanting to meet his eyes for mine are wet and I bite my cheek.

"Get a hold of yourself. Tears don't work on me. I'm a battle-hardened soldier." He reaches in a pocket and hands me a tissue.

I can't reply, just stand there mortified at my inability to gain control. He and his brother are ruining my life. I wipe my nose and eyes with the tissue and then glance around at the setting, anything to keep from looking at him.

"There," he says. "Better now? Enough sniveling. I hate sniveling."

"I hate you."

He grins at that and laughs out loud. Then he casually takes my arm and gently escorts me towards my hotel.

"Ahhh," he says, amusement back in his voice. "No you don't."

"Yes, I do."

"No you *don't*," he says and there's just a hint of darkness in his voice. "Tell the truth, Eve. You hate that I have control and that you don't. You don't hate me. You hate the fact that I can do whatever I want and you can't."

We walk along for a moment in silence, him holding my arm, me trying to stay as far away from him as possible.

"I don't blame you," he says. "I'd hate to be in that position. I'd like to say I sympathize, but I don't, do I? I mean, vampires can't sympathize, can we? You're just prey animals to us, food, a means to an end, sources of pleasure – toys. I'm just damn glad we're not weak and afraid and helpless like ordinary humans are."

"Have you never felt weak and afraid and helpless?"

"Oh, yes." The hotel is about a block away and I'm beginning to wonder if he'll expect to be invited into my room.

"When?"

"When I was a boy. I determined I'd never be in that position again."

"I wasn't afraid and helpless and weak until you and Michel came along. I was doing just fine."

"Eve," he says and clucks his tongue. "Remember, I've read you."

Heat rises to my cheeks. He squeezes my arm. I tug it away, but it's futile.

"You enjoy this, don't you?"

"What – fighting with you? Oh, yes. It's going to make your inevitable surrender so much sweeter."

"Don't count on it." It enrages me that he's so certain I will.

He just grins. We reach the walkway leading to the front entrance of my hotel. He stops and a sense of relief washes over me. He isn't going to come in.

"You go on in. I'll be up in about five minutes. Then we can talk."

"I won't let you in."

"You will."

"I won't."

He takes my arm, squeezes it just hard enough to make his point.

"Look, Eve," he says, his voice harsh, "Do I have to use force to remind you what I am?"

I look away.

"You go on up," he says and takes off his hat. "I have to sign in and get a key to my own room."

"How come you're here? I thought you had work to do."

"I rearranged things. I thought it would be good for us to get away by ourselves. Just the two of us. Well, there's Vasily, but he's pretty good at keeping his distance when appropriate."

"We don't need to get away by ourselves," I say. "I live in your warehouse, in case you forgot."

"You are so saucy." He turns me around, standing behind me, and bends down, his lips at my ear. "I love saucy, Eve, so keep it up." He opens the door for me. "Now, be a good girl and go to your room."

Once inside I see Vasily sitting on the plush furniture, reading a local newspaper. He stands when I walk by.

"Eve," he says, frowning. "You should have waited for me. Now we are both in the shit from Julien."

I shrug. "What's new?"

Once upstairs, I pace my room. When the knock on my door comes, I don't answer.

He repeats the knock and I hold my breath.

"Eve, let me in."

No response.

"Eve. I'm getting angry. This is not a good thing. Open the door."

"I won't," I say, barely able to speak.

"Just do it. *Now.*" His voice is deadly quiet. "Eve, if I have to kill a desk clerk to get a duplicate key, I will. Do you want that on your conscience?"

"Just go away," I whisper.

"Just go away? Jesus *Christ.*" Silence for a moment. "Eve. I'm not going to just go away. Open the door. *Now.*"

I have to do it – there's no other choice. He's too strong. No matter what I do, it'll be the wrong thing. I reach up and turn the lock, pushing down the handle –

He shoulders his way in, practically knocking me over with the force of the door, and grabs my arm, dragging me into the bedroom. He throws me onto the bed and then goes back to the door, locking it, double bolting it.

When he returns he grabs one of my shoes from the floor and throws it across the room. It hits over the desk, causing a painting to fall off, the glass shattering.

I fall into fight mode but he's right there with me, and the time shift seems to give me no advantage. I try to fight him, but it's useless. He straddles me on the bed and takes me by the chin, his face an inch away from mine.

"Who do you think you're dealing with Eve? I told you your little hunter tricks won't work on me anymore. You do what I say when I say it, do you understand?"

By now, I'm a total mess, unable to do anything but nod my head. Time returns to normal and I feel faint.

He starts taking off his clothes, throwing piece after piece against the wall, his trench, his jacket, his tie, his shirt, ripping at them, his movements rough. When he reaches for my clothes, I hit at him, refusing to let this happen regardless of his anger.

"Stop! You said you weren't a rapist!"

"I *lied*."

Then he seems to regain control and just lies on top of me, one of his hands holding mine over my head, his knee between my legs, his ragged breath in my ear.

We remain in this position for a few minutes, his breath slowing, but he doesn't move off me. Gradually, his grip on my hands lessens, the pressure of his knee between my thighs slacks off. He rubs his nose against my neck, presses his lips beneath my ear.

"I need you, Eve," he whispers, his breath on my skin. His mouth moves lower; he presses his tongue on his bite mark. "Once you taste a human, you want them. Once you feed them your blood, you want them even more."

He inhales again, rubbing his face in my hair. He rises up and looks in my eyes, and he's so much like Michel, but so much not like him. His scar is a thin silvery line on his cheek beside his hairline. His hair is shorter. But everything else is Michel – the thick black eyelashes fringing clear blue eyes. The square jaw, the soft lips. Dark brows, which are now furrowed. I see the determination in his eyes, the anger mixed with lust. It's almost overwhelming, his body on mine, his weight, his hardness, his blue eyes so intense.

He leans down to kiss me. I turn my face away.

His whole body stiffens. I can almost feel the anger radiating off him.

"What is wrong with you?" He grabs my chin and turns my face back to him. I close my eyes. "You want me. I *know* you do. Your body's ready."

I just close my eyes.

"Look at me."

I refuse.

"You had sex with Michel."

"I wanted him," I say and close my eyes. "I don't want you."

"You want me, Eve. Just give in."

I struggle beneath him, flailing around as much as I can. Finally, he releases me.

"What's wrong with you? I can't see it. It's blocked."

He takes my hands and examines them – I've done it again. Dug my nails into my palms.

"*Damn*," he says. "What happened to you to make you this way?"

I roll away from him, my stomach clenching, stomach contents rising in my throat.

"My first foster father raped me. That's what's wrong with me."

I roll off the bed and onto the floor, then drag myself to the small bathroom, to vomit in the toilet.

He holds my head, pulling my long hair back so it doesn't get wet. I retch and retch until there's nothing left. He doesn't say anything, just hands me a tissue so I can wipe off my mouth. I lie down on the bathroom floor, the tile cool against my flushed cheeks. He kneels down and just looks at me while I recover.

"How old were you?" he says quietly. I don't respond, unable to speak. He touches my foot, rubs it. "How old?"

I shake my head, take in a deep breath. "Eleven."

He doesn't say anything, just kneels beside me, a hand on my foot. The memories are too much and I get up, push my way past Julien, who for once seems immobilized. I go to his coat, which is discarded on the floor. I search through his pockets. I feel such a frantic need. I need to find a blade. I need to have one, now. I find one, a long switchblade with an ebony handle and hide it in my sleeve.

He comes to the doorway. "What are you doing?"

I scramble past him into the bathroom and shut the door before he can enter, locking it, knowing how futile it is, but I do it anyway. I remove my blouse, climb onto the vanity, my back to the mirror, and flip open the knife, the blade long and sharp and polished.

"Eve, open the door."

But I say nothing, just slice my skin an inch below the crease in my arm opposite my elbow. I pull the knife down, drawing a straight line about two inches long, the cut not very deep for the knife is deadly sharp, but deep enough so that the blood trickles down over the curve of my muscle. He breaks the lock, the door banging open, and he's inside the bathroom, standing there, watching me.

"There," I say, calm now, the pain cutting through all the fear and panic and anger, holding my arm with the bloody line out for him to see. "Does that make you happy?"

He steps closer, leans against the vanity where I sit, my knees up to my chin, and takes my arm in his hands. He bends down and runs his tongue through my blood and then looks at me, his face transformed, eyes blood red, teeth long. He licks the wound several times and soon, I see the incision start to clot and seal from the healing effects of his saliva. He pulls back and examines it. And then he pulls me into his arms and I don't resist.

He doesn't kiss me. Just holds me, my arm marked with a bloody line caught between us.

# CHAPTER 4

"So, I love you because the entire universe conspired to help me find you."

Paul Coelho

"I'll go down to the front desk and get a bandage for that." He leaves me sitting on the vanity. I watch as he dresses, putting on his shirt and tie, then his jacket.

The door closes and I'm alone.

I examine the cut on my arm, feeling all foolish now that I've been so histrionic but I was so confused, so torn between fear and anger and pain and desire, it was like I blanked out. It's always that way. Darkness overtakes me, I find a blade and cut and feel better. Then I see what I've done and I can't believe I'm so screwed up.

A knock at the door signals his return and I let him in without a thought, in stark contrast to earlier.

The world – my world –shifts.

"I had to tell them you stepped on a razor."

I sit on the bed while he bandages my cut, applying a stick-free pad to cover the wound and then wrapping my arm with gauze to keep it in place. He ties it off expertly, as if he's done this before.

"You're good at that."

"Army Ranger training comes in handy now and then."

I can't hide my admiration as I examine his face. Rangers are the best soldiers, the top, superior, enduring extensive physical and mental training, tactics, strategy, planning. Only someone physically superior and mentally stable could survive and complete Ranger school.

"I thought you were a Navy SEAL. Are you a Ranger, too?"

"Not officially, but I took the training, passed the course. Even Hell Week. Now, I don't know about you, but I'm starved." He cracks a grin when he sees my frown. "I don't mean for blood, although that little taste was a treat…"

I shake my head, unable to stop from smiling a bit.

"There's that smile," he says and brushes my cheek. "Don't worry. That mark on your neck is just for show. I won't drink your blood – unless you offer it because I'm just that kinda guy." He puts on his overcoat and scarf. "You're not fit to go out to eat, so I'll go out and get us some food from the little chicken and rib restaurant down the wharf. I know, I know. You don't eat meat. I'll get you a salad. Do you at least eat cheese? I don't know if they'll have tofu."

"I'm vegetarian, not vegan. I can have cheese. If they have pasta, that's good, too."

He goes to the door and before he leaves he turns to face me

"You might want to pull yourself together. We have a lot to talk about."

He puts on his hat and leaves me, the door closing behind him.

Later, he sits across from me at the little table in the room and eats with a single-mindedness he seems to apply to everything he does. I pick at my linguine Alfredo, biting at my food, chewing it but barely able to swallow, not really enjoying it. My stomach's still raw from vomiting.

When he's done, he goes into the washroom and washes his hands.

He stands in the doorway, drying his hands on a towel, watching as I pretend to eat. He looks incredibly handsome in his expensive suit, his dark hair shining in the overhead pot light. He looks like a CEO of some multi-million dollar company instead of a vampire-hunting vampire.

"You're not hungry."

I put down the fork. "Not really."

"Then why are you eating?"

"Um," I say and stumble. "I didn't want to make you mad again."

He shakes his head and throws down the towel.

"You think it doesn't make me mad to see you pushing your food around, pretending? You see, that's your problem, Eve," he says and sits back at the table across from me. "You're living a lie. Just be honest with yourself and everything will be a whole lot better. Try it sometime."

He watches as I wrap up my food and throw it in the trash. I go to the bathroom, splash water on my face and look in the mirror. My eyes are still red from crying. I have to pull it together. I return to sit back down at the table across from him. I keep my head down, not wanting to meet his gaze.

"I'm sorry about what happened," I start, wanting to explain. "I was so afraid you'd –"

He leans forward, interrupting me, his hand taking mine.

"Look, Eve. I'm not your therapist. I know," he says, shaking his head. "What that bastard did to you, what was it? Ten years ago? What he did to you was really sick and bad. But it's ten years and you're still cutting yourself while he's off probably still screwing up pretty little girls. You need to move on if it's keeping you from enjoying your life."

I look away from him. He really doesn't understand why I reacted that way. He doesn't understand that it isn't just that I feel damaged, that my memories of what happened resurface when I'm bored or afraid and cutting helps anesthetize me.

Cutting is what I do when my feelings overwhelm me. It helps me cope. I know he doesn't want to hear it so I sit there, mute. I can't even start to explain why except that for the past few weeks, he and Michel have been my life. Vampires. Monsters. Like the one who killed my mother. How sick does that make me?

After a while, I speak, defending myself.

"I'm doing pretty well. I've been accepted into the combined MD/PhD program, I have a scholarship to finish my B.Sc. I'll be one of the youngest graduates."

"I know your credentials. You're gifted. You're smart. With training, you'll be amazing. But you *suck* at life. You live alone in your little cat apartment, have no lover, or at least, had none other than a screwed-up vampire priest. You cut yourself. Look," he says, impatience in his voice. "Eve, you have to understand one thing. We're at war. *I'm* at war."

I look up.

"Yes, at war. I'm in the middle of a battle right now, planning out my strategy, refining my tactics. I don't have time for this," he says and twirls his fingers, "this battle of wills thing that's going on between us. I didn't expect you to be so unmanageable. With most humans, we get to just compel you into compliance, but you're impossible."

"I can't help it. I don't know why I can't be compelled. I have to do what I think is right."

"Look," he leans back, his finger tracing a pattern in the fake laminate wood grain of the table. "I admit I've had a real big hard-on for you since we met, what with your fair hair and hazel-eyed dancer body, sweet little pussy, gifted Adept - *thing* - you got going on."

I look in his eyes to see if he's playing me again, but he seems serious.

"I was in love with her too, Eve. But this little *pas de deux* has affected my performance and that's my fault. I've been sniffing around you like a dog after a bitch in heat, only you're not in heat, are you? Not yet," he says and leans forward, his elbows on the table, his arms crossed. He cricks his finger for me to come closer. "I have this policy of only being with women who are gagging for it. I know you're still mourning Michel. But I also know you find me attractive."

He nods and I feel heat rise to my cheeks.

"I thought, given a little encouragement, you'd be gagging for it as much as me, considering Michel's the first guy you've been with since that guy – whatshisname – *Grant* – back in your freshman year and he was less than adequate, wasn't he? Trying to get you to replicate all his favorite porn videos?"

Dammit! I hate how these brothers can just read my mind, find out things about me I don't want anyone to know.

"Your body needs it, but your mind's fighting it," he says. "And that doesn't work for me. Consider us back to business. No more of this little dance we've been doing, skirting around the issue. I thought," he says and pauses, licking his teeth. "I thought if I gave you a little encouragement, that if we could get here alone, that you'd come to your senses and realize what we could have, and I still think it might be possible. But I'm no therapist. I can't help you with this – *problem* - you have. You have to fix it yourself."

I can't help it. Tears spring to my eyes.

"Now, look at *that*," he says, waving a hand at me. "Instead of taking my advice and admitting I'm right, you start to cry. It doesn't work on me, Eve. Seriously. I'm a hardened soldier, a vampire hunter. I'm used to eating sweet young things like you for breakfast."

"I'm sorry, I—"

"*Don't*," he says and grabs my hand, squeezing it – hard. Hard enough that it hurts. "Don't be sorry. Be angry. Believe me, anger is so much better than sorrow or pain. You got an issue – *deal with it*. It's getting in the way of you living your life. You know, we could have a sweet thing going on here between us. But we can't – not when dear old foster dad," he says and waves his hand, "what was his name?"

"Bob."

"Dear old foster dad Bob Hayden-"

"No, that was my real dad's last name," I say, barely able to remember my first foster dad without a shiver of revulsion. "His name was Robert John Thompson." I pull my hand away from him, saying it with as much disgust as I can muster.

"Not when 'dear old foster dad Robert' is still screwing you over ten years later all the way from Boston."

"He's not in Boston. He's in Providence..." I stop and glance at him, but his eyes are hooded. I realize what he just did – what he got me to do. He said he did interrogations. I've told him who my enemy is and where he is without even knowing it. He's so skilled.

"What you *should* have done," he says and leans forward even closer. "What someone should do, is slip a knife between his ribs and cut the bastard's heart out. Instead, you're cutting yourself."

I look into his eyes and know he's right about me.

"You really don't live in the same world as me, do you?" I say. Now it's time for me to shake my head. "You think I can just have sex with you because you look like Michel. I can't."

"You see, Eve, you're still not telling yourself the truth." He takes my hand and holds it in his, softly this time. "Be honest with yourself at least, even if you're not honest with everyone else. You wanted me right from the start. I could tell when I touched you. I wanted you. By all rights, there was nothing keeping us from screwing our brains out – except convention and society and ethics."

"Those things matter."

"What *matters*, Eve, is what's right here right now." He turns my hand over in his, running his fingers over it. "That's all we've got. You're mortal. You die. Before I know it, you'll be dead and I'll be alone – again. I want to enjoy you. *Now*. I'm not my brother. I don't feel a need to wait until everything's perfect."

He lets go of my hand and leans back again. His gaze travels over my face.

"How can I," I say, swallowing. "Have sex with you when Michel will know?"

"Listen, you've got to stop holding out hope that he'll come back. He's not. I'm here. I look just like him, Eve. I'll grow my hair, act all pious, if you want." He gives that lopsided grin, but it just makes me more upset.

I shake my head, unable to express what I feel. I know he can't understand.

"It's true, Eve. If you want Michel, I'm a pretty good substitute. Just pretend I'm all *soulful* and regretful about having sex with you. Like Michel. I won't be regretful but by all means, pretend that I am."

"You could never replace Michel,'" I say, his tone getting my back up.

He shakes his head. "Don't worry," he says quickly. "Everything in its own time. Like I say, one day you'll come and offer it. And I'll take it. Ohhh," he says and mimes a shiver. "I'll take it."

He sits up and clasps his hands on the table, his face all serious.

"So, what do you know about this research Ed's got you doing?"

My head almost spins at the shift in topic and tone. I struggle for a moment, trying to focus.

"Um, he wants me to check into research on vampire immunity. Something about why the sun affects you. How are you able to daywalk? When did that happen?"

"Let me tell you a little story," he says, staring at me from under those dark brows. "Once upon a time, there was a private organization in South Carolina," he says, his voice quiet. "A very private organization. Funded by a number of very powerful political, business and military interests. Oversaw a corporation that was a combination security operation with big no-bid off-the-books defense and civilian contracts. Had a large population of vampires on which to experiment – all those incarcerated by the SCU and in tanks, waiting for their sentences to be up. One of the really cutting edge research projects was trying to turn us into daywalkers. You know, to use us all the time instead of just at night." He leans forward. "At least, that was the justification for the experiments. They took vampires – guys used to using killing to stay alive – and tried to turn them into high functioning operatives with no fear, no qualms about using violence, and no remorse. Hard as fuck to kill."

"You were one of them."

He nods.

"The organization wanted me. I was already working for the Council. I was a star candidate with hundreds of years as a knight and soldier. I scored high on IQ tests, had superior hand-eye coordination, spatial orientation, verbal skills. I was healthy. I could see fifteen steps ahead instead of just what was directly in front of me the way most grunts are. We were going to be super warriors. A group of us went to

Ranger training camp. Even got some good clandestine training courtesy of the CIA."

"How did they use you? The wars?"

"Iraq. Iran. Saudi. Russia. Oilandgasistan. Wherever there was a need to take people out to ensure the direction of the flow of petroleum was favorable to us, keeping the machinery of power working."

"What happened?"

"We got into a situation – an op in Iraq with too many civilian casualties. Real messy. Some of my soldiers left bodies behind. Then, the organization took care of us. Cleaned house. They terminated everyone with, shall I say, extreme prejudice so they could start it back up in another guise. I was betrayed, turned over to the enemy. I survived. Luckily, although sometimes I wonder, I really wonder. Luckily, I was picked up by another survivor, and we hid out. That's why I went to live at the monastery. Hiding out."

He shakes his head disgustedly.

I sat in silence for a moment, trying to take it all in.

"So you're fighting those in the organization who betrayed you?"

"Blackstone."

Blackstone?  "I heard Michel talk about it before. They're out for Dominion."

He nods.

"Now, Eve," he says and leans forward. "I'm going to tell you what Michel didn't want to tell you. He wanted to protect you, but I figure you're mine now. I want you to know. To understand. Maybe you'll stop fighting me."

I nod, a bit ill at ease because I'm scared now by his tone.

"To achieve Dominion, the Blackstone group plans to destroy modern electronic technology and send humans back to the steam age. Then, vampires will no longer be under threat. You humans have just developed too much advanced technology and now it's a threat to us."

I sit in silence, a sick feeling in the pit of my stomach.

"How?"

"That's the question. We don't know the details. Just the broad strokes."

"Destroying all electronic technology? That would kill so many people. People rely on technology to keep them alive. People on ventilators. People with pacemakers. Airplanes, navigation."

"Humans have to get real, Eve. Vampires are coming for you. You need people like Michel and me to fight them."

I cover my mouth with a hand and look away.

"Is Blackstone a vampire group?"

"Not just vampires. Humans as well. Collaborators who want a place in the new order. Blackstone wanted to create this super vampire warrior to use in this war against humans. You see, even with recruits offering to fight for Dominion – and there are – you'd be surprised. Even with them, war is hard on your average human," Julien continues, his voice taking on an amused tone. "There's a real need for warriors who can kill without all that messy emotional stuff to hold them back. Why not create a special private army of natural born killers? Hunters of humans? I thought I was going to be a warrior protecting the Treaty and I find out I'm protecting those out for Dominion. I have to prevent that at all costs." He stares at me. "That's what my whole life – *Michel's* whole life – is about. Preventing Dominion. Michel and I? We're infiltrators. We're fighting from within."

"Soren's part of Blackstone?"

"No," he says. "Soren's out to control Blackstone. He has his own agenda."

"Can we fight them?"

"We have to. I don't want Dominion."

"Why not? Wouldn't it mean you vampires would have power? Isn't that what you want? Power over us?"

He leans forward, his face intense.

"Eve, I was a priest. Sure, I wasn't a good one, but I was. Sure, I love blood. I love the hunt. I love feeding. But I don't want you to be like factory-farmed cows. What makes it so sweet," he says and closes his eyes, inhaling deeply. "What makes it so sweet is when you're free and you choose it. Choose *us*." He shakes his head. "You can't possibly understand. But know this, what Blackstone wants is for you to be nothing more than slaves and cows."

Tears sting at the corner of my eyes and I bite down hard on my lip to stop them. I know he has no patience for sniveling, and really, if what he says is true, anger is the only proper response to his story. I can't summon it. My overwhelming response is horror and grief.

Fighting Dominion is what killed my mother.

I don't want to even look at him and show my weakness. I leave him in the main bedroom and try to close myself in the bathroom but the lock is broken and the door won't shut. I sit on the toilet, covering my face with a towel so he won't hear me cry.

He knocks on the door, and it opens on its own. He comes in, looks at me sitting there with a wet facecloth in my hands to mop up my eyes, and he picks up the knife, pocketing it as if concerned I'll use it again.

I wipe my eyes once more, get control over myself.

"So, you'll help me?" he says. "No more resistance?"

He stands there in the bathroom doorway, his figure taking up most of its space, his shirt opened a few buttons, his hair tousled and he looked so damn strong and desirable. I know that if I'd met him first, I'd want him. I go to him and put my arms around his waist, not intending it in a sexual way, but out of care for him, for the human he once was and for how honorable he is now. He's startled at first by my embrace – I can tell by the slight hesitation before he returns it. Then he pulls me closer, his breath hitching just a bit.

"Eve," he says, amusement in his voice. "If I'd have known this would be your response, I'd have told you the whole sob story right away."

I squeeze harder, my head fitting perfectly in the space beneath his chin. Then I pull away when I feel his body respond to me.

"That wasn't me offering anything except compassion, Sir Julien, Knight defender of humans." I smile up at him and I mean it. He *is* a knight, despite the rough demeanor. I know he's honorable. I dart out of the bathroom, exhaling with relief and some regret as I escape his arms. I turn to face him when he enters the room. "It was just one person to another."

"Whatever you say, Eve," he says and chuckles. "Whatever you say. But I like it when you call me Sir. Maybe a bit too much."

I glance at my watch. It reads 9:20 – too early to go to bed, but I'm completely wiped after everything that's happened since my walk home from work. My knees actually shake just a bit, my eyes feel swollen and itchy. I need to wash my face, brush my teeth and go to bed.

"I'm really tired. Could we discuss this tomorrow? I have to go to the lab tomorrow morning. I need to sleep."

He nods and then picks up the channel changer.

"Go ahead. I'll keep the sound down."

"You're not staying."

"Yes I am. Don't worry. I'll sleep in this bed. You can take the other one."

"No, you have your own room."

"Uh, uh." He looks at me and shakes his head, then flicks on the television and searches channels. "Not a chance. You think I'm going to leave you alone after what I've told you? I don't think so. For one, you could run away and tell someone and then I'd be exposed, all my plans for nothing. For another, I don't know if you realize this but I do have enemies. They've probably seen me sniffing around you like a hungry dog. I expect that I've been followed. That's why Vasily's sitting down in the lobby."

"That's crazy."

"Eve, you're vulnerable. They could take you and try to use you to get to me. Like Luke did." He kicks off his shoes and stretches out on the other bed, one hand behind his head, the other wielding the channel changer as he surfs the news. "I'm not honorable enough to risk my life to save your life, so I'd rather not be put in that position. I need you alive."

I stand with my hands on my hips, fighting with myself over my response. On the one hand, he's right. I could run and tell. I might very well be in danger. On the other, he might also just be using this as a clever ruse.

"How do I know you won't try to use this opportunity to give me more encouragement?"

He rolls his eyes. "Eve, if I wanted to, I could tie you up in about oh, six seconds, and have my way with you and there'd be nothing – *nothing* – you could do about it except enjoy it." He looks at me, the intensity of his gaze imparting the truth of it. "I've told you more than enough. Now, I don't get off on rape so rest your little mind. Get in bed. Go to sleep."

I sigh. He'll do what he wants and there's nothing I can really do about it, short of getting myself killed. I take my overnight bag into the bathroom and try to keep the door closed with the ice bucket and my bag. After my usual routine of washing my face, brushing my teeth and hair, I put on my nightgown – a simple white cotton nightgown with delicate lace on the neckline and straps – more pretty than sexy. The one I wore when Michel came into my apartment that first time. I hold my bag in front of me as I return to the main room.

"Nice." He glances over briefly when I enter. I throw back the covers to the bed next to the bathroom and jump underneath so he can't see me for more than a second. "I had you pegged as more the granny gown type, Eve, but I'm not disappointed to be wrong."

"Goodnight, *Sir* Julien." I say, emphasizing the 'sir' part to remind him he's supposed to be honorable. I turn off the lamp on my bedside table, pressing my reluctant smile into my pillow.

"Sweet dreams, Eve." He chuckles. "I know mine will be rather tortured."


I wake up, my eyes adjusting to the low light in the hotel room. Julien's body is spooned against mine, one arm thrown over me. He snores softly behind me. I panic just a bit, then try to keep my breathing slow and steady, hoping to appear as if I'm still asleep just in case he's also pretending. I don't want to deal with this now – this little *pas de deux* as he called it – whatever it is. I turn over and he turns over with me, his arm withdrawn. His breathing changes its pattern. He's awake.

I wait, wondering what he'll do, torn between wanting him to roll back over and lie on top of me and him doing nothing.

He does nothing, just lies there. Maybe he's asleep after all. I keep still, breathing in slowly, out slowly. I try to focus on something other than the body next to mine – thinking of the tests I'll be setting up tomorrow, the PCA analysis, the biochemical screens. I think of hundreds of test tubes, one after another, hundreds of pipettes filling with liquids, Bunsen burners, gas chromatography . . .

When I next awaken, the bed's empty beside me. I have to pee and tiptoe over to the bathroom. Before I open it, I see through the crack that he's inside. My immediate response is to pull away, but the image I see makes me stay for a second longer than is polite.

He stands over the toilet, pants and boxers around his ankles, leaning against the wall with one arm supporting his weight, his hand spread out on the wall while the other hand strokes himself. Jammed into his mouth is a rolled up facecloth.

I tiptoe back to my bed and silently slip beneath the covers. I lie there, my heart pounding.

The thrill of it clashes with the sense of warning in my heart. The two of us are like trains approaching each other on the same track. Right now, I'm pretty much stationary, but he's hurtling towards me, picking up speed. I knew if I move towards him with any speed, the inevitable crash could destroy us both.

# CHAPTER 5

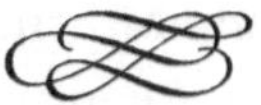

"Nobody has ever measured, not even poets, how much the heart can hold."
Zelda Fitzgerald

The next morning when I wake up, Julien's sitting on the end of his bed watching television. He's dressed in his suit, a cup of coffee in one hand, the channel changer in the other. The sound's on mute; he's reading news headlines. For a moment, the unreality of the scene strikes and I have to remind myself that the sense of tranquil domesticity is a mirage. He's probably thinking of his next move, which enemy he'll attack, what tactics he'll use in this war he's fighting.

Underneath the expensive suit and trappings of modernity is a knight itching to get his battle plan finalized.

I sit up and rub my eyes. My memories of the previous evening's events add to the sense of unreality that fills me – the walk along the waterfront was the last moment when I felt truly myself. After that, it was as if I've been transported to a different world – Julien's world. The confrontation when I almost denied him entrance to the room, the cutting, the revelations, his body next to mine on the bed, the image of him in the bathroom struggling against the sound of his own desire – only a few weeks ago, I could never imagine how any of it could happen to someone like me.

I get out of bed and go into the bathroom, needing a shower. I lodge my overnight bag against the door – not that it will keep him out if he truly wants to come, but it might keep the door from opening a crack. I undress and turn on the water, enjoying the hot sting of it.

As I wash, I think about him, remember moments from last night. Intimacy's a strange thing – the man's embraced me, lain on top of me, rubbed his face on my neck, in my hair, kissed me, and yet he's a stranger emotionally to me. I know more about his life than most people, and yet he's an unknown. He's another creature. I feel inexorably bound to him and yet he's a stranger. It's Stockholm Syndrome. He's been holding me emotional hostage since that day he rescued me. I'm starting to identify with him, as captives eventually do their hostage-taker.

As I shampoo my hair, I think about having sex with him. The truth is that in the few disappointing relationships I've had, being drunk was about the only way I could relax enough to do it and even then it was a blur. Oh, I felt desire, sometimes so much I felt it would suffocate me, but when it came to doing it, I balked like a frightened doe at the sound of a cocked gun. I couldn't let myself go. Michel was right about me. I need someone strong to take responsibility for my desire. Or therapy.

Or both.

I finish and dry off, dressing in my change of clothes that hangs on the back of the bathroom door so the steam will draw out the wrinkles. I wear little makeup – just a bit of mascara and lipstick. I pull my hair back into a ponytail. If you looked at me, you'd never know I spent the night with a vampire warrior next to me.

When I emerge from the bathroom, he's reading the local paper, holding it up for closer inspection while sipping his coffee. I can't help myself and smile as I fold my nightgown and tuck my things back into my overnight bag.

He glances over. "What are you smiling about?"

I shake my head, biting my lip to stop my smile from broadening.

"You sitting there, looking like Clark Kent ready to go out to the world in your business suit disguise, superhero hiding underneath."

"It's a good analogy except for the 'hero' part." He turns back to the paper, a smile on his lips. "I'm offended. Antihero, thank you very much. They're so much more fun."

I zip up the bag and then pick up my briefcase and sort through the papers inside. He puts his paper down and turns to face me.

"So, how are you today? Recovered from last night?"

"Have you?" I say, thinking of him in the bathroom.

He turns away and shakes his paper, folding it up. "Never better."

"I have to pack up. My flight's this afternoon. I'll be going to the lab for the morning then I'll go right to the airport after lunch."

He stands and buttons his jacket. "Vasily will take you to the lab and stay with you. Then he'll go with you on the flight. I don't fly commercial."

"I don't want him following me around everywhere, Sir Julien."

"Mmm, *Sir*. How I love that." He comes over to me and brushes a strand of hair from my face. "You have to promise me that when you finally offer yourself to me, you'll call me that."

I turn away from him and fumble with my shoes.

"What am I supposed to say, 'Here I am? Come and get it?'" His certainty that I will do it irritates me and I can't keep the frustration and anger out of my voice.

"That's nice," he says and turns me around, bending down to look in my face, "but I was thinking more like, *Oh, please, I need you now*." He lifts my chin. "That'll do it, yes it will. Why, I imagine if you say it with that sweet little voice of yours, I might not even make it across the room."

I brush by him. "Don't hold your breath."

He laughs. "I'd have been dead dead long ago if I'd done that."

I pick up my coat and scarf and then look around the room.

"I've already paid and its automatic checkout so I'll just go now."

"Vasily can drive us over to the lab."

"I'd prefer to walk."

"Eve, you just can't walk around by yourself anymore."

"Why not? This is Norfolk, not Boston. I'm walking."

He shakes his head and holds the door for me. "Not gonna happen."

"Sir *Julien*, I need the exercise."

"Stop calling me Sir," he says. "Save it for when you beg, thanks."

"I won't be begging." I stand firm. "I'm walking."

He holds his hands up.

"All right. Fool yourself if you want. You can put your bags in the car and Vasily can follow us."

I finally give in. There's no point in arguing. But I'm determined our walk isn't going to be an idyllic stroll along the waterfront.

I grab a muffin and bottle of juice from the free breakfast buffet on my way out and wait outside the front entrance as Julien speaks with Vasily and makes arrangements for him to follow us. Julien puts on his coat and his fedora and dons some sunglasses. I wouldn't have known he was Julien if I met him on the street.

As he approaches, I start walking ahead, determined not to let him lead or take my arm as I imagine he'll try to do. Although I'm wearing heels, I'm adept in them due to my years of dance and can walk at quite a brisk pace if I need to. He hurries to catch up.

We walk in silence. I keep my focus on the water, watching the gulls circle around, eating my muffin.

"So it's going to be like that, is it Eve?"

I don't reply. We walk along the waterfront, and near the lab. I'm relieved that soon, we'll part and I can try to return to a normal life. *My* normal life. When we reach the walkway that leads to the lab, we stop.

"I don't get you, Eve," he says and turns to me. "One minute, you're smiling with me over something amusing. The next you won't even look at me."

"I was reminded that you've taken over my life – pretty much against my will."

"You said all in."

"As a researcher interested in understanding vampirism. As

someone who wants to find out the truth. Not as your personal sex toy."

"It's a package deal."

I glance at him, see the mischievous grin on his face, and have to turn my own face away so he can't see my smile. *Damn him.* I start walking to the lab.

"Eve, Eve, *Eve,*" he says and grabs my arm, stopping me. He puts his arms around me and forces me into an embrace, looking around as if to see if someone might think he was forcing me against my will. He takes off his sunglasses and looks down into my face. "You *like* me. You really do."

I try to turn away, hiding my face from those too-intense blue eyes, but he grabs my chin and stops me.

"You *want* me. You really do."

I close my eyes, but in truth, I feel like a small child plugging my ears at something I don't want to hear.

"Look at me," he says quickly, his voice soft. I open my eyes with reluctance. "I'm right here. Any time you decide that you *need* me, you just have to call."

I actually feel dizzy standing there in his arms, his voice so strong and certain, his gaze so intense.

An abyss. That's what he is. And I'm too close to the edge.

He leans down and kisses my cheek, pressing his lips there, squeezing my arms.

When he lets me go, I walk away without a word, not trusting my voice.

"Don't wait too long," he says, just loud enough for me to hear. "If I die on some operation, it'll be too late and then you won't have either of us."

I stop in my tracks, anger and frustration filling me. That's emotional blackmail. I turn on my heel and storm back to where he stands and when I reach him, I hit his chest with a closed fist – not hard, just to make a point.

"Don't you make me feel guilty! You aren't going to use emotional blackmail to get me to be your little pet."

He grabs hold of my shoulders and glances around, then shakes me.

"Calm down."

"No, I'm not going to calm down," I say. "I've had it up to here with this! You and your *I need you Eve*. You're in my face wherever I go, trying to tempt me to be your little squeeze while you fight your war. Do you really think I'm looking for heartbreak? Do you really think I'll choose it?"

I hit him again, but it's a paltry attempt.

"Eve," he says and shakes me just a bit harder. "Listen, look at me. Let me tell you about something." I try to leave, but he won't let me, pulling me back into his arms. Finally I give in and stand there, fighting back tears.

"I have a telescope, a nice telescope. I attach a camera to the tripod and take pictures of stars and planets. I took one once of Tycho's Nova with a long exposure to let in as much light as possible. It's all purple and green and red, like a giant celestial flower on acid."

I look at the water, at the birds sitting along the lampposts, anywhere but in his eyes.

"It's a remnant of one of the brightest explosions in the universe - a Type 1a supernova. It happens when a star explodes after millions of years circling another, sucking up the other's matter until it passes critical mass. The small one's a dwarf, a pretty little thing, all shiny and burning bright white. The larger one is a giant, a big red seething angry fellow."

"Look," I say, fighting against the hypnotizing effect of his voice. "I'm sure this is a nice story, but I have to go."

"Just wait. Let me finish. The dwarf," he says and turns my face to his, smoothing my hair. "The dwarf isn't the kind that explodes on its own. It's too small, but put it next to the giant, bring them together close enough and a maelstrom forms, a violent convection that pulls them even closer until they're together so tightly that the giant's mass flows into the dwarf. Eventually, the dwarf passes this critical mass called the Chandrasekhar Limit. When it does, the explosion is five billion times brighter than the Sun."

I look up at him, unable to turn away.

"Eve, if the dwarf stays alone, it never passes that limit. It slowly dies, becoming so faint that no one can even see it anymore. But when that red giant gets close enough? For a brief second, a thing of beauty seen right across the universe."

A sense of deep anguish fills me.

"But it's destroyed, isn't it? The dwarf dies."

He sighs. "Every human dies. What counts is how you live."

"I was living before you and Michel came along," I say, but I know it's a lie.

"You were alive. You weren't really living. This," he says and pulls me closer, his lips almost touching mine. "This is living." He kisses me, pressing his mouth against mine – softly at first, and then with more passion, his lips parting, his tongue touching mine, his embrace tightening. A connection forms between us and I feel his desire for me, his need, and it makes me dizzy in its intensity. Finally, he lets me go and he's the one to turn away. He walks to the car where Vasily stands with the door open. He sits in the back seat, the door closing, the darkened windows blocking my view of him.

The morning goes slowly for me. I don't feel the enthusiasm for the work the way I did only yesterday. Julien's words at our parting haunt me, the image of the colliding stars, the explosion – it's a scary metaphor for the two of us. Part of me says to run, to call the police and enter the witness protection program, go into exile. The other part says to run to him, to lose myself in him, to feel completely possessed for once in my life – the way I thought I'd feel with Michel.

After lunch is ordered in, I say my goodbyes and promise to return, then go outside the building to find Vasily sitting there in his rental car reading a paper. He hops out of the vehicle and opens the back door, waving me inside.

"There's an envelope on seat beside you, Eve."

I pick up the envelope and open the flap. Inside is a receipt from a local printing shop, and a photographic image with fiery reds, brilliant violet purples, luminous greens all roiling together against a black background. Tycho's Nova. On the back, hand-scrawled, is a simple note:

*Imagine it. Julien*

I put the photograph down and watch out the car window as the streets of Norfolk pass by.

# CHAPTER 6

<br>

"*A very small degree of hope is sufficient to cause the birth of love.*"

Stendahl

We arrive home in the late afternoon and my head aches so I go to the fridge for a bottle of OJ to wash down my Tylenol. I wander over to the office where Vasily sits, drinking his coffee and watching the video cameras.

"Where's Julien?"

"Meetings," Vasily replies, turning to me and smiling.

"Is this his warehouse? Does he own the whole thing?"

Vasily nods. "Has owned for long time. Before staking, he lived at monastery but has office in apartment downstairs. Now he lives here."

Outside on one of the monitors, I see a van drive up and park on the curb. Vasily points to one monitor.

"Cleaners are here," he says. "Come to clean up construction mess. Clean carpets and floors on each level."

"Should I do anything?"

"Just play piano or watch TV. They do this floor first and won't take long – maybe one hour."

The cleaners consist of a couple of men dressed in white overalls with a large industrial vacuum and carpet cleaners. They move through the large space with amazing efficiency and then clean the carpets in the entry, which have accumulated dust from the drywalling that's been done in the loft.

While they're still cleaning, I become bored of hearing about the latest armed robbery and murders, so I turn off the television and play piano for a while, practicing *Ballade* like a good servant.

Suddenly, I hear a tremendous crash from outside. I go to the row of video monitors and check out the screens. Then I see it – a car smashed into the cleaning van and the vehicle was knocked into the street, the other car's hood crumpled, its engine smoking. Someone slumps out of the driver's seat and onto the road.

Vasily grabs a cell phone off his desk.

"Let me help," I say. "I've taken first aid."

He shakes his head. "No," he dials a number. "You stay safe. I'm calling it in now. You stay here."

He leaves me alone and I go back to the video monitors and watch as Vasily and the cleaners discuss the situation on the sidewalk and someone else speaks with the driver of the errant car.

I go to the door and see that it's held open by a corner of the carpet that the cleaners were working on. I go through the empty anteroom and to the elevator. Beside it is a stairwell with a glass door and window. When I press the elevator button, nothing happens – Vasily must have had it stay on the main floor for security reasons. I try the door to the stairs, not really knowing why, but checking to see if it's open. It is.

I can't help it – I go down to the lower floor and to the door to the apartment where Julien has his office. I try the door, my heart in my throat, and it's unlocked. For a moment, I debate with myself whether I should open the door. If I do and someone's there, Julien will be angry that I left the apartment. Perhaps Vasily will get in trouble – but it really wouldn't be his fault that the cleaners accidentally left the door ajar.

I'm just so curious about Julien – this vampire who's claimed me in Michel's absence. Inside, the apartment is Spartan – just a massive open space with hardwoods and exposed brick and ductwork like upstairs. A platform bed sits in one corner, messy, unmade. Piles of papers, books, magazines, boxes, and what looked like scrap furniture lay about, giving the space a cluttered look. A telescope sits in a window.

As I stand there, a naked woman comes out of a room. A shock goes through me – at first, I think it's either a model or a drug addict, for she's tall and thin, her eyes hollow, her skin grey. Long brown hair, greasy. Dark eyes. Tattoos on her arms and one on her hip. About my age, but she looks ill, pale, skinny.

I can see bite marks on her neck and shoulder.

"Who are you?" the woman says, stopping in the center of the space.

"I'm Eve. I'm staying upstairs," I say. "Who are you?"

"I live here," the woman says.

"You live here?"

"Yeah. I'm with Mike. I'm Kate."

"You and - *Mike*?" I stare at the floor, my muscles tightening. "Don't you mean Julien?"

"No, you know. Mike. French guy. Vamp. With the big teeth?" She coughs, a raspy sound. "Julien's the monk. Are you one of his pets?"

A feeling of numbness floods through me.

"No." I grind my teeth, dig my nails into my palm. "I'm no one's pet."

"Oh, yeah?" The woman seems unconcerned that she's naked. "Then what's that bite on your neck?"

"How long," I say, barely able to get the words out, "how long have you been living with Michel?"

"Six months but I just got back from County last week." The

woman looks at her arm, rubs it. Even from where I stand, I can see needle tracks in her arm. "The court gave me an option of rehab or 30 days, so I did the time. Forget that shit." She wipes her nose on a wrist.

"Did Michel pick you up?"

She frowns. "Yeah. Of course he did."

So that's where Michel was.

"You always go around naked?"

"Hey, it's my place. Besides, Mike likes it." She coughs again. "You got any smokes? I'm out."

"No." I shake my head. "Sorry. I have to go."

I leave the apartment, feeling numb – completely numb, my knees weak. I walk back up the stairs. Go inside. Find my shoes. My backpack. My coat.

I leave, taking the stairs. Glance out the front doors to see a crowd of people around the car, its engine flaming, Vasily spraying it with a fire extinguisher.

I find a rear exit and try the knob. It opens. There's no one outside watching the door, so I open it and leave the building.

The streets bordering the waterfront are narrow, with old deserted warehouses and buildings that have been abandoned and are rusting with age and the salt air. I walk as fast as I can, my mind blank, just wanting to escape. I get about five blocks away and go down a narrow alley and stop by a trash bin and vomit.

A car drives down the street and I wave at it, hoping that the person will give me a lift but the car drives by and the driver doesn't even glance at me.

Although I've lived in Boston now for almost a decade, I don't know this area of town well, and have no idea how to get back to civilization. I just walk towards the city center, hoping that I'll find a telephone booth or someone who will give me a ride to Boston PD. I'll ask for witness protection.

As I turn a corner down another deserted street, I see Vasily's car coming in the other direction. I duck down the alley and run, searching for a door I can enter and a place to hide. I'm sure Vasily saw me. Now it's only a matter of time before he comes for me.

I find an open door and enter an old brownstone warehouse, and am assaulted by a stench so bad I think I must be in a garbage dump. On the floor are dozens of needles, bags of trash, filthy mattresses, used take-out containers. It is – or has been at one time a flop-house for addicts.

I climb the stairs, hoping to find a place to hide, but each level is wide open, the floors abandoned and empty. There's nowhere to go but up. Finally at the top floor, I see a ladder going up to a skylight in the roof and climb up.

"Eve!"

It's Vasily. I try the skylight and it opens so I climb out and find myself on a platform about a floor above the rest of the roof, twenty feet square. An old rusting HVAC system perches on one edge. I close the skylight and hide behind the old tin housing.

It takes about five minutes for him to find me. I don't know what I was thinking – there's no escape. I sit and shiver, my coat not warm enough against the unusually cool weather.

The skylight opens and Vasily pops out, glancing around in search of me. He walks over and kneels down beside me.

"Come," he says, holding out his hand. "You must come back with me before Julien returns or there will be paying hell."

"Hell to pay," I say. "I'm not going back, Vasily. Just let me go."

Vasily shakes his head. "If I did, Michel would surely send someone to kill me. Julien too."

"Don't tell him, then. Say you couldn't find me. It was the cleaners – they left the door open, not you."

"No, I am your protector. The bucks come to me. You are in danger now because of being Michel's woman."

"I'm not his 'woman'. Kate is." I can't believe that Michel lied to me about being celibate. He kept a woman in his home and now keeps her in the warehouse? A junkie?

Vasily frowns for a moment.

"Ahh," he says, covering his eyes with a hand. "You went downstairs. No," he says and shakes his head. "You don't understand. Kate is junkie friend of Michel's. From way back, when he was working as priest with street people. He," Vasily says and shrugs. "Michel keeps her supplied with good drugs, doctors, a place to sleep so she doesn't walk streets. Live in place like this." He points to the building. "Now that the mansion is being fixed, she had to come stay at Julien's."

"She said Michel was her lover. Are you telling me she and Michel aren't lovers?"

"Lovers?" Vasily makes a face. "Not lovers. You," he says and points to me. "You and Michel are lovers."

"Not anymore." Even as I say it, grief bites at my heart.

"Come back, Eve. You can't leave."

"Am I a prisoner?"

"Prisoner, no. Unsafe outside of warehouse, yes. Didn't Luke teach you that? Come back with me now before Julien finds out. He will punish you for this."

"I'm not coming. You'll have to drag me."

"I will."

"I'll kick you."

He leans over and grabs one foot and pulls but only succeeds in removing my shoe.

"Eve," he says, throwing the shoe down. "Enough foolishness. If you wait too long, he will come himself and then I will pay Hell. And now, I am getting mad."

"I won't come back. I'm not letting Julien claim me like some spoil of war."

Vasily takes out his cell phone and dials a number. He speaks in Russian to someone on the other line, his voice angered. It's quite a long conversation. Finally, Vasily rubs his forehead and looks at his watch. Then he hangs up, and dials another number, listens, presses buttons, and listens some more – as if he's listening to voice mail.

"You come now," he says, waving his hand at me. "Julien is out of town for the rest of week. He left message. He knows nothing – left straight from meeting. Come."

I close my eyes. I can't stay on the roof forever and Vasily's getting angrier but I can't go back willingly.

"I'm not leaving."

"*Ebanatyi pidaraz!*" Vasily says, stomping his foot. "That means fucking motherfucker. That means I'm getting very mad. Do I have to call Ivan and get him to bring Taser? Maybe tranquillizer gun? He was with Russian Secret Police before Vory. Do you want him to use his techniques on you? This is no game, Eve."

I wrap my coat around myself more tightly.

"I won't go willingly." I turn my face away from Vasily. "I'm not cooperating any longer. If you take me back, it will be by force."

He throws his hands up. "So be it."

Vasily dials a number on his cell phone. He speaks once more in Russian and gesticulates in an angry fashion. He snaps the phone shut and climbs down the ladder, closing the skylight behind him.

After about ten minutes, I hear a car drive up and I climb to the edge that looks over the side of the building and glance down. A large black SUV – two men get out. As I watch, Vasily points up at the roof and the men follow his hand.

Vasily shades his eyes.

I stand up and walk along the edge, looking down at them.

"Eve," Vasily shouts up. "Stay away from edge!"

I raise my arms up, feeling the wind blowing around me. The two other men run into the building.

"Eve, no!" Vasily waves his hands. "Don't!"

They think I'm going to jump. It almost makes me laugh. Good. Let them worry. I've been put through a wringer in the past few weeks. The man I'm in love with is a lying vampire who thinks I'm a possession he can just give to his brother, who's a first-class jerk. I can't leave the warehouse without Vasily in escort. I'm not to ask questions, complain or expect anything. By all rights, I should jump.

The skylight opens and a man climbs out. He has a shaved head and ice blue eyes and is wearing a leather trench that looks like something out of Nazi Germany. Ivan perhaps.

"Come, Eve. Move away from the edge," he says, his accent not quite as thick as Vasily's, more cultured. "You don't want to do that."

I shrug. "Why not?"

I cover my eyes and try not to cry, but finally, my emotions over-whelm me. Then the man grabs my arm roughly, and despite every-thing, I fall into fight mode, and I have him down and on his stomach, in a second. I'm just about to pull his gun away from his hand when I feel something press in the back of my neck. I realize the one who holds the gun must be an adept as well, to be able to beat me. I have a lot to learn about fighting.

"I wouldn't try, Eve," the voice says and the speaker has a Russian accent. I turn to look at him. He's got dark hair slicked back and a goatee. He has a gun to my head and so I put my hands up and he grabs one and twists it behind my back, keeping the gun at my neck.

He practically pulls me down the stairs with him. When we reach the bottom, we emerge out of the building and are met by a concerned Vasily, who opens the door to the black SUV while the man who grabbed me shoves me inside. The men speak in Russian, exchanging angry words, Vasily shaking his head.

I sit staring out the windshield, completely numb.


Vasily escorts me up the elevator, and enters the code to the lock before pushing me into the apartment. When I emerge into the main area, I see Julien standing there, his hands on his hips, a scowl on his face.

"Vasily," I say to him. "You said he was gone."

"I lied."

Vasily enters a code on the lock and leaves the apartment. I turn and face the door, covering my mouth.

"You know, Eve," Julien says from behind me, his voice hard. "I was right in the middle of something important, interviewing someone from South Carolina, someone involved in research on vampirism, when I get this panicked call from Vasily telling me that you'd gone missing. Right away, I think that Luke has taken you, or worse, that Soren's gone back on our bargain, and I'm *sick*. Then Vasily calls me back and tells me you're hiding out on top of a building, threatening to jump? Here I was, thinking someone came to harm you and I find out you're pouting over sick little junkie *Kate?*"

He grabs me by the arm and spins me around to face him. I close my eyes.

"You look at me when I'm talking to you."

I open my eyes.

"What have you got to say for yourself?"

I shake my head.

"I can't do this," I say, my voice breaking. "All of this." I wave at the apartment. "I'm not yours. I don't want you."

"I hate to break it to you, but you *are* mine. You have no choice about it. Once Soren learned you were alive, your fate was determined. You're just lucky I'm giving you time to adjust."

"I'm leaving. You have no right to force me and I'm not staying with you."

"You're staying, Eve," he says and squeezes my hand - hard. "You're worth too much to our enemies to let you leave. I paid too high a price – *Michel* paid too high a price – to have you be taken by someone else."

"I'm not cooperating any longer."

"You never did."

I pull my hand away and clench my fists, dig my nails into my palms.

"All this over Kate?" He squeezes my arm. "Running away, climbing on a roof, threatening to jump?"

I try to wrestle free, but it's futile.

"No, she just made it all crystal clear."

"OK, bright girl," he says. "You tell me what's so crystal clear now that you've met Kate." He drags me over to the couch and pushes me down onto it. He stands in front of me and waits, hands on hips.

"I'll help you," I say, breathing slowly, in control now. "I'll do research. I'll work as a blood witness. But the rest – I can't do it anymore. I won't be your Adept or your little pet."

"Eve, why are you doing this? Kate's a junkie from Michel's past when he was looking after street people. He found her on the street and tried to save her life. He supports her financially. Nothing more. You saw her. For God's sake – even with good dope and medical care, she's dead."

"You're trying to tell me that he's supporting her out of compassion? I saw bites all over her and she said he liked it when she walked around naked."

"Eve," he says, bending down, grabbing my arms. "Did you see her? She's sick, dying. Michel … Ah, screw it," he says and closes his eyes. "He bit her so he wouldn't bite you. *Dieu.*" He shakes his head. "There. I said it. Michel's a morally-fucked-up former priest who didn't want to feed on you to keep you pure. So he fed on sick little Kate who's donated her blood to him so he'll give her a good death." He shakes his head slowly, and he looks truly pained. "Being with you made him need it from someone. She wants him to kill her when she's ready to die. Now, I have to do it, just like I have to take you. There. He didn't have sex with her. He gave her nice sex dreams like I gave you. He made her feel good about herself in her last days. That's all." He lets go of my arms. "It's the one thing we vampires do that has any value."

I sit in silence, not knowing what to believe but I didn't feel deceit when he touched me. He rubs his forehead as if exasperated.

"You have to understand about vampires," he says, looking at me. "We don't survive on blood alone. We can, but we become dead to the world of humans, seeing them only as prey. We need the physical contact, the connection, to prevent that. We need to feed on a warm body and feel some kind of human connection or else we lose our humanity. Michel was so intent on keeping you pure that he bit her, so he wouldn't bite you. Saint and sinner," he says, shrugging. "That's my totally fucked-up brother."

I look away from him because he's being so honest, it's hard to meet his eye.

"Now Soren's got him in payment for your life and I'm a monster, and all I want is to protect you and make you happy in his place. And I think I can make you happy."

"You can't."

He just stares at me, shaking his head slowly.

"What is it with you? You're more trouble than you're worth. Screwed up. You actually think this is all about you. It isn't. But, OK," he says and his voice sounds as if he's on the edge of losing control. "If you want it totally professional, so be it. Just remember this – this is war. People don't get to be happy." He just stands there. "Grow up, Eve," he says. "Grow up."

With that, he leaves the apartment, slamming the door behind him.

# CHAPTER 7

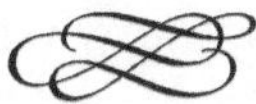

"Fear may induce the show of submission, but love only can truly subjugate a haughty spirit."
Mary Cowden Clarke

JULIEN'S BEEN OUT OF TOWN FOR THE PAST DAY on some business and Vasily has kept a low profile so I've been alone most of the time. Vasily makes me meals but barely looks at me. I notice a bruise on his cheek and a butterfly suture on his lip.

"Did Julien hurt you?" I say when he hands me a plate of food at supper.

Vasily shrugs. "He was very upset. Thought Soren had taken you. Thought you were suicidal. I was wrong to have left you alone."

I shake my head, disgusted with Julien, filled with guilt that Vasily paid for my disobedience.

When he arrives back later that night, Julien strides in the apartment looking all chipper and rubs his hands together, as if excited to be home.

"Vasily," he says, his voice almost ebullient. "I've made plans for our little outing later. Perhaps you could go downstairs and finish the arrangements. I have some work to do here."

Vasily nods.

"Keep stiff upper lip," Vasily says quietly as he passes by.

I frown, not knowing what he means. Once the door closes and we're alone, Julien takes my hand, pulling me to one of the over-stuffed couches in the small sitting area. He sits in the middle and before I can react, he pulls me face down over his lap, one arm pinning me across the upper back, the other fumbling with the zipper to my skirt.

"What are you-" I stop, gasping when I realize what he intends to do – he's going to *spank* me. "Don't you dare!" I try with all my might to wrestle my way free, expecting to fall into fight trance, but nothing happens. He's disarmed me before I can respond. "Don't you touch me!"

"Oh, I'm going to do more than touch you, Eve," he says, yanking my skirt down below my knees, my panties following. "I'm going to spank your bottom just like I said. You disobeyed my orders and you have to be punished. But don't worry - it's going to please me far more than it hurts you."

"I could kill you," I say. "I will kill you if you hit me."

"Spare me the false threats. You can't beat me any longer," he says. "I'm going to spank you like a good Master should when his slave disobeys. And you're just going to take it."

"I'm not your slave!" I try to fight, but he's already grabbed hold of my body using his powers, making me unable to resist except for a paltry struggle.

"Oh, I like it when you wiggle like that," he says, his voice all lusty. "It'll make this even more enjoyable for me." He holds me down and whispers in my ear. "But the more you fight, the angrier I get. The angrier I get, the harder I'll spank."

"You're too strong," I say, my heart racing. "You'll hurt me."

"I can feel what you feel, in case you forgot. I'll know when to stop."

"My pain will block you from knowing when to stop," I say.

He's still for a moment, and I stop struggling, thinking that he's realized that my pain block nullifies any advantage he has through touch telepathy. My buttocks are now completely bare, and he's stroking his hand over them softly.

"I'll just have to take that chance," he says, but even now, I feel his reluctance when he touches me, as if he's worried that what I say is right. "You need this. You want this, even if you don't admit it to yourself. So, give me a safe word, Eve, just in case I can't read you."

"No," I say. "I'm not playing along."

He doesn't hit me just yet. Instead he strokes his hand over me, cupping my cheeks.

"All right then, I'll give you one. Red. If you need me to stop, say red."

I don't reply.

"You know, Eve, I'm not really into this whole pain/pleasure thing," he says, his voice all husky. "I tend to just like the pleasure part. However, I think I might just enjoy this a little too much because you have a very nice ass. *Very* nice," he says in a playful voice. "Peaches and cream. It's a shame I have to make it all red but when I'm done, I'll make sure to kiss it all better."

"Don't do it," I say, unable to keep my resolve not to resist, "or I'll hate you."

"I'll just have to take that risk. You have this coming." With that, he brings his hand down on my left buttock with a loud smack, his hand landing down low, the pain sharp. I cover my mouth with my hands, not wanting to make a sound and give him any satisfaction.

"That," he says, rubbing the place where he slapped me. "That's for sneaking away from Vasily the other day. The poor man was frantic when he realized you were gone. He was afraid I'd kill him for it and I probably should have but I'm just too soft-hearted and only punched him."

I tense up, waiting for the next blow.

"And this," he says, another blow on my other buttock. "This is for leaving the apartment and going downstairs, finding Kate. You know you have to just obey, Eve. The rules are there for a reason. They're not arbitrary. You think you need to know everything about everything but this is a military campaign and you know what I *think* you need to know, nothing more."

He rubs the spot gently. I'm determined I won't make a sound, won't give him the pleasure of my tears.

"This—" Smack! "This is for making me tell you the truth about Kate when I didn't want you to know. When you didn't *need* to know."

The spank stings, but it's the helplessness that gets to me – I'm at his total mercy. He could spank me as much or little as he wants, as hard as he wants, and there's nothing I can do about it except use the safe word and that would admit defeat.

"I *hate* you."

"Ah, but I don't hate *you*, Eve, and that's all that matters. I don't hate spanking your sweet little derriere. When I met you that first night in the diner, when I got a look at you as a grown woman, I was so sad to think Michel found you first. But now, I have you all to myself and oh, you have such a nice little ass, all round and jiggly when I slap it. It makes me think of how it'll jiggle when I take you from behind. And look - now it's getting a lovely shade of pink."

"You're a bastard and you'll never take me from behind."

That makes him laugh. "Yes, technically I am and considering what an old letch my father was, how could I be anything else?" After a moment, he bends down and whispers in my ear. "And I *will* take you from behind Eve." He pulls my hair away from my face, presses his cheek against mine. "And you'll love it when I do."

With that, he smacks me even harder than before, and for the first time, I become scared as I realize how powerful he is and how he really could do whatever he wants to me, ignoring any safe word I did use.

"That's for putting yourself in such danger. And this," he says and smacks me even harder without first rubbing, the pain sharp. "This is for making me have to kiss Luke's ass to get you back. Now he's going to be out to get you any way he can and I'll have to watch my back every minute of the day until I kill him."

"Stop it - you're hurting me!"

"I hope so," he says smacking me again, this time so hard that I cry out loud, tears of anger and frustration springing to my eyes. "That's for making me spank you."

"You're a sadist!"

"No, far from it," he says, "but you are a little bit of a masochist, aren't you? I'm up for administering a little spanking now and then to help out, especially when a girl forgets to do as she's told." He starts to rub my buttocks again, his hand moving lightly over my skin.

I can't help it – I cry, my hands covering my eyes.

"Shhh," he whispers. "I hope you've learned your lesson. If you have, I'll stop."

I don't respond, just try to hold back the tears, wiping my eyes on my sleeve.

"Tell me what lesson you've learned, Eve."

"I hate you!"

"Wrong answer." He strikes me again, and I jam my fist in my mouth to stop from giving him the satisfaction of hearing me cry out. He rubs my buttocks again, his hands moving in slow circles over each one. "That was for scaring me half to death by your stunt on the roof and for making me think Soren had you. Now, try again."

I refuse to answer, biting down hard in anticipation of the next blow.

"I assure you, Eve, that I'll keep spanking you until you give me the right answer. I love spanking your nice little ass, imagining all the other things I'm going to do to your sweet little body when I'm done. Now tell me, what lesson have you learned today?"

Finally, I give in. "Not to leave without permission."

"That's right. You know you're not to go out by yourself because it's dangerous. You went out anyway and got into trouble. You could have died." He strokes my skin and then leans down and kisses one buttock, then the other. He lays his cheek against me, and it's cool and soothing. "You could have *died*."

I lie still, my breath shallow, my face flushed.

"I'm happy to be spanking you at all," he says. "I was afraid I'd lose you. I can't let that happen."

I lie quietly, barely able to breathe. When he turns me over, I don't resist, feeling almost drugged. When he lies fully on top of me, I'm still, my eyes closed, letting him touch me, letting him kiss me, his mouth on mine, his tongue touching mine. He feels so much like Michel, he looks so much like Michel, that I let him.

Finally, he rises up on his elbows and I open my eyes. He looks down, one hand wiping the tears from my cheeks. He's so beautiful in every way – just like Michel. The blue eyes, the thick black lashes, the black hair, pale skin, the square jaw, the stubble.

But he has that scar. His hair is short. He's *not* Michel.

"Eve," he whispers, leaning back down to nuzzle my neck, his breath in my ear. "You have to obey. It'll make everything so much easier. Now, just let me in."

I lie beneath him, naked except for the blouse around my shoulders and the skirt and panties around my knees. My body responds despite my mind refusing him and I don't let him in, my nails digging into my palms again. He hangs his head, his eyes closed. Then he climbs off the couch and leaves me alone.

I lie there for a few moments trying to understand what happened, my body so ready but my mind so unwilling. Finally, I get up, adjusting my clothes. I go to my bed and crawl back in it, pulling the covers over my head, crying as silently as I can manage.

I sleep for several hours, waking up when the sun goes down. I get out of bed and go to the bathroom to inspect my ass, to see what damage Julien did to me. My butt is no longer red but it's tender to the touch. I have a bath and get into my nightgown and socks. I remember how I felt after the spank and can't tell if it was from him affecting my brain or from the spanking. I felt as if I had to make him suffer.

And then I think I'm seriously in deep. Part of me just wants to give in and let this happen between us. But I still fight it, not yet sure if I'm ready. I barely know him, no matter how much he looks like Michel. It scares me.

Later, Julien arrives while I'm sitting at the piano, practicing alone in the darkened living area, playing a Bach piece I know by heart,

Prelude in C Sharp Minor. I always loved Bach when I was first learning piano – the perfection of his work, the precision needed to play it properly. I loved the discipline involved.

He doesn't come over but I know he's standing at the kitchen, drinking a glass of blood, listening to me. I finish playing and just sit in the stillness, wondering what he's going to do next. He comes to me and takes my hand, pulling me with him to the seating area again.

"Stop," I say, afraid he's going to spank me again.

"I'm not going to spank you."

He pulls me down onto his lap so that I'm straddling him, one knee on either side of his hips and it's far too intimate for his face is only a foot away from mine and I can't help but stare into his blue eyes.

He says nothing for a moment, just looking at me, his gaze moving over my face. I have to look away because his eyes are just too intense. I sit there, my hands resting on his shoulders, my face turned away.

"I shouldn't have spanked you when your pain block means I won't know when to stop."

"Julien, I…" I say, hesitating, for my emotions are just too close to the surface. I'm not really sure what I feel. "It scares me."

"I know," he says and I can just detect a slight bit of hurt in his voice. "I'm really not into this whole obedience thing in a relationship. Sure, I'm used to using compulsion to get my way with humans, but I don't consider that a true relationship. Humans are tools. Your immunity to compulsion makes this so much harder. I just can't make you do what I want."

"Would you have just compelled me to have sex with you if you could?"

He runs his fingers through my hair.

"I don't tend to become involved with humans any more."

"Why?"

He pauses for a moment, running his fingers along my chin.

"Humans die. After the first dozen or so who died after I fell in love with them, I gave up trying and stick to other vampires."

"That's probably wise."

He nods and leans his head back.

"Because Michel and I can't compel you, it's like we're forced to see you as a person instead of as just a tool. We have to reason with you, argue with you, talk to you. You're complicated. Anyway, I thought you were ready because your body was but your mind is so damn rebellious. I can access your body but I couldn't tell if I'd done too much or too little for your mind, so if I did too much, I apologize. I thought that it would help bring us together because, well," he says and trails his fingers down my neck and over his bite mark on my throat. "Michel's gone and I'm all you've got. I hate that I can't read you whenever I need to. Michel warned me."

I shake my head. "You two actually *talked* about this?"

"Of course. He wanted you protected, cared for." He takes my chin in his hand so I have to look in his eyes. "We have to get on the same page and quick. Partners?" he says, and tilts his head to the side. "Work together?"

I nod and feel my breath hitch for that's what I suggested to Michel and what he rejected. These two are so different...

"On one condition," I say, wondering how to phrase my proposal. "My condition is that you have to help me find a way to kill Soren and bring Michel back. I can't have him do this, Julien. It's not fair."

He tightens his arms around me.

"You're so good, Eve," he says, his voice soft. "But killing Soren? That's a huge thing. Do you think for a *moment* that if there was a way, I wouldn't have already done it? You're not strong enough. I don't know if anyone's strong enough. He's probably four thousand years old and something else entirely. You think vampires are hard to kill? Ancients are motherfuckers. I don't know if one's ever died."

"He was created," I say. "He can be destroyed. We just have to find a way."

He shakes his head.

"I won't risk your life. Michel's tolerating his servitude to Soren because he wants you to be safe. And you just can't stop from trying to put yourself in danger." He tucks a strand of hair behind my ear, smiling softly as he does. He runs the back of his fingers against my cheek and he's so much like Michel with those black-lashed blue eyes and black hair that before I know it's happening, he pulls me down to him and we kiss, the kiss starting off soft, chaste, then deepening, his lips parting mine, his tongue finding mine.

My body responds to him in an instant, but I push him away.

"Stop," I say. "I don't *want* you, Julien. I can't give up on Michel. You said partners. We can be partners. Nothing more."

He shakes his head and exhales. Then he gets up, lifting me up with him and I slide down  his body. He pushes me away.

"Fine," he says, adjusting himself, not meeting my eyes. "Purely professional from here on in."  He turns away and leaves me standing alone.

# CHAPTER 8

"Absence diminishes mediocre passions and increases great ones, as the wind extinguishes candles and fans fires."

Rochefoucauld

THE NEXT AFTERNOON, VASILY COMES OUT of his office and calls me to the door, holds out my coat.

"We're going out. Boss wants you to meet someone."

"Who?"

"Someone from South Carolina."

I take my coat and put on my shoes. South Carolina – it must be the person he had been 'interviewing' when the whole business with Kate happened. Despite myself, I'm curious about who it could be. One of the staff working for Blackstone? A doctor involved in the research?

I follow Vasily down to the car and sit beside him in silence as we drive towards the more run-down areas of the waterfront that hasn't yet been revitalized.

We pull up beside an old warehouse whose bricks are so old

they're black from years of soot and pollution. Vasily escorts me inside and into a room in the basement. The room is hot and stuffy. On a chair in the center of the room is a man, his shirt off, his arms behind his back. He's sweating, but his skin is pale, his face bruised and his lip split. Blood has dripped on his chest. One eye is swollen shut.

Julien walks around him, some kind of implement in his hand, which he slaps against his palm. He stops when he sees me, but his expression is still dark.

"Ah, here she is – my little Adept. Colonel Reynolds, meet Ms. Eve Hayden."

Vasily pushes me forward and I stop a few feet away from Reynolds, who looks me up and down.

"This is your *Adept?*" He whistles, causing my cheeks to burn in the already hot room. "God, how can you possibly focus?"

"Tell me about it."

Reynolds nods to me.

"Pardon my slurred speech," he says in a soft southern drawl, "but my lip is a bit fat right now. Sorry I can't shake your hand."

Julien turns to me but doesn't meet my eyes.

"Besides being a former special ops officer, Colonel Reynolds is also a clinical scientist, Ms. Hayden," he says, emphasizing the formal title, his tone reminding me of the new status of our relationship. "He worked on that very special project in early 90s. I thought you two might have a chat and share stories."

"I wasn't directly involved in the research that was used on you," Reynolds says. "But on the larger project. I do know some who were."

Julien pulls up a chair and motions to me to sit. I do, glad to focus on something other than Julien and this icy chill between us.

"What we need to know is what they were using to alter my DNA so I could daywalk and how the drug was delivered."

"I think, from what I do know," Reynolds says, "that it was done to regulate gene expression in the skin's immune system. They either turned on genes that were dormant in order to offset the effect of the deficient or mutated genes that vampires receive when they're infected, or insert corrected versions of the defective gene. How they did it? Nanotech to deliver to the cells, having discovered Bucky balls in the mid-80s."

"What do you know about the skin's immune system?" Julien asks.

"All I know," Reynolds said, "is that people with extreme light sensitivity are prone to extreme responses to the sun. Their skin literally bubbles when exposed to ultraviolet light in certain wavelengths."

I think for a moment. "The drug given to the daywalkers must activate or suppress the genes in some way," I say, remembering my class in immunology. "The drug must be delivered to the cells through the blood and is released into the cell, altering the DNA at the cellular level."

"Exactly," Reynolds says. "Genes that protect are either shut on or defective genes are shut off. I don't know which it was."

"I knew vampirism was a set of genetic mutations," I say, turning to Julien. "Not a curse from some vengeful god."

Julien nods but doesn't meet my eyes.

"Or a set of genetic mutations unleashed on mortals by a vengeful God," he says.

I shake my head at his willingness to put it all down to God.

"Military researchers seem to know a lot more about the genetics of vampirism than the rest of science," I say to Reynolds.

Reynolds smiles.

"The military started doing genome research at Los Alamos and through the Department of Energy in the early 80s – a kind of genetic Manhattan Project, and just as secret. Working for government directly gets results. The civilian genome project was years behind the military's own secret project. It was important to delay civilian research until the military could ensure any knowledge gained that could potentially be used for military purposes could be controlled."

"And used to create a super warrior," Julien says.

Reynolds turns to Julien. "You were in the first group."

I turn to look at Julien, who is leaning back against a table on which are a bunch of nasty looking implements. I realize they're used for torture. There are metal rods and knives and prongs and syringes in a black case. It looks designed for inflicting pain – a torture kit.

"I was given the drugs when I signed up for duty in the Persian Gulf the first time."

"You have to remember that this research started during the Cold War, when our biggest threat was from the Soviets," Reynolds says. "They were doing research. We had to do it so that there would be no gap."

"A genetics gap?" I say. "Or a vampire warrior gap?"

"Either. Both. Whatever they did, we did and vice versa," Reynolds says, a touch of humor in his voice. "The logic of mutual deterrence was inexorable. The idea of an enhanced warrior has always been the holy grail of the military – one who lacked the usual barriers to high performance. Other than their weakness to daylight and their need for blood, vampires are superior in every way to humans. Self-healing, ruthless, especially if they've lost a grip on their humanity, like psychopaths. Give them proper rules of engagement, proper weapons and wide latitude and they can get the job done. No qualms. No messy moral conundrums."

I cover my eyes with the heels of my palms. The horror of the whole project comes home to me once more. I shake my head, momentarily overcome.

Finally, I glance up, looking at Reynolds through blurry eyes.

"I hate you bastards."

Reynolds says nothing, shrugs. The room is silent for a moment.

Finally, I take in a breath, try to regain control.

"I wanted to go into medicine to study vampirism in order to prevent it, eradicate it. Your type studied it to refine it, exploit it."

"I was just doing research I thought would help prevent them from taking over. I only learned about its real use later. But I gotta tell you, as a military man, I came to appreciate what an asset it was for our side. The problem is that now the vampires out for Dominion have it, too."

I wipe my eyes.

"This knowledge of genetics and gene therapy could be used to improve humanity, reduce disease in humans, extend longevity," I say. "But it's been delayed for a decade so the military could abuse it?"

Reynolds nods. "Pretty much, yeah." He doesn't flinch under my gaze. "Guys like Julien are irreplaceable, except by more of his kind. You could throw anything at them – any situation however novel or threatening and they were unfazed. Unafraid of pain. No fear of dying – there aren't many stakes on the battlefield and unless they get hit by a freak stray shard of wood, they won't die permanently. Kill an enemy without a thought. Fight and most often, win in any hand-to-hand combat. Isn't that right?"

"Absofuckinglutely. A war hog's wet dream." Julien's tone is sarcastic. "So," he says, turning to me without looking at me in the eye. "Ms. Hayden, Colonel Reynolds has decided he wants to continue to live and will cooperate." He turns to Reynolds. "What level of clearance do you still have? Can you get into some of the research for her?"

"You give me a clean PC and I can tap into the database through my clearance. As long as it's related to my work, I can access it."

Julien nods, his arms crossed.

"Thank you. Ms. Hayden," he says without looking at me directly. "You and Colonel Reynolds will spend a bit of time in the next few days doing research. I'll call Ed and tell him you won't be coming in to work. I want action on this as soon as possible." He waves a hand at Vasily. "Find out what they did to us. I can still go out in the light, but others from my group – those who are still alive, that is, started to lose the ability. I don't think I have much time left."

With that, Vasily comes to me and I stand. I stop beside Julien, wanting to say something but there's no opportunity. Vasily takes my arm and pulls me out of the room. I follow him out to the car, regret heavy like an iron weight in my gut.


"So," Reynolds says as we sit in the office the next day and work on the computer. "Why are you helping him?"

I press my nails into my palm. "Stockholm Syndrome?"

"Oh, yeah?" Reynolds smiles. "I could see it. What's your interest in helping the Council?"

"My mother worked for the Council before she died. I hate what's being done. We should be curing vampirism, not use them as some kind of killing machines. It's immoral. It's criminal. It should be exposed."

Reynolds laughs. "Good luck with that. If anyone does expose the program and its escapades, you're implicated along with Julien by helping him, and you're dead. The guys who work for Blackstone? Not very pleasant. You think Julien's a psychopathic vampire killer? The guys who head Blackstone are worse."

"I don't think Julien's a psychopath."

"Oh he is, rest assured. All vampires fit the definition. They all want to drink you dry, no matter how they feel about you."

I shake my head. Not Michel. He cared about humans. He wanted to protect us and prevent Dominion. I sit in silence for a few minutes while Reynolds searches through a government intranet virtual library for research.

"You're implicated as well," I say. "You were willing to help create this army of psychopathic vampire killers. Now, if you help Julien, you're at risk and will be condemned with him if he's caught."

Reynolds shrugs. "It's either die now because I won't help, or die later for helping him. I figure if I help him now, I have a fighting chance of staying alive, evading them once this comes out."

"Maybe you'll take pity on a screwed-up college student and help me evade them as well."

He nods. "I promise you that if I survive and there's a chance of my helping, I will. I have SERE training and know a few clandestine tricks." He turns and glances at me, his eyes moving over my body. "I could use a little research assistant myself."

"What do you mean by that?"

He smiles.

"I'm a trained observer, Eve. I saw the way you look at each other, despite the chilly reception you gave each other. The way he looked at you?" He shakes his head. "Like a wolf looks at a doe. Hungry. Drooling for a piece. But most does are afraid of wolves, not wanting to be closer to them. I'd say there's one hell of a lot more than Stockholm Syndrome going on."

I rub my forehead. "It's pretty screwed up."

"I can see that." He reads a few abstracts. "He's a very nasty vampire, you know. Once he found out I actually worked on the project, his appetite for inflicting pain on me increased exponentially. I'm surprised he was able to stop and actually let me go. I don't get why you're helping him or even with a guy like him."

"I'm not *with* him," I say, "at least, not by choice." I look at my hands, which are folded in my lap.

"I don't know if I believe that," he says. "I'm a trained observer. I saw something between you."

"Let's say I have issues."

"Hate to use a cliché but moth to a flame?" He clicks on a link and opens a new window. "You know the score and yet you still can't end it?"

"I did – the non-professional part. I'm pretty much committed to the professional part."

"You were able to end it and you're still alive?" Reynolds raises his eyebrows. "That's a surprise. Vampires are used to absolute control. They call the shots, not mortals, and they use their powers to get compliance."

"I'm the exception to the rule. I can't be compelled. I'm still alive because he needs my help." I sigh, wanting to change the subject. "As to his hurting you when he found out you were in the program? Can you blame him? I mean, seriously? They not only turned him into a daywalking vampire, they used him for their dirty work and then tried to destroy him when he became a liability."

"I don't blame him at all. Not one bit," Reynolds says. "I've always figured the program would come back to haunt us. The powers that be thought they could control these vampires, thought they had it all figured out. But you don't give predators free rein, knowledge of military ops, clandestine procedures and weapons and expect to control them. Pride goeth before a fall, as the saying goes."

Reynolds downloads and prints off a half-dozen research papers that are classified and that detail procedures used in Operation Black Knight, as it was called. I look at the insignia at the top of some correspondence Reynolds shows me and think about the Lorraine Cross tattoo on Julien's neck.

After Reynolds leaves with one of Julien's other employees, I sit in the seating area and read the papers, one after the other, studying the methods, the materials, and wonder how to replicate any of it. It's far beyond anything I've done in my labs in university, although I'm able to grasp the basic science. If the Council really wants to do this, they'll have to set up an ultra-modern lab and hire professionals.

I make notes in a lab notebook I asked Vasily to buy for me, and try to think of all the technology and equipment such a lab would need. Some of this is very advanced. There are some less technological things they could do in the short term – to depress a vampire's immune system, to allow them to daywalk – but if they really want to replicate what the military did to vampires like Julien, they really need more of that drug they gave him to start. The nanotech.

As I dig deeper into the research papers Reynolds found, I realize the military scientists hadn't altered his genes permanently – they either suppressed the action of the defective genes on a temporary basis or activated others on a temporary basis. The plan was to implant slow-release nanoparticles that would keep a steady level of drug in the vampire's blood, withdrawing treatment if they felt a need for whatever tactical reasons. They'd get boosters every six months, to ensure that a certain level of drug remained in their blood. They could withdraw treatment if the vampires failed to cooperate. Julien must have stopped working for them within the past six months if he's still able to daywalk.

The Council has the money, apparently, to afford to build a lab for this. What they lacked was the knowledge of how to deliver the gene therapy agent. I figure for the right amount of money, they could probably convince some researchers to do the necessary lab work. It could be done. The work absorbs me for the rest of the evening. It's well beyond my pay grade, but I give it a shot. If I'm not going to be

Julien's little pet, I have to do something of value. Besides, this is what my mother did. In doing this, at least I'm following in her footsteps, which is what I wanted from the start.

Except there's one little complication. I don't have Michel. But I have Julien walking around me, looking almost identical to him, looking at me like I'm a piece of meat he can't wait to eat. I can practically feel his lust for me from a distance and it's distracting.

It's arousing.

# CHAPTER 9

Later that afternoon, Julien arrives and takes off his trench coat, hanging it on the coat tree by the door. He's in his casual clothes, a pair of faded jeans and a long white linen shirt open at the collar. Reynolds is with him. He speaks with Vasily and then comes over to where I'm seated, working on my summary of the literature.

"The Colonel reports you two had some luck today. We're going downstairs to celebrate a bit."

I look at him, wondering why he's including me. Probably just to rub it into me how wrong I've been about Kate.

"I probably should keep working. I don't know if it would be good for me to go down there, considering."

"Considering that Kate will be there? No, it would be a good thing. I insist."

I shake my head, already feeling my gut knot at the idea of having to meet her again. "I think I'd be bad company."

"Humor me, Eve. Considering what trouble you caused me over this, I think a little penance is in order."

I sigh. "Why not just give me a hair shirt to wear."

"Nah," he says and smiles. "This will be much more fun."

I relent with extreme reluctance and follow him back to the door, where Vasily and Reynolds stand.

Down in the fourth-floor apartment, Kate is waiting for us. I'm surprised to see her dressed, although her clothes hardly cover her. She's wearing a tiny black muscle shirt that shows how thin she is, her ribs sticking out, her breasts small, her hip bones sharp angles, visible from beneath a short jean skirt. She looks like some kind of sick punker, with her dark hair in a mess, dark circles under her eyes.

"Hey, where the fuck have you been? You got my stuff? I'm sick." She coughs, the sound so wet and raspy that I think she must have pneumonia.

"Yes, love, never fear," Julien says. "I have your stuff. Go get your kit. It's party time."

Kate goes over to the kitchen and returns with a small leather case.

"Come in, friends," Julien said, his voice ebullient, "and have a seat while my brother's dear angel Kate gives herself a little taste of heaven." He sits on one of the couches and Kate sits next to him.

"Who the fuck are you talking about?" Kate says, frowning. "Jesus, quit with the theatrics. And who are these people?" She barely glances at Reynolds and me, before grabbing the package of powder Julien takes out of his pocket, almost shoving him out of the way in her haste to spread out her drug paraphernalia.

"Just some acquaintances of Michel's. Sit!" Julien says, pointing to the couch across from him. Reynolds looks at me with wide eyes and complies, sitting down across from Julien. I sit next to Reynolds.

"Vasily – music. We need some sweet music for Kate to shoot up to."

Vasily goes over to the sound system. He flips through satellite radio channels, and then finally selects one. Soon, mellow jazz plays, the music not too loud, just background – it sounds like Miles Davis. He remains there, as if he can't bear to watch Kate. I wish I could do the same. I've never seen junkies actually shooting up in person – only in television reality shows. It's even worse in real life when you're not separated by a screen.

"What is this?" Kate says, looking at the packet.

"Only the best," Julien says. "Michel insists I get you pharmaceutical grade."

On her part, Kate is busy arranging her equipment, spreading it out, lining it up, her actions jerky, impatient. Out of the case comes a new short tip insulin syringe, a spoon, two small vials of liquid – one clear, one slightly yellow. A lighter. A blue rubber tourniquet. Some small balls of cotton about the size of the end of a cotton swab. A couple of packages of alcohol swabs.

"How was your day, Kate?" Julien says, his voice playful. He watches me intently.

Kate ignores him.

"Where the fuck is Michel?"

"He's going to be away for a while," Julien says. "Remember I told you I'll be looking after you now?"

"What-the-fuck-ever."

She focuses on the process, her hands almost shaking. She cleans off the spoon with a swab, dumps the powder into the spoon, draws up some of the clear liquid in the syringe, and then uses the plunger of the syringe to mix it up. Next, she holds the spoon over the lighter flame until the liquid boils. She drops a small piece of cotton into the mix and draws up the liquid in the syringe through the cotton.

"Nothing to say to your sugar daddy, Kate?"

"What the fuck took you so long? I told you I'm sick."

"Just trying to keep you alive, love," Julien says, smiling. He looks at Reynolds. "If she had as much as she wanted when she wanted, she'd have OD'd by now."

She grabs the tourniquet and wraps it around her upper arm in a slipknot, pulling the end tight with her teeth. She slaps her upper arm to reveal a vein but I can see a half-dozen needle marks already there. She then cleans her arm with another alcohol swab, inserts the needle, pulls back on the plunger to ensure she has a vein, dark red blood filling the tip, and releases the tourniquet, slowly injecting the liquid into her vein, pulling a bit more blood back before finishing.

I'm horrified and mesmerized at the same time.

Kate sits back, closes her eyes and sighs, the empty needle on the couch beside her hand. Julien picks up the needle and places it on the table.

"There you go," he says, stroking Kate's hair. "Feeling better?"

Kate doesn't respond, just lies back slack-jawed.

"So," Julien says, turning to Reynolds. "How goes the battle?"

Reynolds is still agog at Kate's shooting up in front of us and struggles to speak. He opens his mouth a few times, and then looks at me. I look away, at my feet, and the far windows – anywhere but at Julien and Kate. It's about the saddest thing I've seen for a long while, and makes me feel like an incredibly small and petty jerk.

"Oh, don't mind Kate," Julien says. "She has a bit of a smack habit. She decided to go out and get some extra for herself one day – against the rules, I might add – and got arrested. She went to jail instead of rehab, because you can get junk in jail but not in a hospital and she didn't want to detox or do methadone seeing as she's on her way out. She shoots up two or three times a day – four on a bad day. We won't hear much out of her now. I just like to keep her around for a while, in case she stops breathing," he says and looks at her, his head tilted to one side. "One of these days though. . ."

At that, I stand and leave the seating area, unable to sit and watch any longer.

"Where are you going?" Julien says, his voice low. "Come back and sit down."

I swallow hard, biting my lip to keep control. "I'm going to the bathroom."

"Be quick."

I find the bathroom and close the door and lean against it, my emotions at the edge. What a bastard! He arranged all this just to make me feel like the petty jealous female that I am. He could have told me that Kate was dying. Why Vasily didn't tell me is confusing. Perhaps he didn't know how bad she is.

My hands shake, my stomach in knots, tears stinging the corners of my eyes. I won't cry. I won't.

I grab some toilet paper and hold it to my eyes, mopping up the moisture, blowing my nose.

"Eve . . ."

"Be right there."

I flush the toilet and run the water, drying off my hands on the cleanest-looking towel there is and then take in a deep breath. I go back to the seating area and sit back down beside Reynolds. When I look up, Julien has a joint out and is lighting it. He offers it to Reynolds, who shakes his head.

"No thanks," he says. "Makes me throw up."

"You must be sensitive to THC," Julien says, taking a hit. "What's your poison?"

"Do you have any scotch?"

Julien blows out the smoke and turns to the sound system where Vasily stands.

"Vasily, my dear man. Do we have any scotch?"

Vasily bends down and opens a cabinet on the dry bar. He holds up a bottle of Glenfiddich. Reynolds nods.

"Good man," Reynolds says when Vasily brings over a glass and the bottle.

Julien sucks on the joint, inhaling deeply, holding the smoke in his lungs, and then blows it out slowly. He takes another hit and then holds the joint out to me. "Here, have some."

I shake my head, avoiding his eyes.

"That wasn't an offer."

"I don't do drugs," I say.

He shakes the joint in front of me.

"That wasn't a request. It was an order, Eve."

"Do you have any vodka? I'd prefer a drink."

"Smoke this."

"You can't force me."

"Oh, I can." He extends his hand to me again. "Would you like to see me? There are ways."

I relent, not wanting to see him try, for I suspect he could easily do it and I don't want the evening to devolve into some kind of strange drug assault. I take in a weak puff of smoke and inhale it briefly before coughing it out. I try to hand it back to him.

"No, you finish it," he says. "I've got another one all ready for myself." He lights another joint and pulls hard on it as if he's desperate to get stoned. He blows out a lungful of smoke and leans back. "Vasily, what are you having? Don't tell me it's vodka or I'll throw something at you."

"I'm Russian. Drinking vodka is like breathing." Vasily sits on the third couch, bringing his bottle of vodka and an icy shot glass with him. He pours a shot and then holds the glass up to the group. "*Vashe Zdorovie* –your health."

Julien and Reynolds hold up their respective poisons and I follow suit, holding my joint up.

"Your health," Julien says.

Vasily then downs the shot and smacks his lips.

"Oh *Khorosho* – it feels so good." He winks at me. At least he still likes me.

"Eve," Julien says, pointing at me with his joint. "You're letting it burn out. Smoke it. It's some really good stuff."

I take another puff but try not to hold the smoke in too long. I don't want to lose control for fear I say something really stupid.

"Come on," he says, waving his hand. "Finish it off. I don't want it wasted. Besides, you look all uptight like you don't enjoy our company." He turns to Reynolds. "Do you think she looks a bit uptight tonight?"

Reynolds takes a sip of scotch and leans back, his arm on the back of the couch behind me.

"She could use a bit of lightening up."

I finish off the joint and then hand the tiny stub to Julien.

Kate moves, lifting up her head for a moment, her eyes still closed. "Get me a smoke."

Julien makes a surprised face.

"The sleeper awakens. Yes, dear Kate. A cigarette for my little lady." He grabs the pack of cigarettes and lights one, then places it between Kate's fingers. She just sits there with it in her hand, not even bothering to smoke it.

Julien and Reynolds talk about the research and I just sit there, listening. I'm starting to feel the pot, my body feeling languid, liquid, my limbs filled with a pleasant heaviness, my mouth a bit numb. I lean back and close my eyes as well, enjoying the feeling of euphoria despite my best intentions.

"Ah, Kate. Isn't she just the life of the party?" Julien says to Reynolds. "A laugh a minute is dear Kate."

"Stop it," I say, the words slipping out of me almost without my knowing it. "Just stop it."

A silence. "Excuse me?"

I open my eyes with great effort.

"You made your point." When I see Julien's expression, I shut them again. Damn.

"Oh?" His voice is amused, that lopsided grin on his face. "And what point was that?"

I shake my head.

"No," I say, waving at him, my arm feeling like it's made of cement. "We're not getting into this now."

"Into what?"

"You know very well what."

"No, I don't think I do. Why don't you explain to us what this is?"

"Nope." I shake my head, which is a bad idea, because the room spins.

"Oh, I think you better."

"Uh, uh."

"Colonel," Julien says, his tone one of exaggerated confusion. "Do you know what Ms. Hayden is referring to?"

"I have my suspicions."

"Oh, that's right. You're a psychiatrist on top of being a grunt. So tell me, what do you think she's talking about?"

I open my eyes and glance beside me to Reynolds. I shake my head. "Don't."

Vasily speaks up.

"I thought pot supposed to make people happy. Is not working."

"Whatever do you mean, Vasily? Why, I'm happy as a lark, here with little Kate by my side."

I stand up again.

"I've had enough." I'm on the verge of saying something I might regret. My legs are unsteady and I wobble a bit. "I want to go back upstairs."

"I think that's a great idea, Eve," Julien says, his voice mock happy. "The little woman here wants to sleep anyway."

Julien takes the burning cigarette out of Kate's hand and crushes it out. Then he picks her up and carries her over to the bed, covering her up. He feels her carotid pulse for a moment and then tucks her in before returning to the group.

"Shall we?" He motions to the door. "Bring your bottles gentlemen. I've got the bud."

I wait for them to lead the way, my head swimming a bit from the buzz. He's rubbing it in, grinding my face in it. I feel terrible for Kate, but most of all, I feel like a total idiot. I lean against the elevator wall on the way up.

Once inside the fifth floor apartment, Julien leads us over to the seating area and we sit down around the coffee table. This time, Vasily sits beside me and rubs my shoulder affectionately.

"Would you like some vodka? It will warm your blood."

"No, thanks," I say, shaking my head.

"She doesn't need vodka," Julien says, pulling out the bag of weed and extracting another joint, "when she has some really high quality very potent White Widow Indica. Vasily, you should give it a try."

"No," Vasily says, holding his hand out. "My lungs getting too old to be sucking in dirty air. Was enough living in St. Petersburg all those years."

"Well, this stuff gives a really powerful buzz. Here," he says, lighting the joint and handing it to me. "Do some more. You're not stoned enough yet."

"I don't need anymore."

"Ah, but I want you to have some more." He pushes the joint towards me. "That's what matters."

"Is there no music?" Reynolds says, pouring some more scotch in his glass.

"Let her finish her joint and then Eve can play for us," Julien says. "Won't you play for us, Eve?"

"If you make me smoke the whole joint, I probably won't be able to even stand up."

"No, this isn't that kind of buzz."

I take in another lungful of smoke and blow it out quickly. By the time the joint is half-gone, I'm starting to feel the buzz he referred to – not a giggly dreamy buzz like I've had before when I smoked pot as a teenager, but instead an intense feeling of euphoria, as if the world is just perfect. I lean back as it takes hold of me and close my eyes, feeling as if I'm riding on a wave of pure peace. Gone are my concerns about the day, about Julien, even poor tragic Kate – she's a lovely junkie, really, poor thing. Julien is so good to her. He really is so sweet, looking after me in my illness, feeding me his blood, looking after Kate.

Someone takes the joint out of my hand and I open my eyes. It's Julien, bending over me, smiling.

"Come on, Ballerina Girl." He takes my hand and pulls me up. "Play some Russian music for Vasily. I have to pay him back for something."

I stand and try to follow him, glad he's leading for my legs feel a bit leaden. Vasily follows us over to the piano and stands to the side, resting his hand on the piano.

"This is for you, Vasily." I sift through the sheet music to find Variations on a Theme by Chopin by Rachmaninoff, the sheets falling onto my lap. "It's the only Russian work I have. I want to apologize to you for the trouble I caused the other day and for the cut on your face." I have trouble locating the music, and Julien leans over to help, taking the sheets from me, picking out the piece and setting it on the stand for me.

"I don't know if I can play," I say as I peer at the music and find the first notes.

"Nonsense," Julien says. "Musicians have been playing stoned for decades – drunk for centuries. Why even Berlioz composed on opium."

I make an attempt, doing well at the outset, playing the main theme from memory, but then having to focus on the first four variations, which are the more difficult parts I haven't memorized. My fingers don't respond as well as normal and I trip over some of the more difficult parts and then start over when I get to the part I haven't yet learned well.

"Sorry," I say, turning to Vasily. "That's all I can do." Vasily has his hand over his heart and his expression is thanks enough.

"Play this for me. You owe me as well." Julien puts Chopin's Ballade on the stand. "Big time."

I ignore his comment and play, getting caught up in its beauty. When I finish as far as I can go, he takes in a deep breath.

"Again."

I play it again from the start, and the sound of his voice, the music and the high from the joint combine to make me forgive him for everything. It's the saddest thing, to play this piece for him, knowing it must be painful to know I played it for Michel –that it's Michel I want, and it's for Michel I practiced, yet he seems to want me to play it anyway.

The euphoria from the high keeps me going, keeps me from feeling sad. I feel happy to be able to play it, to listen to its sweetness. I think of Kate, so high she can't even talk, lying in the messy bed, so insubstantial that she's like an empty scarecrow. I feel my heart swell for Kate and mostly for Michel that he was so willing to take care of her. And now Julien, trying to make her last days comfortable, keeping her off the street, getting her medical care.

When I stop playing, I turn to him, shaking my head, my emotions rising. He finally looks at me directly and it's the first time we've really made eye contact since yesterday.

"I'm so sorry."

He nods but says nothing, looking away from me to Vasily.

"I think it's time to go."

Vasily raises his eyebrows, but nods. He motions to Reynolds, who's eyeing Julien and me, a hint of a smile on his lips.

"Cheers." He chugs the remaining scotch in his glass. "See you tomorrow, Eve. We've got more work to do."

I nod, feeling like the moment could go on and on.

Vasily and Reynolds leave, and Julien follows. I stand and grab his arm.

"Wait." I have to say something more to him —my apology isn't enough. "Don't go."

He stops and looks at me, glancing up and down.

"I don't see you on your hands and knees."

"I don't mean that. I just wanted to say something to you. To apologize—."

"You already did."

He turns, pulling his arm away.

"I was wrong," I say, trying to get the words out before he's gone. "I was foolish, stupid." I stand there and close my eyes, feeling borne on a wave of acceptance. When I open my eyes again, he's at the door, saying nothing in response. "Screwed up," I say, the warm feeling from the White Widow keeping me from despairing. "More trouble than I'm worth."

He stops, the door open. "Everything that's worth anything in life is hard." He looks back at me. "You know what to do."

I nod, but it isn't going to happen. I just had to say I was sorry, to make things right.

After a moment, he goes to his coat on the coat tree and retrieves some papers from an inside pocket. He stands there for a moment as if deciding, and then he comes to stand before me and holds out the papers.

"Here," he says, handing them to me, closing my fingers around the folded papers. "I'm going out later and don't know when or if I'll be back. I hoped that our little party tonight might straighten a few things out for you, but you need more. You wanted to read it all. These are some parts of the manuscript Michel didn't want you to read. I went to his place and found them, tucked away in his desk. Read them. I know you think you love him, but you have to let him go. He's no saint and he's a great actor. At least with me, you know what you're getting."

Then the door closes, and he's gone.

# CHAPTER 10

"Looking back, I have this to regret, that too often when I loved, I did not say so."

David Grayson

I take the papers and go to my bedroom, creeping under the covers, and start to read.

*"Nous séjour avec Soren pour l'année prochaine,"* the manuscript starts. *"We stay with Soren for the next year."*

*I see such a transformation in my brother that I barely recognize him. He has become Soren's servant as he did Marguerite before him. But even more, he has become Soren's confidant and partner in crime.*

*I kill mortals. I don't apologize for it. I drink their blood with relish, for I am a hunter now. But I have not forgotten that they are humans, and that I was once one as well. That I once loved and felt pain and had hopes and dreams just as they do. Michel seems to have forgotten this entirely or he plays this role so convincingly that even I start to hate him.*

*I keep telling myself that he is merely trying to learn as much as is possible from Soren – about his kind in the hopes of finding a way to kill him, but it is difficult to see him act in such a base and heartless manner.*

*Only last night, we were sitting around the salon in Soren's Paris home after a day of rest, and Soren turned to Michel, who was lounging on a divan after a bath, preparing for the night's conquests.*

*"I want you to do something to impress me, Michel," he says. Soren's dressed in his finery, black trousers, tunic and belt, black boots, and it contrasts against his pale skin and white-blond hair. He enjoys looking like a vampire and does whatever he can to enhance it, relishing the fear his appearance elicits in his victims. Indeed, it seems as if their fear gives him as much delight as does their blood.*

*He motions to the servant and holds out his goblet for more wine.*

*"Do something out of the ordinary. Show me how far you've come. How you've adopted the spirit of our kind."*

*Michel shrugs his shoulders.*

*"What could possibly surprise you? You've been in existence for thousands of years."*

*Soren purses his lips.*

*"Nothing in itself. You could surprise me with your willingness to do it. That would be the novelty. Think of it – Michel de Cernay, former Domini canis, Hound of God. Priest, Bishop of Carcassonne. God's Beloved – isn't that what the name Michel stands for in your language?"*

*Michel's face is impassive. "Not so beloved after all I expect."*

*Soren only grins.*

*Later, we're out strolling down along the river, enjoying the night. The sky is clear, the stars barely visible because it's a full moon, and this one is blue, its edges blurred by high cloud. A strong wind blew in over the land earlier in the week, carrying on it darkness during the day. Reports from travelers bring news of an eruption of a volcano in Italy and the sun takes on a violet hue during the daylight hours.*

*A bad omen during a time when every sign seems dark.*

*"So, Michel," Soren says as we stroll along, admiring the humans as*

*they're out walking along the Seine, taking the air, escaping the stink of the city. "What are you going to do to surprise me? I'm bored."*

*Michel walks ahead of us, his hands clasped behind his back, his gaze moving over the mortals we pass, eyeing them, sizing them up. A few of the women eye him, for he's beautiful with his long hair pulled back, in his black clothing.*

*"I'm still thinking," he says.*

*We leave the more refined part of the city for the stretch of the Seine bordering slums, where no one in authority notices drained corpses thrown into the river. We come across a man begging on the street, crouched down in the gutter, asking for money to help feed his starving family.*

*"How many are there in your family?" Michel asks as he digs into his pocket for a coin.*

*"Six, my Lord," the man says, his hand shaking so badly he can barely take the coin Michel offers. "The wife died in childbirth and I have five children."*

*"Where are they?" he says, glancing around. "Where do you live?"*

*"We stay under the bridge, my Lord," the man says. His face is filthy, his hair matted, his clothes stiff with sweat and dirt.*

*Michel turns to us. "It would be a mercy, don't you think? How can a family survive without a mother?"*

*Soren nods. "Truly a mercy."*

*I stop in my tracks. Michel's going to kill an entire family?*

*"Take me to them. I want to see them. Perhaps if your story is true, I'll take care of you. I need a special project."*

*The man is so grateful, he fawns at Michel's feet, kissing his legs, hobbling down the stairs to the space under the bridge.*

*There we find the family, the children ranging in age from twelve to two, three girls and two boys. The youngest is a tiny girl with a filthy face, sleeping in her older sister's arms.*

*Michel knees down and looks the sleeping children over.*

*"You've done your best," he says to the man. "You can't be expected to care for them all alone. What will they do without a mother?"*

*"I do what I can, my Lord. I do what I can."*

*"That's all we can do," Michel replies. He reaches into his pocket, appearing to remove more money, but when he extends his hand it's empty. Instead, he grabs the man by the scruff of his neck, and he calms the man. Then, his fangs extended, his eyes red, Michel bites the man's neck, drinking him dry in a few short minutes.*

*Next, he kills the oldest girl, who is sleeping peacefully and never wakes then he moves on to the next oldest child – the oldest boy and does the same. Not a single sound is heard from any of them as he kills them for he silences them first so they don't awaken. Finally, he takes the baby in his arms – a lovely child with pale curling hair, and kills her as well. He's taken so much blood that his skin has a rosy hue, the first time I've seen him so since we were turned.*

*He looks up at Soren, his mouth bloody.*

*"What next?"*

*Soren smiles as if he approves.*

*"Good, but I would have preferred if you'd killed them in reverse order – the children taken in front of the father. So much more dramatic. Plus you were too kind, calming them first. I always like to see a fair fight. The chase. The conquest. If you had chased them down and killed them one by one in front of the father, like a lion kills a baby gazelle in front of its family, now that would have surprised me. But this was better than your usual kill. Dying soldiers? What sport is that? You're improving."*

*We walk on under the bridge and find a young girl and her sister asleep beside a support pillar, an old ragged blanket all that keeps them warm and off the dirt.*

*"There's your chance to redeem yourself. Take them. Chase them. Kill the one in front of the other."*

*Michel does. He stands over them, menacingly, and kicks the older girl's foot. She wakes, sees his hunter face, and screams, clutching her sister who also wakes and screams.*

*"Run," Michel says, his voice a growl. "RUN!"*

*They run along the riverbank in the darkness. The youngest girl trips and falls and Michel is there, picking her up. She's no more than eight, her face still baby-soft despite the grime that covers her. He carries her as he chases the older girl. When she sees he has her sister, the older girl stops and pleads with him to release her.*

*"Don't hurt her," she begs. Older, perhaps ten or eleven, she kneels on the riverbank, her hands clasped. "Please, Sir, don't hurt her!"*

*He kills the child in his arms and I watch in horror as her tiny body struggles, their forms silhouetted against the blue moon. Then he throws her down on the ground. The older girl tries to crawl away on her hands and knees but Michel grabs her from behind and lifts her up, taking her, killing her in moments before dumping her body in the Seine.*

*Now, he has drunk the blood of seven humans, most only children, but still, he's gorged himself on human life.*

*I hate him as I stand there, tears in my eyes.*

*"Well done," Soren says. "Why, you've so much fresh blood in you, you could fool a human into thinking you are alive. That you have a soul. Maybe we should go to one of the more popular salons and watch you try. Convince some lovely and high-born marquess of your humanity, and then kill her. Oh, to see the horror on her face..."*

*Michel says nothing. He merely climbs the bank back to the bridge and we continue on our evening stroll.*

*"Yes, let's," he says finally. I watch him from behind as he and Soren walk side by side.*

*For the first time since we were turned, I truly don't believe he has a soul anymore. I don't know anymore what is act and what is real. I don't know my brother anymore. I make a pact with myself to never become like him – acting as if he's heartless, soulless.*

*Even if it means my death.*

I throw the pages onto the floor beside my bed and lie back on the pillows, my stomach sick at the story I've just read. I can't believe Michel would act that way – he seemed so moral, so ethical, when I was with him. Fighting for humanity, to protect us from Dominion. How could he be so heartless? Was it an act or did he relish the kills he made?

I toss and turn for hours, unable to get the images of him chasing the poor children and then killing them with such little care – all of it to impress Soren.

I suspect that was Julien's goal.

I don't see Julien again for the rest of the week, and by Friday, I'm feeling exceptionally blue. Reynolds does most of the work requiring discussions directly with Julien, so I have no reason to even see him. Instead, I return to work and try to catch up with the case and any developments I missed while I was away.

Every night I go to bed, thinking of Michel, about Julien, wondering where Julien is, and how Michel is doing. On my part, I feel a certain level of frustration knowing I could have Julien in my bed if only I was willing to get down on my hands and knees. I just can't do it.

I'm worth more than that.

Finally, late on Friday night after I've gone to bed and have been sleeping for a while, I wake when he sits on the bed beside me.

"Eve," he says, shaking me lightly. "Wake up."

I startle awake and sit up, rubbing my eyes.

"What's the matter?"

"An interesting development turned up in my travels."

I wait, but he seems distracted.

"What is it?"

"Are you wearing your perfume?"

"Yes," I say and touch my neck.

"Please stop. It's penetrated everything and I can't get away from it even if I try."

I lift my pillow and the soft cotton pillowcase is infused with it.

"It's the sheets."

He nods and glances away, his gaze on the far windows.

"I'm sorry, I didn't realize you hate it. Michel liked it and I wear it because it reminds me of him."

"No, no," he said finally. "It's just a constant reminder, that's all."

He exhales. "How have you been?" he says. "I haven't seen you all week."

I shrug my shoulder.

"I'm fine. I've been busy at the SCU."

He reaches out and touches my cheek, and I know he's trying to read me.

"You miss me," he says, his voice soft. "That's a start. You feel regret."

My cheeks heat that he knows how I feel.

"I feel a lot of things. Sadness. Loneliness." I sigh. "Self-respect – not much, but enough."

"What does self-respect have to do with it?" He sounds so frustrated. "If you want something bad enough, you do what it takes to get it."

I shake my head. "Even if I crawled on my hands and knees, I still wouldn't get what I want so why bother? Why humiliate myself?"

"Why would it humiliate you? What would you think of me if I crawled on my hands and knees to you, asking for your forgiveness so that you and I could be together?" He says nothing for a moment. "It would be a big turn-on. Admit it."

I hold my hand to my forehead. "You really don't understand, do you?"

"I understand that you caused a hell of a mess because you were jealous of Kate – Kate! Poor little junkie Kate who's dying, for Christ's sake. You foolishly gave me an ultimatum saying that it had to be your way or no way. I think crawling on your hands and knees and admitting you regret it would be nothing more than righting a wrong and proving how you felt."

"I don't want to just," I say. "Have sex with you. It's not enough."

"Do you want to have sex with me?"

I close my eyes in frustration.

"Answer me."

"Of course. But that's not all I want."

"I can't give you what you think you want." He takes my hand. "Why can't you want what I can give?"

"I need more." I squeeze his hand back. "You're the most," I stop, my throat constricting.

"What?"

"You're so," I say, still unable to say it, express it. "I feel so-." He waits. I close my eyes. "I forget everything when I'm with you. Everything. It's just so . . . powerful. You're so powerful." I search for words. "There's so much inside of you. So much more than I ever thought possible." I pull my hand away and cover my eyes, my cheeks burning. "I'm sorry – but for me? With you? It's all or nothing."

"I'm going out in a few minutes," he says after a pause, his voice sounding as if he hasn't even heard what I said. "Going to run a little errand. It may help me get more information from the Blackstone group if I succeed. Get right inside the Blackstone if so."

A jolt of fear goes through me. "How do you get inside Blackstone?"

"Oh, I have ways of getting inside places," Julien says and smiles.

"How will you do it?"

"Most people have a price," he says. "The trick is to find out what that price is and offer just a bit more so they bite."

I look away, wondering what price he's going to pay.

"Unfortunately, I haven't figured out your price yet or I'd be rolling around under the sheets right now, smelling your sweet perfume instead of sitting here all cold and lonely."

I smile even though I feel more like crying.

"Well, it's time to go." Before he stands up to go, I turn to him, reach out and touch his arm.

"Be careful." I can't hide the fear in my voice. "I wish you hadn't told me. I won't be able to sleep now." Then he pulls me into his arms, buries his face in my neck. I can't help but respond, my arms slipping around him, tears in my eyes. His mouth is next to my ear.

"It should be me," he says, his voice so quiet I'm not sure if I hear him right.

He pulls back, looks at my face. Rubs my cheek with his thumb.

"It should be you what?"

He stands and leaves, stopping in the office for a few moments before leaving the apartment. I sit with my head in my hands, fighting my emotions, unable to understand what he meant. When I regain control, I rise and go to the bathroom.

On my way back, Vasily's waiting for me by the bed. He hands me an envelope.

"What's this?"

"Boss said to give it to you after he left."

"Thanks." I switch on the lamp beside my bed and open the envelope. Inside is a small slip of paper folded in half. I spread it out.

*On _my_ hands and knees.*

*J.*

# CHAPTER 11

"The truth is rarely pure and never simple."<br>
Oscar Wilde

I WAKE TO MY CELLPHONE RINGING instead of my alarm. Four a.m. I've barely even been asleep. I grab the phone from my nightstand, my heart already thumping in alarm. The call display reads, O'Neil, Ed.

"Hello?"

Ed speaks on the other end, his voice rushed. "Sorry to call you so late, but we need you in here, right now. Something happened, and, well, you'll see when you get in."

"OK," I say, my brain barely functional. "Should I get Julien?"

"Eve, Vasily knows about this. Just come down and meet me as soon as you're ready. I'm outside waiting."

The line goes dead.

I rush around the room, dressing on the run, and then go to the bathroom where I give my teeth a hasty brush and rake a comb through my long messy hair before clipping it up in a makeshift bun. I glanced in the mirror at my face. I look tired with dark circles under my eyes. Makeup would help to make me look presentable but there's no time.

I go out to the living area to find Vasily there, his face ashen. He holds out my coat.

"What is it, Vasily?"

He shakes his head. I take my coat and shoulder bag.

"Just go. O'Neil is outside waiting for you. Now is test, Eve. I hope you pass."

"Tell me!" I say, but he shakes his head and opens the door.

I follow him down and out to the street where Ed waits in the car. I get in and watch Vasily as we drive off. He looks scared and his expression makes me terrified. My first thought is that Soren's killed Michel.

"What is it? Is it Michel?"

Ed shakes his head. "Julien. He's in custody. We caught him with a dead body and he's now a suspect in the case."

"What?" A rush of adrenaline goes through me. "That's crazy! It's Soren, Ed. I already told you. I felt him, I know it's Soren!"

"Nope," Ed says, shaking his head. "Caught him red-handed. An adept dead, head not sawed off yet though so we caught him before he was finished."

We drive in silence, me trying to figure out what Soren's doing.

"Ed, this is some kind of diversion. It's meant to keep us from focusing on Soren. I'm sure Julien didn't do it. I've touched him and I never saw anything like his involvement in the case."

"You weren't trying. You have to really look for kills, to see them. They don't just come to you unless you look."


We arrive at the Foster Building and Ed leads me inside to the elevator.

"We got a tip that a man was down by the waterfront carrying something that looked like a body. We sent an operative who was able to immobilize the suspect, who turned out to be Julien. He killed a priest who was also an adept and was carrying the body to the shore."

"But all the others were decapitated before they were dumped.

This isn't the right MO. The killer – Soren – drained and decapitated and then transported them to the dump sites."

Ed leads me down the hall to a small basement observation room with a window that looks into another larger room. In the center is an old boiler emitting a warm red glow from the inferno in its interior. A hooded figure sits on a huge wooden chair while a guard shackles him and another man attaches an I.V. The chair looks like one of those old electric chairs I'd seen in movies – Old Sparky.

"This is another test, right?" I say, doubt filling me. "You want to see how gullible I am."

"No, this is real, Eve."

"What's the man doing to him?"

"That's filled with colloidal silver. If Julien tries anything, we can activate the drip and he'll be immobilized in a matter of moments."

"Will it kill him?"

Ed shakes his head. "Nope, just give him a hell of a hangover."

I can see that it's Julien despite the hood. He's wearing the same Navy Seal t-shirt and cammo pants he wore the first day in the warehouse. Silver chains circle his ankles and silver clamps hold his arms in place on the wide armrests. I watch from the shadows, my palms sweaty, my pulse elevated.

"I need you to read him," Ed says. "Witness his kills. I want you to really explore his memories to see if he was involved in these latest murders. This last one in particular. I want to give him the benefit of the doubt, but he's not being very cooperative. If he were innocent I expect he'd be all too happy to explain what he was doing at the waterfront with a dead body."

"He's been compelled," I say, my stomach already tightening in anticipation. "Just like you've been. Both of you. Don't you see, Ed? Soren did this. He set all this up."

"Just give it a try," Ed says as if he doesn't hear me. "Besides, you're all we have. We're under higher security due to a threat against Adepts and there's no one who can come at the last moment and assist. It's you or nothing."

While they prepare Julien, I sit on a chair and try to regain control over my rapidly beating heart. After a few deep breaths, I'm starting to feel a bit better, although my stomach is still tense.

"Are you ready?" Ed lays a hand on my shoulder as if giving me strength. "I wouldn't ask you to do this under normal circumstances. Besides the fact you know him, we don't normally use Adepts on cases for the first six months while they train, but we have no other options."

"There isn't anyone else you can use?"

"Nope. You're it. If he's guilty," Ed says, "he'll try to intimidate you, threaten you, try to play with your mind when you read him, convince you to lie. You don't have to take long – just see if you can find one unsanctioned kill that's part of this case, even if it isn't this current murder. Catch him killing any one of them. That's all we need to start the process. You can find more and document them later."

"How will I know if they're unsanctioned?"

"You'll know. When a kill is sanctioned, there's documents to sign and an inspection of the corpse to make sure the kill was clean."

I nod and my hands shake just a bit. "I think you're making a mistake."

"If Terri thinks you're up to it," Ed says, "you're up to it. She's the expert."

I glance at the I.V. "Is that really necessary? He's not going to hurt me."

"It is necessary. It acts in seconds. One move to hurt you and he'll be immobilized. He knows there's no escape for him."

Ed passes me a clipboard. On the top is a bold title 'Oath of Office'.

"You'll have to read this out loud and I'll witness. Once you read it, you'll be bound to it. You have to agree to faithfully report what you see when you witness his kills, revealing those that are unsanctioned so we can begin prosecution. If you don't, you'll be charged with treason and put in prison for an undetermined time – or executed if the treason is considered high."

"Why would I lie?"

"People have chosen sides. Even some humans have sided with vampires if you can believe it. They want vampires to be rulers." He shakes his head. "It's like a drug with them. They see vampires as god-like and want something to worship."

"People worship vampires?"

"Believe it. They have an underground cult following."

I swallow hard and read the oath of office out loud, my throat constricting so much that I can barely speak. I sign, indicating that I understand the penalties for lying. I try to smile and hand it back to him. He witnesses the form.

"Might as well jump right in," he says. "You can talk while you read him. We'll record everything and you can add to it later."

Ed goes into the other room and nods to the guard, who removes the earphones and hood.

"He has color in his cheeks," I say to Ed when he returns.

"Recently fed on whole human blood and a whole human's worth. There wasn't time for it to dissipate. Takes a few hours."

As I wait for guards to finish removing the hood and earphones, sadness fills me. Soren has manipulated everyone and is probably now laughing.

Julien sits behind a heavy oak table, a two-way mirror on the wall across from him, a video camera in a corner of the ceiling taping everything. Dried blood speckles his chin, marring the otherwise perfect strong jaw and symmetrical features. Finally, Ed escorts me into the room and Julien turns to face me.

"You must be joking." He turns away as if in disgust then glares at Ed. "You can't use her as my witness for God's sake. She's never done one case. Besides, we're intimate. That breaks the ethics rules. Can't Western send someone?"

My cheeks burn when he mentions our intimacy.

Ed turns to me and shakes his head. "Suspects don't get to choose their interrogators."

"Interrogator my ass." Julien glances away. "She's nothing more than a girl."

Ed shrugs. "This girl could have killed Michel in the dojo if she'd had a stake. The depth of her gift is all that matters. You said yourself that hers is very deep despite her age."

Julien says nothing, turning away as if he can't bear to even look at me. I focus on the notes Ed has given me. Before administering the test, I'm required to take a verbal statement from Julien, to get him to confess.

"Tell me what happened," I say, trying to keep my voice neutral. "What were you doing with the body?"

"Oh, that?" he says, his eyes narrowing. "Just a little lunch." He lunges forward just enough to make the cuffs jangle on his ankles. I flinch, hurt that he's treating me like this. The guard steps forward, ready to activate the hypodermic, but Ed holds his hand up. "Don't give the bastard what he wants." The guard backs off.

Julien smiles, but his eyes gave lie to it.

"How old are you, Eve? Twenty? Are they so desperate for talent that they're sending neophytes in to do adult work now?"

"I'm old enough." I frown. He knows how old I am. Why is he acting like this? Is this a performance? Did Soren compel him to act this way?

Ed speaks over the intercom. "You know how old she is."

"How many of us will you destroy during your career," he says and leans forward, "because you will destroy us. Even if you don't put the stake in them yourself, their deaths will be on your hands. You'll have taken away the gift of immortality from vampires with decades, centuries, maybe even millennia of experience. That's an awful burden, Eve. It will weigh on your conscience." He sits back, his eyes on me. "Superior beings. You'll help destroy them."

I shrug, not having really had time to think about it.

"I thought you supported the Council."

"Obviously, you didn't know me as well as you thought."

I say nothing, my hands gripping the chair's armrests. His words make me warm, my face flushing in embarrassment. He's right. I obviously didn't know him. I thought he was honorable. He's really just a predator. I fight to regain control, biting the inside of my cheek until I taste blood, using the pain to focus.

I take in a deep breath and try to shift back to him.

"Tell me about the kills. Why did you kill the priest?"

"Hypocrisy."

"What do you mean?"

After a moment, he shrugs. "This is a waste of time." He turns away. "I'm guilty. Just read me and get it over with."

I write his words down in my notes.

"I need you to confess to one kill publicly if you want your sentence reduced."

"I killed them all. How's that?"

"No, I need one kill detailed. A confession."

"Fuck the confession. I'm no longer Catholic and you're not a priest." He turns and faces me directly. "Come on, executioner. Read me and get this farce over with. I'm bored."

"Why are you being so nasty to me?"

"That's the wrong question," he says. "You should ask why was I so nice to you before?"

I shake my head, not knowing what he means. Was his friendly demeanor when we first met just an act?

He leans closer.

"I'll tell you something," he says, his voice conspiratorial. "Don't ever think that any vampire is your friend, Eve. None of us. The truth is, no matter how we act, or how nice we behave, we want to kill you, *all* of you. We're nasty motherfuckers. We are psychopaths. All of us. That's why we'll win. That's why Dominion is inevitable."

I take in a deep breath and close my file, my mind registering shock, my body numb. I approach him, and when I do, the guard moves closer, holding out the mechanism in case Julien makes a threatening move. I look into Julien's eyes before I touch him, afraid now of what I'll see in his mind. He smiles as if he relishes the prospect of my touch, but for just a second, his lips betray him and his smile falters.

I touch the bare skin above his wrist on the arm not attached to the IV, and for a moment, all I feel is cool flesh. Then, a falling sensation overtakes me and the rest of the world, the room, my own flesh, disappears into the distance. I see his recent kills – dozens, one after the other as if he's assembled them on purpose just to show me how many. In the few seconds that I'm able to focus on each one, I know they're all either pardoned or sanctioned kills, done in the service of the Council. There are witnesses, there are documents signed and stamped. Inspections completed. Even the latest kill – the young priest – was Council-approved. A dour-faced human stamped a letter. The beheading hadn't happened yet, but was meant to mimic the real killer.

Julien is a killer and enjoys each one, relishing in his victim's blood. But he isn't *the* killer. He isn't the River Man.

When I try to pull away to proclaim his innocence of the charges against him, to attest that his kills are all just, he twists his hand and is able to grasp mine before the guard can react. In those few seconds before the guard depresses the switch to trigger the flow of liquid silver, Julien pleads with me in his mind.

*Find me guilty.*

I hear it in my mind, just a whisper, but his voice is pleading.

I fight against such an idea. He *is* a killer, a contract killer working for the Council, an infiltrator as he said to me in Virginia. His kills are all sanctioned. He wants me to find him guilty but I don't know why.

The guard steps forward and I pull myself momentarily out of contact with Julien's mind.

"Don't!" I shout as he starts to depress the lever to releases the flow of the colloidal silver. "I'm fine." The guard steps back and glances at Ed, who nods.

Then Julien's other memories overwhelm me, moments and times beyond his kills, carnal memories of his lust for the women he's loved, their bodies entwined. I try to catch my breath, sorting through the darkness of his mind as he chases down his targets and takes them out, one by one and the erotic scenes I happen on. When he feeds, I feel his bloodlust as if it's my own, the beating of the victim's heart so loud in his head, the warmth of the victim's body against his coldness, the coppery taste of blood acting like an aphrodisiac. Soon, sex and death blended into one mélange until I can't separate them and my mind rebels.

Julien, a warrior who sees the horror of the coming war between vampires and humans and refuses to accept it, who changed allegiance and now kills to ensure the continued existence of the Council. Who takes life with pleasure, without fear or care, feeding on his victims, feasting on them. Every kill justified and in service of the greater good. He wants me to trust him. To lie. I haven't found a reason for it; he presents no evidence to explain it when our minds touch, and so I have to decide and fast.

I breathe in a ragged breath. "He's guilty."

Finally, the guard pries Julien's fingers away from mine and I step back, tripping into Ed who rushes in to help me. I almost collapse as my own senses rush back to fill the gap when Julien and I part minds. Overwhelmed, I bend over, head between my knees, on the verge of passing out. Ed sits me down and then strikes Julien across the face with so much force that I can hear bone breaking.

"Son of a fucking bitch," he shouts and bends over at the waist, rubbing his knuckles, which are stained with blood. "I forgot how indestructible you bloodsuckers are."

Julien turns his face back, and I notice there's blood on his lips. "Is that your blood or mine?" He licks the corners of his mouth. "Oh, it's yours," he says and smiles. "Thanks for the snack."

Ed makes a fist again. "I'm going to enjoy pulling the plug on you, you traitorous sonofabitch. You had us all sucked in. What a expert liar you are."

"My pleasure, but really," Julien says and the menace in his voice sends a chill down my spine, "you're being too kind."

I pick up my notebook and pen from where they fell, my hands still shaking as I try to grasp what I've just done. I've broken my oath of office within moments of taking it. I've lied about Julien's innocence – at his request, but it's still a lie. I search his face for something, but he won't look at me. His eyes are fixed on Ed.

"The truth is," Julien says, his voice mocking. "You were too accepting of what I said. You wanted to crack the case so badly you ignored those little red flags, that nagging doubt you felt at me being so willing to help in Michel's place."

"Let that be a lesson to you," Ed says and points to me. "It takes a while to become a battle-hardened skeptic. Just remember to keep your guard up. Guys like him," he says and gestures towards Julien, "are adept at assessing a mortal's weaknesses and then exploiting them to get what they want. Pure psychopaths."

I nod, pretending to agree with him, but I know that Julien isn't what Ed imagines. At least, I hope that's the case.

Ed stands beside me

"You always were a bit thick," Julien says and smiles. "Good enough for a grunt and for police work but you're obviously way over your head. No match for an eight-hundred year old vampire."

At that, Ed grabs the switch from the guard's hand and depresses the button. Julien laughs when he sees what Ed's planning, but soon his face contorts into a grimace and his body arches backwards as if he's in terrible pain.

"Is that necessary?" I say, the pain on Julien's face making me cringe.

"Don't worry," Ed said, his voice dripping with disgust. "There's not enough silver in it to destroy him. Let's go," Ed said, taking my arm, leading me out of the room. "You don't need to watch this."

I can't help but feel sick at this game he's playing with Ed. He has to look guilty and is inciting Ed's wrath on purpose.

"What'll happen to him?"

"I'll let my guys practice aggressive interrogation techniques on him, you know, just for the experience. Then, when he recovers, you'll have to question him again. Detail at least one kill so we can put him away. You need to document one kill, how he did it, where he did it, and lead us to some physical evidence we can use. It shouldn't take more than a few moments direct contact."

We go upstairs to the SCU offices and I sit on the chair across from Ed's desk, glad for the rest. Strapped into the old electric chair, the silver IV attached to his arm, he looks so vulnerable. I wonder what he was like before he had been turned. A warrior – that much I know from the manuscript, but before even that, he was a priest like Michel. Loyal to his father who died fighting a war against the Church, his mortality taken from him.

Ed glances at the clock. "It's almost dawn. We'll keep him busy for a few hours, soften him up for you later. Why don't you go home and get some shuteye? You better go back to your own place. I don't want you staying at Julien's warehouse any longer. I'll put 24/7 surveillance on you starting now. Obviously, Julien wasn't on our side so I don't trust any of his men. Report back here at dusk."

A driver takes me to my apartment. He points out the unmarked car stationed outside my building to check on everyone coming and going. I go upstairs and after I feed the cats and check my email, I creep under the covers and sleep like the dead.

# CHAPTER 12

"*L*ove does not dominate: it cultivates."

Goethe

I SPEND THE DAY IN A BROKEN SLEEP, waking up and turning over and over in my bed, getting up during the middle of the day to check outside where I see an unmarked sedan still on the street, the man inside smoking, a newspaper opened in his hand.

I have few of my things at my apartment – they're all at Julien's warehouse and so I have to find something from my really old clothes.

My world is now completely upside-down. Michel's gone for good. Julien is posing as a traitor and I'm no longer in protective custody. I have a stake in my coat pocket and that's about the only protection I have that I feel I can count on. I wonder if it would kill Soren, if he were to come after me.

Ed seems impatient to get going when I arrive back at the SCU after dusk.

"We kept him up all day, so he'll be less able to influence you when you read him."

We go down to the basement and I catch sight of Julien sitting in the chair through the two-way mirror. My heart does a little flip-flop and my palms are already starting to sweat.

"Go ahead," Ed says, a hand at my back. "Might as well get it over with. Sooner you write him up, the sooner I can tank the monster."

I take the clipboard on which is attached the declaration form I'm to fill out, detailing the 'confession' if there is any and whatever I witness when reading him.

Julien raises his eyebrows when I enter the room. He tilts his head to the side, a tiny bit of a grin on his face. Blood spatters his cheek and he looks even more undead than before but I see no bruising or damage to him. Of course, he heals so quickly, any wounds would be gone in a matter of minutes.

"Hello, Eve. How'd you sleep last night? I hear you were back in your apartment. I'm sure you have good surveillance on you, so don't worry your little head about it." He nods briefly as if reassuring me. Does he have his own security on me and this is what he's telling me?

I smile back, trying to play whatever game he wants me to play, and take my seat, then focus on my work, flipping open the witness report file, reviewing the directions.

"Where did we leave off? You were bragging about your superiority, if I recall correctly."

Julien says nothing, just nods slightly as if confirming that I'm right to play along. Then he smacks his lips suggestively.

"I'm going to enjoy tasting you again," he says.

Ed steps into the room and slaps Julien across the face.

"The only thing you're gonna taste, asshole, is tank gel, you animal. I'm gonna enjoy shoving the tube down your throat and filling you full of it."

"You see what kind of human he is?" Julien says and lifts his chin towards Ed. "He wants to kill us all, every last one of us. Doesn't that sound a bit -- genocidal?"

After a moment of silence passes he smiles.

"I was wondering why they sent you in to interview me instead of putting me in stasis and waiting until a more experienced witness is available. You can't seriously think they sent you in because you're so skilled."

He's playing a game, pretending to be a real asshole. I have to play along, and do my best, but it's hard because half the time, I'm really not certain it is a game.

"I'm not skilled," I say. "Not yet. But I am fascinated about why you choose to break the treaty that protects your kind from vigilante justice."

"The treaty keeps us in servitude," he says. "We aren't free to be true to our nature."

"Your nature as serial killers."

"As hunters," he says. "Keeping the prey population in check."

"Immoral killers who kill with no concern."

"Oh, I don't kill with a lack of concern," he says and shakes his head, then gestures with his chin as if to draw me nearer. I lean forward. "Exactly the opposite," he says, his voice soft. "I kill with deep concern. I cherish every single kill. When I'm sucking the life out of my victim?" He sighs audibly and leans back. "I know that God is good."

"Get on with it. I know you hate having to do it," Ed says to me from the observation room. "Please read this monster and let me do my job and put him away."

Julien shakes his head. He glowers at Ed and then turns back to me.

"These idiots think that if they can understand vampires they'll be able to kill us all off. That's what you really want, isn't it Ed?" he says and turns to the two-way mirror. "You want to control us. You want power over us. Mortals are weak, and vampires strong, and you're afraid. You can't and you won't destroy us because God himself ordained that we're to be punished forever." He leans forward and whispers to me. "God himself condemned us all and any that we love."

He says it with all earnestness and I almost believe him. He tilts his head to the side and examines me.

"He condemned you, didn't he, pretty little Eve. Pure little Eve, full of promise, child prodigy on the piano, little ballerina, weren't you, before all this caught up with you? Made your father weep when you played so well when you were only five. Father had big plans for you to become a modern-day Mozart, but fate intervened, isn't that right? Fate in the form of a vampire who killed your mother and sent your father into an institution."

"I said shut the fuck up," Ed said and punches Julien once more.

I shake my head and look away from them, turning pages in my file with a shaking hand, wondering at what a great actor he is or whether he's serious about all the God talk.

"I imagine the Accord was meant to control you because you're a danger to humans."

He glowers at me. "You can't really control us. We're a force of God's will. Vampires were created to prey on you in punishment for your transgressions against God."

"Let's get this over with."

"Look," he says and leans forward. "Eve. I can see you're clearly over your head. It's not your fault. You should have been spared this. I blame men like Ed who want to exploit you. They think they've outsmarted God himself, figuring out some way to destroy us with their genetic technology. But I'll let you in on a little secret," he says and nods for me to move closer. I do without thinking. "It's you they'll destroy." He leans back, as if satisfied. "Now go ahead and read me. Get this over with." He smiles.

I check the box on the form that reads 'Subject Fails to Disclose Details Voluntarily' and put the clipboard down on the table. I take in a deep breath and lay my hand on the exposed skin on the inside of his wrist. His skin is soft there, velvety, and cool.

Then, that familiar sensation of falling into a chasm overtakes me and I'm inside his mind. I see him with the dead priest, meeting him in a dark wooded area somewhere outside the city, the monastery, the priest kneeling down before him. Then the pleasure when he sinks his teeth into the man's neck, drinking deeply of his blood, the sensation of the man's heart as it speeds up while the blood drains out of his body.

I'm drawn into his bloodlust briefly, the sensations of drinking the blood now familiar. I watch the next part – the part where he carries the body to the waterfront. Then, I pull out of the vision, using every bit of energy I can.

"I got it all," I say, waiting for the vertigo to pass.

Ed comes to my side and puts his arm around my shoulder in an avuncular fashion. "Just record what you saw. Give us details that we can use. Did you get the location of the kill site?"

I nod. "The monastery where he used to live."

Ed snaps his fingers and points to someone in the observation room. "Get a team and check it out."

"Poor sweet Eve," Julien says as the guard starts to unshackle his chains, preparing to move him. "Trying so hard to please your parents, playing the piano like an angel to get their approval. Your father's approval. Your mother really did love you." He shakes his head. "Isn't that the story of all our lives? Doing whatever it takes to get the father's approval when all he really cares about is his own aggrandizement?"

"I don't know what you're talking about," I say in anger. "My father loved me."

"That's what I thought as well. Common mistake."

He smiles and stretches in an exaggerated fashion in spite of his restraints. "Now enough about our bastard fathers. There are plans afoot. I have to keep on top of things. Why don't you just ask me something more interesting, like – can I predict the future? Can I tell you what's going to happen next?"

"What do you mean? After I read you or after the Council sentences you?"

"Not that long. . . " He cranes his head to see the clock. "Not nearly that long."

I frown. "What are you talking about?"

"You'll see." He smiles.

Then a huge explosion shakes the building and the lights flicker out so that we sit in complete darkness. I hear a scuffle, and when my eyes adjust, I see that Julien has taken down both guards who were in to move him.

"What happened?" I say, breathless.

"Don't worry," he says, his voice steely. "You're safe."

After about ten seconds, the emergency generator starts and the lights switch on.

Julien leans forward. His face is dark, his expression stern. "Listen to me," he says. "Just don't fight."

"What are you doing?"

He closes his eyes tightly.

It all happens too fast for me to take in. A bright flash of light blinds me and a loud bang dulls my hearing. Someone pulls a fabric hood over my face before my vision returns and wrenches my arms behind my back, binding them with some hard plastic ties.

I blink as I'm pulled along, and soon, the sparkles that impeded my sight are replaced by the darkness of the hood.

"Where are we going?"

"Shush," he says, his face next to mine, his voice a little lighter. He pulls me along, my heels falling off so that I'm barefoot.

"Help!" I call out, barely able to make any noise from the fear constricting my throat. Am I supposed to go along with this – pretend I'm a hostage? Or is this real?

He shakes me, squeezing my arms tighter.

"Quiet!" His voice is deep now, angered and he's either really mad or he's acting. I don't know what it is, but I do know that a camera is catching everything.

My breath catches in my lungs when he picks me up, throws me over his shoulder, and then carries me up a flight of stairs. I feel cool air against the skin of my legs, and am deposited somewhere, perhaps the back of a vehicle, the floor hard against my ribs. Doors slam shut. An engine roars into life, tires screech. Rapid movement, bumps in the road, muted conversation from the front of the vehicle.

I lie on my side, a hood covering my head, my arms bound behind me.

I wonder what the hell Julien has got me into.

We drive around for a long time – I'm not able to gauge how long. Finally, the van stops, the engine idling. A door slams and I wait for something else to happen. After another much shorter wait, the door opens and I hear a familiar voice. Julien. He and the other man speak, their conversation muted.

"The back entry's open. It's three flights up. I'll carry her."

Next, I'm lifted out of the vehicle and thrown back over his shoulder. Up stairs, I don't know how many, for my heart is beating far too fast. I hear a door close and then am plopped onto a bed.

Some more discussion takes place between Julien and someone else and then another silence after a door shuts. I hear a meow and my heart jumps. The mattress depresses and the hood is removed from my head.

My apartment! I glance past Julien's face through the open door to the living room, to my small upright grand piano, to the cat apartment by the bay window.

"Why are we here? Won't they look here first?"

"Why would they look here? Who'd be dumb enough to take a hostage to her own apartment?" He leaves me on the bed. "I always say, hide in plain sight. People are too stupid to look there. Besides, I wanted to remind them you're not safe," he says and turns to face me. "Ed thinks he can protect you from me and all the other vampires out there. I'm trying to prove he can't so he'll put you in protective custody."

"Can you at least take these off?"

"No can do. You have to look like you've been abducted. I have to sever ties to you so you can keep working for the SCU. I need you inside if I'm no longer there."

"Why did you have to kill that priest?" I say.

"He's very dangerous to the peace," Julien says, pausing to pick up a book from my bookshelf on Freud, then moving to my closet. "He chose the wrong side. That can't be allowed – for all our sakes."  He takes out one of my blouses and holds it up to his nose, breathing in deeply.

"Why did he have to die? Wasn't there another way? Couldn't you talk to him, imprison him?"

"Eve, there's a lot you don't understand," he says and turns to face me. "You're a weapon. In the wrong hands, you could be a threat to us all. When one of you is taken to the other side, when you're corrupted, compelled, the only solution is death. We've tried hiding them, but their masters hunt them down unrelentingly. This is the only way."

I shake my head. "It sounds like genocide."

Julien moves to my piano and plays a key. "It isn't," he says. "It's targeted assassination. If Adepts go on the wrong side, we have to kill them."

I frown. "You'd kill me?"

He remains silent.

"You didn't answer me."

"Don't make the wrong choice," he says. "Then I won't have to."

I can't let it go. "So, you would kill me."

He gives me a weary look.

"Eve. I'm a soldier. I kill enemies. Don't become my enemy. Lying psychopaths aren't the best enemies to have."

"You're not a psychopath."

He seems amused at that.

"Oh, yes, I am," he says, shaking his head. " Yes. I. Am. Vampires can't help it. We like to kill humans. We love it. It takes a hell of a lot to keep us from being monsters. Didn't you read your mother's files?"

"Maybe some of you are, but you don't have to be. You're not," I say, remembering him with Kate. "Michel's not. You both care. You look after Kate. A psychopath wouldn't do that."

"It serves our purposes to keep her alive. I already told you that she was a source of blood for Michel so he wouldn't have you. That's it, Eve. Mortals are a means to an end for us."

"I don't believe it."

"Whatever. It's true."

He leaves the bedroom and I can barely see him through the open door. He stops by my desk. Oh, hell. He's reading my letter to Cecile.

He comes back and climbs on top of me and leans down, sniffing my neck. Presses his nose under my ear where I daubed perfume and he inhales deeply.

"That's why Michel didn't want to have sex with you. He wanted to keep his distance, so he could use you like a tool. A weapon. If he did, his feelings would soften him, make him less likely to use you properly. But he's always been such a softie. I can have sex with you and it won't matter. I'm tougher than he ever was."

"Why are you telling me this?"

He plays with my hair, twirling it in his fingers.

"So you don't get the wrong idea. I want you, sure. I'll enjoy you. I'll enjoy making you my pet. But I won't love you."

"I don't want you to," I say, trying to sound as if I don't care, but my heart squeezes at that and sadness fills me.

"Good. I don't want to either." I say it but I know it's a lie. A blush rises to my cheeks.

"Oh, poor Eve. Did it hurt you to hear the truth?"

I can't say anything for tears bite at the corners of my eyes. He already knows.

"Don't worry," he mouths against my neck. "I told you I'm not a rapist. Sex has to be freely chosen. It has to be offered. In your case, it has to be begged for."

I try to pull away from him but he tightens his grip on me. "If you think I'll beg," I gasp. "You're crazy."

He presses against me even harder, his mouth poised over mine. "I'm not crazy. And you will beg, Eve. You will. I know you. And you know what?" he says and takes my bottom lip between his teeth for a moment before letting go. "When you do, I won't even have to remind you that I told you so. When you do beg me, you'll look in my eyes," he says, sniffing my neck, "and you'll remember this precise moment, word for word. And. It. Will. Be. So. Good." His lips just touch mine, his breath on my skin, and then he kisses me, his lips crushing mine, his tongue finding mine, his breathing harsh. Then, it's like he switches off and he hops off the bed, leaving me lying there, aroused, and reaches into a bag and pulls out a roll of duct tape.

"I hate to do this, but I have to make this look real. If you try real hard, you might get loose by morning – you know, just in case I miscalculate and die in an unfortunate stake accident. I don't want you starving to death, the police breaking down your door to find your rotting bloated corpse. I'll call in an anonymous tip that you're here so you won't be here too long."

He tapes my mouth shut and then sits beside me, a hand brushing my hair from my face.

"Don't miss me too much. Pretty soon, you'll be back at the warehouse and we'll start Act Two of this farce."

And then he's gone.

# CHAPTER 13

"*L*ove is all we have, the only way that each can help the other."

Euripides

I lie on the bed and listen to the sounds of my quiet apartment now that Julien's gone. I can't do anything about the plastic ties that bind my wrists, but I can jiggle those attaching my feet to the bedpost. The bed frame's constructed so that the ball-shaped top of the corner post is screwed on. I try to shimmy my way down towards the bedpost in the hopes I can find a way to unscrew it. I work my feet up so that my toes just touch the ball at the top of the post and try to turn it, but it's screwed on too tight.

I pull at my restraints with all my might, but all that does is cause them to bite into my flesh, leaving raw welts around my ankles and wrists.

Hours pass – the slant of the light through my window tells me that. Finally, I hear footsteps in the hallway – is it Julien? I hear a knock at the door and then a crackled voice.

"Eve? Eve? Are you in there?"

Mrs. Barnes from down the hall – God bless her! I try to call out, but all I'm able to manage is a muffled groan that deaf old Mrs. Barnes is surely not able to hear.

I glance around in a panic – what can I do to get Mrs. Barnes' attention? I turn to the night table and wonder . . . perhaps I could wriggle my way over to the side of the bed and somehow make the lamp fall over . . .

After tremendous effort, I succeed in worming my way over closer to the edge of the bed and start rocking it, hoping that the bed will knock the night table and then the lamp . . .

It falls with a crash.

"Eve? Is that you?"

Silence. *Damn.* She mustn't have heard the sound and has gone away. Resignation fills me. Julien said he'd call this in, but in how long? Then I hear keys at the lock and my hopes rise. My heart races and I feel a surge of adrenaline as the door opens and . . . it's the Super! He has a master key.

He takes one look at me and picks up a cell phone from his belt.

"Send the police over to number 3b, 14 Parkside Lane. I just found Eve Hayden and it looks like she's been harmed."

Relief floods me and tears filled my eyes, obscuring my vision.

Now I have to act all scared and surprised that Julien would kidnap me. This worries me. I am not an actor.

The Super removes the duct tape with a quick tug and it hurts like hell.

"Ow," I say. "Thank you. I thought I was going to die here."

Ed arrives and rushes in to me.

"Are you OK?"

I nod. "Just a bit raw where the restraints were."

He stands with hands on hips and glances around the room. "I don't understand why he brought you here. We would have eventually checked out your apartment as a matter of course. In fact, I had a few men scheduled to come over here in the morning. It's like he wanted you to be found."

He looks me over.

"Did he," Ed says, his voice soft. "Did he harm you in any way? Did he assault you," he hesitates, "sexually?"

I shake my head. "No. Why do you ask?"

"It's just that," he says and points to my face. "Your lipstick. It's smeared."

"Oh," I say, wiping my mouth with my fingers. I shake my head. "It must have been when he was putting the duct tape on."

"Why would he take you hostage?"

I shrug. "He said it was just to show you that he could and that I wasn't safe."

"Yeah," Ed says. "He likes rubbing our faces in our mistakes. I'm glad your neighbor saw someone leave your apartment and thought to come and check. She said you never had men over."

Being a spinster had some benefits after all.

"No, I," I say and falter, embarrassed to admit it. "I'm not very . . . active socially, what with finishing my degree."

"Well, it's lucky for us you have such a good neighbor and we were able to get here before he returned."

I rub my ankles, the skin red and raw where the plastic chafed.

"What happens now? Do I need to hide? Should I go to stay with my foster parents or something? They live in Ipswich in the summer."

Ed helps me off the bed. "We need to debrief you and then yes, please, stay with a friend or family member. I think you should take some time off work until we get Julien back into custody."

"Do you think you'll be able? He escaped from the SCU."

"I know – it was an operation carried out with military precision. Disabled the alarms, knocked out security, power. Used flash-bangs to startle everyone."

"He told me he has military training."

"He or one of his gang." Ed motions me to my bathroom. "Maybe you want to pack a small bag with your things. If you have nowhere else to go, we can put you up in a safe house."

"I'll call my friend Frances, from school. Maybe she can pick me up from the SCU when we're done. I," I say and glance around. "I can't leave my cats alone for too long – I'll have to get someone to come by and feed them and . . . "

"Don't worry about that now. We'll take care of the details later."

I go to my small bathroom and throw my few things that remain into an overnight bag.


I call Frances when we get to the SCU. She's also a pre-med student. I'll stay with her rather than go to a safe house. When we arrive back at the SCU, Ed gives me a lecture about safety.

"He may be gone," Ed says, his voice soft. "Or he may still be in the city. If he is, you're not safe. I got the feeling he has a sweet spot for you. Whatever happens, don't let him bite you or in any way taste your blood. If he did that, you'd be tied to him. Don't let any vampire bite you unless it's to save your life. You do and they consider you theirs for life.  They taste your blood, and they're connected to you. Word to the wise."

He can't see my bite? Has Julien compelled him?

"Don't worry," I say. "That's the last thing I want." Of course, it's already too late. I'm his if that's the case. Not Michel's as I want to be. Or, as I thought I wanted to be. After reading the pages Julien gave me, I don't know if I want either of them.

"He's very dangerous." Ed says, removing his glasses and rubbing his eyes. "But we'll get him, one way or the other." He puts his glasses back on and regards me steadily. "What's your assessment of what's motivating him? What is his goal?"

I put on my most professional face.

"We hadn't really gotten that far in the interview but I'd say he wants Dominion but he also wants to show how much smarter and stronger he is than everyone else."

"Yeah, but the thing is," Ed says ruefully. "He is."

"Do you think so?"

"Like other vampires, he has no fear. He doesn't believe he'll be defeated and he doesn't believe that the normal laws and morals apply to him, so he's free to do whatever he can get away with to achieve his ends. And most of the old ones are very smart. Above average intelligence. Julien? From what I heard he's fought in pretty much every war in the western world since he was made. He isn't stupid at all. Call your friend," Ed says. "Get her to come and pick you up. We'll put a detail on you, watch you in case he tries something else."

"He won't. He told me he was going out of town and wouldn't be back."

"Yeah, like I believe that." Ed leads me out of the interview room. "He'd like us to believe it and get all complacent with you. Then he'd come right back under our noses just to prove that he could and snatch you. Remember, you Adepts are like gold."

A week passes. I'm in lockdown mode at Frances's apartment. I make two trips to my apartment accompanied by some Council guards assigned to me. The cats go crazy, rubbing against my legs, almost tripping me in their enthusiasm for my presence.

"I'm sorry, kitties," I say as I fill their water and food dish. "I won't be gone for much longer."

Tucked in the corner of my mirror in my bedroom is a card. I open it. One of my guards comes over to me.

"What is it?"

I hand it to him. A card a huge white peony in the center. Beneath it black script.

'Remember me.'

Ed calls me at Frances's place later that afternoon.

"I take that as an indication he doesn't want to forget you," he says. "He must have snuck into your apartment when one of our guys wasn't looking. We're searching your apartment for anything else, a bug or something but so far, nothing's shown up."

"Thanks." I feel strangely violated knowing that Julien had been inside my apartment again. "I think it means he's actually leaving town. Why else ask me to remember him?"

I hang up.

Later, before supper, I go to the window in France's apartment and see the unmarked car on the street – Ed insisted on having the apartment watched 24/7. Frances is at work and isn't due back for an hour or so. I call one of the guards and ask if he'll take me out for a while.

"Where to? We have to call in for our log."

"Anywhere. I just want to get out for a while."

"I'm sorry, but I need a destination."

I think for a moment. What do I feel like doing?

"The conservatory," I say. "I miss having a piano around. I can rent some time and go and practice for a while."

"Ok. Whenever you're ready."

I call the conservatory but they had no small sound rooms left. I'll have to make do with an empty lecture hall that has an old grand piano on the stage. I pull on a sweater and my jeans and brush my hair. Before I leave, I write a note to Frances, just in case she comes home before I return.

"Out for a bit – be back soon. XOXOX"

The two guards take up positions at the front and back doors of the building to keep an eye out in case I've been followed.

It's good to feel the keyboard under my hands again. I have to play the old stuff – pieces I know by heart without my sheet music. Alone in the empty lecture theatre, I play my entire repertory, and soon became lost in the music. Years ago, when I was younger, before my mother's death, they dreamed of me being a soloist. My father taught me for a few years when I was age three to five, but he found new teachers because I learned so quickly. Music is tied to my father so intimately that I can't play without feeling some grief for his loss to insanity.

I finish playing and rest my head on the piano. It brings back memories of my childhood and gives me a choky feeling of regret. I start to play another piece but then feel someone sit down beside me and turn only to be staring into Julien's face. Before I can react, he has a hand over my mouth and a finger to his lips.

"Shh."

I nod and he withdraws his hand.

"Sorry to startle you. Go ahead," he says and motions to the piano. "Play some more. I was enjoying it."

"How did you know I was here?"

He smiles. "Do you really think I'm going to answer that?"

I don't respond. Of course he must have someone on the inside of the SCU feeding him information.

"Why are you here?"

He points to the keys.

"I heard you were coming to play. I rearranged a meeting so I could listen."

"I already finished playing."

He points to the instrument. "Play some more."

I shake my head.

"I don't feel like it."

"Eve," he says and I can hear exasperation in his voice. "I don't want to have to force the issue. Just play something. Do you know any Bach?"

"You don't like Chopin?"

"I prefer Bach."

I play a Bach Prelude – C Sharp Minor – and he closes his eyes until the piece is over. He opens his eyes and smiles at me, but his smile is sad.

"I heard it played a few years after he wrote it," he says. "After it was published, all the students in Vienna learned to play pieces from The Well Tempered Clavier."

I shake my head.

"God, I can't imagine what its like to live so long."

"It's wonderful and terrible at the same time.  My kind call it the curse of immortality. To watch people you love grow old and die. Most of us refuse to make connections with humans as a result other than through feeding, but sometimes, you meet someone and you're helpless."

"That's happened to you before?"

"Too often."

"I thought you're a cold-hearted psychopath."

"Not cold hearted."

I sigh and try to play something else but I don't have the heart and stop, folding my hands in my lap. "I'm sorry," I said. "I've played enough."

"Thank you for letting me listen. It's more than I deserve, considering everything."

I shake my head, but don't trust my voice.

"But part of the reason I came was to warn you that if I could find you this easily, so could others – those who want your skills as much as we do. You're in danger and now that I'm not working with you, I feel you're vulnerable. Ed's decent, but he's still just a mortal."

"What can I do?"

"Don't trust anyone besides Starr and Ed," Julien says, his brow furrowed. "Don't even trust them. If you were mine," he says his voice dropping lower, "I'd always know where you were and could protect you."

"If I were yours?" I say. "What does that mean?" But then I remember about blood slaves.

Julien shakes his head as if he's changed his mind.

"It's time to go," he says and stands. "I'd like to say we'll meet again, but I can't. How things will go in the next few days will determine if you can come back to the warehouse."

I don't respond. What can I say?

"Eve, I," he says and then stops as if he's reconsidered something. He leans closer, his face beside my ear, his lips pressed against his bite on my neck. I can't help but respond to his touch.

Then, he's gone.


I return the key to the office then walk to the exit, my knees shaking. One of the guards stands with his back to the door, his hands folded behind him.

So much for protection.

I open the door and he turns and tips his hat. "Ready to go back?"

"He was in the building, sitting right next to me."

The guard's face drops.

"What?" He pulls out his gun and picks up his two-way radio. "Hey, Bailey – she says he was inside the building. Call in backup. I'll go inside and check. You keep watch over the rear of the building."

He points to the unmarked car. "You better go and sit inside."

I do, knowing this is all just a performance. A moment later, a dark figure slips out the door and down the street.

"I'm going home." I pack my things, stuffing my clothes into my small travel bag.

Ed stands in the doorway, the grey of his rumpled trench coat matching the bags under his eyes.

"We're short of staff," he says. "You shouldn't have gone out."

"Ed, he can get me no matter where I am. I'm going home."

He shakes his head. "Just give us a few more days."

"Look. You don't seem to be able to stop him. You can't protect me."

"We're looking into who might have alerted him to your presence at the conservatory. I really don't know who I can trust anymore."

"Try to understand," I say and continue packing. "He can do pretty much what he likes, so why shouldn't I just go back to my apartment? If he's coming for me, he's coming for me."

"I don't think it's wise for you to do this, but I can't stop you." Ed's face betrays exasperation. "If you were anyone else, I'd say there's the witness protection program but you're too valuable to us."

"Thanks. Too valuable to let go, but not too valuable to protect."

Ed sighs.

"Call me, anytime of the day or night if you feel in danger and I'll have a car over in five minutes, just in case he does come by. You can consider this a time to catch up on reading material."

"Oh, I'm confident that if he wants to, he'll come by. I'm also confident that no matter what you do, he'll be able to get to me."

I walk him to the door and lock the deadbolt behind him. What Julien taught me by coming to hear me play was that a vampire is able to get by mortal defenses. Someone as well-trained as Julien more than most.

The first night I'm home, I sleep with a knife beside me. During the day, I stay inside and check the street frequently to see the unmarked car. The second night I'm home, I get a call from Vasily.

"Come downstairs, Eve. You are not safe in apartment. Come to warehouse."

"There's a security detail on me," I say. "They'll know I've left."

"No," Vasily says. "They are Julien's. They will report you were home all the time."

And so I return to the warehouse and the ostentatious bed, but other than Vasily, the apartment's empty. Julien isn't there.

# CHAPTER 14

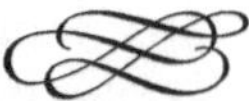



Aristotle

I sit alone in the small living area and switch on the television. The local news is on and I watch a reporter and his cameraman standing at a police barricade about two blocks from the SCU, cameras rolling. A crowd assembled to watch and overhead comes the sound of helicopters. Police cars with lights flashing and uniformed officers line the barricades to keep onlookers from entering the protected areas.

I sit on the couch, my feet tucked under me, and wait, flipping from channel to channel to follow the commentary, my nerves on edge. The anchor for Channel 7 speaks while the camera zooms in on the scene, the image enlarging to show the empty street across from the SCU, the other buildings like granite caverns all around it.

"We're here live at the scene of a standoff at a building near the waterfront. Right now, there's some kind of hostage situation. Boston SWAT have surrounded the building. It looks as if a man's stepping out of the front of the building – yes, there is a man stepping out."

The camera zooms in for a closer shot, and I gasp as I recognize Ed's characteristic shiny dome head. It has to be him.

Julien enters the apartment at that moment, distracting me from the television.

"You're here," he says.

"Vasily picked me up last night," I say. "Ed's involved in some kind of stand-off with the police."

"Oh, that," Julien says, making a face. "I was going to tell you. Ed became a liability. I had to take care of things."

I turn to him and he shrugs, raising his eyebrows as if he's sorry but helpless.

"You *what?*"

"I had to turn him over to the police for some nasty business he was involved in. Killing a police officer, if I recall correctly. Shame. He was a good asset while he lasted."

"They're going to take him into custody?"

"No," Julien says, shaking his head. "That wouldn't be a good idea. He knows too much."

"What do you mean?"

I sit at the edge of my chair, wondering what will happen next. Then, Ed stumbles, his arms flailing outward, his head thrown back as if he's tripped. He goes to his knees, remains in that position for a moment, and then falls face forward onto the street. No sound, just Ed falling and then a wild scramble as police and emergency personnel move in.

"Ladies and gentlemen," the reporter says, his voice struggling to maintain control. "I believe he's been shot. The man has been shot before our eyes."

I cover my mouth, unable to process what I've just seen. Julien had Ed executed on television on some trumped up charge.

Police run towards a building overlooking the scene, firing at a window. Sirens blare and all hell breaks loose as gunfire erupted, shots echoing throughout the area.

I sit in utter silence for a moment. Then I turn to him, my eyes filled with tears.

"How could you?"

"Eve," he says, his voice irritated. "I told you we're at war. People die in war. I had no choice."

"There's always a choice." I stand and brush by him, making a beeline for the bedroom, wanting to escape.

"Not in this case," he says, following me. "Besides, what do you know about how to fight a war?"

"I know what's right, and wrong and this was cold-blooded murder."

He grabs my arm, stopping me in my tracks.

"No," he says, his voice deep, edged with anger. "It was an operation to terminate a compromised contact. I didn't want to do it, but tactically, I had no choice."

"He *helped* Michel. For years. Soren compelled him. And you set him up."

"He didn't even know what hit him. Dead in an instant. We should all be so lucky, Eve."

"He's dead!" I struggle to pull away, trying to pry my arm away from him, but he's too strong. "You always have a choice and you chose to kill him. Why not rescue him and hide him somewhere?"

He grabs me and drags me over to the bed, throws me onto it and looms over me, one hand holding my hands over my head.

"You don't know what you're talking about so shut up."

"You killed a colleague," I say, turning my face away from him. "Someone who helped you."

"Eve," he says, grabbing my chin and turning my face to his. "This is the big league now. He has information. He knows about the Blackstone Group. There were operatives sniffing around the SCU. It was only a matter of time before they took him and he gave them something that could trace back to me. I can't let that happen." He shakes his head as if in frustration. "Can't you understand that?"

I lie beneath him, my heart pounding.

"I have information," I say, barely able to speak. "You ensured that I do. Will you kill me, too?"

He just looks at me, shaking his head slowly.

Then, he closes his eyes, his breath ragged. He leans down, his face in the crook of my neck, his arms sliding underneath me, almost crushing me against him.

"That's why," he says and presses his lips against the skin on my neck where he bit me, "you can't be free."

I push him away.

"You're a monster!"

Then he pulls back, his whole body stiffening.

"That's right, Eve," he says, breathing hard. "Did you forget that fact in this little romantic fantasy world you're living in?"

I cover my eyes, unable to stop my tears.

"Goddammit!" He lets go of me and storms away from the bed to the bathroom. He emerges from it a few moments later and he's dressed once more. He goes into the living area and I hear something crashing and glance out the open door. He's kicked over a table by the seating area on his way past, and now throws a lamp against the wall, the glass shattering into hundreds of pieces.

He comes back to me and grabs me once more, this time around the neck.

"I am a monster and you better be afraid of me because I will kill you if you ever betray me. Without a thought."

With that, he leaves.

Vasily goes downstairs, leaving me alone. I'm still lying on the bed, the apartment dark except for the lights over the office and kitchen. I cry, lying curled up on my side, the image of Julien's rage-filled face playing back in my mind, the anger as he kicked over the table, threw the lamp making my heart race, his hand at my throat, the threat – he's dangerous. He would kill me – I'm certain of it.

I replay the scene of Ed being shot over and over and it fills me with despair. There's nowhere for me to go, and I begin to feel panic rising inside. I've been living in a dream world, my reason and logic blinded by this ridiculous lust both he and Michel have been creating in me with their little games. I dig my fingers into my palm, hoping that the pain will help erase the fear, but it does nothing. I feel as if

I'm going to hyperventilate and so I leave the bed, going to the kitchen, searching through the drawers for something to dull the pain.

A small knife with a sharp edge will have to do, for the rest are either too large or serrated. I go into the bathroom and sit on the floor with my back against the vanity, the knife in my hand, breathing fast as panic threatens to overtake me. After I roll up my sleeve, I examine the lines I've carved into my skin over the past few months. The cuts have scabbed over. I start working on the skin using the sharp tip of the blade. It's a bit dull, and so I have to press hard. Soon, the outline of a J takes shape, blood welling up in the thin seam. J for Julien.

Finally calm, I put the knife down on the counter and look in the mirror – at my red eyes, streaked makeup, the bloody self-imposed brand on my arm. What a screwed up freak. A stupid woman living in a fantasy world, just like Julien said. Michel's not coming back and Julien is a poor substitute – a monster and now that I've read some of the missing manuscript pages, I'm not too sure about Michel either. I'm nothing more than some pawn in a war between vampires.

All I want to do is run away, to go somewhere where he can't find me, where I can forget I ever knew him or Michel or anything about vampires. I open the large windowpane in the bedroom and look down – five stories would kill me and there isn't any way to climb down. I can't get by Vasily – the door is alarmed, and I don't know the code.

There's nowhere to run.

I crawl underneath the bed itself, as I used to do when I was a girl after I was put into foster care and lived through very dark times, crowding up against the wall at the top, my face resting on my arm.

Julien returns later that night. I fell asleep under the bed, and wake at the sound of his voice. My body tenses as I watch from under the bed skirt. He walks into the apartment, his boots and jeans the only visible part of his body from my position, and goes to speak with Vasily. Then he wanders over to the bed, standing beside it for a moment. Next, he goes to the bathroom and I lose sight of him, my breath held, my heart pounding.

"Jesus *Christ*."

He returns from the bathroom and then goes to the seating area, checks the kitchen and yells at Vasily, kicking over a barstool.

"Goddammit – where's Eve?"

"Isn't she in bed?"

"No, she's gone. What have you been doing all night? How did she get out?"

Vasily comes out of the office and the two search the apartment.

"She got a goddamned knife. Jesus Christ Vasily, what the *fuck* were you doing? Playing with your dick?"

"I want to leave her to herself – she was very upset. She can't have escaped – is no way possible."

"She's *gone*, Vasily. Did she watch you enter the security code? Did she climb out the window? She can't have jumped – it would kill her."

The two go back into the office and I can hear Julien give directions to replay videotapes monitoring the interior and the door and watching the building itself.

"She can't have escaped. She has to be here."

Julien stands in the middle of the room while Vasily makes another circuit. I hear him inhale deeply as if he's trying to smell for me. Tears fill my eyes – hiding under the bed is stupid but I just wanted to escape. I wanted to disappear.

"Oh, Jesus *Christ*," Julien says, his voice hushed.

Vasily stops. "What is it?"

But Julien doesn't respond. After a moment, he comes over to the bed and stands still, saying nothing. I cover my mouth, trying to keep from making a noise. I hear him sigh, and then he pushes the bedside table out of the way and sits down on the floor beside the bed, his back to the wall. I can see his shoes on the floor a few feet away from my face.

"Eve," he says, his voice soft, a note of regret in it. "I'm sorry."

I press my hand over my mouth even more firmly.

After a moment of silence, he starts to speak, his voice low.

"When I was a boy, Michel and I knew not to say a word when my parents yelled at each other. Sometimes, that's all it would be – just yelling. But sometimes, he'd hit her," he says, "and we knew if that happened to get out, fast, because he never hit her only once. And sometimes, he'd go after Michel, so I'd step in between them and I'd get it instead of her or him. When we hid, I always took a knife with me, just in case he came after us."

I picture it in my mind's eye, the two boys running for safety. The father slapping the mother, pushing her, hitting her. An over-whelming feeling of sadness fills me – I don't want to hear the story, but I can't help but listen.

"One night, when it started, after he came home really drunk and belligerent, I took Michel and we went to the bedroom and climbed beneath our bed. He came looking for us, couldn't see us and was too drunk to bend down and look under the bed, so I knew that whenever he came home like that, to grab Michel and hide under the bed. This one night, when we were twelve, he grabbed the knife from me and slashed me. You might think my scar is a battle wound I got fighting a war but you'd be wrong."

I lie on the floor, my eyes closed, tears on my cheeks, picturing the scene in my mind, and my heart breaks once more for him. I slide out from under the bed and crawl into his lap, my arms slipping around his neck. He pulls me tightly against him, his face in my hair, his lips against my neck.

"I'm so sorry," I say, unable to stop my tears. I just hold him tightly, wishing that we lived in a different world and that none of this had happened.

"I don't want to scare you," he says, "but you have to understand this is serious. This isn't a democracy, and you don't have a vote on what's done. You don't even get to complain about my decisions."

I don't say anything, just hold him, unable to get the image out of my mind of him as a little boy lying under his bed with a knife in his hand, protecting Michel from their drunken father, bleeding from the wound on his face.

After a few minutes, he takes my arm in his hands and runs his fingers over my skin.

"Eve." He bends down, covering the cut with his mouth, licking it and it's so sexual, I can't help but respond. "Why do you hurt yourself?"

"Because I'm such an idiot."

"Shh," he says and takes my face in his hands and kisses me softly. Soon, the kiss becomes more intense, his arms more tightly around me, pulling my body against his.

When his hand reaches up under my dress, which has bunched up around my waist, touching my bare skin, I gasp and pull away, but he keeps me there, his cheek against mine, his hand on my skin. His breathing is heavy in my ear.

"Still not interested?"

"Julien, I-" I say, trying to find the words.

"No, it's OK." He pulls away, his hand withdrawing from under my dress. He takes my hand. "It's late. You're tired. Go to bed. I have to go out anyway."

I nod and wipe my eyes.

He stands and holds me in his arms for a moment then he releases me and leaves me alone.

When he's gone, I slip into the shower and wash off the tears from my face and dust from the floor under the bed then brush my teeth, staring at the red eyes and nose of my reflection in the mirror. I slip into my nightgown and go outside, tiptoeing to my bed. As I lie under the covers, I remember our kiss in the bedroom, how tender it had been at the start, and how both of us moved so easily into desire. The natural thing would be for me to have had sex with him, and I once more shut him out – even after he opened up and told me about his own pain. It makes my throat tight with emotion, my heart filled once more with regret.

I wake in the middle of the night, uncertain of what woke me at first, and then I realize Julien's standing by the bed, just watching me. I close my eyes quickly and try not to give any sign that I'm awake.

After a few moments, he leaves and goes over to the seating area, sitting in the darkness facing the windows.

As I lie there wondering what he's doing, why he isn't asleep, I remember his kiss, I remember how passionate he'd been and how willing he was to let me decide, not pushing any longer. Maybe he does care about me just a little. Maybe more than he expected.

I feel so incredibly lonely lying there in the huge empty bed with him sitting all alone just a few yards away. In truth, I realize I want him. I want to have him on top of me, I want to feel his skin against my skin, to kiss him, to feel him inside of me, in my mind and in my body. To feel that sweet oblivion with him that I felt with Michel.

He's not Michel. He's himself. I want him.

I fight with myself, torn between desire and guilt. But the overwhelming sense I have is one of want for him, a need for him that finally overcomes my sense of what's right, what's acceptable.

Breathless, I slip out of bed and remove my panties, dropping them beside the bed, determining to leave my anxiety behind as well. I cross the floor to where he sits. When he sees me standing there, he startles a bit.

"Eve. What's the matter-"

I kneel down between his thighs, my arms slipping around his waist. He exhales loudly as I press myself against him and his hands slide down my back, then up beneath my nightgown and along my back.

"Oh, *God*," he says. His hands slip back and he pulls me closer. We stay like this for a few minutes, not kissing, just touching, and I can see his startled expression, and it sends a thrill through my body.

"How did you know?" I whisper, watching his face, remembering the words he spoke to me in my apartment when he broke out of the SCU. "Why were you so sure this would happen?"

He shakes his head.

"I didn't know. I only wanted. And when I want something," he says and runs his hands up along my back again. "I do everything in my power to get it."

"I want you," I say and lean in, my lips searching for his, finding them soft and open, his tongue right there, touching mine. My body responds immediately to the feel of it, of his hands on my bare skin. This is the moment – he told me I'd remember what he said, word for word, and I do.

"Julien," I whisper when the kiss ends, and he just sits there waiting. "Please," but he stops me, pressing his finger against my lips.

"Shh," he says. "Don't say it." He pulls me up and into his lap, kissing me deeply.

Then he stops. "This is no good," he says, his voice thick.

"What?" Alarm fills me – what's he doing? Will he reject me now in some kind of twisted revenge?

"No, this won't work." He shakes his head. "I need more light. I'm not doing this in the dark."

He stands, lifting me up with him, and I wrap my legs around his waist. He carries me over to the office. "Vasily," he calls out. "Wake up."

Vasily sleeps on a fold-out cot in a corner of the office space. He sputters awake. I press my face in Julien's shoulder, embarrassed that Vasily will know what's happening.

"What's wrong?"

"Go sleep downstairs and turn on all the lights on your way out."

"Turn them *on?*"

"Yes. Hurry." Julien carries me over to the bed. "Hurry, Goddammit," he whispers in my ear. I can't stop from smiling, my body responding to the urgency in his voice.

The lights flash on, one bank after another, making me blink in pain from the abrupt change.

He lays me down on the side of the bed, leaning over me, kissing me, his kiss intense from the start, his tongue insistent. Then, he stops to pull my nightgown up and off me, so that I lie naked beneath him, my arms beside my head. He stands up, pulling my legs away from his waist, one hand on each of my knees so that I lie completely open for him to see every part of me. His face takes on such an expression of desire that I can't help but respond.

He runs his hands down the inside of my thighs, his fingers soft, slipping beside but not touching my sex, then up over my belly, sending a sensation of such lust through me that I gasp, my breath hitching in my throat.

He touches me all over, my breasts, my nipples, my neck, down my arms to my hands, kissing me as he lies on top of me for a moment, then his hands move back down again, his eyes hungry, and he starts to remove his clothes, ripping open his shirt and removing his pants, his underwear and socks. Then, his fingers explore my sex, slipping over my mound, fingers sliding between my outer lips, his thumb finding my hard clit, his groan of delight when he does, the sensation making my back arch.

"You're so perfect." He lies back on top of me, his mouth now moving over my body, kissing me, the skin on my neck where he bit me, my throat, tonguing my nipples as he cups my breasts, running his teeth softly over each nipple, coaxing them to hardness, sucking each one in turn, each time making me gasp with increased desire.

He pulls me up farther on the bed, and I lean back on my elbows, watching as he begins kissing my belly, his hands pushing my thighs apart, kissing each thigh in turn, his fingers searching out my sex, spreading me open, finding my clit once more with his tongue, the sensation so sweet that I feel momentarily dizzy and I lie back, letting the feelings of his mouth on me, his tongue on me, wash over me, building my lust even higher.

"Eve," he says, between kissing and tonguing me. "Why did you deny me for so long?"

I gasp when he slips fingers inside of me, stroking me while he tongues my clit, sucks it, and I can feel my orgasm is close.

"I'm going to—" I say, biting my bottom lip.

"Oh, no you're not," he says and stops what he's doing. "Not yet."

I groan when the sensations stop, unconsciously moving my hips, searching for the sensations of his fingers moving inside me, of his mouth on me.

"Just relax for a minute," he says. "This is too fast, even if I've waited too damn long. Breathe."

I swallow hard, trying to comply, but my flesh aches so much, feels so swollen, ready to burst, that I can't help but move just a bit.

"You're a greedy little thing," he says, his voice a mix of amusement and lust. "I like that."

I lie waiting, wanting him to continue, my breathing shallow, my body so ready.

"Please."

"Please, what?"

I'm barely able to think let alone talk,

"Please don't stop."

He lowers his mouth to me once more and soon, the pleasure builds inside.

"Tell me when you're close again," he says, stopping his motions.

His tongue touches me lightly then withdraws and I can't help it – I strain, pressing my hips up, searching for the sensation. My body's shaking as I try to find him, my face flushed.

"I'm going to come," I say once more and he stops, withdrawing his fingers, rising up to lean back over me, kissing me.

"Just breathe, Eve. The longer you wait, the better it'll be."

"I've waited long enough."

"Oh, you have," he says and leans over me, pulling me back down so that I'm positioned at the end of the bed once more. "And so have I."

He kisses me again and presses his erection against me, pressing it between the lips of my sex, and I thrust against him, hungry to feel him inside of me. He stands up and rubs the head against me, the slick wetness of it feeling almost as good as his mouth. He thrusts his hips, running his length against me, stopping to tease the opening to my body, repeating the motion until I feel as if my head will burst.

He enters me finally, his entire length filling me up, and begins thrusting, and it feels so good, so sweet, that I feel as if I'll pass out, groaning, closing my eyes when our minds connect and I feel his lust on top of my own.

"I'm going to-"

"No, don't close your eyes," he says, his voice shaking as he leans over me. He takes my chin in his hand. "Look at me. Look at me when you come."

I open my eyes and watch him above me, his eyes on me, sweat on his forehead, and feel the sensations build until the sweetness of it overtakes me, making me tense up, my body spasming around him as he thrusts, my eyes closing despite my best intentions, a cry escaping my lips.

He groans as my orgasm crests and starts to subside, and he rises up, pulling my hips lower, thrusting harder, his hands gripping my hips, pulling me to meet him with each thrust. Then he grimaces in pleasure, grunting as he comes, his body shaking.

He collapses on top of me and kisses me. My emotions overwhelm me, tears stinging at the corners of my eyes because as much as I enjoyed this, it should be Michel. I turn my head to the side, not wanting him to see me, but he turns my face back and kisses me.

He already knows how I feel.


He leaves me in the night while I'm asleep. When I wake, the empty bed makes me feel empty inside. I wanted him here when I woke. I've been alone so long.

When I get up for the day, I peer out into the main living area, where Vasily is sitting drinking coffee.

"Where's Julien?"

"Gone out of town."

I frown. "For how long?"

Vasily shrugs. "He didn't say. Maybe one week."

I go back into my room and sit on the bed, an empty feeling in the pit of my stomach.

# CHAPTER 15

Khalil Gibran

THE WEEK GOES BY, each day the same as the one preceding it. No word from Julien, nothing from Vasily. I'm now angry as well as hurt. By Saturday, I'm numb to the whole business. My feelings about him – whatever they were – were misplaced. Of course they were – he's a vampire and once again I think about my traitorous heart. Like Michel, the mission comes before everything else.

I decide to blot him out of my memory. I needed a dose of reality. He gave it to me. I should thank him. I'll act as if nothing happened between us if he does come back. That his being gone was noted but that I haven't fallen apart. If he tries to touch me, I'll just let him, and not respond positively or negatively. I'll just let him do whatever he wants. It won't be because I've begged him or chosen him.

That's what he wants, after all. My compliance.

It's while I'm practicing the Ballade that he arrives back at the apartment. When I hear the door open, I know it's him, and for a moment, just a second, I wonder how to respond. Should I stop playing and wait for him to come over? Should I keep playing as if I didn't notice him being back?

I decide to keep playing but to acknowledge his presence when he comes over.

He takes his coat off and boots and comes to join me at the piano. I try with all my might not to trip up in my playing. I don't want to give him the pleasure of knowing how upset I am, and I realize I am upset.

And I am so upset, despite all my best intentions. I breathe deeply when he approaches to calm my beating heart. He stands at the side of the piano watching as I play. When I come to the end of the piece I stop and just sit there.

He says nothing, and so finally I look directly at him. He looks haggard, if a vampire can look tired. He's dressed in something a bit more formal, black pants, a black jacket and a white shirt open at the collar, the tie undone. He's so attractive that my heart does a flip-flop and I hate myself.

He smiles, his eyes hooded.

"You've been practicing like a good girl."

"I'm not a girl. Besides, I want to play it better – for myself."

"Why don't you put something pretty on? We're going out for dinner."

A shock goes through me at that. He's just going to act as if nothing happened?

"We are? What about security?"

"Don't worry about that," Julien says. "All taken care of. I'm hungry and I'd bet a thousand that you've barely eaten anything but rabbit food today."

"You go ahead. I'm not really hungry." I touch the keys. I play the beginning of Ballade again. I feel as if I couldn't swallow a morsel.

"That's fine. You don't have to eat. I want company. Just go," he says and waves his hand towards the bathroom, "and put something pretty on. My eyes are hungry, too."

I stand and comply without a word. I wonder what game he's

playing – is he just reinforcing how he's in control and I have no choice but to comply?

Does it really give him that much pleasure?

Of course it does. I'm such a fool. Give up your silly romantic fantasy world. He's a vampire and a killer. A monster, as even he admitted – he'd kill me if he felt it was justified. Yeah, he'd have sex with me and enjoy it. But he'd kill me, too.

Period.

I sort through my clothes, unsure what to wear. I don't have a lot of pretty things, as most of my money during college went to rent and expenses. The only piece of clothing I have other than Luke's gift that is the least bit pretty is a black dress I wore last Christmas for the party for students in the pre-med program. It's a bit too dressy, knee-length, with a sleeveless wrap bodice made out of black lace with a deep cut neckline and fitted skirt.

Whatever. I put it on, glance at myself in the mirror. I decide to put my hair up, clipping it up in back with a barrette.

Damn him. I'm his hostage even if I've been with him. That's Stockholm Syndrome. I've been totally dependent on him and am at his mercy.

I walk back out to the living area and wait while Julien finishes speaking on his cell. When he looks up, he tilts his head to one side as if appraising my choice. He comes to me and takes my hand, then turns me around in a pirouette. He whistles softly.

"You look lovely."

My cheeks burn and I have to glance away.

"But I think your hair should be down." With that, he pulls the clip out of my hair and my hair falls down around my shoulders and down my back. "Look how nice it is against the black lace. It looks like silk."

Julien helps me into my coat. Damn him – why is he being such a gentleman when I want him to be a jerk so I can hate him?

Dinner is a quiet affair, with Julien eating as if he's ravenous, his focus on his meal, while I content myself with nibbling on a salad and drinking a glass of white wine.

The wine does me good, for it relaxes me a bit, warms me up. He pours me another glass from the bottle he ordered, and I drink it down as well while he works on his food, and now, I'm beginning to enjoy the buzz I get from the wine. I've never been a drinker except on the rare occasion when I was with a man and sex was involved. I found that two or three glasses was about all I could handle before becoming a giggling drunk so I stop, covering my glass when he tries to pour more.

"No, really," I say, "I can't drink any more."

"Why? You've only had two glasses. Live a little."

I sigh as he pours yet another glass, but I'm determined not to drink it. I'll just pretend. I don't want to get drunk and lose control for fear I say something I'll regret.

Julien finally pushes his plate away and leans back, his own glass of wine in hand. He appraises me from overtop of his glass as he drinks – his eyes feel so judging. I sip at my wine, trying not to look him in the eye. He doesn't look like a monster tonight. He looks like a very pale and very handsome man.

"So, Eve," he says and leans forward, licking his lips, his tongue lingering a little too long on his bottom lip. "Did you miss me?"

I put my glass down with a bit too much force and the wine sloshes around, a few drops spilling out. Bastard! I mop it up with my napkin and then look at him, trying my best to keep my face neutral.

"Did you miss me?" I say.

"I sure missed those sweet dimples of yours." He smiles, not wide, just a bit, his expression dark, lusty. "And your nice round ass."

I can't help it – my body responds to his words. How is that possible? How could he affect me like that with just a few words when I was hating him?

Despite my resolve, I take a sip of my wine, a big sip. I say nothing, just glance around at the deserted restaurant, at the white tablecloths, the good silver cutlery, the dark mahogany woodwork, the polished hardwood floors. Anything but his leering face.

He holds up his wineglass.

"I propose a toast, to me, to my success on my trip."

I hold my glass up and touch his.

"Congratulations."

I take another sip. The wine is rather nice, not that I know anything about wine, but it feels smooth against my tongue and has a nice aftertaste. I relax a bit more and lean against the deeply cushioned banquette seat.

Julien tries to pour more wine into my glass.

"No, please," I say, trying to cover my glass, but he insists. "Are you trying to get me drunk?"

"You seem to need a bit of softening up so I thought I'd ply you with liquor." He fills my glass almost to the rim. "Besides, all work and no play makes for a dull girl."

"I feel dull," I say, the warmth in my belly and in my veins making me lose my resolve not to engage him. "Mentally dull."

"You think too much. Just 'be'," he says, waving his fingers at me. "Let life happen. Don't always try so hard to be in control. Give in."

"Give in to you."

He smiles, his eyes narrowing.

"Now you're talking."

I sigh, the wine making me feel loose.

"Why should I give in? I need to have some self-respect."

"Eve," he says, leaning forward. "You like it when a man takes control." He leans a little closer, looking at me over his wine glass. "Really."

"I thought you weren't into the whole obedience thing."

"I'm into pleasure. Now, drink up," he says and waves at my glass. "It's time to go."

I take a sip, but there's almost half a glass left and I feel far too warm already.

"No, no, no," he says and shakes his head. "All of it." He mimes lifting a glass to his lips and waits, his eyebrows raised.

I take a deep breath and comply, the wine sliding down my throat, warming my stomach.

"That's my girl," he says and takes my arm, helping me up from the table. He wraps my coat around me from behind and nuzzles his face against the back of my neck for just a moment. He inhales deeply and the touch of his lips on my skin makes my knees feel weak. He practically holds me up as we walk out the door, Vasily paying the bill.

*Damn.* I laugh at myself as I plop onto the back seat of the car.

Julien moves my legs over and buckles me up when I fumble with the latch.

"What's so funny?" he asks, smiling.

"I am," I say, my mouth feeling all cottony. I watch him as he sits back and looks at me from beneath hooded eyes. "I'm so naïve."

"Oh, you *are*," he says and leans over to me, his arm around my shoulder. He plays with a lock of my hair. "I like that. I like the prospect of teaching you the ways of the world, Eve. I like the idea of slowly but ever so surely corrupting you."

The car stops at the warehouse. Julien helps me out, his arm around me. We go up the elevator in silence.

Once inside, he turns on the banks of lights so that the entire floor is brightly lit. He pulls me against him after shooing Vasily downstairs.

He takes me in his arms and tries to kiss me, and part of me wants to just give in but I don't. I dig my fingers into my palm. He presses his lips against mine and holds them there, but I don't respond.

He lets go and just stands there, looking away. He doesn't say anything for a moment, his hands on his hips staring at the apartment. Finally he turns to me.

"You wanted to be with me the other night. You want to now." He shakes his head. "Just have sex with me."

"And if I say no?"

"Why would you say no?"

Now it's my turn to shake my head.

"If someone offers me a line of cocaine, I'd say no. Why? Because it would hurt me."

"You see?" he says, throwing his hands up. "That's where you're wrong. You need to say yes to experiences. How can you know what's good and what's bad unless you try?" He walks in a circle as if he feels trapped. "Do nothing, risk nothing, choose nothing, and nothing is your responsibility. Being 'good' is not really your choice if you never actually make it. If you never really know what's bad – really know – and choose not to do it."

"I don't have to do something bad to know it's bad."

"Eve, how can pleasure be bad?" He stands there, his hands extended to me. "How can having sex with me be bad?"

I'm unable to comprehend how he can't comprehend.

"Because," I say, turning away. "You'll break my heart. I don't need to have it broken to know that."

He grabs me by the arms and turns me to face him.

"Then break your heart. At least then you'll know you have one. Isn't that why you cut yourself? Because you turned off when you were a girl and now you need pain to feel anything other than a desire for revenge?"

"Why did you leave without saying anything?"

There. I said it. Having that last glass of wine was a mistake – I knew it was, but I did it anyway. It's the story of my life since I met him and his brother.

He lets go of me.

"That's what all this is about? Because I didn't leave you a little note saying, *'Dear Eve, Off for a week. Hugs and kisses*, you're in a state?"

"Would it have hurt to do something?"

He takes my coat off and hangs it up, takes his own off and does likewise. Then he grabs my hand.

"Come here," he says and brings me over to the seating area, pulling my down on his lap, my legs straddling him, my arms on his shoulders. Moving so fast makes me dizzy and I have to hold my head for a moment.

"Eve," he says, lifting my chin so I have to try to focus on his face. "I went out of town for important business. Yes, I do actually work. It really doesn't matter why I left. I leave when I have to. I didn't know I'd have to leave for a week at the time. Something came up. An opportunity – one that yielded some good information. I didn't have time to come up and leave you a note. And you can't expect me to. You can't expect anything from me."

He nods, forcing me to look in his eyes.

"You understand? *Nothing*." He holds my gaze and I fight to remain in control. "Nothing except a nice big juicy hard-on and a very willing tongue."

I can't help it. I smile, the corners of my eyes stinging just a bit as my emotions battle.

"There," he says, stroking his fingers against my cheeks. "That's better. I knew that would make you smile. You want me to corrupt you." He smiles for a moment, but then his face becomes serious again and he pulls me closer. "All you have to do is accept the fact that you can expect nothing from me but great sex when the opportunity arises and we'll be fine. But don't expect anything more from me." He runs a finger over my bottom lip. "Because I can't give it."

"What if I fall in love with you?"

He pulls me against him. "Then fall in love with me. I'm not going to say no. But don't expect anything in return."

"So, it's like this – I try to help you, do work for you, have sex with you whenever you feel like it, possibly fall in love with you, and in return I have sex whenever you feel like it."

He nods. "I'll try to make it worthwhile." He brushes my hair from my face.

I shut his words out of my mind. I refuse to respond.

"You went to South Carolina?"

"Yes. I found someone. I turned up some interesting information."

"What?" I say, interested in spite of myself. "Tell me."

"Eve," he says and pulls me closer. "It's late. I've been gone more than a week. I was mostly good the whole time. I think we can talk about this later."

I stiffen. "Mostly good?"

"Well," he says, tilting his head to the side. "There was this woman, but she was necessary. Part of the plot, so to speak."

"You were with someone else while you were away?"

"Yeah," he says, swirling his hand. "It was part of the deal. You know, I was with this guy who had some information he didn't even know he had, he was on a tear, he and I became fast buddies. And there were girls. It was unavoidable, not that I mind that kind of work."

I close my eyes, the thought of him with another woman both arousing me and making me feel as if he's just stabbed me in the heart.

"Eve, I'm not Michel."

"Yeah, I know. You already told me that."

"You can't be upset."

I shake my head.

"How would you feel if I told you that I'd slept with a man while you were away?"

"With who? Vasily?" He smiles.

"No, I don't know - in the broom closet with that new janitor at the SCU."

"It wouldn't happen."

"And it won't tonight either." With that, I extract myself from his lap and stand, then make a beeline for the bathroom.

"Eve, come back."

I close the bathroom door, go to the window and sit on the ledge, my knees tucked under my chin. He's a heartless bastard. He didn't have to admit he'd slept with someone else while he was away. He did it either because he's totally clueless, or because he *wants* me to know. He wants to elicit some kind of response.

He follows me, as I knew he would, but I had to leave - I had to get away from him. It's futile, for there's nowhere to go, no place to hide. I just had to act. The warm buzz from the wine is now gone and all I feel is cold. No tears – there will be none. Just cold.

He comes into the bathroom and removes his suit jacket, and then comes to the window and stands beside me.

"Eve, I don't feel like any drama tonight. You're going to have sex with me and I'm going to enjoy it. So are you. You want it, and you need it. So come."

He holds out his hand and waits. I push it away.

"Go to hell."

"I'm not going to hell. I'm going to be fucked. I want you to do all the work. I'm tired." He yawns and stretches. "But I'm glad you came in here because I need a soak."

He goes to the huge claw foot bathtub and turns the taps on, drizzling in some bath salts that fill the room with a pleasant spicy scent - sandalwood. The tub's large and deep, and the water fast, so soon it's filling with steamy soapy water. He wastes no time getting undressed, removing his shirt and then his belt and pants.

I can barely believe him. He's so damn certain I'll have sex with him.

He removes his socks and then his boxers, and doesn't hesitate to get into the water, exhaling loudly as he does.

"Come," he says, motioning me over. "Get in. I made Vasily get an extra large tub so we both could sit in it."

I shake my head in amazement. "You had it all planned out."

He smiles.

"Oh, I spent a lot of time planning for you, Eve. I intend to see those plans to fruition. Every single one." He pats the water, splashing it around. "This was one of them. I really looked forward to this. Come in. I need you to wash my . . . back." He's smiling, broadly, looking like the Cheshire cat, so satisfied with himself – knowing.

I sit on the ledge, my arms around my knees, and seethe. Yet, at the same time, I have to admit that it thrills me to think he imagined this scenario, that he planned to have me in the bath with him, washing his … back. He wanted this. He thought about it and planned it. It gives me a curious sense of power over him. One that sends a delicious jolt of lust through me.

I go to the tub, staring down at him as he lies partially submerged. I turn my back to him.

"Can you unzip me?"

He does and I let the dress puddle on the floor, removing my bra, and then my panties while my back is still towards him, bending over to remove them, knowing that he'll get a good look at my ass in the process.

"Why, Ms. Hayden," he says, his voice deep, throaty. "I do believe there's just a bit of a tease in you after all. I like that."

I turn and step into the tub across from him, then kneel down in the water so that it covers me from the nipples down.

"Tell me what you want me to do," I say.

"Why don't you just come over here and find out?"

I lean forward on my knees. He slips down farther in the water, his arms over the sides, his knees spread. He isn't smiling any longer, and for a moment, I think he's just a bit surprised, maybe even shocked. There's a look of blatant lust on his face, in his eyes, that does something to me and I lose the lingering traces of inhibition that always seem to hold me back from expressing myself.

I wrap my arms around his neck and lie on top of him, the water splashing over the sides of the tub and onto the floor. I just lie there, my lips almost touching his and wait, wanting to see what he'll do. He in turn appears content to wait for me to make a move. Neither of us does anything for a moment and so I just enjoy the feeling of desire that's building inside my body, and it's magnified when he opens up to me and our senses connect.

I pull back and look at his face and his blue eyes are hooded, waiting. His breathlessness fills me, increasing my own until I'm almost dizzy from it.

"It's too much," I say, closing my eyes, trying to catch my breath. He pulls back just a bit and now, his lust doesn't overwhelm me and I'm able to open my eyes once more.

When I do, I'm staring into his, so-blue eyes. I try to imagine him as a human with a flush in his cheeks but his paleness is too much a part of him. Besides, I've come to desire that paleness – it's part of the package. I lean closer and run my tongue over his lips. He closes his eyes as if content to just let me do what I want. Then I kiss him, my mouth on his, lips parting, my tongue seeking out his.

What do I want to do to him? Up till now, I've been so passive – with both Michel and him. Now, I want to watch his response to what I do. While I kiss him, I slip one arm away from around his neck, my hand trailing down his chest between our bodies, running over a nipple, over his stomach, his navel, and he makes a little sound in his throat – a sound I thought belonged to Michel, but it doesn't. My hand slides lower, touching the thatch of hair that reaches down from his navel to his groin. I slip my fingers around to his inner thigh, taking care not to touch his erection – not yet.

He likes to be teased? I'll try to tease him.

My hand strokes down his thigh and back up, around his groin, then up his chest to the other nipple. I end the kiss and lie to the side, my mouth on his neck below his ear where I'd bite him if I were a vampire. He groans. My hand slips back down over his belly, then traces his hip bone down to his groin once more.

"Eve, I didn't know you had it in you."

"Shh," I say. "You talk too much."

I kiss him once more and let my hand brush him, which elicits another murmur from him from deep in his throat. I change sides, moving over in the tub and start to nuzzle his other ear and then suck on the skin beneath it. He groans again and arches his back. I explore his body, teasing a nipple, then once more slip my fingers down to his thigh and up, and this time, I let my fingers brush his erection lightly. It jumps against my hand.

I don't have a lot of experience with men's bodies – my early experiences I tried to block and my later ones were a drunken blur. I just do what he and Michel did to me – touching him, avoiding direct contact at first but then touching him more directly. When I grasp his shaft and curl my fingers around its length, he exhales, his breath shaky. The water's a bit slippery from the bath salts and I slide my fingers up and down slowly, my eyes closed, just enjoying the feel of him in my hand.

"Enough teasing," he says, his voice low. "Let's get out."

He starts to stand, his hands under my arms to help me up.

"I didn't even get to wash you," I say. "I thought you liked to be teased."

"Only so much. Besides, the water's getting cold."

We stand and step out of the bath, shivering in the chill air of the bathroom. He pulls me out of the bathroom and over to the bed, sitting on the side, his slick body shining in the bright light, his erection thick and wet. "But if you want to wash me," he says, breathless. "Use your tongue."

"Now, now," I say and push him back onto the bed, lying on top of him, his hard length pressing against my groin. "I'm the one doing. You're the one being done. Lie still and no talking."

He closes his eyes and smiles, lying back. "Eve the little dominatrix. Who would have thought?"

"Shh, I said no talking. You're always trying to control everything."

I kiss him in passing, my mouth trailing down his chest to his belly, then lower, so that my face is above his erection. I breathe on it, and he tenses, then I run my tongue up from the base of the shaft to the tip and he groans out loud. He rises up on his elbows and I try to push him back down. "Lie back and just relax," I say, trying to sound a bit pushy.

"I need to watch you."

I move my mouth over him, trying to take as much as I can without gagging, trying to suck at the same time. He lets a little more of himself connect with me and I feel how good it is, how good my mouth feels on him.

After a while of alternating stroking him and sucking, he's breathing more deeply.

"Stop," he says, his breath ragged. When I look up, my mouth full of him, his eyes are closed. He pulls me up and off him, his salty taste on my tongue. "Do me now."

"But I'm the one in control and -."

"*Now.*"

I rise up and climb onto his lap as he sits up, leaning back on his hands.

"I've never done this before," I say, feeling breathless at the prospect but not knowing really the best way to have ride a man.

"You've *never* been on top?"

I shake my head, not caring if it shows my inexperience.

"Oh, *God.*" He closes his eyes for a moment. He holds his erection up with a hand. "I thought you always wanted to do Michel like this."

"I did."

He stares at me, shaking his head slowly.

"Just sit on me."

I rise up and position myself over him, knowing how wet I'll be, I'm so aroused. I miss the first time, and it feels so good as his erection slides against me that I gasp and deliberately repeat the movement. I close my eyes and do it once more, hungry for the feelings. "Just a minute, I want to —."

"Hey," he says. "Just fuck me, you greedy thing." He does something when I try to rub against him again, and I miss and he enters me instead, the sensation so great I shudder. I sit down on him as far as I can, and exhale heavily. I just sit there, enjoying the sensation of him filling me up so completely.

"Now fuck me," he says, all alpha.

I try, moving up and down on him. At first it's easy, but then my thighs shake a bit. "I need some leverage."

"Lean on me."

I do, but it only helps for a few thrusts. He lies back completely and I lean my hands on his chest and find a better position, so that I can ride him.

He reaches down and works his fingers between our bodies so that with each thrust, my clit rubs against his fingers. He begins to thrust as well, meeting my body with each of my own thrusts. With his other hand he teases one nipple, then the other and it's enough, with him inside of me, his fingers on my clit, his others touching my breasts.

"I'm going to come," I say, and stop, but he kept thrusting.

"Keep going," he says, and I tense as the sweetness overcomes me, my body spasming around him and then he does something to me, like a time shift when I'm fighting, and my orgasm goes on and on. He turns me over and in my delirium, I wrap my legs around his waist and lie back, my eyes closed as he starts thrusting fast and hard and soon he comes as well, his mouth by my ear, grunting with each thrust.

Later, as we lie in each other's arms, he kisses me and runs his fingers through my hair, the ends still damp from the bath.

"I have to go."

I frown. "Where?"

He shakes his head.

"No questions. I just have to go."

I bite back another question. I was going to ask him how long he'd be gone.

He rolls off the bed and goes to the bathroom. I lie there, my feelings conflicted. I want to throw something at him, I want to ask him to stay. I realize that neither would be appropriate. I crawl under the covers instead.

He emerges fully dressed in a few moments, putting his tie back on, his jacket over his arm. He stops at the bedside and stands for a moment, tying the knot in his tie. He leans over and kisses me. "Next time, we'll smoke a little pot. I want to see you stoned again."

Then he's gone.

I lie back and rub my eyes. There are no tears. Frustration, some anger. But my body feels so well used.

It will have to be enough for now.

# CHAPTER 16

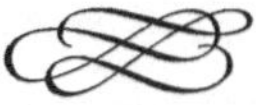

"Love takes off masks that we fear we cannot live without
and know we cannot live within."
James A. Baldwin

THE NEXT NIGHT, JULIEN RETURNS, sitting on the bed beside me, waking me up from a dead sleep. I turn over and face him and he smiles, brushing hair off my face.

I smile back.

"That's what I want to see," he says, running the backs of his fingers over my cheek. He leans down and nuzzles my neck, licking his bite mark, which is almost healed. The touch of his tongue on my skin sends a shock of lust through me, and I want him immediately. I think he's going to have sex with me, but he doesn't. He just sits there, smiling at me, running his fingers through my hair.

"Sorry I'm waking you so late but I had work to do."

"That's OK."

"Get up," he says and takes my hand. He pulls me out of bed and leads me over to the seating area in the living room. This time, he doesn't pull me down onto his lap as he has on other occasions. He just sits down and looks at me expectantly.

"Sit," he says finally.

I sit on the couch beside him.

"How are you?" he says, and runs his hand down my arm to my hand, which he squeezes.

"Fine. How are you?" I say.

"Never better."

We sit for a moment, looking at each other, each of us waiting for the other to speak. He leans back, one elbow resting on the armrest, his chin in his hand and watches me for a moment.

"Oh, I brought something for us." He goes to the coat tree and removes something from a pocket in his coat. A bag of dope and some paraphernalia. He sits back down and holds it out in front of me, smiling. "Something to lighten the mood."

"Oh, no, thanks," I say and shake my head. "The other night was enough."

He pulls out rolling papers and prepares to roll a joint.

"I feel like relaxing. I want you completely relaxed as well."

"When did you become a pot smoker?"

"Oh, since about when it was invented. Soldiers do a lot of drugs. Helps get you through the long stretches of total boredom and brief but intense moments of utter fear."

"Aren't you afraid of becoming addicted?"

"Can't," he says. "Body heals of every insult. Even drugs."

He pulls me over to him, across his lap, so that I'm sitting to the side with my legs over his lap rather than straddling him. He keeps working on the joint, rolling it together, twisting the ends. He picks up a lighter and lights it, takes a puff and then offers it to me.

I wave it away.

"No, I don't think so. Unlike you, I don't heal."

"You could," he says, his voice playful. "All you have to do is drink my blood…"

"Not a chance, " I say, my arms crossed. He smiles.

"You loved it."

"It's a drug. That's all. I couldn't help but—"

"Quit lying to yourself," he says and turns my face to his. "You loved the idea as well."

I don't say anything. What can I do? I can't deny it – he knows my thoughts.

"Now smoke this. It's an order."

I shake my head.

"Luke was right when he said you'd be difficult to control. Eve," he says. "Obedience…"

"Do we have to tonight?"

"Yes." He holds it in front of my face. "This is very mild stuff and I rolled it pretty thin, so don't worry. You're not going to freak out or anything."

He lights the joint and holds it out to me. I relent and take a puff, sucking in the smoke, holding it in my lungs as long as I can before coughing it out.

"There are so many things you want to do and try that you're afraid to admit to yourself. You don't have to be afraid with me. For example, you want to get stoned and let yourself go. I aim to please."

He takes it back and does a small hit, and then quickly hands it back to me. I do another hit, coughing even more this time, tears in the corners of my eyes. He hands the joint back to me after a tiny puff. I comply and take in another lungful of smoke.

"You're not inhaling," I observe when he lets the smoke curl out of his mouth.

"Nonsense. What do you know about smoking pot anyway?" He takes another tiny hit and hands it back to me. "Besides," he says, the smoke coming out of his mouth without inhaling, "when you're experienced like me, you don't need as much to get high."

Somehow, I don't believe it.

"Liar." I take another hit, the smoke not bothering me nearly as much as it first did. "You just want me stoned and you sober so you can take advantage of me."

"Am I that transparent?" he says, that devilish grin on his face. Soon, the joint's just a tiny smoldering stub. I hand it back to him and he clips the end and then sucks.

"Here," he says, blowing the smoke out before inhaling. "Finish this off."

I giggle. "You're not inhaling."

"Eve, there aren't very many people who can get away with calling me a liar, or even suggesting it. Consider yourself lucky."

"You're a big fat liar." I suck on the tiny ember, holding the smoke in my lungs as long as I can.

"I am not fat." He starts to roll another joint.

"I can't smoke any more," I say, and then lean back, closing my eyes. I feel giddy, a bit dim as if I have a screen between me and the world.

"That's hardly anything. I thought I'd start off slow, since you're not very experienced."

I peer through my eyelashes and watch as he puts the joint down and then runs his hand up my bare leg, from my ankle to my knee and then up my outer thigh to my hip, underneath my nightgown. He turns to look at me and I don't hide that I'm watching him.

"You have beautiful legs."

"My ballet teacher told me I had the perfect dancer's body, but maybe a bit too short," I say, my tongue feeling a bit fuzzy already but I feel good. I stand up, and teeter a bit, but regain my balance. I stand a few feet away from the couch on the other side of the coffee table and take the first position in ballet, my feet turned out to one-hundred and eighty degrees, my arms softy curved, hands in proper position. I move through each position and back with only a slight wobble. "Not too tall, thin, legs in proportion to my torso."

He leans back, watching me with his head cocked to one side.

"Why did you stop dancing?"

I attempt an arabesque, succeeding for a moment and then try to move into a second one and lose my balance, falling into a very undignified position before trying to right myself. He stands quickly and holds out his arm, which I take, using it for balance.

"Eve, why did you stop?"

"I don't like to talk about it," I say and do another arabesque, determined to get it right.

"Obedience..." he says, frowning, a lopsided grin on his face.

"You keep saying that word," I say, and do a plié. "But you also said 'partners'. Partners don't force each other against their will."

"And you said 'all in'."

Finally I relent.

"I spent a year in and out of court after my current foster parents got custody of me. You can spot me," I say, pulling him around the table, his arm out so I can use it for balance, performing *battement tendus*, holding my body still while one leg moves into the three positions, front, side and to the rear. Then I perform *battements*, lifting my leg to the level of my hip and then moving down rapidly, repeating it several times, front, side and back, my arm moving into the correct position each time.

"Court?"

I perform a *passé developpe*, ignoring his question, not wanting to get into it. I start in first position, my arm out in front, my right leg moving to the front then back, and then to the side and then finally into an *arabesque*, using his arm as a bar for support.

"You didn't answer."

"I don't want to talk about it."

"You're still too sober." He pulls me back to the couch and I collapse onto it, my legs across his lap once more. He leans forward and takes the fresh joint, lighting it and taking a small puff to get it going. "I think I made them a little too thin because you should be feeling it more."

He hands it to me and I take it, feeling relaxed enough that I don't care how stoned I get. I inhale deeply, hold it in as long as possible, and then blow out the smoke, lying back, my eyes closed. I hand it back, peering at him under my eyelashes, pretending to keep my eyes closed, and he takes the joint and puts it between his lips but doesn't even puff on it, a smile on his face.

"Hey," I say, indignant. "You aren't even pretending to inhale."

"No, no," he says and hands it back to me. "This is about you, not me. You need to chill out. Mellow." He motions to the joint. "Go ahead. Finish this."

I take in another lungful, and then exhale. I glance at the joint. It's half gone. I'm definitely starting to feel it now, my arms and legs heavier, my mouth feeling like it doesn't really belong on my face. I take one more hit and when I exhale, I shake my head.

"I can't do any more."

I hold it out for him, turning my head away. He takes it back and taps it out, leaving it on a dish. I get up awkwardly, intent on trying out more dance steps. I hold onto the back of the other couch and try another *plié*, a deep knee bend and then lean back in a stretch, my arm extended. I lose my balance, laughing as I do, and he's once again at my side, catching me and holding me up.

"Hold your hand out," I say, "just in case I fall." Then I attempt a pirouette. It's a big mistake, for I knock into him, falling over into his arms, and then have to watch his wide grin at my clumsiness. I extract myself from him and pretend to be Odette from Swan Lake dancing around Prince Siegfried.

"Eve, you better sit down," he says, following me as I dance away from him. "You're going to hurt yourself."

I imagine I have on a costume with long flowing skirt, moving my nightgown as if it were a full costume. I don't care – I feel giddy, laughing as I run, my face flushed, cheeks hot. He's smiling as he comes after me and I try to elude him but he's far too fast, then I collapse into a fit of laughter when he catches me from behind, leaning back when he turns me around to face him, my arms out, my head to the side, eyes closed.

"That's more like it," he says, letting me lean back as far as possible, so that I feel as if I'm floating, falling, not caring what happens.

"I think I'm stoned," I say, my arms starting to feel unwieldy, my head spinning.

"Oh, yes. You are *definitely* stoned."

Finally, I stand up straight and he pulls me close and I feel so loose and free that I don't care what happens. He bends down and picks me up and carries me back to the couch, sitting down with me so that I'm once more lying with my legs over his lap, my head leaning on the armrest.

"Tell me about court," he says, his voice soft, one hand stroking my calf.

"I don't really remember," I say. "But it was very scary." I nod, my eyes closed. I feel so good lying there, so free. "I was supposed to testify about him, but he scared me and I didn't. They got custody, and then there were no more dance lessons. No more piano. Just martial arts and science."

"That's too bad."

"No," I say, wistful, listening to Debussy's *Arabesque* in my mind, my hand directing. I dance the steps I learned as a young girl in my mind's eye and hum the music. "I'm glad. Dance and music are pointless. Who cares? I prefer science."

"They aren't pointless. They make humanity beautiful. Worth saving."

I sigh. Such sweet thoughts.

"I wish he was dead."

"He will be."

He sits and just stares at me, his face dark.

"You're so serious," I say, giggling at the frown on his face, barely able to open my eyes. "I want to dance again, with you as my evil prince."

"I'm not evil."

"In the play – you have to be evil, the dark prince. The vampire prince. And I'm your captive, a tiny white swan held against my will." I laugh to myself, imagining him with a crown on his head, in a dancer's costume. "You were a vicomte after all." I hold my hand up to my forehead in my best damsel-in-distress mode.

"And if I let you go?"

"Oh," I say, filled with theatrics. "What would the swan do? She'd fly away. Away to the police and enter the witness protection program, never to be seen again."

He says nothing for a long while. Finally, I force my eyes open and see him sitting there, no longer smiling.

"What?" I say, poking his arm, laughing. "The world is so smooooth. Why are you frowning?"

"Would you?"

I feel my mind tumbling, my sense of time unreal as if reality is stretched out thin.

"Would I what?" I laugh at the world.

"Would you join the witness protection program if I let you go?"

"Oh, you won't let me go, silly," I say, the thought ridiculous, making me giggle. "You'd kill me first." I tilt my throat to the side and laugh at myself. "I'm too valuable to fall into enemy hands." I make an exaggerated face of pain, my tongue lolling out to the side, then go into a fit of hysterics at the sight of him, frowning like a spoil-sport.

He leans over me, his arms on the armrests beside my head. "Is that what you really think of me, Eve? That I'll kill you?"

"Eventually," I say. I open my eyes, look up into his hooded ones. "You're a killer. That's what you do."

I burst out laughing at his frown.

"What do I really think of you? Let's see," I say and smile, closing my eyes again, suppressing a giggle. "I think you have a very nice big thick . . ." I open my eyes and glance up, then convulse in laughter at the sight of his face, "piece of steak in the freezer that I feel like eating!"

"Oh you do, do you?" He smiles finally. "I thought you were a vegetarian."

"You've given me a taste for meat," I say, grinning. "We'd have to heat it up first." I practically roll around on the couch in hysterics. "Get it nice and hot!" Hold my belly. "Not too well done, though," I add, tears in my eyes, "cause I like it all nice and dripping juice!"

"Oh, believe me, it's already dripping," he says, leaning down closer, his face just an inch away from mine, smile now broad.

I scream at that. "Well you better get it out," I laugh so hard I can barely speak, "cause I got the munchies!"

I lie beneath him, his face against my neck, his nose beneath my ear, snuffling me like I'm some kind of exotic flower, the laughter slowly subsides, leaving me in a state of near bliss. It just feels so good, lying there with him on top of me, his weight comforting, his lips on my neck, his hair on my cheek.

"What do you *really* think of me, Eve?" His voice is so soft that I'm not sure if he actually said it. It sounds as if it's distant, as if we're under water.

"You already know."

"Say it."

"Why? Just read me."

"I want to hear you say the words."

I inhale slowly.

"What do I really think of you?" I say, now serious, my eyes still closed, my lids too heavy to open. "I think I could love you, even though you're not Michel," I say, nodding to myself. "And I hate you both. I wish I'd never met either of you."

He doesn't say anything for a while, and I just enjoy the moment, the way it seems to stretch like warm taffy, sweet and soothing.

"And if I said you were free to go? Right now? If I said you could just get up and leave, and I gave you a plane ticket and money to go wherever you wanted, start a new life?"

"Mmm," I say, imagining, shaking my head slowly. "If I could go anywhere?" I think for a moment, my eyes closed. "Wales," I say finally. "The Northern coast." I see it in my mind's eye. A rocky coast. "There's a medieval ruin there. Dolwyddelan Castle. Some days, when there's a storm, the clouds roll in off the sea and fill it up." I sigh. "I want to go back and feel the clouds in Dolwyddelan Castle."

I lie still, imagining what clouds would feel like.

"They must feel like fog." I remember fog lying thick on the ground when I lived in Wales. I remember a poem from public school I had to memorize and repeat to the class. "The fog," I say, reciting it out loud, "comes on little cat feet. It sits over the harbor and city on silent haunches and then moves on."

"Carl Sandburg," Julien says.

"Yes," I say and frown, my mood shifting at the memory. "Mrs. Peacock made me memorize it in Grade Five. I cried when I had to recite it in front of everyone. I hated people looking at me, as if they could see . . . "

"See what?"

"The blood." I shake my head, remembering. "He made me bleed." I swallow. "He took pictures."

"Shh," he says, rubbing my cheek.

I close my eyes and my feelings of bliss vanish as if clouds blown away by the wind at the top of a mountain in Wales.

"Time for more," Julien says, sitting up. "You're coming down fast."

I sit up beside him and rub my eyes. "I don't want any more."

He shakes his head and picks up the joint that lies in the dish on the coffee table and lights it. "Here. Smoke the rest."

"What if I don't want to?"

"*Eve.*"

I relent and take a hit, sucking in the smoke, holding it in for as long as possible. The buzz I get from before is nice. I like the feeling – as if there's nothing wrong in the world. As if everything's fine, happy, sweet. No troubles. When I'm done with the joint, I turn to him and watch him as he finishes up the end, the ember blazing for a brief moment before dying out completely.

He isn't Julien the vampire anymore – he's Julien the sweet man who smiles a lot and wants to nuzzle my neck – wants to replace his brother in my arms, between my thighs. When he turns back to me after closing up the baggie, I lean in and kiss him, my hand cupping his cheek, my fingers tracing his jaw.

"Sir Julien," I say, pulling him down to me. He kisses me.

# CHAPTER 17

"*R*evenge is a dish best served cold."

Pierre Choderlos de Laclos

I WAKE IN BED, MY HEAD POUNDING. Julien must have put me here when I fell asleep. I get up and go to the bathroom and wash my face, brush my teeth for my mouth feels like garbage. Julien opens the door and peeks his head around.

"How are you feeling?"

"Like I was stoned last night and have a hangover."

He smiles. "You were. I didn't even get anything out of you because you fell asleep before I could get you into bed and all my plans were ruined."

"You and your brother have so many plans," I say.

"We do. Get dressed," he says, his expression suddenly serious. "We're going somewhere."

"Where?"

"Just get dressed."

I bite back a protest and finish cleaning myself up, dressing in a pair of jeans and a black t-shirt. When I return to the main area, he's sitting at a counter in the small kitchen, drinking blood. He glances over at me, his expression unreadable under the hunter's face. When he's finished, he comes to me.

"Come." He reaches out and grabs my hand, pulling me with him,

"Where are we going?"

"We've got work to do."

We get our coats and leave the warehouse. Down on the street, Vasily's waiting with the car. I don't know what to expect as we drive along the streets. A cold front blew in and the skies are overcast, thick dark clouds blotting out the moonlight. I shiver, burnt out from the events of the previous night.

The car slows as we approach one of the oldest parts of the waterfront, the buildings falling down, ramshackle, rusting into pieces, this section not yet having been reclaimed. I want to ask what's happening, but am reluctant. Julien hasn't said a word to either Vasily or me, nor does he look at me. He just stares out the car window at the passing scenery, his fingers tapping on the door.

The car stops at one huge building made of corrugated metal. Inside, the building is empty and dark except for a floodlight which shines down on a figure sitting in the middle of the space with his back to us, his hands tied, a mound of small objects littered on the floor around him. To the side is a can of gas.

Once we're closer, Julien stops in the shadows, pressing his finger over my lips, motioning for me to stay where I am. He goes to the seated figure – a man dressed in a white shirt and dark pants, greying hair, his head forward.

Julien pulls out a knife and starts to circle the man, waving the knife around so that its blade catches the light and glints like a diamond. I tense, wondering what he's doing.

"Who are you?" the man says, fear in his voice once he sees Julien.

"No, the question is, who are you, or should I say, *what* are you?"

"What do you mean?"

"Your name," Julien says, edging closer to the man, his knife flashing. "Tell me your name."

"Bob," the man says, his voice breaking. "Bob Thompson."

I gasp and cover my mouth.

"Bob." A deadly serious voice. "Do you know why you're here?"

"No," he says, "I don't."

"You don't?" Julien steps closer, and picks up one of the dark objects off the floor. "Can you tell me what this is?"

The man shakes his head. "I don't know."

"Come on, Bob. Tell us what's inside. Is it a tape? A porno tape maybe? A kiddie porn tape?"

"I said I don't know."

"Well, that's strange. You see, after a few of my associates invited you along for a ride out to Boston for a visit, they went to your little den of iniquity and found these on your shelves. So I'm a little confused. Are you sure you don't recognize them?"

Thompson shakes his head. "Some guy gave them to me. I don't know what's in them."

"Oh, I think you do. You see, Bob, a few of my men took a look. They say you were in them with little girls. Doing all sorts of very *very* bad things. Now do you recognize them?"

"What do you want from me?"

"I want the truth, Bob. The absolute honest-to-God unblemished truth. You see, that's my mission in life – to get to the truth, every dirty filthy ugly bit of it. I want it all. Do you think a pervert can do that if it'll save your neck?"

Thompson doesn't respond, whimpering, his head down. Julien circles around, closer now, his knife touching Thompson on the neck.

"That's what you are, Bob. A pervert."

Julien comes over to me where I stand frozen with horror. He pulls me over to stand in front of Thompson, one arm around me from behind, squeezing me.

"Do you recognize her?"

Thompson looks at me but shakes his head.

"No?" Julien's voice is quiet, and I realize that the more quiet his voice, the deadlier his intent. "You don't recognize sweet little Eve? Look at her – the pretty hazel eyes, the lovely soft lips, the long fair hair, the ballerina body? How could you ever forget that?"

"Whatever she told you was a lie."

Julien lets go of me and goes back to Thompson. "You're calling Eve a liar? Oh, come now, Bob. You know and I know that's a lie. My men tell me there are tapes in that pile, at least one of them with a girl in a tutu, a little girl with shiny fair hair, with such pretty hazel eyes. Why, she looks like a fucking angel, doesn't she?" Julien's voice is close to breaking. He runs the knife under Thompson's neck, pressing it against his jugular. "Isn't that right?"

"I don't know what's there."

"Now, Bob," Julien says. "I'm going to be honest with you. Eve's already told me everything. Every ugly little detail. I want you to tell me, too, just so I know you're telling the truth. So that you and I both know what kind of animal you really are. Remember, I already know what you did. If I catch you telling a lie, something's going to get cut off, and I can assure you it will hurt."

I cover my face and turn away, unable to stand there any longer. Julien returns and holds me. "Shh," he says and strokes my head. "Just a little longer, and it will all be over."

He lets go of me and approaches Thompson once again. He bends forward and flashes the knife in the man's face.

"When did you first touch Eve in a bad way? You better tell the truth. Remember, Eve told me everything. If you lie, I'll get mad, and believe me, you don't want to see me mad." Thompson panics. He glances around as if looking for someone to help him.

"Answer me, Bob. I'm waiting."

Thompson's face is red, his mouth slobbering.

"I don't know, I don't know – maybe eleven. I'm sick. I need help."

"Oh, yes, you are sick. *Very* sick. But don't worry, I'm going to help you." He comes back to me. "You're a disease, Bob. And I'm the cure.

Look at her. She's an angel, and because you're such a dirty pervert and hurt her, she's all messed up. Twelve years later and she's still getting screwed by you in her mind. Now that's not fair, is it?"

Thompson's weeping, perhaps knowing there's no way out for him.

"Answer me!"

"No!" Thompson cries.

"And all the other little girls," Julien says, his knife ripping Thompson's pants in the crotch. "How many of them are fucked up because of you?

"I don't know," Thompson says. "Don't hurt me, please God don't hurt me!"

"Oh, God's got nothing to do with this now. God isn't going come and help you, Bob. He didn't come to help me, or Eve and he's not coming to help you. I'm the only one here, Bob. I'm your god now and it's just you and me."

I cover my face with my hands.

"Look at her!" Julien says, twisting Thompson's neck towards me. "I love her, and she needs pain to block out the memories of you! What do you think, Bob, should I hurt you?"

"No, no," he gasps, barely able to speak through the blubbering. "Please don't hurt me."

"Did Eve ask you not to hurt her?"

"I'm sorry," he cries.

Julien holds the knife under Thompson's chin. "Well Bob, it's too late for sorry now. You see, I'm here to do an exorcism. I'm here to cast the devil out. In fact, why shouldn't Eve be the one to do it? Here," he says and puts the knife in my hand, closing my fingers around it, his voice almost a whisper. "Take it. Do what I said you want to do and cut the bastard's heart out."

I just hold the knife in my hand, shaking my head, the tears rolling down my face.

"Don't," Thompson says. "Please don't."

"I can't," I say, barely able to speak.

"Didn't he hurt you, Eve? Didn't he make you hate yourself? Didn't he make it so that you can't get through a week without cutting yourself?"

"Yes."

"Doesn't he deserve to be punished? Doesn't he deserve to be stopped?"

"Yes," I say, but shake my head. "I can't."

"No, of course you can't. You're not a killer." Julien takes the knife back from me. "But I am."

He grabs Thompson's neck and twists it to the side, then bites down. I cry out, covering my face but watch through my fingers. Thompson groans, a strangled cry escaping his lips as Julien drinks his blood, almost ripping Thompson's neck apart. A moment passes before Julien stands up, his mouth and chin covered in blood. He wipes his mouth on a sleeve and then reaches down to feel Thompson's neck for a pulse. Then he turns to Vasily, who stands off to the side of the room in shadows. "Throw me your gun."

Vasily complies, and Julien catches the weapon and shoots Thompson point blank in the forehead, the force of the bullet rocking his head back. Then Julien kicks the body over onto the pile of tapes. He takes the can of gas and spreads it over everything, throws a lit match on the pile. Flames shoot up, igniting the gasoline, the fire licking at Thompson's body.

Julien takes me by the arm, leading me out of the building and to the car where Vasily stands at the ready. We drive back to the warehouse in silence, Julien just holding my hand in his, and he's released something in my brain so that I'm numb, feeling nothing.

I stand in the bedroom by the window overlooking the waterfront. Outside, the city lights across the river sparkle like a thousand crystals of yellow and white. A wind picks up and blows the stoplight on the street below back and forth. Through an open windowpane, I can hear it creak as it rocks in the wind – a lonely sound that arouses in me such a feeling of regret and sadness.

The streets in the surrounding area are bare; no traffic passes by. I realize I don't even know what time it is – I'd forgotten my watch at my apartment and haven't thought to look for it in the boxes Julien brought over.

Julien comes in, the open door throwing a sliver of light from the hall, briefly illuminating the hardwood floor. He closes it behind him and the room is once again in darkness and comes to my side.

"I'm sorry, Eve," he says. "That was difficult for you."

I feel numb, but I nod.

"Did you have permission to kill him?"

Julien shakes his head. "No," he says. "But he needed to die."

"I thought you only killed within the terms of the Treaty."

"I'm beyond that now," he says and sighs.

"What does that mean?"

He shakes his head. "Need to know, Eve."

Frustration fills me. How can I know whether to obey if I can't know why?

"I don't know if I can do this," I say when he leans against the windowsill, looking out across the skyline. "I feel so conflicted, so guilty, like being with you is wrong. Like it's a betrayal of my mother."

He says nothing, just runs his hand down from my shoulder to my hand, which he squeezes and that small show of caring makes my heart soften to him.

"It's like the world I grew up believing in doesn't really exist," I say. "It's all just a façade, and underneath is this really horrible world where monsters run things in collusion with bad humans. I always believed we lived with a system of justice. That our laws were what kept us from barbarism and arbitrary power. Without that system," I struggle to express myself. "Then, life becomes so insecure, dangerous, meaningless except for brute survival of the strongest."

"It's always been that way," he says, turning to face me and I can hear frustration in his voice. "Those laws are just meant to assuage your fears, keep you in line so that you live your lives out without causing those in power any problems. That's the truth."

"I realize that now," I say. "There is no meaning, no reason – for anything. No universal rights. Rights are what the strong say they are.

Your life and my life? Accidents. Eyeblinks in the life of the universe. Random collisions between molecules. Nothing more. Your vampire mutation? Just a random accident of random radiation and cellular biomechanics. In the long run, nature doesn't care and will probably weed it out as unfit. The universe doesn't care. Life has no meaning and all that matters is power."

"Do you really believe that?"

"I do." I run my fingers along the glass windowpane. "Events would seem to bear me out. Soren has power. He can force you to do what he wants. The rest of us are helpless and nothing we can do will change it."

We stand in silence for a moment.

"Come here," he says and takes my hand. "I want to show you something." He pulls me behind him and I resist, not wanting to talk, not wanting to think. We enter into the main room and he pulls me over to the office area. Vasily sits at a desk, watching the monitors, playing solitaire on his computer.

"Can you excuse us for a while?" Julien says.

Vasily stands and leaves without a word.

Julien sits at a desk, an old oak dinosaur, the top worn and scratched. He opens a file drawer and searches through a dozen files in a holder.

"Here it is," he says, pulling out a worn folder, thick with contents. He opens it on the desk and on the top is a folded image from a glossy magazine. The edges and folds are worn from repeated use. It must have been folded and unfolded hundreds of times.

Spread out, the image is of a dark sky with what appears to be thousands of tiny blurs of light. I lean closer and see that amidst the points of light are small galaxies resembling images of the Milky Way I've seen before, some on their side, some face on, yellow, white, pink, blue.

"Is that the whole universe?" I say in awe. "There are thousands of galaxies."

He shakes his head and touches the image, his fingers running over it almost with reverence.

"No. This was taken of the emptiest part of the night sky. It's called the Hubble Ultra Deep Field Image. If you held your hand up at arm's length, the area of the night sky they studied for this would cover only the tip of your little finger."

I lean over and examine it more closely. Galaxies of every conceivable size, shape and color are strewn against a black background. In the middle, one large bright star, its light refracted into points.

"I never knew there were so many."

"Each one of those specks? They aren't stars, Eve. They're galaxies with hundreds of millions of stars." He pulls me down so that I sit on his lap, his arms around me and although I want to resist, he prevents me.

"Look at it. That," he says, pointing to the bright star in the center of the image. "That is the only star. The rest are galaxies. The star's close – maybe thousands of light-years away in our own galaxy. The galaxies? Millions of light-years away. There are billions of galaxies. Each one has hundreds of millions of stars. They took that image from that position because they thought it was empty. Look at what they found in the emptiest part of the sky. Imagine that image taken and repeated to cover the entire sky."

He looks down at the image and shakes his head.

"There are too many stars – too many for us to be skeptical of the existence of God. Humans create such beauty and wonder that I can't believe that there's no meaning, no purpose. God may be beyond any of our puny minds but I do believe God exists, Eve. If I didn't, I couldn't imagine existence."

He squeezes me.

I don't want to hear his philosophy. I want to crawl into the bed and pull the covers over my head, block out the real world.

"That's so anthropocentric," I say, repeating some word I've learned in a class at university, never having a reason to even use it before. "What about all the other animals?"

"You can't compare that way, Eve. They're like steps on a ladder to us. The universe is billions of years old and in all that time it's been moving towards us. You've studied science. You should see it clearly –

increasing physical complexity starting with hydrogen and helium, all the way to the creation of biological life and then consciousness, and finally an intelligence that can actually see back to the beginning. And now one that's immortal. It's like we are the universe's consciousness and given immortality, what can we do? It's limitless."

"That's a beautiful thought," I say and shake my head, my breath catching in my throat. "I thought you wanted all vampires dead. I can't believe it. It's too self-serving, to see us as the reason for the universe to exist."

"God put us here for a reason," he says. "I don't want all vampires dead. Just those who want Dominion."

"Evolution put you here and it doesn't care about us."

"You Atheists are so brave, able to exist in a Godless universe," he says and squeezes me. "I know there's a God, although my faith has been challenged at times." He's silent for a moment. "I don't believe in the Church any longer, but I know that what it claims about the divine is real."

I look at him, at the white skin, and I remember the story of his making, and how he was taken off the battlefield, turned in the tent where medics tended the wounded, then transformed in the old castle. I take his face in my hands, and imagine him as a child, with dark hair, those huge blue eyes, praying to a god who never answered and yet he still believes, even now, and something breaks inside of me – I can almost feel it crack, rip apart.

I lean down and kiss him, pressing my lips against his, the kiss remaining chaste, the connection between us forming as our lips meet.

"I want you," I say.

"Not tonight."

"Why?"

He shakes his head, his face solemn. "Obedience, Eve. Just obey."

"Are you going out?"

He nods. "Yes. I can't tell you about it."

Then he stands and I extract myself from his arms. He lets me go.

I go to my bed, my knees weak, a choky feeling gripping my chest, and creep under the covers, closing my eyes.

I'm too tired to even cry.

I don't care any longer about this vampire war. I don't want vengeance. I don't feel any better with Thompson dead. It won't make what happened disappear.

# CHAPTER 18

o not seek the because - in love there is no because, no reason, no explanation, no solutions."

Anaïs Nin

THE NEXT DAY DAWNS GREY, overcast. I sit up in bed and through the open bedroom door, I watch as Vasily and Julien stand outside the office space and speak in hushed voices. I wondered if Julien ever sleeps and where he does, because after that night we had sex, he hasn't joined me in bed. I get up and go to the bathroom. In need of a shower, I step inside and the hot water that falls in a cascade over me from the huge showerhead stings.

When I'm finished, I dry off and search through the box of clothes, selecting a clean pair of jeans and a sweater. Brushing my fine hair is hard, for it tangles so easily, but after a few minutes of effort, it's tangle-free. I look at my reflection in the mirror. I look the same, with the exception of the scabbed cut on my forehead and the now-fading bruise on my cheek, but I'm not the same person inside.

I go to the kitchen and eat with little interest for there's a kind of emptiness inside me that feels like nausea. There's coffee in a coffeepot but I can't face it with my stomach the way it is. I drink some juice instead.

I wander to the piano and sit down, touching a few keys hesitantly, not really sure that I feel like playing. Usually my solace, now every piece I know just makes me feel incredibly sad. Instead of playing, I sit and stare out the window at the grey clouds scudding across the sky.

A noise from the entrance draws my attention away from the windows. A few of Julien's men come inside. He speaks with them, and then they leave. Julien returns to his office, retrieves a canvas bag. He stops near the exit and drops his bag, then comes over to me as I sit at the piano. He takes my hand and leads me away, over to a couch in the seating area.

He sits and pulls me down on his lap so that I straddle his hips, and I rest my hands on his shoulders. His arms slip around my waist, pulling me closer. There's nowhere for me to look except in his eyes.

He says nothing for a moment, just looks at me, touches my hair, holds it up to his face and inhales.

"I'm going now," he says, his voice quiet. "There are plans in place. The game's afoot."

"What are you going to do?"

He shakes his head.

"I can't tell you details, but it's big. Look, I don't have much time. Once the clock starts, we have everything mapped out in thirty second intervals, and I have," he said and glances at his watch, "about two minutes and thirty seconds left. But if I succeed and make it back," he says and squeezes me, "there'll be one less threat towards you."

"If you make it back?" I shake my head.

"There's always the chance when a soldier goes into battle that he'll die. I'm not expecting it," he says, and runs his fingers through my hair. "But just in case, I wanted to tell you something."

I shake my head, not sure if I want to hear it, whatever it is.

"I want you to know," he says, taking my hand in his, "that I wanted you from the moment I saw you in the diner." His fingers trace my bottom lip. "I was ready to break all my own rules for you. It hurt to even look at you. So delicate, so lovely, and so in danger from us monsters. You just really don't have any idea." He takes in a breath, holds it, then lets it escape slowly. "At first, it was just lust. There you were, so pretty, so young and fresh. I felt like such a," he says nothing, shakes his head. "Like such a monster compared to you. You're so good. I don't deserve you."

I try to pull away from him, feeling too much emotion rising in me, tears stinging in the corners of my eyes. I've cried too much. Too much. I bite my lip to stop.

"When I heard you play piano that first day you were in the warehouse, you had me." He touches my cheek. "I want to say this to you before I go. I may not ever be able to say it again."

I turn my head away, feeling like I'm at the breaking point.

"Stop."

"No," he says and turns my face back. "I want you to know. Just in case."

"Please," I say and cover my eyes." Don't say that."

"Eve, when I heard you play, I felt so – cheated. No, listen," he says when I struggle to leave. "In another life, I would have deserved you. If we'd met when I was human, I could have won you."

He says nothing for a moment. I can't speak. I can't look at his face, in his eyes.

"But there are just too many stars for me to care about what's right and wrong anymore, what I do deserve and what I don't. I want you. I could have made you happy. And now, time's up." He stands, lifting me up, my arms still around his neck. "Will the queen at least give her knight a pity-kiss goodbye?"

I pull him down to me, my lips meeting his, my tongue searching his out, the touch of it sending a shock of desire through my body. When our lips part, he presses his forehead against mine.

"Remember me, if I don't make it back."

"Don't say that."

He buries his face in my hair.

"You're an angel." And then he's gone.

Later that afternoon, Terri calls me and asks if I want to attend the memorial for Ed. His body was cremated but now the SCU is holding a small memorial for staff and friends at the graveside where his ashes were buried. Of course I want to go, and I get leave from Vasily to go. He'll be escorting me and we dress in our best and bring raincoats and umbrellas, then stand in the rain as the small graveside ceremony takes place. Ed was divorced, with no kids, his life completely dedicated to the SCU so only his colleagues and a few old friends attend.

I go into the SCU that night. I stroll into Terri's office in time for tea and flop down on the couch to talk with her. Terri and I reminisce about Ed, and she tells me about him and I feel as if I'm learning about an uncle I knew but never really knew. We're watching the television news clips of the peace talks in the Palestinian Territories. After months of random shelling between Israel and Palestinian groups, they're meeting to discuss peace.

Terri waters her plants, looking over her glasses at the television screen, mumbling a running commentary - none of it complimentary to the participants. The camera shows a large briefing room filled in the rear with reporters and at the front a large table with a panel of officials. Terri brings me a cup of tea and we watch the question and answer session.

It's quite boring - just an opportunity for the press to ask questions about process - who, what, where and when questions about the negotiations. I have little real faith in the possibility of peace - this is just a new government's attempt to garner favor at home. The camera focuses in on the Israeli official – I can see a number of advisors standing behind him, but none of their faces. The official's asked a question from one of the reporters about support from Zionist groups in the United States. The official covers his microphone and leans back and I'm amazed as Soren himself bends down and whispers in the official's ear.

"Holy crap," I say. "There he is."

"Who?" Terri says, her voice alarmed. "Where?"

"Soren. The pale one."

She comes quickly to my side and watches the television.

"Where is he – oh, I see him. Hard to miss."

"He's talking to officials at the briefing table."

"Is he an advisor? But our reports..."

"Our reports said certain ex-members of his group were involved in selling arms to militant factions who were out to end the peace process," I reply.

"Maybe they were traitors - going against his wishes. It might explain the deaths in Montana. Maybe he's playing both sides against each other. Who can say what his motives are? We don't know enough about him to even guess."

Michel and Julien know all about Soren...

The camera pans back as the two discuss the question. Soren stands back up and leans against the wall, the officers on either side of him leaning in to listen to him. The official replies, saying that the purpose of the meeting was to answer procedural questions, not discuss policy but that the new government enjoys the support of sympathetic people and groups from around the world. That he couldn't mention any names in particular to protect them from potential backlash.

How has Soren worked his way into the upper echelons of the military establishment? He established his own private security company in Montana, training recruits and mercenaries. Reports from the CIA suspect that he hires them out to the highest bidder. Now here he is - involved in the most current round of peace talks?

"Who in the hell is this guy?" Terri shakes her head and looks at me. "He's damn visible for an ancient. Almost like he's purposely drawing attention to himself. I don't know. That's not how Ancients act. They hide from the limelight. If I were more religious, I'd say he was Grigori."

"Grigori?"

She nods. "A fallen angel. They were said to be the most mighty demons on earth - set to rise up when the apocalypse neared, acting as Satan's minions in the final battle against Christ."

"You believe that stuff?" I can't keep the ridicule out of my voice. "I thought you were a scientist."

She shrugs. "I've seen too many cases of men with unnatural power -- power to alter the thinking and beliefs of their followers, seemingly able to manipulate matter and induce psychoses in their disciples. I've begun once again to believe in evil."

"I don't believe in God and I don't subscribe to any religion. Evil is just immorality. Conscious immorality."

"I'm a scientist," she says. "But there are things science just can't explain."

"*Yet*," I say. "Science can't explain it yet, but that doesn't mean we have to run to religion to explain it."

"Some of our advisors are members of the Church, Eve. I have to admit that I'm convinced there is more to this than what the science tells us and religion seems the best explanation."

I sigh, surprised by her admission. Soren didn't look like a demon when I met him. Other than the brief flash of darkness surrounding him that day at his compound, he looks like a competent military officer with very pale skin. I don't believe in angels any more than I believe the moon is made of green cheese. But If I accept the existence of vampires, why not fallen angels? That's probably just a name we gave to a sub-species of humans with greater powers than other humans have. Like vampires.

"We'll have to contact Vasquez. He'll want us to go there," Terri said. "Eve, it's time you met him."

"Who's Vasquez?"

"Bishop Miguel Vasquez. He's the Eastern Representative for humans on the Council."

"Soren..." I hesitate, not wanting yet to tell her about the clay seal fragment. "He entered my dreams while I was in Montana."

"How do you mean?"

"I had a dream of him. He told me we're wrong if we think we know who he is. He gave me something. I think it's a clue to his identity."

"Why didn't you tell my this immediately? This is critical. You can't keep information back like this!" She sits down beside me on the sofa and waits for me to tell her the whole story. I go to my backpack and retrieve the small piece of pottery, ashamed that I've kept this from her. I tell her everything.

She takes the pottery in hand and examines it.

"We'll have to find someone to check this out. I'll courier this over to Vasquez. He'll have someone familiar with this kind of artifact check it out," she says. "Whatever this seal is, it's part of the case, not your personal property. Soren may have given it to you, he knows who you are so he gave it to us as well."

"I'm worried about Julien," I say to Terri. "I'm afraid he's under Soren's control."

"Julien knows him more than any of us. We have to trust that he knows what he's doing. If he doesn't, we're screwed."

I lean back and close my eyes. That worries me, too.

# CHAPTER 19

"*L*ove that is not madness is not love."

de la Barca

We drive over to the Cathedral to meet with Vasquez later the next evening. He's a small man with dark close-set eyes framed by thick eyebrows. He's busy on the phone when we walk into the office. I scan the books in the bookshelves and some are so old, the bindings are falling apart. I sit beside Terri on a velvet couch. A cool breeze brushes my cheeks, flowing in through open leaded windows.

Vasquez sits behind his desk, hands clasped together, waiting for us to speak. On the desk in front of him is the piece of clay Soren gave me.

"Tell me about your trip," he says after we're introduced.

I tell him of our trip to Montana and of my suspicions regarding Soren – his ability to change his appearance. Of our flight and the turbulence. Of our parting at the airport and the seal he'd given me.

"It could mean anything, his words to you. We can't jump to any conclusions," he says, taking his glasses off and cleaning them with a handkerchief extracted from a pocket.

"She's had dreams, Miguel. He seems to be projecting into her mind."

Vasquez looks at me and leans forward.

"This wasn't in your report. If it's relevant to the case, it should be included. I have to have all the facts before I can determine the proper course of action. This is not personal - none of your work for the SCU or our group is."

I flush, knowing what he says is true, but I was so damn embarrassed to admit my response to the dreams.

"I've talked to Terri about this. I realize I should've put it in my report, but I didn't want it in writing."

"It's a perfect form of torture, to tempt us with desire. You're no different than any other person in this," he says, watching my face closely for my response.  I nod at his words. On the way over, I read a brief biography of Vasquez that was part of my files. He knows just what to say - he practiced psychiatry before joining the clergy, and had lived a normal life before becoming a priest.

"I'm sorry that you are faced with this test. Most Adepts are never faced with such temptation. We were so pleased to find you again, Eve.  You have so much to offer us because of your gifts. I'm counting on you to weather this and carry on." He rises from his chair and comes in front of me, leaning back on his desk, his hands folded on his lap. "I want you to go to the Palestinian Territories and let him know you're there. Do you feel able to meet this challenge?"

"I..." I hesitate. "I don't know. Michel seemed really worried about my going near him."

Vasquez nods. "He's not unbiased in this. He wanted you for himself. But you serve the Council first and foremost, Eve. As the representative for the Council, I want you to go. Michel's on leave. Julien is a fugitive. I'm your supervisor now. Pray for strength to help you through this. I'll pray for you as I'm sure Terri is already. Call me at any time should you feel a need. Other than that, you'll have to fly to the Palestinian Territories and check out Soren. Place yourself where he can see you so he knows you're following him, that you're aware of his involvement in the peace talks. He may contact you, he may not," he shrugs.

"What about that?" I say and point to the artifact.

"It's nothing important," Vasquez says. "Terri," he says, turning to her. "I want you to stay behind and help me. I'm sending someone to Montana to infiltrate the group, to watch Soren first hand. I'm reviewing candidates now and could use your input."

He goes back behind his desk and turns to his files. When I don't get up, he glances at me.

"Was there something else?"

"Soren said the clay was important. What is it?"

"He's trying to confuse us. This is not your concern."

"But it is. He gave it to me."

"When he did, he gave it directly to me. It's just a diversion. That's all you need to know."

I sit there, frustrated. I know Soren wanted me to know what that was.

"Who will come with me to Ramallah?"

"I'm sending one of our older Adepts from Central with you."

I nod, unwilling to challenge his decision. Vasquez's silence is our dismissal and we leave him and go back to our own offices at the SCU. As we drive back, Terri shakes her head, admitting shock at Vasquez's attitude towards my dreams.

"I can't understand why he's sending you. It's like he's dangling you out as bait."

I have the same feeling.

"Will you be all right?" she asks when I get out of the car outside my apartment.

"The security is crazy here."

"Call me if you need to talk. If you want to stay at my place, feel free. I have an extra room now that Joseph's gone to college."

"It won't do any good," I sigh. "But thanks anyway. You're good to me."

"I don't like what I think Vasquez is doing with you. Michel would never allow it. Keep that in mind when you encounter Soren. You may be bait." She looks in the rear- view mirror at the traffic building behind me and I know she has to leave.

"We seem to be caught up in the idea that the demon is tempting you, but Vasquez may want you to tempt the demon. If so, I fear for you."

I fear for myself as well.

As soon as she drives off, Vasily arrives in his car and I get in and go back to the warehouse.

"Vasily, is there any way you can contact Julien? My new boss wants me to go to Ramallah and make contact with Soren. I don't think either Julien or Michel would want that."

"I'll try, but Julien said he'd be out of contact for maybe a week."

I watch the scenery as we drive to the warehouse. Now is not a good time for Julien to go black.


With no word from Julien to stop me, I make plans to leave for Ramallah. I have nothing to do but pack my small case and leave an extra bowl of water and food for the cats at my flat. Once that's done, I pace the warehouse, wondering what will happen in Ramallah and who this older Adept is. Finally, I go to bed and roll up in the blankets, doing my progressive relaxation to try to fall asleep.

The first sensation is movement on the bed as he sits beside me, the pressure of his hard thigh along my hip. I lift my head off the pillow, to look at him, expecting to find Julien and am shocked to find Michel instead.

He's dressed in a loose black robe open at the neck, his pale skin glowing in the moonlight shining in from the window.

"You're mine," he says, his voice warm and deep. His eyes move over my body. "So lovely. So much loneliness."

He leans over and kisses my neck. His mouth is so cool, his tongue soft and wet - they feel so incredibly erotic on my skin.

"I've known loneliness," he whispers in my ear. "Hundreds of years. They chose you so well, I just might give in to temptation."

Then he kisses me and I feel such a surge of desire go through me I think I'll explode from it even as I feel tears fill my eyes. I miss him so much and kiss him back and my arms circling his neck, pulling him closer to me.

"Dear sweet Eve," he whispers, pulling back and raising himself up on his hands. He wipes my cheeks with a finger and slips the finger in his mouth, his eyes closing as he tastes my tears. "So much need..." He bends down and kisses me once again, the touch of his tongue on mine taking my breath away. "Can you believe?"

He waits for an answer.

"Yes," I say, not knowing what it is I'm asked to believe. I only know I want him more than anything. Then, he exhales heavily and bends down, his open mouth pressing on my neck and then a searing pain as he bites down.

I wake with a start, still on my side, my blankets twisted around me. I reach for my neck and feel only smooth skin, the wound where Julien bit me almost healed. Thankful that the dream ended there, I get up and go to the washroom, drink some water and go back to bed. I spend the rest of the night tossing and turning, waking only partially rested, but I have no more dreams.

Twenty hours of flight after we leave Boston, and Ramallah shines like burnished copper in the mid-day sun. Its light gilds the building tops and glints off the domes and minarets spread over the city. The heat of the morning blends the scents of the city to produce the overwhelming odor of humanity.

My handler from the Council is Sharon Blake, an older Adept, heavy-set and assuringly strong, dressed in grey pantsuit, a scarf around her head to honor the local customs. I wear one as well, not wanting to draw attention to myself.

Although assigned to escort me, she's given me wide latitude, even leaving me alone while she returns to the hotel to retrieve her laptop that she forgot in the suite. While she's gone, I meet with our contact in the office assigned to American officials and I use my guise as an FBI Special Agent, flashing my badge, which I keep in my jacket pocket. The staffer hands me the latest reports on the peace talks. I sit on the couch and read through the reports. It's uncertain if Soren is here to sell his mercenaries or arms. Is this part of his plan for Dominion?

My head aches from too little sleep the previous night and I feel hung-over and can't stop yawning.

"Is there someplace to get lunch?" I ask Crosby, the staffer in charge of logistics when I return from the washroom. He shakes his head.

"You have to go out to the market and buy your food. Only official participants get food."

I head out. I don't really feel like being here, sitting in the cramped room with Crosby. He's wearing headphones and listens to the proceedings of the talks. There's nothing to do but sit and read the international English language newspapers.

I take the closest exit to the street and walk to a nearby market, wondering if Soren's here today. The streets are scorching hot, and the wind blasts me, sand gritting between my teeth. I shiver, feeling suddenly feverish and faint so I sit on a bench, and put my head between my knees.

Before I'd accepted the job at the SCU, I had episodes of vertigo and had them checked out by a neurologist, including a CAT scan, but it was negative. As I sit there, trying to focus, I see what looks like rose petals on the ground before me. Where did those come from? A local man stops in front of me, speaking in some dialect. I shake my head.

He points to his nose and I realized my nose is bleeding. Blood drips down my chin onto the street. I hold my arm up, staunching the blood with the sleeve of my jacket. Then someone hands me a handkerchief and I noticed the signet ring on the man's index finger.

*Soren.*

I lean my head forward to stem the flow of blood.

"You don't look well, *Agent* Hayden."

He lays his hand on my head and I'm filled with euphoria, warmth emanating from his fingers. Soon, the flow of blood slows and then dries up.

"Seems to have stopped," he says. Soren hooks his hand under my arm, helping me to my feet. The light-headedness is gone. "See your neurologist or ENT when you return to Boston, Eve," he says, his voice soft. "Get that CAT Scan repeated. You had a benign tumor in your sinuses causing those headaches and dizziness. It's gone."

"How do you know?"

He smiles at me. "I just have the gift. You need something to eat. Let me take you to my favorite food stall."

I'm too shocked to argue and let him lead me through the thronging crowds, which seem to part just for him. The vendor sells flat bread and spicy meat and vegetables, and I eat a plate with the bread and vegetables, glad that my dizziness is gone, whatever the cause.

"So, Eve," he says as we walk back to the building where the talks are being held. "The Council sent you to watch me?"

"Why are you here? Is Michel here with you?"

He shrugs. "Work. And no, Michel isn't here. Don't get your little hopes up." He opens a door to an office, ushering me inside and stands directly in front of me, his hands splayed on his hips. "Well, here I am. I'm yours. Ask me anything."

He can't be serious. He's just taunting me again. A knock on the door interrupts us.

"Come."

A uniformed man enters and nods politely when he sees me.

"Sorry to interrupt, Colonel, but the General wants to speak with you in his office."

"I'll be right there."

The man nods and leaves us alone.

"We'll have to talk some other time. What about a late supper tonight? I'll be in conference all day, and we won't be breaking until 2100 hours. We could talk then, then maybe I'll get you off my back."

He smiles and I stutter something incomprehensible and realize I've agreed to meet him later at the hotel. He shows me out of the office, one hand on my back as if I'm a prized secretary.

"Until later."

The door closes behind me and I wander back to the office to find Sharon waiting.

"Where the heck were you? You shouldn't leave the grounds without me."

I sit on the couch and check to make sure Agent Crosby has his earphones on.

"I just spoke with Soren. He bought me lunch in the market."

She raises her eyebrows. "Well, I guess we can report that you made contact with our target."

"I'm meeting him for dinner at the hotel. I hope you'll be there somewhere in the background."

"Count on it."


The peace talks go on all afternoon. I sit in the foyer across from the main conference room, waiting for the talks to end so I can see and hear Soren and the other officials answer questions from members of the international press. The halls are deserted. Everyone is in the conference room, and it isn't slated to end for another quarter of an hour, but the small office to which Crosby and I have been relegated is hot and cramped. I sit in the cool dimness of the corridor and sip a cup of hot tea Sharon purchased in the market.

Then, Soren and a couple of officials emerge from a room and walk down the long halls. Soren stands in the midst of them as if he's the center of importance. I wonder how he's able to weasel his way into the realm of power so easily, as if this is second nature to him. His face is turned to talk with one official beside him. They speak to each other, serious about the topic of conversation.

Then a figure emerges from a stairwell and something about the man catches my attention. He carries a jacket over his arm and my muscles tense. Soren looks up and must have seen the same thing I do. The man yells something at Soren in an unintelligible language. Then a white-hot flash fills the hallway followed by a huge concussion that knocks me back against the wall. The ceiling collapses around us and the noise is deafening.

Then blackness.

When I regain consciousness, I'm being carried.  Stars still sparkle in front of my eyes but I can see.  Soren lays me down on a bench and kneels in front of me, wiping blood off my face. At first, an eerie quiet pervades the hallway, but then I realized it's my hearing. My eardrums have been temporarily damaged. Soon, muffled sounds return. Soren holds my head in his hands, checking me, examining my eyes. I feel warmth pervade my skull, and a sense of calmness descends over me.

All around us are bodies and debris. When the dust clears, ambulance personnel come into focus and I watch as they tend to the injured.  Stone from the collapsed wall forms mounds between the fallen. The conference room is in big chunks, and sirens wail.

A bomb.

"How are you feeling?" Soren says.

"What are you doing?" I try to push his hands away.

"Gotta look after you first, Eve," he says. "Of all the people here, you're the most important."

Soren goes to someone else lying on the floor beside me, bloody.

A medic checks me over, examining me with a scope, checking my eyes and ears, while someone put a blood pressure cuff on my arm. Beside me, Soren leans over a man on the ground, blood flowing from a cut on his forehead. He places his hands over the man's head and presses as if to staunch the flow. He turns and catches my eye and for a moment, he seems to struggle as if fighting something.

Sharon arrives and rushes to my side.

"I'm taking you to the hospital," she says as she kneels down beside me.

"I'm fine," I say, waving her off. I want to question Soren, who's busy helping medics treat the wounded.

I follow him to one of the injured. He pushes the medic aside and lays his hands on the man's arm where a wound bleeds. Soon, the bleeding stops.

He's healing the injured...

I step back, shocked at what I'm witnessing. He stands up and tries to walk past me to another of the injured.

"Who are you?"

 Soren pauses and regards me with a look of impatience.

He pushes me aside. "Figure it out yourself. When you do, give me a call and we'll have a little heart to heart. But you can tell Vasquez to stop tempting me. Tell him I have my own plans."

Sharon takes my arm and pulls me away.

"What are you doing? You should be seeing a doctor."

"I'm fine," I say.

She drags me outside the building where we stand, trying to collect ourselves. She checks me over, and then we take a taxi to the hotel.

Back at the hotel, I go to the bathroom to inspect myself and see the extent of my injuries.  I run a finger over my forehead, remembering falling rock and flying shrapnel, warm blood on my hands when I touched the wound. There's only a thin silvery line stretching from my scalp to my ear where the wound was. It looks like a very old scar, barely visible – like Julien's. I run a finger along it and feel an almost imperceptible seam.

Soren healed the cut with his own hands. There's no other explanation.

I sit on my bed and try to comprehend what happened and what exactly Soren is. While I do, there's a knock at my door. I open it to admit Sharon.

"How are you?" she says, inspecting my face. "You look pretty good considering the amount of blood on your clothes."

"Soren healed me." I point to the scar and she peers at it closely.

"Are you sure?" She touches the scar gently.

I nod. "That wasn't there before."

She sits on the bed and shakes her head.

"I don't know what the heck he is, but no vampire I know of can do that. We have to contact someone in the SCU with this information."

I rub my new scar.

"He said I should tell Vasquez to stop tempting him. That he has his own plans."

Sharon raises her eyebrows. "That's cryptic."

"I expect Vasquez will understand."

So, Vasquez *was* trying to tempt him. By sending me? Why am I temptation? Does Vasquez want me to be Soren's Adept?

I check my watch. It's ten o'clock and I haven't heard from Soren. I guess our late dinner is off, given the bomb.

Finally, I go to bed and hope for a dreamless sleep. Before I fall asleep, I think of Michel and wonder where he is and whether he's with Soren. It's with Michel on my mind that I finally fall asleep.

In the middle of the night, I wake to see a mist flowing in through the open window, and a hooded man with wings materializes from out of the mist. I expect to see Soren's face beneath the hood but when the hood falls, it's Michel and adrenaline surges through me.

"Michel!"

He sits on the bed beside me and I'm almost breathless, wondering what he'll do, hoping he'll get into bed with me. He brushes hair from my face, traces the scar on my forehead.

"You're alive," he says and leans down, his face by mine, his lips on the skin under my ear. "I thought you'd died. I didn't want any of this for you, but they've forced my hand."

"What do you mean?"

"I have to choose," he says and shakes his head. "I hoped to delay this, give you time, but I can't wait any longer."

Desire fills me at his touch, and I'm not sure whether it's my own or his, or some combination. I feel his tongue on my neck, feel his lips tugging at my skin, and then intense pain as he bites down.

I want it. I want the pain.

I wake, my heart pounding, my body aroused. I feel my neck but there's no mark, of course. It must have been another dream. Must have been because I wake soon after to a dream of Soren dressed in armor, bearing a flag with a Lion and Raven locked in battle. In my dream, he approaches me, holding out his hand to me, and for some reason that I cannot perceive, I take it willingly and follow him down a narrow path between trees in a dark forest.

Above us, the moon shines, it's silvery light illuminating the path. We walk to a clearing where a huge stone altar stands. Faceless people in hoods surround the altar and at the head of the altar is a throne made out of rock, carved with two animals on either side – one a rearing lion, the other a huge raven with wings outstretched.

Soren brings me to the altar and I willingly hold onto his shoulders as he lifts me up. I lay down and wait, but for what I don't know. I only know that I do it with breathless acceptance. I want it.

A figure approaches dressed all in black, his face obscured. Behind him stretch huge black wings. He pulls the cloak off but with the cloak gone, he transforms from dark to light, shining so brightly, the air around him glimmering like the sparks off an acetylene torch, so that I can't see his face. He pulls me to the edge of the altar and I willingly spread my thighs for him.

I wake with a gasp, my heart pounding. After the adrenaline subsides, I get up and go to my purse to get a sleeping pill. I don't want to go back to that dream, no matter how willing I seemed to be for what was going to take place. I want to escape into the blackness of drug-induced sleep.

"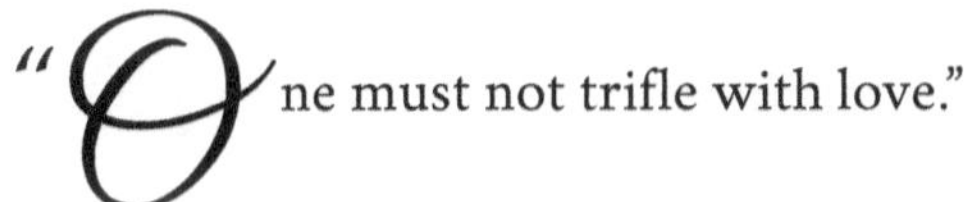ne must not trifle with love."

Alfred de Musset

THE BRIGHTNESS OF THE EARLY MORNING LIGHT that streams in between the drapes wakes me. For a while I try to convince myself that the events of the previous day were just a dream, but when I stretch, my muscles all ache as if I've been hit by a truck.

When I go down to check my messages, the front desk clerk says I have one from Soren. I read it:

"Sorry we missed our dinner date. I'm leaving tomorrow, and will be unavailable until I return to Montana. Call me next week. I'm looking forward to our little heart to heart."

"Soren's gone," I say to Sharon when I go back up to my room. Just when I wanted more information from him, when I felt I could approach him and demand he reveal who and what he is, he leaves. I stand at the window and look out over the sunrise, wondering what's true, unable to judge any longer.

I return to the site of the conference, to the makeshift headquarters in another wing of the building that was untouched when the bomb exploded. There's no need to linger in the city. With Soren gone, Sharon and I make plans to return to Boston to meet with Terri and Vasquez, to decide on a new course in this case, but I hesitate, wanting to hear more about the blast.

There isn't much for me to do but sit and listen to the other agents discussing the bombing. Since I don't have an official role, I make one last walk around the building to the wing where the bomb went off.

I catch sight of Soren out of the corner of my eye. Before I realize it, he's walking beside me down the long marble hall. Our footsteps echo against the stone walls and ceiling and I wait for him to say something, but he doesn't. He just walks beside me. I finally stop and look at him, searching his face for some clue to his thoughts.

"Tell me what's going on," I say and grab his arm. He glances down at my hand on his bicep.

"It's not that I mind when you touch me, but you'd better let go or there'll be several men with weapons here in a second."

I take my hand away quickly and glance around.

"I don't see bodyguards."

"They're well hidden," he says. "They know what you are, even if you don't. They see you as a threat to me."

I laugh in disbelief. "Me, a threat to you?"

He merely smiles and begins walking down the hall. Then, he stops and turns around.

"Like I said, Eve, when you figure out what I am, you come and talk to me. Until then, you're just a pretty little bit of temptation and a waste of my time."

"Why am I a temptation?"

He shakes his head.

"You really don't know much, do you?" He stands, hands on his hips, and looks away for a moment. "I'd say that's bad management on Michel's part. He's too damn stubborn. But I have a feeling he's going to change his mind. Soon."

He leaves me standing in the middle of the hallway.

I'm not sad to see the city grow smaller below us as I look out the window of the jet. We're on a busy flight to Rome and I'm unable to get an aisle seat, my usual refuge when on a passenger jet. So distracted from the events of the preceding two days, I forget to count to one-hundred and twenty and think instead about my report to Vasquez: what I'll include and what I'll leave out.

I swallow down a scotch and ask for another, needing the heat of the silky liquid to calm me before I have to meet with Vasquez and Terri. They've arranged to meet me at the airport, and I have to build up my courage to tell them the truth.

More than twenty hours later, after a layover in Rome, I arrive at the airport in Boston.

"Oh, God, Eve. You look terrible."

Terri clucks over me like a mother hen, examining me, checking for injuries. I let her fuss over me. She's the closest thing I have to family and I relish her honest concern for my welfare.

"I'm fine, just shaken."

The driver retrieves my bags and escorts us to Vasquez's car. On the way to Vasquez's office, we discuss the events of my trip. Vasquez doesn't look at me even though he sits in the seat directly opposite me. He holds his hands folded as if in prayer and touches the tips of his index finders against his bottom lip. He looks like the Pontiff himself as I relate the facts of the bombing and the way Soren healed me.

"That scar was there from when you were a child, Eve." He looks at me finally, and the conviction on his face is so strong, I have to reassess my experience.

"You're wrong. I never had a scar on my face."

"That scar you have is very old. Ask any surgeon and he'll confirm that for a scar to look like that, it takes years. Decades."

"You think I imagined this?" I say, anger filling me. "I felt his hands on me, I felt warmth from his touch. I saw him heal others right after the bomb."

"You were obviously upset and in shock. The mind often plays tricks on us when we're under duress. Only the Saints themselves can heal."

I shake my head and look out the window as the city speeds by. His religious explanation for everything irritates me.

"I know what I saw. I know what happened."

"By now, Eve," he says, his tone dismissive, "I'd have thought you'd know not to trust your own senses. Your own prejudices."

Terri reaches out and her warm hand is a comfort in the silence of the rest of the trip.


Back in his office, I look around as Vasquez rustles through his files and then speaks on the phone. The leather chair creaks under my weight as I shift nervously, waiting for the real interrogation to begin.

"The bombing.  Please relate the events for me." He turns on a small tape recorder, and smiles at me.  "I hope you don't mind, but I want to record your words for our records."

I tell them everything I can remember – meeting Soren in the market, him saying he'd healed my benign tumor. The bombing and his healing me and then others while I watched. Him saying he wasn't what we thought and that I should figure it out before contacting him again.

Vasquez sits, hands folded once again as if in prayer.

"We have to let you go, Eve," he says and his words shock me.  His small eyes finally come to rest on me, and as he speaks, he takes off his glasses and folds them in one hand.  I look at Terri. She's staring at the floor in front of her.  She doesn't look up at me, even when she must feel my panicked eyes on her. "You're now a liability to the Council and will be unable to fulfill your responsibilities to us any longer. You'll return to University and continue your studies."

I don't know what to say. He stands and comes to me, leaning against the desk.

"I'm so sorry.  I was wrong about your value to us. I thought you were stronger. I blame myself entirely for this mishap. In your condition, we can't afford to allow you to work with us."

"What do you mean, my condition?"

"Your fantasies of Soren healing you. This notion that he healed you of a wound that you received a decade ago. It's clearly psychosis. Only the saints heal."

A long silence ensues, during which I'm unable to speak. When I realize I've been dismissed, I stand.

"So that's it? I'm fired?"

"Yes, I'm truly sorry, Eve." Vasquez moves to shake my hand, his arm clapping my back. I don't reciprocate. "You weren't strong enough for this work. Time to retreat, take stock and enjoy some serenity for a while."

I turn to leave, and then look back at Terri. I want her to come with me, to talk with me.

"Terri?"

She doesn't look at me. Vasquez smiles and cocks his head sideways as if he feels guilty.

"Sorry, but I need Terri for the rest of the afternoon. I'm sure you two will talk soon enough. Good-bye, Eve." Vasquez presses a hand against the small of my back and gently propels me outside the office. The ornate wooden door closes with a soft thud behind me.


I go to my office at the SCU to begin the process of packing up my personal items. I have a feeling people are trying to avoid me. Word must have gotten around that I was fired and I can't blame them if they want to avoid having to face me. Still, it's pretty cowardly.

I collect what little there is of my personal effects and check my e-mail one last time. There's only one -- from Seth. One of the techs who mines data for the SCU. He's not working this evening.

*I need to talk with you about the relic. Can we meet as soon as possible? This is very important. Please call me. Thanks.*

*Seth.*

I phone the number he's included right away. His voice is strained, as if he's tired or ill.

"We need to talk somewhere private. Can we meet at your place? I'm staying at a friends for a few days so we can't meet at my place."

I agree and after glancing around the empty office, I go home. It feels strange to be on my own, without Vasily or anyone trailing me. Although I'm pleased at the prospect of hearing what Seth has to tell me about the artifact, I feel numb.

Once back at my flat, I turn the television on and watch the news coverage of the bombing of the embassy. Seth arrives, knocking at the door. He's about twenty-eight, tall and skinny, with rimless glasses. He has fair hair and eyes and looks every inch the geeky IT guy. He comes in and stands in the middle of the living room awkwardly.

"I heard you were there," he says, pointing to the television news report. The camera shows the blast scene, the floodlights picking up debris, bloodstains and emergency personnel as they rush to tend to the wounded. The press had been on site, preparing to cover the news conference and so both camera crews and reporters were primed and ready to cover the carnage once the explosion occurred. They're playing it in endless loops on the news networks.

"I was at the wrong place at the wrong time, I guess."

"You're lucky to be alive."

I nod and sit down, planning on turning the television off so we can talk about the clay fragment.

"I'm," I say, my voice quiet. "I'm no longer working for the SCU. They took me off the case."

"I heard. That's why I wanted to talk to you. The seal?"

"Yes?"

"It was from a tomb in a cave in Israel, removed about a century ago where they found some old scrolls in a clay pot. There was a lost scripture in it from the third century. Described the apocalypse. The end of days."

I smile. "I'm not a religious person," I say and take the research paper he hands me.

"Read this," he says. "Don't tell anyone I gave it to you but it's a copy of a report someone on the Council prepared. I thought you should know because it involves you and when I heard you were fired, and heard what Vasquez told you about this seal, I thought you were being unfairly treated."

I look over the paper. It's titled *Revelation According to St. Therese of the Reeds.*

"I have to go," he says. "I don't want to stay in any one place for very long, just in case someone's watching me."

"Why would they be watching you?"

He shrugs. "Who knows? I know they watch everyone so if anyone asks why I was here, say it was because we were friends or something and I was saying goodbye."

"How do you know about the tomb seal?"

"I mine data. All of it, even SCU data. I have a few tracers of my own included in the official search terms. I stumbled over some conversations and it scared me. Now I have to go."

I lead him to the door.

"Take care," he says. "Watch your back. I know you can fight, but I also know you haven't been fully trained. I don't know what's coming, but I have a bad feeling about it."

I close the door behind him.

*Join the group.*

*Revelation According to St. Therese of the Reeds...* I tuck the paper into a mental file marked *Superstitious Nonsense* and plan to read it later, when I have nothing else better to do.

# CHAPTER 21

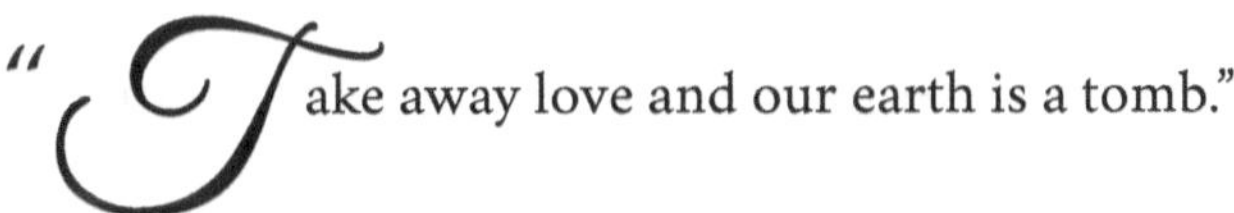

"Take away love and our earth is a tomb."

Robert Browning

THE NEXT FEW DAYS PASS SLOWLY as I try to adapt to my new life no longer employed by the SCU. I tried to go back to the warehouse but there was no response when I went to the service entrance and rang the bell. I couldn't get in and Vasily never answered my calls. Instead, I go back to my tiny apartment, feeling completely abandoned by everyone. I haven't heard from Julien or Vasily and I feel completely cut off from my life of the past few months.

Finally, I hear a knock at my door and I check the peephole. It's Vasily. I open the door.

"Eve," he says. "Why haven't you answered my calls? I've been so worried about you."

"What do you mean? You never answered *my* calls!" I go to my cell and check, but there are no calls registered on my phone from Vasily. "There's nothing here..."

He shakes his head. "I've been calling and calling. I came by your apartment but there was no answer. You weren't at SCU."

"I'm fired."

"What?"

I close the door behind him and we sit on my couch.

"I went to Ramallah to track Soren and when I got back, Vasquez fired me. I went to the warehouse but there was no one there."

"You went to track *Soren?*"

"I told you before I went. Don't you remember?"

He rubs his head, grimacing as if the very idea hurts him.

"You must come back to Julien's. You are not safe here. I can't believe you've been alone all this time…"

I sit there, so confused. Once again, I suspect that Soren's at the bottom of this. I fill my cat's dishes with fresh food and water and leave my tiny flat for Julien's warehouse.

"Where's Julien?" I say as we drive through the narrow streets bordering the waterfront. "I thought he'd at least call me."

"He is on operation."

"When will he be back?"

He shrugs. "I can't say. He hasn't contacted me."


I feel strangely at home at Julien's warehouse and spend the evening reading or watching television news and staring at the cityscape. I remember the last words Julien spoke to me, wondering what he meant when he said he's taking out one threat against me. Does he mean Luke? Finally, I'm too tired to stay up and say good-night to Vasily. I fall asleep quickly, feeling for the first time in a while that there's nothing I can do to change things, and so I stop even trying to figure out how. All I know is that I'm falling in love with Julien. I miss him. I worry about him, and I want him back safe.


Noise from the apartment wakes me sometime in the middle of the night. I go to the bedroom door and crack it open enough to look into the main foyer. Julien has returned and is standing with Vasily, the two men speaking in low voices. His shirt is off and his chest bare. There's a bandage on his arm stained crimson.

I go to him immediately and cup his face, kissing him, not caring if Vasily and his other men see me.

"You're hurt," I say. "Can I check it?" He nods so I peel back the bandage to reveal a laceration several inches long, clean edges, the cut at least a quarter inch deep. "What happened?"

"Luke and I fought. He used a silver blade."

"Luke fought you?"

"Don't worry," he says and cracks a lopsided grin. "He got the worst of it."

Before my eyes, the wound begins to heal, very slowly, but it's apparent even to my eyes. The blood seeping from it slows, and then the edges pull together so that soon, it's just a thin seam of white.

I daub the wound and the gauze comes back clean.

"Your skin isn't cold," I say and run my hands over his chest. I notice a light pink blush to his cheeks. "You have some color. You just fed."

"Luke," he says, grinning. "To the victor, the spoils."

I smile and put my arms around him, pulling him down to me, my mouth by his ear.

"I'm so glad you're alive," I whisper, tears making my vision blurry, my throat choked. He says nothing, just smiles and pulls my arms from around his neck. Then I see movement in the shadows.

Michel.

"*Michel…*" I whisper, my voice breaking. I can't help myself and run to him and he's there, his arms open when he sees me coming and I'm in his embrace and his mouth is on mine. He picks me up, lifting me off the floor, turning around, holding me there, kissing my face and throat and neck.

"You're here," I whisper.

"I'm here."

"How? I thought I'd never see you again."

Over his shoulder I see Julien, a frown on his face.

"How? Tell me!"

"Soren released me."

He glances at Julien. I turn back to Julien and he's not looking at me, his hands in his pockets.

"Why did Soren release you?"

Michel shakes his head and leads me into the bedroom, shutting the door behind us.

"I made a bargain with the devil. I've just done a thing that I detested very much, but I had no choice. When I learned you met Soren in Ramallah, I knew what I had to do. Julien knew what he had to do. I have to be very careful from here on in. Every step has to be taken with complete calculation, every move perfect."

"What do you mean? What did you do? What did Julien do?"

He smiles softly.

"Eve of a thousand questions. I can't tell you. Just accept that I'm back." He brushes hair from my cheek. "I have to sacrifice if you do."

"What do you mean?" I say, confused at his cryptic comments.

Vasily pops his head into the room. "The others have arrived."

Michel closes his eyes briefly. "I have to go. Please put on the black dress Luke gave you and join me."

"Why?"

"Eve, I want you there with me," he says, running his fingers through my hair.

"For what?"

"For our ascension." He goes to the door. "Hurry."

*Ascension?* When he opens the door, I see a group of vampires, their pale skin clear identifiers of their nature. They're a dangerous looking group, all dressed in black, like a group of warriors in leather.

When they see Michel, they all bow. Michel closes the door and I sit on the bed for a moment, a chill going through me at the show of obeisance to him. Then I comply with his request, slipping on the black velvet dress Luke gave me. I go into the bathroom and brush my hair, splashing water on my face. My shoes are outside in the closet in the foyer. I'd have to go barefoot. I take in a deep breath, and then open the door. The scene I witness when I step into the hallway stops me in my tracks, adrenaline flooding through me.

In the main living room, Michel and Julien stand with their backs to the windows, bare from the waist up, what look like huge black wings spread out behind them, the feathers shining iridescent in the light from overhead lamps. Before Michel, one vampire kneels and kisses the golden ring on his hand. He then moves to Julien.

My heart pounds and my legs wobble. I can't take my eyes off the wings and the paleness of their bare skin. All eyes turn to me as if I'm a specimen on display. Michel looks up when I enter the room, then extends his arm and offers his hand.

"Come," he says, his voice soft. "Don't be afraid."

But I *am* afraid and I turn around and go back into the bedroom, closing the door behind me. I slide down the wall to the floor, my heart pounding, my vision closing in. Then the door opens and Vasily enters, closing the door behind him. He kneels down beside me and takes my hand.

"Eve, are you OK?"

"No, I'm not OK." I shake my head. "I feel faint," I say, my voice barely audible.

He takes me over to the bed and makes me lie down to stop from fainting, and then he goes to the bathroom. He returns with a wet facecloth, pressing it against my forehead and neck.

"Rest for moment. Take deep breaths."

I do, and in a few minutes, I start to feel better.

"I saw something," I say and look up at him. "I can't believe it. I thought I saw wings..." I say and shake my head. "But it's impossible."

"If you feel better, Michel wants you with him."

I hold my hand out.

"No," I say. "I'm not going out there."

"You must. He wants you with him."

I turn over, refusing to move. Finally, he leaves the bedroom and I hug my pillow, trying to comprehend what it was that I saw. The door opens again and it's Michel and I see those black wings spread out behind him and I close my eyes, pressing my face into the pillow.

"Eve," he says, his voice soft. He sits on the bed beside me, but I refuse to look at him, keeping my eyes shut tightly.

"Go away," I say.

"I want you to come with me. I want the others to see me claim you."

I shake my head quickly. Then, he lays his hand on my head and my fear dissipates, replaced by calm. I exhale slowly and relax, my tense muscles all loose.

"Come," he says, taking my hand. I don't resist.

He pulls me gently outside the bedroom and through a path the vampires make for us.

I stand in front of them with him in front of me, tears welling in my eyes, for Michel and Julien appear so unreal as if they've just stepped out of a Renaissance painting. While they look like the twins I know and have the same features, they seem otherworldly in a way that's entirely new, their bodies larger, more powerful, their skin more luminous. I can't find a word for it but it's as if they've been transformed.

Michel turns me around to face the other vampires. I feel their gaze on me as an almost physical force – as if they could smell me and taste me from a distance like predators sensing their prey. Despite their differences in coloring – some are fair haired, others are dark haired – they are uniformly tall and well-built, their skin the same luminous quality, whether they were dark-skinned or fair as Michel and Julien's.

Michel pulls my hair back, smoothing it, exposing my neck. He's almost a foot taller than me and when he pulls me against his body, his chin touches the top of my head.

"So this is the one?" one of the vampires in the back says, his accent heavily British.

"She's Natalia's daughter, Eve. In case there's any doubt, she's ours. If any one of you dares to even come within arm's reach of her without our leave, we'll destroy you."

He tilts my head to the side, exposing Julien's bite wound, running his fingers over it tenderly. Then he bends down and covers the wound with his mouth. I close my eyes at the feel of his lips on my neck, the touch of his tongue on my skin sending a stab of desire through me. My knees give out from the intensity of his emotions flooding through me from his touch, but he grabs me and holds me up, one arm around my waist.

He bites me, his teeth sharp, breaking through the skin where Julien bit me earlier as if he's trying to overwrite what Julien did. Despite the pain, I feel what he feels, his overwhelming bloodlust, and he hates that Julien had me first but he also feels that finally he's having me the way he wants me, even if he has to share this moment with Julien. He takes in a mouthful of my blood, savoring it like its some rare old wine and he doesn't want to let go. He didn't want it to be like this, in front of everyone but when we were alone, our bodies naked, joined in pleasure.

Soon, the pain recedes. He hates this, drinking my blood and claiming me like some spoil of war in front of everyone but he feels he must. He pulls his mouth away and our connection breaks. My eyes open, only to stare into those of a dozen vampires, watching hungrily as blood trickles down my neck. Then Julien takes my hand and bites the other side of my neck and I feel him at the edge of my consciousness. He's glad that Michel's back but unhappy that he has to share and afraid of what this means – the two of them now Soren's possessions, one a bishop and one a knight like they were in 13th century France.

Julien pulls away, and Michel motions to Vasily, who comes to my side and takes my arm.

I turn back. Julien's in hunter mode, his eyes blood red, his pupils huge, fangs extended. He licks my blood off his lips and that image makes me so weak that I stumble and Vasily has to hold me up. Michel and Julien are now clearly the most powerful vampires – or whatever it is that they have become – showing them all that I'm their pet. That they own me – the two of them.

Vasily leads me through the vampires and I feel their gaze on me as a barely repressed current of hunger, jealousy, and desire. I glance back and the procession of vampires bowing before Michel begins once more. One vampire with pale hair kneels before them and takes Michel's hand, kissing his ring as if Michel were the Pope himself. Then he moves to Julien and repeats the gesture.

"What are they doing?" I whisper as we leave.

"Swearing fealty to their new Lords."

"They were Luke's before?"

"Yes," Vasily says.

The evening's events finally catch up to me, and my composure crumbles. The sight of the vampires kneeling before Michel and Julien, whose huge wings make them resemble angels instead of vampires, the perfection to their faces and forms, the otherworldliness to them, overwhelms me.

I look up at Vasily, my vision blurry.

"What are they?"

"What do you think they are?"

They resemble angels, but what are angels? Are they shape shifters, able to change their form at will? One moment they were both ordinary, and the next they had wings, and I wonder if this isn't some kind of psychic projection.

"I'm going insane," I say. "They're projecting into my mind," I add, remembering what I've read about telepathy. "They have telepathy and are sending images, making me think I see wings."

"If that comforts you, believe it," Vasily says.

"Do you see wings?" I say, staring at Vasily.

"Seeing is believing," Vasily replies.

The other vampires take seats around the room, murmuring in muted conversation as they wait for Michel and Julien to finish. Michel comes to me and lifts my chin so that I have to look in his eyes

"How are you?"

I shake my head, unable to speak.

"Come," Michel says, offering me his hand, leading into the bedroom. When the door closes, he pulls me against his body and leans against the closed door. His wings curve around us as if in protection and when he presses his lips against my neck, a connection forms between us. I'm overwhelmed with his emotions – pain and longing, desire for me, hunger for my blood, frustration at the way he can't completely control any of his emotions. The intensity makes me momentarily dizzy, but then he begins to recede until he's only a presence at the edges of my awareness.

He strokes my neck. Pressed against him as I am, I lay my hands on his skin, which feels as cool and smooth as marble, yet vital rather than unyielding. Almost touching me are feathers from the wings and I long to reach out and touch one to see if it's real.

"Tell me what you are," I say. "You and Julien."

"We're still us," he says. "What do you think we are?"

I shake my head, not wanting to sound stupid. He says nothing, just waits. Finally, I take a chance.

"I haven't read anything about vampires having wings. There are stories of vampires turning into bats, or even ravens, but not," I say, hesitating, knowing it sounds ridiculous. "Not angels."

"Why is it so hard to believe?"

"I don't believe any of it," I say. "I'm a scientist."

He tips my chin up so I look directly into his eyes.

"And when a scientist is confronted with new evidence, she incorporates it into her understanding of how the world works."

I resist his reasoning.

"When you no longer trust your own senses, how can you trust the evidence? There has to be some physical reason for this," I say. "For these." I reach out but don't touch one of the black feathers just inches from his shoulder.

"Go ahead," he says. "They're real."

It feels like any other feather I've touched, only on a much grander scale. The same barbs, woven together to form the fabric of the feather, the thick hollow rib in the center, and an iridescent shine created by the diffraction of light through the layer of pigment molecules. Undeniably a feather and undeniably wings.

His face is calm, so beautiful in its ivory perfection.

"What happened to you? You've changed."

"We finally gave in to what Soren had planned for us."

I take in a deep breath.

"I've gone completely insane." I say, despair welling up inside of me. "You and everything that's happened? A psychotic break."

He presses his forehead against mine briefly.

"Trust yourself." He brushes hair from my face. "This is more real than what you think is reality."

"I give in," I say, tears stinging my eyes, certain that I am in fact insane, the break with reality I had as a child after my mother died returning due to stress. I'm trapped in my delusions. "Whatever this is, I can't fight it."

He cups my cheek with his hand, and wipes away a tear with his thumb.

"Don't despair," he says, his voice filled with emotion. "You aren't insane. You merely see things too well and that's your great tragedy."

He bends down and kisses me, softly, a kiss more of compassion than lust, and I reciprocate, reaching up to hold his face, not caring any longer whether I'm suffering from Stockholm Syndrome or psychosis.

After a moment, he lets more of himself fill me and a wave of raw emotion sweeps over me, almost overwhelming me with its intensity. Need, desire, lust, hunger, fear. Every emotion is mirrored in my own body and mind until I didn't know where I end and he begins, what are his emotions and what are mine. Then he pulls completely back, withdrawing so that all I feel is his physical presence, his skin against my hands, his mouth on mine. He breaks the kiss, but keeps his forehead against mine.

"I have to go back," he says. "They're expecting us to lay out our plans, discuss our strategy. We had to do this to be free," he says, brushing hair off my cheek. "But know this. You're not Julien's. You're mine. He may have marked you first. He may have had your body. But you're mine and he won't touch you again. That was all for show for we need to project a united front." He kisses me again. "We have to become everything we despise. We have to become monsters. Don't hate me, Eve, for what I've done and what I'll do. One day, you'll understand."

He leaves the room, closing the door behind him. In the darkness, I notice a faint shimmer on my hand from touching his wing. In the moonlight flooding in from the window, it shines like diamond dust.

I go to the bathroom and stand in the darkness, letting my eyes adjust. Then, I rub the dust against my neck, the flecks like a spray of faint stars against the endless blackness of space.

# CHAPTER 22

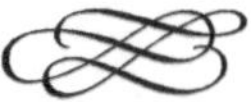

We have to distrust each other. It is our only defense
against betrayal."

Tennessee Williams

I WAKE MUCH LATER and all is quiet in the suite. I expected
Michel to come in with me during the night, but he hasn't. I slip out of
bed and tiptoe to the door, cracking it open to see if Michel or Vasily
are still up. The lights are out and so I leave my room and walk barefoot through the hallway searching for him.

The room is empty. I find him standing at the window in the living
area, looking out over the cityscape in the distance, his wings hidden
and he's now just a man. He turns to me.

"Eve – is something wrong?"

I go to him and take his hand, then I lean on him, my cheek against
his chest. He says nothing, but I hear his sharp intake of breath. He
slips his other arm around my waist and leans down, his lips pressed
on the bite on my neck.

"Since I'm insane now," I whisper. "I might as well just give in. You can have me anyway you want me," I say, my voice cracking from emotion. He pulls back and examines my face. "Whatever you need to do," I say. "It seems like the logical thing for me to do in this little delusional world I've created. I'll be your pet," I say. "That appeals to me so much. Anything you want."

"This isn't a delusion," he says, squeezing my shoulders. "Eve, this is real."

"It can't be real. I don't believe in angels and demons and vampires with wings."

"It's real. I now have the gift of transmutation. I can alter my body at will. That's all. I'm still the same."

"How can that be possible?"

"I told you before about the origin of vampires."

"The myth that fallen angels created you."

"Not a myth. It's all there in *Enoch*. All vampires have this in them, but it's suppressed by our human origins. This is just our nature being brought out. I drank the waters of life and have been purified."

"You took some kind of drug that activated some kind of psychic ability so you can project images at will. There's no way you can alter matter like this. It's not physically possible."

"It's not a delusion or a projection."

"I've gone insane," I say. "That's the only explanation. I don't even believe in mental projection. It's not possible according to the laws of physics."

"The laws as humans know them you mean." He sighs. "How can I explain this in terms you'll understand?" He shakes his head for a moment. "Imagine self-assembling nanobots, controlled by an intelligence, converting energy into matter and back again."

"Occam's Razor – the simplest explanation is the most likely. I'm insane."

He sits on the couch and pulls me between his legs. I put my arms around his neck and lean in, pressing my cheek against his.

"How can I prove that you're not imagining this?"

"You can't," I say, rubbing my cheek against his. "You could do anything, and it could just be my own mind making it up. So I give up. I give in. Since this is a delusion, I might as well enjoy it. I might as well go for everything."

I reach up and slide my hand behind his head, pulling him to me, kissing him, the feel of his cool lips on mine sending a wave of desire through me. He kisses me back, and for a moment, we connect and the kiss deepens, but just as my lips part, he pulls away.

"No," he says, "not like this. I don't want you like *this*."

"With me like what?" I run my fingers through his long bangs, brushing them out of his eyes, tucking his hair behind his ears. "Ready and willing? Can't you tell that I want you? I want it all. All in, like I said. No more doubt. No more resistance. I'm your little pet, your little blood slave."

"With you thinking you're psychotic. You think this is a delusion but I'm real. This," he says, placing my hand on his chest, "is *real*."

"Of course you'd say that." I wrap my arms around his neck again. "But real or delusion – who can tell? There's no way, so why bother to even try?"

He removes my hands from around his neck and pushes me away.

"Stop," he says, his voice a harsh whisper.

"Don't argue with me, Michel. I'm offering freely. Here," I say and pull my hair to the side, pulling down the strap of my nightgown, offering my neck, shoulder, and breast.

He shakes his head and I can see the desire in his eyes.

"I know you want it, Michel. I can tell when you touch me. You hate that Julien fed on me and fed me his blood. That I've tasted him and not you. Do it. Feed on me. Feed me your blood. Make me your little blood slave. You can't prove to me that this is real. I could be a brain in a vat and this is all just a simulation for all I know."

I close my eyes and wait. When he doesn't reply, I open my eyes. He holds a hand to his forehead as if thinking. He fixes my strap, and then pulls me out of the room and to the closet, handing me my coat. I slip it on, content to just let him do what he will with me.

"There is a way. Come."

"Nothing you do can prove this is real," I say, smiling at his sour expression.

"Care to bet on that?"

We go down the elevator to the first floor and he speaks to one of the guards, who removes a set of keys from a cabinet.

"Let's go," he says and pulls me outside into the chill night air. "I have something to show you."

We take the highway to Franklin Park. It's very late and the parking lot is empty. Michel helps me out of the car and takes my hand, leading me into the heart of the park beneath the trees. I'm following him in my nightgown and trench coat.

Deeper in the grove of trees, the scent of wet pine is strong. Memories of pine trees and the crash of surf against the rocks brings a feeling of melancholy that chases away my sense of abandon from earlier. We come upon people, some alone, some in pairs or small groups. They're smoking crack and shooting up. Others watch, waiting their turn. Michel releases my hand and motions for me to stay where I am.

I can see him despite the darkness, but the others can't. He stands behind the small group, his wings unfurled completely. The moonlight casts a soft silvery light on his skin, so that he resembles a cemetery angel standing watch over the dead. He bends down to one young man who sits alone on the grass and touches him briefly on the neck, but after a moment, passes him by. The young man doesn't even notice, just keeps staring off into the distance.

Michel slips through the tree and I follow, keeping him in sight. He goes to a scraggly young man fastening a belt around his bicep, preparing to shoot up. A young man sits on the ground in front of him, a lighter and spoon in hand. Michel goes to both men, his hand resting on their necks for a fleeting moment. Neither man notices his touch, as if Michel were nothing more than a light breeze on their skin instead of some kind of vampire fallen angel measuring their souls.

In a clearing deeper in the trees, another man stands off to the side counting money, licking his thumb as he flips the bills. Michel stands behind him, his wings spread out wide, and lays his hand on the man's neck. He closes his eyes for a moment, his head tilting to the side as if deciding. Then, the man drops the money on the ground as if his muscles have all relaxed, his mouth opening, his neck lolling back. I knew *that* feeling. Michel pulls him deeper into the trees and I follow, amazed at my own mind as it creates this strange scenario.

When Michel releases his grip, the man blinks as if awakening from a dream. He glances down for his wad of bills then searches around in alarm when he notices it's missing.

"My money—" He sees me and frowns. "Did you take my fucking money?"

I back away and he lunges at me, grabbing me by the hair when I turn to run.

"Give me my fucking money, bitch, or I'll fucking cut you."

He pulls a knife out of his pocket and wrenches my neck to the side. My heart races as I feel the coolness of the blade against the skin over my jugular and I realize how close to death I am. I fall into fight mode, time shifting, and I have him down on the grass, the knife out of his hand and in my hand at his neck instead. Michel appears before us, his wings stretched out full.

"Let him go, Eve," Michel says and I release him. Time returns to normal and the man stands and tries to run, but Michel's too fast, faster than me, grabbing him by the neck, lifting him up as if he weighs nothing, his feet dangling. The man tries to grab hold of Michel's hands but can't budge them.

"You're paying tonight, Alan," Michel says, his voice a harsh whisper. "For everything wrong you've done."

"What? What have I done?"

"For the man under the loading dock," Michel says. "For the girl in the flop house. For all of them." He throws Alan down, and Alan sprawls on the ground, scrabbling in the dirt, trying to stand up and run. Michel stands over him, a menacing figure of black wings, red eyes and long fangs. He follows Alan, never letting him get more than a few feet away before tripping him, kicking his feet out from underneath him each time he manages to rise. Soon, Alan's weeping, tears and snot mingling on his face, his expression one of pure terror.

"Stop! Oh my God, please stop!"

"Your God's forsaken you, Alan, and sent me instead," Michel says, his voice dripping with contempt. "I'm your god now. Your judge, jury and executioner."

I stand a few feet away, covering my mouth, not wanting to watch but unable to take my eyes off the scene playing out in front of me. I will Michel to stop, determined to have this end peacefully with Michel merely drinking the man's blood to satiate his thirst. Michel picks up Alan from behind and twists his neck to the side. He looks at me, his face so dark, his once-beautiful features such a hideous mask of rage that I barely recognize him.

"If this is a dream, Eve, wake up. If this is a delusion, will me to show mercy."

"Please," I say, wanting him to stop. "Don't hurt him."

"Time to die," he says, and then his fangs rip into Alan's neck. Alan screams in pain, wrestling around, his arms flailing, his legs kicking helplessly as he tries to escape Michel's grasp.

"Please God" Alan gasps, "please God stop!"

I will Michel to stop but he doesn't and soon, Alan's spraying blood out of his mouth, choking on blood, frothing red out of his mouth, his windpipe severed so that blood fills his lungs. Then his efforts flag and he goes limp in Michel's arms, emitting a hideous croak as he dies. Finally, Michel rips his head off and drops his body to the ground like he's no more than a sack of coal. He throws the head towards me and it comes to rest next to my foot. He looks at me, his mouth a bloody gash, his long teeth glinting in the moonlight.

"This," he says and wipes his mouth. "This is real."

I stand frozen in place, hands covering my mouth to keep from crying out loud, tears blurring my vision. Alan's eyes are half-lidded in his severed head, and bloody froth bubbles cover his mouth.

"Why?" I glance up at Michel, but he doesn't respond. Instead, he brushes past me and I follow, not knowing what else to do. He stops at the edge of the grove of trees, just outside the streetlights that line the parking lot. I'm too horrified to even look at his face.

"Why did you do that?"

"So you'd know what you were getting when you offered yourself to me." He turns to face me, wiping his lips with a hand. "Not quite as beautiful and dreamlike as you imagined."

"I don't want you to kill me."

"But I could. Another vampire would have by now because there's nothing we like more than draining a human to the point of death. Nothing else satisfies quite as much." He looks away and shakes his head, an expression of dismay on his face. "You think this is some kind of psychotic episode – a delusion – and you can say and do anything because it won't matter. It's all just a dream. You offered yourself to me, offered to let me make you my pet, my blood slave. You can't imagine how much license that gives me. Once given you can't take it back. I just want you to know what you're getting."

"What am I getting?"

"Me."

Michel, black wings, bloody fangs, red eyes. A killer.

Numbness descends over me and the glib feeling I had back at the loft dissipates completely – shocked out of me when Michel tormented Alan the way a cat plays with a mouse. Terrifying the poor creature as it fought for its life then killing it in a most inhumane manner. I remember the manuscript and the description of him chasing down the two girls, killing them in front of each other.

"Is this another kill outside the treaty?"

He nods and stares at me from under a frown.

"I'm beyond that now."

"What do you mean?"

He doesn't answer. Instead, he folds his wings until they disappear, and opens the door on the passenger side of the car, motioning for me to get in. We drive back to the warehouse with only the sound of the engine to accompany us. Once back, I run up the stairs before him, waiting for him to open the door. I go to the door to the bedroom without looking at him.

"Not going to invite me into your bed now, are you?" he says from the hallway.

I turn to him, tears in my eyes.

"Why did you do that?"

He comes to me, leaning down so he's just inches from my face. He traces my bottom lip with a finger but the touch of his hand imparts nothing of his emotions.

"When you give yourself to me," he says, his voice barely above a whisper. "I don't want it to be because you think you're insane or that it doesn't matter. I want it to be because you mean it. I want you to know that it matters." He turns and walks away, leaving me alone in the darkness.

I spend the next day in a funk, wrapped in a blanket on my bed. Not even the bright sun shining on the Charles River can please me. I was so certain that this was all a psychotic delusion, but the sight of Michel torturing the man destroyed that belief. Why did he treat the man so heartlessly? I imagine it's a form of punishment. He found someone he felt deserved death and killed him to show me what a monster he is. I know that in my own little fantasy world, he would have been kind, he wouldn't have been a vampire or fallen angel or demon – whatever he is. He would have been a priest. He would have shown mercy.

I rise from bed late in the afternoon and other than looking over the daily papers and watching some afternoon news on television, I keep to myself in my bedroom, licking my emotional wounds. In the evening, I sit alone in the library and stare out at the cityscape as the sun sets. Soon, the lights from the buildings across the Charles River flicker into view like so many stars in the growing night sky.

Indecision about my situation nags me – should I just give in to Michel and let him have me as he wants? Or should I hold out until I know more? All I know is that he hasn't come to me the way he promised when he left and so I know something's changed.

These thoughts occupy my mind during the evening and I begin to wonder if Michel stayed somewhere else. Maybe with Kate. Only much later does Michel appear as I'm deep into a book that I found on the Council tucked away in the shelves. A history written in the 18th century, the book ancient, the binding threadbare from much use.

I close it when he enters the living area. He looks like the old Michel I remember, his hair a bit wild, tucked behind his ears, dressed in black.

"I was wondering if you'd gone away."

"I've been busy," he says. "Planning, getting ready for an operation."

"Consolidating your grip on power?" I say, with only a tiny hint of humor in my voice.

He glances at me. "Something like that." He stands and just looks at me.

"I wanted to talk to you," I say finally, debating with myself over whether to bring it up now or later.

"And I you, but right now, I don't have time."

I sigh. He'll be out all night and I'll be alone once more.

"Is this one of those 'I may not come back' missions?"

"They all are, but the risks I face are fewer and fewer the more power I get."

"As in fewer other vampires who can beat you in a fight?"

"Precisely." He glances at his watch.

"Are you going to kill them all, one by one?"

He turns away. "If that's what it takes to prevent what I know is coming, yes."

"What's coming?"

He shakes his head. "You already know."

"Dominion," I say and he nods. "Julien told me the Blackstone Group's plans. I feel so alone," I say, regretting it instantly, for I sound like a spoiled child upset that her parents are going out. He's at my side in an instant, sitting beside me, one arm around me on the back of the sofa.

"I know," he says, stroking my cheek with a finger. "I didn't mean it to be this way, but it has to be for now. This is war, Eve. People have to make sacrifices."

"I wish you'd tell me more," I say, my voice wavering just a bit. " I don't know who to trust, what to believe. What to decide."

"I've told you as much as I feel I safely can. You must understand that the more you know, the more danger I put you in. On this, I disagree with Julien."

"I found this book," I say, hoping to keep him with me a bit longer. I open it and flip through a few pages. "It says that if a vampire kills outside the Treaty, they're banned from the Council. You killed that man last night and Julien killed Luke. Which means..."

"Which means we're out of the Council," he said. "But that was a foregone conclusion when Julien was staked and I had to go to Soren. I was just in denial."

"Michel, you have to tell me what's going on." I put my hand on his arm, hoping to sense something in him but he's a blank. "Why are Adepts so important? What happened to you to change you?"

He runs his finger over my bottom lip.

"This is war and you're the weapon."

"What's the endgame?"

"Ah, now that is the question," he says and smiles. "The one I can't answer without endangering you even more than you already are."

"Why?"

"Because if you knew, you'd be dead if anyone found out." He leans over and kisses my cheek. "You'll know soon enough, depending on how things go in the next while. Just remember, I didn't want any of this for you. But you had to be so damned strong willed that I couldn't erase your memories of me."

"So damn cryptic," I say as he stands up. I follow him to the door. "Tell me this one thing," I say and take his arm. "When I drink your blood, I experience telepathy for a short time, right?"

"Yes, but only as long as the blood remains in your system."

"You once said if I were your blood slave, we could connect even at a distance."

"I'd know where you were," he says. "How you were. You could call me, even just in your mind, and I'd hear you."

"I never read about that in any of the material at the SCU. What else aren't you telling me? Why am I so important?"

"You're the conduit."

"What does that mean?"

"I can't tell you. I don't want you to know." He shakes his head and presses his finger against my lips. "That's enough for now."

"Feed me your blood before you go."

He says nothing for a very long moment.

"Eve," he says. "Don't." He shakes his head. "Don't tempt me or yourself. Once you get a taste for it, you'll want more and down that road lies addiction."

I step closer. "I'm not trying to tempt you," I say, slipping my arms around his neck. "At least this way if anyone comes and I can't fight them off, you'll know about it."

He stands in silence as if trying to decide.

"Not like this," he says finally, chopping his hand down.

"Not like this?" I say, barely able to control my frustration. "Yesterday, I offered myself to you and you refused because I thought this was just a psychotic episode and you wanted me to understand it's real. So now I do. You showed me that last night. Now," I say, clenching my fists, "You scare the shit out of me about the danger I'm in." I rub my forehead, the twinge of a migraine threatening. "If you feed me your blood now and you're killed, at least I'll know and can prepare to be claimed by whoever finds me like a cheap bottle of plonk."

I cover my eyes, tears of frustration biting at the corners.

"No, no," he says, taking me in his arms, crushing me against him, burying his face in my neck, his lips beside my ear. "I'd never let that happen," he whispers. "Never. I'd destroy every vampire in existence to stop it."

I let him hold me. I let him comfort me, rocking me slowly in his arms, brushing my hair back. I slip my arms around his neck and pull him down in a kiss that starts out soft, chaste, just a pure expression of a need to touch him, but very soon becomes more passionate.

When his tongue touches mine, I feel one agonizingly intense surge of lust and desire.

"This," he says, his voice husky as he bends down and picks me up in his arms. "This is how I want you."

He carries me over to the side of the bed and lies on top of me. I wrap my legs around him, pulling him against me. As we kiss, the connection between us deepens until I can barely tell my own senses and emotions from his. He needs no words, for I know what he feels. I feel it as well – his intense desire for me as a woman, for my blood, and for this union. His need to touch me, to taste me, to lose himself even momentarily in this connection we form like some salve for all the centuries of existence. He presses his mouth against the beating pulse at my neck, lingering over it, delighting in the feel of it under his lips and against his tongue. He bites me, and the short sharp pain is counteracted by the pleasure.

Soon, the edges of my vision blur and it isn't from tears. My heart beats so rapidly that I'm sure I'm dying. Which I am.

# CHAPTER 23

"We choose our joys and sorrows long before we experience them."

Khalil Gibran

"NO, NO, *NO!*" MICHEL PULLS AWAY, our connection diminishing, his presence receding while the world rushes back in. Blood loss saps me of all strength and I struggle to see past the fog that clouds my vision. Michel looms over me, his mouth bloody. He runs to the door. "Vasily!" he shouts into the hallway. "Transfusion! Now!"

He returns and bites his own wrist, holding it to my mouth, pressing the gash against my lips.

"Drink," he said. "You must drink."

"I don't want to be a vampire. I'd rather die."

"You won't be," he says, trying once more to get me to drink. "I promise you. Just drink."

I can't see his face clearly, for it goes in and out of focus, but I know he's there, his huge black wings open behind him, his blue eyes visible through the fog.

"Don't lie to me," I say.

"I'm not," he replies.

Finally, I comply and swallow a few mouthfuls. Vasily comes in and works on me, tying a tourniquet around my upper arm, struggling to find a vein, then the tiny prick as the needle enters my vein for the I.V.

"How many units do you have?" Michel says.

"Several of O negative."

"That might not do." Michel turns back to me, bending down close. "Eve, you must drink more. If you don't, you'll die. *Drink*."

"I can't feel my arms and legs." Tears spring to my eyes. "I don't want to be a vampire," I say, barely able to speak.

"You won't be," he says, shaking his head. He leans over me, his face darkened by fear. He keeps pressing his wrist to my lips, urging me on. On my other side, Vasily attaches a second bag of blood to the I.V. pole as if he's done this before and is an expert.

Finally, I drink more, the tangy coppery tang pleasant, but it doesn't have the effect on me that Julien's blood had. Michel doesn't need to speak for I know what he's thinking. *Don't leave me*. I don't hear his voice in my head as if he were speaking to me. I just know his thoughts.

Soon, some of my strength returns and my vision clears.

"Are you a nurse as well?" I ask Vasily, smiling at him while he works away with such efficiency.

"You're feeling better," he says and smiles back, but it's forced, his lips thin.

Michel leans down and presses his forehead against mine. *You're alive*.

My mouth feels dry, and an incredible thirst hits me.

"Water," I say to Vasily. He leaves the room. "What have you done to me?" I say to Michel. But whatever connection has formed between us, Michel seems able to control it for he doesn't answer me. He's a blank. But then I know – I know because I saw it when we were connected so deeply. When Michel lost all control over himself, for a brief moment, I saw into his memories – memories he tried hard to block when I touched him that day in the SCU and has been blocking ever since.

He knew Soren killed my mother because she wouldn't turn over her research to him. Michel knew it had been Soren all along. He lost my file on purpose so Soren couldn't have me. So Julien couldn't have me. So I wouldn't be a weapon.

One thing Michel was certain of – Soren was out to claim Dominion for the Ancients, enslave us all to them, using me as a tool.

Even in my weakened state, I know then that my motivation in life has changed permanently. I no longer need to kill vampires. I needed to understand Ancients and their plans to enslave humanity.

*I don't want it. That's what I'm fighting.*

Whatever connection forms between us by my drinking his blood seems to be two-way for I can hear his thoughts, but apparently only when he wants me to.

"It's not fair," I say. "That you can hear everything I think at all times, but I can only hear your thoughts when you let me."

"Existence isn't fair." He says out loud. "Now drink more."

I take another mouthful of the blood that drips out of the wound on his wrist, enjoying the taste for it makes me dreamy. "What will this do to me?"

"Save your life. Now drink."

I do, but only because it will save me so I can fight the Ancients. Time passes with me in a sleepy daze, swallowing the occasional mouthful of Michel's blood, watching while Vasily attaches yet another bag of blood to the I.V. Sensation returns to my limbs and I can lift my head off the pillow briefly to glance around the room. I reach down and pull a sheet up to cover my nakedness. Blood stains the bed beside my neck.

"You almost killed me," I say to Michel, who sits on the bed beside me.

"I lost myself," he says. "Or Soren compelled me to kill you. It won't happen again."

*You're right it won't.*

He lets me in at that, and I can feel his pain and regret.

*Eve... Please...*

"I could know everything right now, and you won't let me in."

"You can't know everything."

"Why?" Anger fills me despite my weakness. "Why not tell me the truth? Because it might ruin your plans?"

"If you knew and they took you, they'd know everything as well through you. Compartmentalization is key to keeping a plan secret. You just can't know."

I try to block him, but have no idea how. Will pain work now? I bite my cheek hard, feeling the sharp intense pain of it.

He takes my face in his hands and looks in my eyes.

"Eve, I love you. Don't shut me out."

"Then tell me what you're planning."

He shakes his head, and then kisses me.

"I can't," he says. "Even if it costs me your affection. One day, you'll understand and forgive me."

He turns away, staring through the open drapes to the night sky. I don't know if I can block him, but if he can't trust me enough to tell me the truth, I can't know that his motives are honorable. I close my eyes and turn my face away.

*You're a monster.*

I say it in my mind to see his reaction. When he does nothing, when nothing in his bearing makes me think he can hear me, I relax.

"When I recover, you're going to let me go free," I say plainly.

He turns back, sadness in his eyes.

"What do you think you're going to do with this newfound freedom?"

"I'm going to kill Soren," I say, remembering something else I picked up when he'd lost control. I can kill them – the Ancients. The Council has a way. My mother was involved in its development but Michel's afraid to use it.

"You're going to show me how."


I recover enough to sit up in bed and drink a cup of hot tea Vasily brings to me along with some toast. Michel sits on the bed beside me, watching me eat and drink, an expression of resignation on his face. He disapproves of my desire to kill Soren, but I'm not going to let up unless he lets me do what my mother was hoping to do – stop those out for Dominion when vampires rule over mortals.

Michel's pretending to be on Soren's side, his lieutenant, helping him gain power. Their relationship is one of subservience – Master and slave for Michel is now his creation. He gave Michel the waters of life – a substance derived from Ancient blood that transformed Michel, bringing out the traits of the fallen angels who created vampires. They used these same traits to create me. I have fallen angel in me.

"Tell me about this nanotechnology the Council's developed using my mother's research," I say as I down another piece of toast.

It's what Reynolds was working on.

"It targets specific vampires using their DNA. Each of us has a unique DNA pattern. The nanotechnology seeks out certain sections on their DNA and attaches to it, then releases micron-sized particles of silver, which weakens the vampire at the cellular level. There's nothing left but molecules. Virtually impossible to reconstitute because of the damage done to the DNA."

"So it won't hurt someone without that DNA sequence?"

He shakes his head.

"Your mother was searching for one specific sequence of DNA common to all Ancients but absent in made vampires so she could kill all Ancients permanently. All made Vampires would be preserved because while we have Ancient  DNA in us, we don't have the exact sequences."

I think about this for a moment. "You took the waters of life. How does that affect you?"

"It causes dormant genes to become active, giving us greater powers of transubstantiation. So I can create these at will. And other things."

"I drank your blood," I said. "So I have your DNA in me?"

He nods. "It wrote itself into your genome and has become part of you, altering your abilities. Your mother was searching for one specific sequence that all vampires and all Ancients possess that we could use to target us all, destroy us all."

The thought repulses me. As much as I hate vampires, as much as I hate Soren for what he did to my mother, I don't hate those who abide by the treaty. To kill them all – to exterminate them as a species – seems barbaric.

"Why do you support this plan? It's terrible. It's genocide."

He shrugs and glances away.

"The Ancients have betrayed mortals from the time they first encountered you. They've done you no good, infecting you with this disease, bringing you into their battles, ruling over you like gods. Vampires are parasites. They rely on human blood for existence and that takes it away from humans who need it. They give nothing back. Why should either continue to exist?"

The thought almost turns my stomach.

"I don't like the fact that vampires have been killing mortals for thousands of years but I don't agree with the plan. There must be another way for both to exist without either vampires ruling us or preying on us."

"If there is, no one's found it. There are many who can't deny their predatory ways. They don't want to deny it. They love it."

I put my cup down. "They're the minority, and like any other psychopath they're the aberration and we have to deal with them the way we do with all killers – try to stop them, try to diminish the harm they are able to do. But to just wipe out the entire species..." I can't accept it.

"You're more generous than many," he says to me, his head tilted to one side.

"Do you deny what I say is true?"

He shakes his head.

"How do you effectively control them? That's the problem. They're a powerful group. Humans are powerful technologically, but even so, they haven't been able to completely control vampires. I don't know if they ever will be able."

"Well," I say and dangle my legs over the side of the bed. "I don't like it and I won't work for the Council if that's their endgame."

"So generous," he says, coming around to my side of the bed to help me up. "But can you avoid it? The Council created you, protected you, made you what you are. They have plans for you."

"You rejected those plans."

"Yes," he says. "Because I have power. Without me, you're powerless. Just a weapon without a hand to guide you."

"Then I need your help."

"Eve," he says and cups my face with his hand. "I went to all this trouble to keep you from this fate. Why do you think I'll help you meet it?"

I stand up on my own, pushing away his hand. "You'll help me because it's the only way you'll have me or my blood."

"I don't need your blood. Nor do I need you. Wanting you is entirely different."

I lean on the door to the bathroom. "If you want me, you'll have to help me or else imprison me and take me by force. And believe me, if you do that? You think I've been uncooperative? You've no idea."

I go into the bathroom and close the door. He stays outside.

"Call me if you feel faint."

"I'll be fine," I say. "Give me some privacy, please."

After a moment, I hear the door to my bedroom close. I lean down, my head in my hands. I was feeling somewhat faint but I have to get away from him for even a moment. He's been hovering over me like I'm going to die at any time and I can't even use the washroom without him standing outside.

I sit like that for a while, just trying to think straight without him there watching me. There's been no mental intrusions since I tried to block him out, and I wonder if I have to actually let him in consciously.

My plan is to recover my strength, and then meet with the Council and talk them into getting me the nanotechnology so I can use it to kill Soren. I'm not at all concerned on a moral level with destroying him. He wants to enslave all humans, have us as slaves to vampires, with him and other ancients as our rulers. They would no longer fear the machinations of the Council and its rules and treaties.

Michel might not like it. That's too bad for him. He's kept the truth from me – claiming it was because he wanted to save me from this fate I was contemplating, but he'll just have to give up that hope. I know he wants me for himself as much as he doesn't want me to be the Adept who kills Soren. One of us has to. I have more reason than most to be the one.

That's what I'll plead before the Council, if I have to. Of course, Soren will know I'm Michel's 'pet' so we'll have to find some way to break us up – have Michel lose me, maybe reject me so that I'm available. Soren can then claim me. Then once I'm safely ensconced in his circle, I'll destroy him.

I don't know how it will happen. The Council has a plan. Michel won't tell me what it is, but I want to hear it.

All my life, the idea that one day I'll find a way to stop vampires kept me alive through all the pain in my life. Soren's planning on being the single-largest mass murderer ever. It's a very strong motivation. If I'm able to kill him, and if I have to die in the process, so be it.

I sleep all the next day and other than eating the light meals Vasily brings me, I do nothing more strenuous than making the short trip to the washroom. During the first hours, I recover fairly well, considering I've almost lost all my blood to Michel's lack of control – or Soren's compulsion.

Michel comes to me later in the night as I lie in the darkness, thinking about what I'm going to do. I'm not feeling well again, the sense that I'm recovering wanes as the day passes and darkness falls. I'm worn out. It'll probably take me several days to fully recover.

Michel stands in the darkness at the foot of my bed and says nothing.

"I can see you," I say.

"I know," he says, his voice soft. "How are you feeling?"

"Like crap." I turn over, my muscles aching from the effort, my hands shaking. "Maybe I need something more to eat. Can you ask

Vasily to come in? I feel like something more substantial than tea and toast. Like meat or something."

Michel sits on the bed beside me and takes my hand.

"You need my blood," he says, his tone serious.

"I hardly had any of it," I say, shifting on the bed, trying to find a position that doesn't hurt. "Did I drink enough to become addicted?"

"Yes," he says. "Because you lost so much of your own, mine had that much more effect on you. You felt fine for a while, but now you're starting to feel unwell again."

A sense of dread washes over me. "I thought it would take more than one feed."

He says nothing for a moment. "One big feed will do it."

"What happens if I don't have more?"

"You'll feel sicker and sicker."

"Will it kill me?"

He clears his throat. "No, but you'll wish it would."

"It's not permanent is it?" I say. "I can get clean?"

"I'm sorry," he says and shakes his head.

I cover my face. Nausea rises up inside of me at the idea that I'd need to drink blood to keep from feeling sick, like some junkie.

"I had no other choice," he says "I had to save your life."

I turn my back to him.

"Are you sure you didn't drink too much of my blood accidentally on purpose?"

He leans over me, his arms around me.

"Remember, you gave yourself to me. As much as I want you, I never wanted any of this for you."

"Leave me alone," I say, pulling away from him, the pain when I do growing by the moment. He sits up.

"Just drink now. You'll feel better immediately."

"Go away."

He does nothing for a moment, but finally, leaves the bed. "Call me when you can't take it any longer."

He leaves me to my misery. And misery it is. I roll around on the bed for hours, sweating, pains in my arms and legs, my stomach aching, my muscles all jerking. I fight for as long as I can before calling for Vasily.

He sits on the bed beside me and feeds me some tea.

"Give in, Eve," he says. "There's nothing else you can do. It'll only get worse."

"He ruined my life," I say, tears of frustration running down my cheeks.

"No, he saved it. He saved you from Soren. He saved it again yesterday."

"Only after he put it in danger."

"You offered yourself to him."

"Because I had no choice," I say. "It was him or Soren. Or every damn vampire in the county."

"You're right, of course, but he had no choice either. He could leave you to Soren, or other vampires, or take you himself and at least protect you."

I can't argue any longer. My nightgown's soaked with perspiration. My gut feels like I have burning coals inside. I roll over on my side and bring my knees up to my chin.

"Oh, God, tell him to come."

He's there in a second, taking me into his arms, his wrist already open to provide me with blood. At that point, I don't care any more what I'm doing. I only need for the pain to stop. I know what it means to be an addict going through withdrawal and it's pure hell. I swallow a mouthful and then two, the taste so sweet and almost immediately, the pain ebbs, the anxiety and fear dissipating. My body feels better, my hands stop shaking, but I cry.

I weep and Michel wraps his arms around me even more tightly. I can't last twenty-four hours without drinking his blood.

"Just kill me now," I say.

"Don't talk like that."

"I mean it. What's the difference between what I am and a vampire? Nothing."

"No," he says. "You aren't a vampire. You won't die if you don't get blood. You don't need much – just a few mouthfuls. You can walk in the sunlight. You're not damned."

"How will I ever leave you?"

"What do you mean?"

"If I can't go a day without your blood, how can I ever have my own life? Do I have to drink it from you directly? Can you put it in a vial and bring it to me?"

"Why would you want to do that?"

"In case I need to be away from you for longer than a day. It might happen."

"Not if I can help it."

"Michel," I say and shake my head in frustration. "There will be times when I can't be with you. What will happen then?"

He closes his eyes as if deciding whether to tell me. "It's not just my blood," he says finally. "Any vampire will do. Mine's just more potent. You need less of it."

I lie in the darkness for a while with his arms around me, trying to get my mind around it. Finally, I sit up and face him, wiping my eyes.

"So, Julien's will do? Any vampire? Will Soren still take me, even if I'm addicted?"

"In a heartbeat," he says, his voice almost a whisper. "You'd be even more desirable."

"Why?"

He shakes his head. "The connection. It's one thing for us to know how a mortal feels, what they think, have access to their memories. It's another for you to know us. Feel our emotions. He'd guard you like a treasure, just as I will."

"Why hasn't he taken me yet?"

"He wanted me to have you, for Julien to have you, and for both Julien and I to be his creatures. You were the bait used to ensnare us both. He has us where he wants us now."

That makes me feel somewhat better. It will make me more desirable. I'll still be able to get close to Soren – close enough to kill him. Thing is, how?

I'm done with feeling sorry for myself. I wipe my eyes.

"Tell me how I can kill him."

He rubs his forehead for a moment, and then looks at me.

"Eve, you don't want to do this. It'll be very dangerous to go to him. Besides, if you drink his blood, you'll be at risk because for at least twenty-four hours, his blood would be inside of you. You could be destroyed when he is."

"Tell me how. I don't care what happens to me as long as he dies. How does this nanotech solution work?"

He sighs. "It's like an infection, except it's not an organism. Molecular machines meant to deliver a poison. You need to infect him in some way – get it into his lungs or into his blood."

"So if I were to ingest this nanosolution, and he drank my blood…"

"I won't let you go." His voice is firm. "I'm not letting you commit suicide. There are others willing to fight him. Besides, the Council's plans are for more than just Soren. He's only one of a group who share his goal. You could kill him, but someone would step up to take his place."

"I only care about him," I say and cross my arms. "Others can kill the rest of them."

"The Council will be unlikely to approve a move against Soren alone. It would alert them to our plans."

"I want the chance to make the offer," I say.

"I won't let you," he says, his voice pained. "I didn't become this monster so you could commit suicide."

I turn away.

"Then you can leave. Is there any reason why Vasily can't bring me your blood in a vial when I need it tomorrow?"

He shakes his head and goes to the door.

"Consider yourself a prisoner, then."

He closes the door, and I hear the lock click.

# CHAPTER 24

" *B* etter a cruel truth than a comfortable delusion".

Edward Abbe

THE NEXT DAY PASSES SLOWLY and I prepare to fight – and win – a battle of wills with Michel. I don't expect to see or hear from him during the day, but I do expect he'll show up and try to talk some sense into me in the evening. I'll be prepared with a counter argument.

Vasily tends to me, bringing me my meals on a tray now that I'm a prisoner of my own bedroom. He doesn't say much to me, but I can feel his disapproval. Finally, I decide to confront him.

"You think I'm wrong," I say as he pours me a cup of tea later in the afternoon.

"I understand you want Soren dead," he says. "We all do. Council is already planning to destroy him and others who are part of Black-stone. This is why Michel accepted this. You should be thankful you have Michel taking care of you."

"How can you say that? He almost killed me. Now, I'm no better than an addict."

"You offered yourself to him," he says, stirring sugar into my cup. "Soren would have done it immediately. Luke as well. There are only a few who are as honorable as Michel. And Julien." He places the cup on my tray. "I wish you'd open your eyes to what you have. It's far better than anything you would have outside these walls and outside of their domain."

"Their domain? You talk about them as if they are gods."

Vasily doesn't respond.

"You really think Michel didn't do this on purpose?"

Vasily frowns at me. "Of course not. You don't know him the way I do. He didn't want this for you at all. He feels terrible that he almost killed you. I know he deeply regrets what happened, but you're very lucky to be in his care. In *their* care."

"You can't understand," I say, unwilling to admit that what he said might be true. "All of these vampires should have just left us alone. I would have had a real life with my mother and father instead of the hell I did have."

"You were fated to this Eve, from the moment you were conceived. Make no mistake about it," he says and sits on the chair by the door. "There's only so many ways to escape your destiny. You were lucky that fate brought you together with Michel and Julien instead of letting you get caught up by others. You were meant to play music, not fight vampires and that's why he lost your file. When you found manuscript, it changed everything. He tried to wipe your memory, send you back into obscurity, but it didn't work. Events thwarted his plans."

"You know what they say – the road to hell is paved with good intentions."

Vasily shakes his head. "I wish you understood how lucky you really are but you're very young. One day you will understand and then you will kneel down to Michel and thank him. Thank Julien."

"I'll never kneel down to anyone," I say with contempt. "Michel and Julien included. I don't believe in kings or gods. Or fallen angels."

"Famous last words?" He folds his arms, a patronizing expression on his face.

I turn to my meal without further argument. What was the use? Vasily obviously admires Michel and Julien. I eat in silence, hoping that Vasily will get up and leave, but he doesn't. Finally, I put my fork down.

"It's not that I don't think they're better than the others. But try to understand – I'm pretty much enslaved to Michel now, aren't I? Or at least one of them." I hold my hand out. It's already starting to tremble, the familiar tension building in my body. The food no longer appeals. "I'm an addict. Nothing more."

"You," he says and comes to me, taking the tray away. "You are a rare gem. You've already been able to block Michel, despite his own very great powers. If Soren got hold of you…"

So I *have* been successful in blocking Michel. That thought gives me some comfort. I might be able to plan without worry about him knowing what I'm doing. What have I done to achieve this? Do I only need to will him out of my mind? Can I let him back in just as easily? I decide to try an experiment – later, when I really am in need of his blood, I'll call his name in my mind and see if he responds. It will be good to know for when – *when* – I go to kill Soren.

"What if Soren got hold of me?"

He stops at the door, tray in hand. "It's not for me to tell you. Talk to Michel." He opens the door. "I expect you'll be needing to feed soon and can ask him then. Like I said, is not my role to tell you these things."

"He won't tell me either," I say, rubbing my aching head. "You're both bastards."


I fight it as long as I can. After standing in the shower with the hot water blasting over me for nearly half an hour, my skin bright red on my shoulders and back, my tears mixed with the water as I weep in despair at my fate. Finally, I towel off and put on a clean nightgown, creeping into bed.

I turn over and roll up in a ball, my wet hair covering my face, my stomach in knots, my muscles aching. I try to do some deep breathing to calm myself, but it's only a momentary distraction from the pain. Then, I try my experiment. I think of him, imagine opening up to him.

*Michel, I need you.*

There's no response from him – neither in my own mind nor does he come to me. Perhaps he's playing a game of psychic chicken with me as well, trying to force me to bend to his will. I hate him for it.

*Michel!*

Nothing. I have this sense that he's resisting me. He can hear me – I'm sure of it. He wants to teach me a lesson. I know what Vasily says was probably true – that Michel wanted me to escape this fate, but I can't help but feel he's just as happy to have me as his little blood slave as not. That makes me choke up in anger, this feeling of helplessness. This sense of being trapped, having no escape.

I feel like throwing myself out of a window, and contemplate just that. I roll over, staring at the far window, wondering if it will open. I imagine the plunge, relishing the pain of impact – at least it will end this agony.

The door flies open and I wait to see what he'll do. Has be brought me a vial of his blood as I demanded? I try to resist turning to him out of need, I try to resist this terrible desire for his blood, digging my fingernails into my palms, the pain barely even registering.

"You are so *stubborn*."

His voice comes from across the room and I finally turn to face him, unable any longer to stop myself from looking to see if he's brought his blood for me.

"Do you have it?" I say, my throat choking when I don't see it in his hands. "I told you to bring a vial of it."

He sits on a bench by the window, the moonlight flooding in and illuminating his wings, which are spread out behind him. His chest is bare and his hands rest on his knees like some Egyptian half-god half-angel seated on a throne.

"You're in no position to tell me to do anything," he says, his voice cool.

I cover my eyes, tears of sickness and frustration welling up despite my best intentions to be strong. I say nothing, trying to avoid him as long as I can.

*I hate you I hate you I hate you I hate you…*

I toss on the bed, gritting my teeth, my hands shaking so badly that I can barely push myself up.

"Are you going to make me come to you?"

"Yes."

"Why?" I say, barely able to stand. I have to grip onto the post at the foot of the bed for support, my knees are so wobbly. "Just to torture me?"

"Because I can."

I struggle to walk across the floor to the window, holding on to the chest of drawers for a moment to control my dizziness.

"Just to show me how powerful you are? Like a pimp and his junkie prostitute?"

"To teach you some humility."

"Humility?" I say, my fists clenching. "By humiliating me?"

In the moonlight he looks so damn desirable, the silvery light caressing his bare skin, highlighting his cheekbones and lips. He's truly beautiful – it hurts just to look at him. I hate that I need him.

Finally, I stand in front of him on unsteady legs. "Your wrist?"

He shakes his head and then reaches up and runs a fingernail along the skin on his chest over his heart. A thin dark line forms, and blood drips from the wound. "Here. Where you stabbed me that day."

"You're a bastard," I say, my voice breaking. He says nothing, just sits there like some god waiting for his slave to swear obedience. "You want me to kneel?" I say as I crouch down on my hands and knees, barely able to keep my balance. "Then I'll kneel. Don't expect me to call you my god."

I creep the rest of the way, tears of anger and frustration – and need – on my cheeks. Then I crawl up into his lap, my arms around him, and press my mouth against his wound, gasping in relief when I taste the blood, but crying as well. I have to lick the dried blood to get any, and it isn't nearly enough to quell the sickness in my body and mind.

"It's stopped," I say, frantic. "I need more."

"Suck."

I stare up into his face. "I hate you."

"You already said that."

I pull away and glare at him through my tears. "I won't forgive you for this."

"Yes, you will," he says. He leans his head back and closes his eyes, a look of sadness on his face. "Because one day, you'll use this to kill Soren."

I can barely believe what I hear though the fog of pain.

"You're going to let me?"

He hesitates, as if it hurts to say.

"Yes."

I lean in and suck the wound, and soon fresh blood flows again, just a small trickle onto my tongue and into my mouth. When I swallow, the relief is immediate. The pain and sickness flees, draining out of me as Michel's blood drains into me. I soon lose myself in the taste of it, the feel of it, the blessed relief of it – of his skin against my mouth, under my hands, his body pressed against me. Bliss fills me, and all the anger, resentment, and frustration vanishes. I no longer know where I end and he begins, and finally, when I've had enough, I pull away and release him, slipping out of his lap, between his thighs, and onto the floor, lying on my side, satiated.

He picks me up and carries me to the bed, then lies down beside me, his arms wrapping around me, his body spooning against mine. We connect, and I don't care what happened before or what will happen in the future. The experience of his blood in my body, his mind meeting mine, his emotions feeding mine, of our bodies joined through shared blood and touch overwhelms everything that I felt just moments earlier. I know without words his true regret for what happened. He fears this fate even though it gives him the most solace he's felt for eight hundred years. He did everything to prevent it and would have stopped it if he could go back in time.

There is no going back in time. He undresses me and I him, and we roll around on the bed, wrapped in each other's arms, drowning in each other's senses. His mouth is on me, mine on him, the sheets caught up around us. I forgive him.

We lie together, recovering, and while his passions calm, his mind won't leave me, and I feel him probing my memories, searching for something – what it is I can't tell – but the search is determined, focused. He lingers over certain memories and feels my emotions as I re-experience them. I realize he's reliving everything that happened between Julien and me, searching for how I feel about him.

"Stop," I say. "I love you."

"You said you could love him as well."

"I said I *could*. I didn't say that I loved him. And that was only because I thought I might never see you again."

"I don't want you even looking at him."

"You're so jealous," I say, smiling, tucking his hair behind his ear. "But you don't have to be. He was a substitute for you. I fought letting him be that, but in the end, I was so lonely for you."

"I am as jealous as ten jealous men, Eve. You have to understand that. I feel as if I have to banish him from my life now."

"Don't you *dare*," I say. "He loves you. You love him. You've had each other for eight hundred years."

"I don't want you in the same room with him. I don't want you ever to be alone with him."

"Michel!" I take his face in my hands. "I love *you. Period.*"

"You fucked him and you enjoyed it."

I shake my head in exasperation.

"If I could take it back, I would."

He sighs and pulls me back into his embrace.

Then, he starts searching my past life by stimulating my memories.

Happy scenes of my childhood in our cottage west of St. David's in Pembrokeshire on the southwest coast of Wales, the warmth of the large kitchen with the bright yellow curtains at the window over-looking a spray of wildflowers in the garden and beyond it the ocean. The smell of baking bread in the old cooker stove my mother rescued and refurbished at great expense, the heat of the wood stove on my face and hands after playing in the surf. The scent of salt water in the wind as I play along the rocky shore, the seabirds wheeling in the sky above me, diving down in a circuit for the bits of bread I throw to them.

The clear crisp starlit nights when my father took me out to watch the meteor showers, lying on our backs on sleeping bags, oohing and ahhing as the meteors burned across the heavens. Watching the moon through binoculars, joking that it looked like it was made of blue cheese not Swiss, and then later, seeing Saturn through our backyard telescope and taking a long-exposure photograph with our new camera. Hours of piano lessons spent alone in the quiet study, surrounded by floor-to-ceiling shelves of books and family photographs, practicing arpeggios and scales till my fingers hurt.

Then, the trip to Hungary, the narrow streets and limited horizon such a change from the wide-open spaces of the Pembrokeshire coast. Dirty old buildings, the cobblestone streets of the old market square, the babble of an incomprehensible language surrounding me. The crisp white blouse and woolen skirt of my uniform, my mother patiently braiding my long fair hair into coils on my head as was the local fashion among girls of my age. To the one memory I want to deny – Boston, the university, my mother's death. I try to shut him out and he rises up and looks at my face.

"Don't shut me out," he says, his voice thick with emotion.

"Not there," I say, covering my eyes.

His voice pleads.

"I won't go back there, I promise. Just let me in."

I close my eyes and think about him, welcoming him in. It works immediately, and I feel him enter my consciousness as if a wind has blown in through an open window. He begins searching through my memories, and settles on one from before my mother died. I was seated in a salon in Prague just before we moved back to Boston, playing the piano surrounded by my father's friends and some prospective teachers. The huge room has high ceilings and windows, the walls covered in gilded paper and full-sized portraits of eighteenth century lords and ladies. I play on an old grand and those gathered to judge me sit and listen, assessing my skill, my touch, my interpretation of the music. I play a theme from a Beethoven concerto and there are tears in my father's eyes. I'm so happy, pleased that my father's proud of me. I crave his approval and work diligently in order to get it, performing to his standards so I'll get more attention.

Michel moves on, searching for more memories. One from a few years earlier in Wales in which I lie on the couch beside my mother, sick with a cold, my throat aching, my nose plugged. I'm happy though, because she's stroking me, smoothing my hair, my head in her lap. I'm perfectly content to be home from school watching cartoons on television while she reads a book.

Another memory of walking home from school in London with my babysitter. Rain falls and I stop to explore the streams and puddles formed along the gutters, the tiny rivers carrying leaves and twigs along to the drains. We make a boat out of a piece of paper from my backpack and I kneel, umbrella over my head, and watch it float along on the water's surface to the drain, spinning in a circle as it reaches the larger puddle.

Christmas in Boston, attending the cathedral in the city for Mass, the incense, the stained glass, the priest in his colorful vestments, the murmur of the congregation repeating the litany. I enter the church, dipping my fingers in the font, genuflecting at the side of the pew, the wooden bench hard against my bony knees, enjoying the sense of awe I felt being in such a holy place.

It's the last time I go into a church except for her mass and the last time I felt any connection to a god. The next day my mother dies in front of me, gasping from a bite wound on her neck, bright red arterial froth foaming at the wound, dripping from her mouth as I lean over her and try to stem it.

*Stop!* Grief overwhelms me and I shut him out, covering my eyes, the memory far too real, the emotions too intense.

"I'm sorry." He takes me in his arms. "I didn't try to go there," he says. "You went there."

"No I didn't," I say and wipe my eyes. "Why do you want to go there?"

"I don't. You keep thinking of that day as if you really want to go back, but you're afraid to do it alone."

I don't reply, just lie there with his arms around me. Like before, bits of him seep through when he can't hold it back and I understand the great loneliness the vampires feel as immortals, my heart breaking at their despair at ever getting back what they'd lost. Only in these brief moments when they connect with a mortal and even more so with an Adept can they begin to feel as they once did. Human. I have to forgive him because this bliss of union is almost too much for a human to bear. It will be mine for as long as I want it – until it's time for me to leave and kill Soren.

# CHAPTER 25

"We know the truth, not only by reason, but also by the heart."

Pascal

"I WANT TO MEET WITH SOMEONE IN THE COUNCIL," I say the next evening, after the sun sets and Michel comes to me.

"We'll talk of that later," he says, sitting on the sofa in the library, opening his arms to me. "Come, feed."

"I'm fine," I reply and pace the floor in front of the window. "I've been thinking all day. Soren will have to think you and I have parted. We'll have to either break up or I'll have to be taken from you somehow."

"Yes. Now, come here," he says again, patting his lap. "Don't wait until you're sick. Have some now and you'll be good all night. You can feed again before dawn and then you'll be good all day."

He holds his hand out to me, as if impatient to have me comply. I stop and consider his offer.

"If I feed more often, is there any chance that I'll become more addicted?"

"You'll get used to taking less, but more often. To change the schedule would mean you'd be uncomfortable for a while, but no, you won't become more addicted. At least, not physically."

"But mentally? That's possible?"

"Anything's possible, Eve. But not likely. You're too strong."

I step closer, not yet convinced I need to feed yet. "You're not going to make me do the crawl on my knees thing again, are you?"

"Not unless you want to." He smiles, just a quirk on one side of his mouth.

"I'm not into the worship scene. I'm an atheist."

He tilts his head to one side. "Still don't believe in God?"

"Why would I? There's no evidence. I tend to need evidence before I accept something is real." I step a bit closer, enjoying just looking at him sitting there bare-chested. Behind him, his wings are unfurled. The place where I'd fed the previous night has healed.

"What evidence would you accept?"

I take another step in front of him, considering the question only half-seriously.

"A very powerful smite of some kind, I suppose. Maybe a big booming voice from the heavens saying 'I am the I am.'" I grin and he smiles back, shaking his head.

"Even those could be manufactured."

"I was joking."

"I wasn't," he says and pats his knee. "Come."

"I see you haven't brought me a vial of your blood again."

I sit on his lap, my arms slipping around his neck. He looks in my eyes.

"There will be no vials of blood between us."

"You like it when I feed off your body." When I say it, desire surges through me, surprising me with its intensity.

"So do you," he says, his voice dropping to a lower register. "I guarantee drinking blood out of a vial would be a pale substitute for the real thing." He brushes my hair away from my neck and when he licks the skin over the original wound Julien made and over which he bit me, I feel a jolt of desire. It's healed quite well – faster than normal, but there's still a pair of marks where he bit me.

"I need something as well," he says.

I stiffen and pull away.

"Do you think it's wise? Am I well enough to lose more blood?"

"Yes," he says, lowering the strap of my nightgown to expose my shoulder and breast. "You've recovered. You have my blood in you. You'll heal much more quickly and replace your blood volume more rapidly than normal."

His words don't calm my fears.

"Don't you have some donor blood? I don't know if I feel right about this…"

I try to stand, but he stops me.

"Don't be afraid," he says. "What happened the other night won't happen again. I promise you."

I hold a hand over the wound on my neck, unsure.

"How do I know that Soren hasn't compelled you to kill me to punish you?"

"That's not his endgame."

"What is?"

He shakes his head. "Don't ask me what you know I won't tell you, Eve."

Then, my anxiety decreases and I relax, heaving a sigh, but it happens too quickly to be of my own accord. Michel's trying to calm me using his powers so he can feed on me. I block him, shutting him out immediately so that I no longer feel his mind at the edges of my consciousness.

"Don't do that," I say and try once more to stand up. "Don't manipulate me."

"Don't shut me out." For a moment, we just stare each other down. "Eve," he says, pulling me closer, his greater strength easily overcoming my paltry resistance. "You're mine. This is what we do."

I cover my eyes. "I'm not yours. I'm my own."

"So stubborn," he says. "Tell me you don't want me and I'll let you go."

I hit his chest lightly playfully.

"I do want you, but have you ever heard about a thing called equality?"

"We're not equal," he says softly. "Pretending that it's so is, I would think, unscientific."

"Pretending it's so is necessary for this to work," I say and lean in, pressing my cheek against his. "I'm human in that way, I guess." I pull back. "I may not be as powerful as you, or as old, or as wise, but I have just as much right as a sapient being to determine my own wants and desires."

"I know your wants and desires, Eve. Besides, those who have power have the right to take what they desire," he says.

"Might makes right?" Sadness fills me that he can make such a bald assertion. "Might may win, but do you really want to force me?"

"Of course not. I want you to offer yourself willingly as I've said from the start. I'm not a monster. But I know you want this just as I do. Because of your past, you feel this need to fight everything, to reassure yourself that you have power. It's to make up for all those times when you didn't have power."

"Don't remind me."

"Don't you see? That's what your resistance is about. In resisting, you only deprive yourself of what you really want. Being with me is what you really want. Being my Adept is what you really want. It's Fate."

"I don't believe in Fate."

"Nevertheless, like vampires and fallen angels, Fate exists in spite of your refusal to believe. All of us tread a very fine line, trying to influence Fate. She only listens so much, and in the end she has her way despite our best efforts. Just give in."

"Give in to you."

"Yes," he says and closes his eyes. "Give in to me. Acknowledge that this is your fate and your desire and you'll be happy. Finally, you'll be happy."

Emotion wells up inside me. "I can't," I say, my voice breaking.

"You can't what? Be happy?"

"I can't surrender."

"Eve," he says and runs his fingers through my hair. "Wasn't last night good?"

I shake my head. "It was beyond good. It was," I say, struggling with words to describe it. "Bliss."

"Yes, it was." He cups my cheek. "Take the bliss. You deserve it. You've suffered so much pain."

"It scares me," I say, remembering. "I feel as if I'll lose myself. Be consumed. Disappear."

He nods. "I understand. I promise you that you won't." He bends down and kisses the curve of my breast. "If anything, you'll come out stronger."

"Why?"

He runs his hands down my back.

"You'll understand what's important."

He kisses me, and I let him. There's no connection between us and I enjoy the feel of his lips against mine, his tongue touching mine, his arms around me – a separate being experiencing my own emotions and senses. I can almost feel him trying to get in and I know that unlike me, he feels that lack of connection as a painful reminder of his loneliness rather than a sweet pleasure. I want to delay the connection so I can just enjoy as my own desire grows.

He needs to feel my response to his touch – his own desire isn't enough. For him, it feels empty, disconnected. Incomplete. So I let him in.

He trembles as our senses join and for a moment, the wave of desire from him overwhelms me. He pulls his lips away from mine and, with his eyes still closed, he tilts his head to the side and runs his fingernail along the skin beneath his ear, opening up a seam from which his blood flows. I lean down and cover it with my mouth, sucking, his response so strong that my body convulses with pleasure. Coupled with the rush from his blood, I barely needed his touch between my thighs to climax, my body shuddering as he bites my neck and drinks from me.

He lies me back on the sofa and this time, he pulls his mouth away, no longer drinking, having taken only a mouthful. Just enough for the connection between us to deepen, growing stronger as his desire builds until the world falls away and there's only pleasure too sweet to endure.


Michel agrees to let me meet with someone from the Council a few days later. He isn't happy that we're leaving the warehouse and it's only using an armed escort that I'm allowed out. He spends a very long time with me that night after I feed, our arms and legs entwined.

"I hate this," he says, running his fingers over my lips. "To find you, to claim you, and then to have you leave me."

"I'm not leaving you," I say and kiss his neck. "I'm going to kill Soren. It has nothing to do with leaving you. When this is all over, I'll come back."

"With Soren dead, there'll be big changes here. There'll be a turf war over who'll replace him among his coven. I'm thinking of relocating. Maybe leave this place. If you could go anywhere in the world, where would you want to go?"

I sigh, thinking of the places I've been before in my life.

"Somewhere by the ocean," I say without hesitation. "Maybe it's just in my blood. The sea."

He studies my face for a moment with an expression of resignation.

"Things are going to happen that will shock you," he says and strokes my cheek. "Since I agreed to let you try to fight Soren, I've been planning with my remaining contacts in the Council, trying to arrange things, letting certain information slip. Just follow your instincts. You and I will have to part for a time, but Soren won't deny you when he takes you. Just don't fight him and he'll be only too glad to keep you as his pet."

"Can't you tell me what the plan is?"

He shakes his head.

"Just know that you'll be taken from me. It will look like an ambush. You'll become Soren's possession – there's no way that he won't take you as his own given the chance. When the time comes you'll be given what you need to kill him."

"Why didn't he take me before?"

"Don't worry about that," he says. "He'll take you now. The less you know about this, the better, so that's all I can say."

I nod, the solemnity of his voice making me fearful. The prospect of killing Soren doesn't seem so appealing all of a sudden. I pull Michel closer, emotion choking me at the thought I'll be taken away from him soon.

"You agree that this is the way to proceed? Your friends in the Council do as well?"

"There'll be someone to replace him when he's destroyed, but this way we'll have an advantage. He's the most powerful of us now, and as leader of this gambit, without him, there's no one strong enough among his coven to take over and follow through. Just me and Julien. No one strong enough to challenge us. But the plan won't involve your death," he says, and brushes my hair away from my face. "I'll only agree to this if it means you're to survive and come back to me."

I kiss him, my arms tightening around him. There's no bliss for us that evening. Only sadness at the prospect we'd soon part.


Despite my growing ambivalence about leaving on this mission, I'm happy to walk the streets of my old neighborhood, past the bakery directly beneath my apartment where I buy black rye and crusty Italian loaf and the butcher a few rows down where I purchase pickles and ripe olives when I lived there. I bought most of my groceries at a small fruit and vegetable shop that sells fresh flowers.

Seeing the familiar landmarks drives home how much my life has changed in such a short period of time. We stop at my apartment so I can run in and check on my cats. Vasily arranged for somenone to come by and feed them but they've been alone all this time. Michel comes in with me and walks around the room, and it reminds me of that day back in time when all this was brand new. Such a short time, but it seems a lifetime ago. He does the same visual tour of the apartment, picking up my possessions and smiling. He holds up a plastic Nemo fish I keep by my kitchen sink.

"A toy?"

I laugh and pour fresh kibble in the cat bowls. "I had a clownfish once and was very fond of it. When the movie came out I had to get one as a reminder." I spend a few moments giving the cats attention while Michel inspects my bookshelf, picking up my texts and flipping through the pages. I wash out the water dishes and fill them, then look around the tiny apartment. What a difference from the warehouse or mansion. The kitchenette in my apartment is the size of that in an RV. The shower isn't much bigger. But it was home once and I feel a sense of melancholia for my past life. The world seemed so full of promise to me then. I thought I'd actually have a normal life once upon a time, despite my horrible adolescence. Now? I'm not sure how long I'll even live. This is war. My mother died in the cause.

I lock the apartment up, sad that I won't be staying there with the cats.

"Tell me how I'll know what to do."

"You will just know. Someone will contact you and you'll know."

"Is that all you can tell me or all you will tell me?"

Michel places his hand behind my back and ushers me into the vehicle, then sits beside me, one arm around me on the back of the seat.

"Eve, I tell you what I think you need to know, and nothing more. It's strategically important that you not know some things. All you have to know is that there is a plan in place. You'll know what to do when the time comes."

I nod and watch as Michel's guards return from their posts at the front and back doors of my apartment. One stands outside our vehicle with his hand on a weapon at his hip like the Secret Service.

We drive farther south towards the docks. The vehicle slows and I look out the front window to see a traffic jam ahead, the flashing lights of a fire truck in the middle of the street.

"Looks like a fire of some sort," I say.

Michel doesn't look up. He takes my face in his hands.

"Eve, I love you." He kisses me, his emotions washing over me, bringing tears to my eyes. "Don't forget that." He reaches into a pocket and takes out a tiny glass ampoule and breaks the tip off it. Inside is a clear liquid. "Drink this."

I take it from him and examine it. "What is it?"

"It's to make you forget." He pulls me closer.

"Forget what?"

"That this happened – this plan and whatever you know about it. I can't let Soren know you're part of a plan to kill him or he'll kill you."

"If you think that's necessary. I could block him out."

"Not good enough – he may use something on you to force you to reveal information. I can't take the chance. Just drink it. Now."

The urgency in his voice makes me comply and I nod and take in a deep breath, swallowing it down, the bitter taste making me squint.

"Oh God," I say and grimace. "That's terrible, whatever it is."

"You're so brave." He buries his face in my hair, his mouth on my neck. "Whatever happens," he says, his lips at my ear. "Remember that I love you." He pulls his small crucifix over his head. "This is for you," he says and slips it over my head. I examine the crucifix.

"It's beautiful." I look up at him. "It's Marguerite's."

He nods. "It's very old." He holds my face in his hands. "Eve, when you look at the cross, you'll remember that the vampire who gave it to you loved you."

"I'll remember," I say. I smile at him and he makes a sound deep in his throat and kisses my cheeks, his tongue touching each dimple, one after the other.

"I love you," he says.

"You said that already," I say and smile. "Three times."

Then an explosion rocks the car.

"What happened?" I crane my head to look, but Michel takes hold of my face and makes me look in his eyes.

"Tell me you love me."

I smile. "Of course I do."

"Say it."

I kiss him. "I love you, Michel."

He kisses me back, deeply. Then he brushes my hair off my cheek.

"That should start to make you feel a bit dizzy."

As if on cue, I do start to feel a bit strange. The world spins for a second. The last thing I see is Michel's face, his clear blue eyes filled with tears as he lays me down on the seat.

"I'm so sorry…" he says, "…but I can't let you go to him."

Another explosion down the street rocks the car again with its shockwave, this time more intense. Michel wraps his arms around me, covering me with his body. Over his shoulder I see a huge black cloud of smoke and fire coming towards us.

And then, darkness.

# CHAPTER 26

"The first magic of love is our ignorance that it can ever end."

Disraeli

*Ipswich Medical Clinic, Two Months Later*

I BLINK WHEN THE LIGHTS FLICK BACK ON, my head throbbing as if someone hit it with a rubber mallet. I'm sitting in an examination room, dressed in a paper robe, paper slippers on my feet.

"Do the bright lights still bother you?"

I nod.

"You need to wear sunglasses whenever the sun's shining. The headaches will go away soon. The explosion caused quite a concussion."

"Will my memories ever come back?"

The doctor shakes his head.

"Some will never come back. The brain swelling caused some

permanent damage. Others will return. Give yourself time. You're lucky to be alive."

The doctor leads me back to his office in a corner of the clinic. He has a television on, tuned to one of the local news channels.

As he writes in my file, I watch the news. It's been two months since the bombing in downtown Boston and the investigation's still ongoing. I just get so upset by it all, I can't watch. It's just too depressing.

"The case is still open," he says, glancing up at the television from his files.

I nod, feeling a catch in my throat. *My* case.

"Well, Eve, I've written you another prescription. You're getting your supply of tonic all right?"

"Yes," I say, remembering the thick black syrup I drink every day to help build up my blood.

"Good," he says. "Don't miss a dose or you'll feel really sick. If you have any problems, any new symptoms, just give my office a call."

"Thank you."

I take the prescription and go back to the dressing room and change back into my clothes. I step outside into the late afternoon sun and squint, slipping on my sunglasses. The fall has been unusually wet, with fewer days of sun than normal – right up until I needed it. With my extreme sensitivity to light, I hope the cloud cover will soon return.


My foster dad and mom are having a few friends over, trying to introduce me back into polite society, but I've got an excuse to avoid them. I'm setting up a camera down on the beach to take time-lapse photographs of the rise of the Milky Way and so after introductions, I escape. I can't stand the way they look at me as if I'm some kind of mental patient just because I have amnesia from the bombing.

I go to the beach below the cottage, carting my load of equipment. There's a shirtless man in the surf, a hand shading his eyes, looking out to the glittering ocean. I almost don't go down to the water because I don't want to intrude, but I brought my equipment and want to set up so I can do the shoot. This section of beach is the best because it's sheltered, with cliffs and dunes breaking the wind. I take a narrow passageway through the rocks that litter the coastline, descending on a path that's been worn down from years of use.

I walk along the beach, looking for a good spot to set up my tripod, keeping as far from him as possible. I stop near a flat rock where I put down my camera case and equipment. I stand gazing out across Ipswich Bay and then take out the tripod, struggling to get it set up in the sand. When I'm busy fighting the bolt to lock the tripod into place, the man I saw in the surf comes to my side, his pale skin glistening wet in the last rays of sun.

The first thing I notice, other than he's completely gorgeous with black hair and incredible blue eyes, is that he's so pale. Unnaturally pale, and I think he must be ill. Maybe terminal.

"Hello," he says. "Can I help you with that? You look like you're having trouble." He has this soft French accent that sounds more continental than Cajun.

I smile, and step back from the tripod, my cheeks burning.

"I didn't realize my mechanical ineptitude was so obvious. I think the bolt was screwed on a bit too tight and now I can't unlock it."

"I've seen you here before," he says as he bends down to examine the tripod. "You come to this beach a lot. I'm Michel," he says and then holds out a hand. He pronounces it Mee-*shell* like a proper French-man. "I'm staying just up the coast a bit."

I look at his hand, surprised at the formality. People don't usually shake hands but maybe it's some French thing.

"Eve," I manage and he holds my hand in both of his for a bit too long. I try to pull my hand away, and finally, he releases it.

When he turns back to the tripod, I noticed strange marks stretching from one shoulder to the other, browny red like a tattoo but raised like a scar, the marks resemble wings and I can't imagine what caused them. I think maybe it's some kind of kelp that attached to his skin while he was swimming and touch the marks, but they don't brush off.

He glances at me, squinting as if to gauge my response.

"It won't come off," he says. "It's part of me."

"I'm sorry," I say, embarrassed. Then I realize they must be scars – maybe burn marks – and sympathy fills me. He works away at the tripod and manages to get it set up.

"Thanks," I say. "You're a godsend."

"I wouldn't say that." He smiles and then picks up a flat stone from the sand and throws it out, skipping it across the surface of the water. "What are you taking pictures of?"

"I'm going to do some time-lapse photography. I saw this really great time lapse video that shows the Milky Way in Atacama Chile and I thought I'd give it a try," I say, "but given my lack of technical expertise, I think I'm probably a bit too ambitious."

"I saw that video on YouTube," he says. "Amazing. What we only can see using technology. It's there, but our light and time perception prevents us from seeing it."

I smile at him, glad to have found someone else who's interested in such things. I attach the camera and timer.

"I read up on it and the timer is set to take a twenty-second expo-sure with a 2 second pause between images."

"Are you an amateur astronomer?" he says, and I feel his eyes on me, watching me instead of the camera. When I glance up at him, I can't help but blush. God, his eyes are so blue. My heart does a little flip-flop because he's just so beautiful but for some reason, I feel incredibly sad when I look at him.

"No," I say. "I just saw the Hubble Ultra Deep Field Image one day in an old National Geographic at my doctor's office and I couldn't get it out of my mind. I started looking at YouTube videos of stars and saw the Atacama video. I'm recovering from an injury and have some time to kill. I thought I'd give it a try."

"You don't look injured."

"It was my brain," I say. "I was in a coma for a while and now I have memory loss."

"Permanent?"

"The memory loss is, but the brain swelling is down now so every-thing pretty much works."

"That's good."

That's the most I've said to anyone outside of my neurologist and my foster parents since I woke up in the ICU after the bombing.

He goes to his clothes, which are folded on the sand. Once he's dressed, and I have everything set up, I start the timer and we watch as it takes a few exposures.

"Keep your fingers crossed," I say.

He smiles at me, tilting his head to the side.

"You don't have faith?"

"Oh, no," I say. "Atheist. No faith in anything. Just trust in science. And good instructions."

"How long will it continue to take pictures?"

"A few hours."

"Would you like to go for a walk along the beach?"

I take in a breath. I don't know him from a hole in the ground but he seems nice enough and for some reason, I feel no threat from him. We walk along the beach in silence and I examine him from the corner of my eye – he's about a foot taller than me, his body well-muscled but not overly. His straight black hair is longish, beneath his chin and long down his neck. His blue eyes seem to shine with intelligence.

"So what are you doing in the little hamlet of Ipswich, Massachusetts?" I say, awkward with the silence.

"I have a cottage along the coast just about a mile from here. Come to get away from it all."

"What do you do for a living, if you don't mind me asking?"

"Private consulting, research, investigations."

"Sounds cryptic."

He laughs.

"Yes, very. Pointedly so."

"All right," I say, smiling. "I won't ask."

We round the point and I find an injured Gannet, its feathers still dark, a late season fledgling probably flown from the nesting colony in the cliffs in the distance. We kneel in the sand and I pick it up, concern for the young bird flooding through me, making my throat close. Still alive but clearly in pain, its wing hangs at an odd angle. It flops around, breathing heavily, gasping for breath. I hold it in my hands, but it falls limp and still. I can feel the moment it dies and blink away the tears that fill my vision, embarrassed to show emotion in front of a complete stranger.

He tilts my chin up and examines my face. "Not a single sparrow can fall to the ground without your Father knowing it."

I frown for I recognize the biblical reference. He lays his hand on my neck, his skin still cool and wrinkled from swimming, and I feel as if he's inside my mind probing my thoughts, the sensation so clear it feels like a violation. I pull away and avert my eyes for he shouldn't be touching me.

"Here," he says and takes the dead bird from me. "Let me."

He holds the small body in his hands, peers at it closely, then strokes its chest. Before my eyes, it moves and then starts to breathe once more. He rights it and pulls out its wing, straightening it with his hand. The wing folds up into perfect alignment. Then, he throws the young fledgling up into the air and off it flies.

I watch, my mouth gaping open. I turn to him.

"How did you do that?" I whisper, my voice barely registering.

"How do you think I did it?" he says, watching the bird fly off.

"Well, you're either magic or an angel," I say, "and since I don't believe in either, I must have been mistaken about it being dead."

He frowns. "Sad to be so cynical for one so young."

"I don't want to be cynical, but I have my reasons."

He stands and walks along the shore once again, picking up shells, holding them up, turning them over so that they glitter and gleam in the last rays of sunshine.

He holds a shell out. It's a dog whelk.

"*Nucella lapillus.*" He turns it over in his hand. "Look at the shape. Interesting isn't it? It's what's called a Logarithmic Spiral. Mathematics is coded in nature. Like a message to us."

"I don't believe in messages from God. And you didn't answer me."

"Adrenaline got its heart beating again."

"But how did you do it?"

He shrugs. "We all have our secrets."

He sits on the sand a few feet from the surf. I sit beside him.

"I was just wrong about it being dead," I say, not willing to concede any point about magic.

"You lost your faith when your mother died," he says. "It's a very common thing, but death and loss and pain don't mean there is no God."

"Are you a priest or something? How did you know about my mother?"

"I know a lot," he says. "And yes, I was a priest. A long time ago."

"What do you know?" I say, a panicky feeling growing inside of me. Is he someone from my past – the past I can't remember?

"Everything." He gets up and walks back towards the tripod. "And now, I have to go. I've probably already said too much, which is completely unlike me normally, but you've always had that effect on me."

"What do you mean?" I say but he doesn't stop. "Tell me how you know me."

He doesn't reply and I just stand by the tripod and watch him walk away, listening as the timer hums and clicks, recording the heavens as they whirl around us, invisible, inaccessible without these artificial eyes.

I wonder what the heck he is and how he knows everything about me.

I don't see him for a week and my little quiet life goes on as it has for the past month. I get up and eat on the patio, then walk the beach. I spend the afternoon playing music at Grant's music store or reading. My foster parents have no piano at the cottage and so I come to Grant's music store and play on an old baby grand in the back. Mr. Grant lets me, pleased to hear someone play with a modicum of talent. At dusk, I walk the beach again, and at night I gaze at stars. I sleep with the salt air in my nose.

One morning, he's swimming the beach again when I go down for a morning walk.

"Hello, Eve," he says, emerging from the waves and he's so attractive he looks like some god of beauty born in the foam like Venus. "I thought I'd find you here."

"Are you going to be cryptic again and get me all confused? Not tell me how you know me?"

"Probably," he says and grins, his smile lopsided. I can't help but smile back and he makes this little sound in his throat and closes his eyes for a moment. I see the strange marking again, and can't stop myself from asking about it.

"What is it?" I ask as he dries off, pointing to the mark on his back. "Is it a scar?"

"Of a kind, I suppose."

"What's it from?"

He pulls on his sweater.

"Does it matter?"

I'm silent for a few moments, fighting my desire to know, to understand. It's more important for me to have him as a friend so I shake my head.

"No."

"Good," he says. "I'd rather not talk about it. Let's just say that I did something that cost me far more than I anticipated."

I say nothing more about it. Instead, we walk along the beach and I look for the perfect shell to use for a little project I've been working on. I'm making jewelry for my foster mother's birthday, and want the perfect shell for a bracelet.

"What are you looking for?" he asks as I kneel down and pick up one after another empty shell.

"I thought you knew everything."

I glance up and he's grinning. I grin back and the smile falls from his face and it's replaced by something like need.

"Something for my foster mother," I say, glancing away from that naked expression, wondering if I'm misreading him. "I'm making her a present for her birthday."

He kneels down beside me and helps sort through the pile of bivalves and mollusk shells that have collected against a rocky outcropping on the beach. He holds one up – the white shell a smooth spiral, the lip of the shell a beautiful translucent pink nacre like that on a pearl oyster.

"Here," he says, holding it up in the sun so that it shines. "What about this one?"

"It's perfect," I whisper. "So beautiful."

He puts it in my hand and closes my fingers around it with his.

"Like you."

I look at his face, in his so-blue eyes, checking to see if he's teasing me, but he isn't smiling. I think he's going to lean in and kiss me, and he briefly moves closer. I close my eyes, waiting, but then he stops as if thinking better of it.

I open my eyes only to see him pull away, kicking myself mentally for being such a silly female, my cheeks hot.

We walk along the beach, and he finally speaks as if to break the awkward silence.

"How did your time lapse photography work out?"

"Other than clouds moving in at the end, great," I say, forcing a smile to hide my blush. "I'm using a video editor to put it together. Now I just have to choose the music."

"What are you thinking of using? For music?"

I shrug. "Something serene. I'm thinking Debussy. I've only just started playing again after the coma. Maybe *Reverie*."

"It's a beautiful piece," he says. "I'd like to see it when it's done."

I nod. "Sure."

"Would you like to look at stars tonight?" he says as we walk on a little further. "I have a nice telescope. We could set it up and take a few good long-exposure pictures. I've taken some of the Large Magellanic Cloud before that turned out pretty well."

I smile at him, glad we've moved beyond the silliness of a few moments ago.

"That sounds nice."

"Come down here once it's full dark. Say around 10:30."

The sun comes out and the brightness bothers me. A headache strikes out of the blue and I stop and rub my forehead, grimacing.

"Are you OK?" he takes my hand, squeezing. I frown, uncertain what I think about his forwardness. He's beautiful and nice but I only just met him.

I nod and pull my hand away, reaching into a pocket in my sweater to find my sunglasses.

"Just the injury," I say, slipping the sunglasses on. "I'm extremely light sensitive. It's a lot better now."

"What will you do when you recover fully?" he says, staring at me from under a frown. "Will you leave Ipswich?"

"Yes," I say, and we start walking again. "Probably go back to university. I'm in pre-med, just finishing my last year of my Bachelor of Science."

"And when you're done? What field of medicine?"

I shrug. "Probably do a PhD and do medical research," I say. "My mother did medical research."

He nods his head slowly.

"It's a way to keep her with you, I suppose."

"I barely remember her," I say. "She was murdered."

"Did they find her killer?"

I shake my head.

"No, it's still cold. Some freak who'd been stalking her, I guess."

He shakes his head, his face sad and we part, me taking the path up to the cottage and him walking the beach towards his own place.

I go back to the cottage and wonder what tonight will bring. I don't think I'm wrong to assume he's attracted to me and is seeking me out. It sends a little thrill to my belly.

# CHAPTER 27

"There are two tragedies in life. One is to lose your heart's desire. The other is to gain it."
George Bernard Shaw

I MEET HIM DOWN AT THE BEACH where he has a flashlight covered in a red sock and his telescope set up on a tripod.

"I was worried you wouldn't come," he says. He shows me the telescope, explaining how he's set it up so that it takes a series of long-exposure images of a nebula. Then he leads me to a large blanket that he's laid out on the grassy part of the beach closer to the cliffs. He sits down on the blanket and hands me a pair of binoculars.

"Take these," he says. "I have another set. You can see quite a bit of detail with them."

I join him and we lie on the blanket, binoculars in hand, the sound of the surf in the distance and crickets chirping in the long grass. We stare up at the stars and he tells me all about them, naming them, reciting their type and age and class as if he's reading directly from a text.

"That's Kepler's Nova," he says, pointing up into the sky towards the constellation of Ophiuchus. "It's a supernova remnant about twenty-thousand light years from us. The last supernova visible in our galaxy. That's Barnard's Star," he says, moving his hand to another star. "One of the closest stars to Earth. There's another supernova in the Southern Hemisphere, but we can't see it so far north. Eta Carina. It's already gone off, but we won't see the explosion for years. When we do, it'll light up the night sky in the south. It'll be something to witness. I plan to be there when its light finally arrives."

"How do you know it's gone off?"

He says nothing in reply, just points elsewhere in the sky and describes the nebula at the end of Orion's belt.

"Is astronomy one of your areas of research?"

He's silent for a while before answering. "No. I've just had a lot of time to study it and learn."

"You're not that much older than me," I say, my voice chiding.

He just smiles.

I watch him for a moment longer and then turn back to the sky, acutely aware of him lying next to me. I want so much just to take his hand and squeeze it, but I'm not going to repeat the earlier silliness.

He has a map and a flashlight covered in a red sock to protect our eyes. He points to the map to show me the path the space station takes over the earth's surface. After a while, he turns over on his side and watches me. It's strange for I've only now just realized I can see him perfectly in the darkness, his skin silvery gray, looking like a cemetery angel in the moonlight. Finally, he reaches out and runs his finger over my cheek and I wait but he doesn't kiss me. Instead, he keeps his fingers on my cheek, his touch cool and dry.

Part of me feels sad that he doesn't kiss me for something's been growing inside of me – a feeling that I want more from him than just walks on the beach, passing time in a comfortable silence, the stillness broken only when something of note comes up. I want him to lie on top of me and kiss me, my pulse quickening and my body warming at the thought. I wonder if I'll ever meet someone and fall in love. Then he pulls his hand away before rolling onto his back once more.

He sighs heavily and I turn back to the sky and the vast emptiness of space.

In about an hour, after he tells me all about the main stars and constellations, most of which I already know, it's time for me to leave. It's getting late, and he hasn't said anything or done anything to make me think he wants to kiss me or more.

I point up to the cottage. "I better get back. My parents go to bed early and I don't want to disrupt things."

"Thank you for joining me. I enjoyed having company for this. It's usually a very solitary pastime."

I smile and after a bit of an awkward moment, start up the path to the cottage.

We meet in town one afternoon at the music store. That Saturday Michel shows up, and I see his reflection in a picture against the wall. He stands silently behind me and listens to me play a Bach prelude, but his presence causes me to falter and I stop and turn to him.

"Don't stop because of me," he says and motioned for me to continue. "Play something. Play your most favorite piece. The one that breaks your heart."

I turn back and hold my hands over the keys but something stops me, for my most favorite piece is also the one that hurts the most. It's the one piece my father loved more than anything and I'd been learning it when my mother died. Playing it brings back so many memories.

Michel comes up behind me, bending over me, his cheek next to mine, his hands covering mine on the keyboard.

"Just play it," he says softly, his mouth next to my ear. "Even if it makes you sad. I want to feel what it's like to play so beautifully."

I take in a deep breath and play the first bars of the Chopin, *Ballade No. 1*. The opening starts slowly enough and he's able to keep his hands on mine, but as the piece grows more intense, the tempo rising, he can only keep his fingers touching the backs of my hands as they move across the keys. Then, during the slow movement, he's once more able to lay his fingers over mine. As I play, memories of the year before my mother's death and my time studying piano in Budapest fill me with melancholy.

"So beautiful," he whispers when I finish as far as I can go. I can feel his lips against my cheek as he speaks. "That alone makes all of this worth it."

I turn and his lips press against my neck, brushing my skin like the kiss I've been desiring.

"Worth what?" I say, closing my eyes, imagining his arms around me.

But he doesn't reply. Instead, he removes his hands from mine and leaves me sitting at the piano, trailing one hand over my shoulder as he walks away. He stops at the door, the knob in his hand.

"I have to go," he says, leaving without another word.


The weather turns rainy and cold as a storm system moves in. On Sunday, I don't see him down at the beach. Instead of meeting him as I expected, I walk the shore alone, dressed in a rain slicker and rubber boots, feeling like an exile. I think back to the other night watching stars, and the day we found the seashell, and how close he seemed to kissing me. How he didn't. Sadness wells up inside of me as I wander along the coast, cursing myself. I barely know him, but I want more than anything to kiss him – and more.

I climb on the boulders that lead up to the main road but slip on the slick surface of the rocks, my usual sure-footedness gone. I fall between two larger boulders, my ankle twisting as I land badly. I crack my face on one bolder and my lip instantly inflates, the blood dripping down from a cut to my bottom lip. I struggle out from the boulder and sit on the sand, holding my ankle, trying to staunch the flow of blood from my mouth with a sleeve. The rain drips down my face, and a thin bloody stream of it stains the sand on which I sit.

Hot tears sting the corners of my eyes. They aren't from the pain but from disappointment. Then, arms reach down and lift me and I crane my head to see who it is.

Michel, his face dark, a frown creasing his brow.

"What are you doing out here in this weather?" he says, his voice stern. His hair is soaked and his eyelashes clumped together. "Why are you climbing these rocks? It's too slippery."

He sits me on a boulder in the shelter of an overhang against one of the larger hills, its base worn away from the tides.

"I can look after myself," I say, pulling away from him, angry that he's treating me like a child.

"I know you can," he says and tilting my face up. "Me more than anyone," he says, examining my bloody lip. "Oh, *damn…*"

I see his face change as he leans closer, his eyes becoming red, his pupils dilating, and he kisses me, taking my bottom lip in his mouth and I swear he's after my blood, licking the blood from my cut, sucking my lip …

"What are you doing?" I gasp and try to pull away. There's blood on his lips, and he turns his back to me.

"Look at me!" I say but he shakes his head and holds his hand out, stopping me from coming around to look at his face.

When he grabs my hand, my fear evaporates and I just wait. In a moment, he turns back and he looks normal once more, except of course, for being very pale. He runs his fingers over my lip and the pain dissipates. Next, he bends down and removes my boot and sock, cradling my foot in his hands. As he holds my ankle, I touch my lip – the blood's gone, the swelling deflated, almost back to normal. His hands on my ankle feel soothing, and soon, the pain's gone. He twists my ankle back and forth, glancing up at me.

"Does it hurt this way?"

I shake my head.

"How about now?"

"No," I say. "It's better." I move my ankle in a circle but there's no pain. "How did you do that?"

He replaces my sock and boot and stands but doesn't answer.

"You really should know better than to climb among the rocks when it's raining. What's got into you?"

"I like the rain." I stand up, testing my weight on the ankle, unwilling to concede anything. "Why were you here?"

"Looking for you. I had a feeling you'd be out wandering around, nature girl that you are."

The rain starts to fall heavily, the wind whipping the drops against my face, soaking my hair beneath the hood.

"What *are* you?" I say, frowning.

"You should go home," he says, ignoring my question. "The weather's too bad to be out."

"Nonsense." I start walking the beach. "It's invigorating."

I glance back and he's still standing where he found me. I turn and keep walking, wondering if he'll follow me. *Hoping*.

He doesn't.

I want to return to him, but something stops me. I don't want to appear too interested in him. When I turn back again, he's nowhere to be seen.

Disappointment floods through me and I regret being so stubborn. I wonder what it is I saw when he turned away – why his eyes seemed so red. It must have been just my eyes blurring from the rain.

That night, I dream of him. It's a strange dream of him with my lip in his mouth, my blood on his lips. In my dream he's a vampire but one with huge black wings like some kind of fallen angel. He comes to me through an open window, lying with me on the bed in my room at the cottage, his arms wrapped around me, his wings covering us, his lips on my neck, and he's filling me up, lying between my thighs. I feel the short sharp pain as he bites me but the pleasure is so intense that I spasm in my sleep, waking up alone in bed. I reach up and feel my neck but there's nothing there and I think I'm such a freak that I dream about having sex with a vampire.

In the morning, I notice the marks on my neck, and stand at the mirror in the bathroom and lean in close to examine them. From a distance, they look like a couple of freckles, nothing more, but when I get my foster father's magnifying glass and look more closely, the edges are rough, like a bite. There are clearly teeth marks and then my blood feels as if it has turned to ice.

That wasn't a dream.

Is he a *vampire*? That's crazy…

How does he go out during the day?

Why does he have wings?


That afternoon, I find him on the beach, waiting for me in the shelter of an outcropping of rocks near the pathway.

He smiles when he sees me.

"There you are," he says, holding out a piece of beach glass. "Look what I found."

I'm in no mood to look at it.

"I have a bite mark on my neck."

His smile dies and he glances away. He throws the piece of beach glass in the water a few yards away.

I pull my long braid out of the way, arching my neck to the side.

He shrugs. "I don't see anything."

He's lying.

"You didn't even look." He knows about the mark because he put it there. I'm certain of it. "You bit me," I say plainly. "Last night. It's almost all healed. You're a vampire."

He leaves the shelter of the rock outcropping, walking along the surf, his strides long, fast enough to keep just ahead of me.

"You must have been dreaming."

"You *bit* me," I say again, hurrying to keep up. "I know it."

"You don't know what you're talking about."

That hurts and I quit following him.

"No," I say. "It's a bite." I dig my nails into my palms to control my emotions. "What are you? How can you be out in the daylight?"

"You're crazy."

I shake my head, tears springing to my eyes.

"I thought I was dreaming last night, but I wasn't. I'm not crazy."

He stops in his tracks and stands still for a moment. I see the tension drain out of him, his shoulders sagging.

"No you're not," he says, coming to where I stand. "I'm sorry," he whispers. "I didn't mean that." Then he lays his hand on my cheek. "You shouldn't be able to see that. I'm supposed to be able to make you forget when you dream, but it must not have worked." He shakes his head. "This is the second time I screwed up."

"Tell me how you know me," I say softly, looking in his eyes. "Tell me what you are. You can do things. You healed that bird. You healed me. When you touch me, you enter my mind."

He glances away, staring off across the sea. After a moment, he turns back and looks in my eyes. He touches my cheek again.

"Am I in danger from you?" I ask.

He closes his eyes. "I'd never hurt you."

I touch the bite mark. "But you bit me."

"I'm weak," he says, his voice filled with pain. Then he takes my face in his hands, his fingers tangling in my hair and he leans down and kisses me. His lips press mine apart, and the brief wetness as his tongue touches mine makes something surge inside of me. Without knowing I've done so, I slip my arms around his neck, pressing my body against him, and for a moment, the kiss intensifies and a jolt of desire spreads through me from my chest to my belly. I'm feeling his desire as well and it's so intense, I can barely breathe. Then he breaks the kiss and presses his forehead against mine.

"I never wanted you to ever have to know," he whispers. "I thought this time I could let you go for good, but I can't. I just *can't*."

Finally, he lets go of me and turns, walking to the pathway, scrambling up through the rocks to the field that leads back to the cottage.

I follow him but stop at the top of the path.

"Who am I to you?"

He stops as if considering. Finally, he steps closer still and touches my cheek with the backs of his fingers.

"We were lovers."

Disbelief floods through me, my knees feeling suddenly weak.

"Lovers?" I say, shaking my head. "I'd know if we were lovers…"

"No, you lost everything."

My mind's numb. I shake my head and step away from him, then I turn and start back towards the pathway to the cottage.

He follows me.

"Eve," he says when he reaches my side. "You don't have to fear me. I'd never hurt you."

"This is too much," I say and shake my head, holding my hand up to stop him.

He grabs my arm and when he touches me, my anxiety and fear dissipates. I just stand there, waiting, not feeling anything.

"Eve," he says. "I know you don't remember me, but we were lovers. I have photographs to prove it." He reaches into a pocket and removes a wallet. Inside are two small photographs. One is of me as a young girl, waiting in the wings before a recital, my hair up in a bun, my eyes unfocused. The other is a picture of me standing with his arms around me, my forehead pressed against his. It looks real enough, but I'm no fool.

"That's a manipulation for all I know."

"It's real," he says, sighing. "It was taken by a security camera in the warehouse where we lived for a while. Before the bombing."

"Look," I say. "I don't remember you. You could be anyone with a picture of me that's been manipulated telling me you and I were lovers. How can I know it's true if I have no memory? Even if you prove to me it's true, I don't remember!"

"Your foster parents will tell you. And when they do, and when you know the truth, you can come to me. My cottage is up on the cliff about a mile down towards Rockport Bay. 21 Oceanside Drive." He's silent for a moment. "You loved me, Eve. It was the last thing you said to me before the bomb."

Then he turns and walks away, leaving me standing there like a zombie, not knowing what to believe.

# CHAPTER 28

"The greatest happiness of life is our conviction that we are loved; loved for ourselves, or rather, loved in spite of ourselves."

Victor Hugo

THE COTTAGE IS FANTASTIC, WITH HUGE WINDOWS on three sides and a large wrap-around cedar deck. I peer inside the window and the space is rustic, with comfortable couches and a large flagstone fireplace. The door is open and so I knock and step inside.

"Michel?"

There's no answer so I enter and go up the stairs to the living room. In the corner of the room sits a huge Steinway piano - a monster. Concert grand. I walk over and touch a few keys. Sheets of music litter the stand - some of it old and curling - Some works by Chopin.

He walks in and stands in the doorway, watching me.

"You play?" I say.

"Yes."

"Play something for me. I played for you."

He sighs and sits at the piano.

"Play the piece that breaks your heart," I say.

He smiles, wistfully, and I sit beside him on the bench and admire his hands as he holds them above the keyboard. He starts to play and it's familiar but I can't remember the name.

"I know that," I say. "I can't remember the title."

"Nocturne in E Minor," he says. "Chopin wrote it when he was seventeen."

I listen to him play and he plays so well, with such feeling. It brings tears to my eyes for some reason and I have to bite my lip to fight them, covering my mouth with a hand.

When he finishes, he turns to me and I can't hide my tears. I don't know why I'm so sad. He inhales and runs his finger through my tears, and then slips his finger into his mouth, closing his eyes.

"I'm sorry," I say, shaking my head, wiping my cheeks. "I don't know why I'm crying. It happens sometimes, when I see certain things, pictures, hear certain songs. Must be from the brain damage."

"It's okay." He pulls me into an embrace. I let him hug me. We were lovers. My foster parents told me.

He breaks the embrace and wipes my cheeks with his fingers.

"Another bad memory?"

I shake my head, unable to speak for a moment. "No memory at all. Just sadness."

Just then, the door opens to reveal an older man with a salt-and-pepper brush cut and a pale blue button-down shirt and jeans. His face is weathered, with deep lines above his eyes, beside his nose. He has piercing blue eyes.

The man just stares at me for a moment.

"Sorry," he says to Michel. "I have bad timing."

"No," Michel says and motions to the man. "Come in and say hello to Eve."

The man hobbles over, using a cane. "I am Vasily," he says, extending his hand. "Nice to meet you, Ballerina Girl."

"Ballerina Girl?"

"Was my name for you."

"I knew you before, too?"

He nods.

"Nice to meet you." I take his hand and shake it, a smile on my face.

Vasily covers his eyes with a hand. He turns away and goes back to the kitchen and stands with his back to the room. I look at Michel.

"Did I say something?" I ask, keeping my voice down.

"Vasily's an old softie," Michel says and shakes his head, his voice quiet. "He was so worried about you because of the bombing. Play something for him. Play something Russian."

I sit at the piano and play a piece, but I don't remember how I know it.

"Rachmaninoff," Michel says. When I look up at the kitchen, Vasily stands with a tissue at his eyes.

I stop playing. "It's upsetting you."

He looks at me over the tissue, and waves a hand. "No, I am just silly old Russian who loves music. Please don't stop."

I keep playing.

"It's so strange," I say. "I don't even know what I'm playing. I have no memory of it, but my brain knows how to play it."

"Memories aren't made up of one sense," Michel says and clears his throat. "They have layers. Sight. Sound. Smell. Taste. Feel. Emotions. They get cross-referenced to other memories, other senses. You might lose one part of a memory, but not others."

Vasily leaves us alone and I get up from the piano to walk around the room, inspecting his books, the art.

Michel sits on a couch. Finally, I sit on the chair across from him.

After a pause, I take in a deep breath.

"Why me?"

He frowns. "What do you mean, why you?"

"Why did you want me? Why were we lovers?"

"Why?" He shakes his head as if the question's ridiculous and stares at his hands. "Why does a man ever want a woman?" He looks at me. "Because her smile makes his heart hurt." He looks away. "Because being with her, in her arms, inside her body, is about the only time he feels truly happy, like existence is bearable, and all the pain, sadness and disappointment is gone, even if only for a while."

His words make me so sad. "How did we meet?"

He doesn't answer at first, just sits there, shaking his head, looking at me with those way-too-intense eyes.

"We met. That's all that matters. Fate brought us together. We fell in love."

"I don't believe in Fate," I say. "There's just random and non-random events. You made decisions and I made decisions, events happened that led us to meet. That's all."

He smiles, but it's one of tolerance rather than acceptance.

"Fate parted us. Now it's put us back together and I don't ever want us to be parted again."

The sound of his voice makes my throat constrict.

"But you're a vampire… How can we be together? Don't you kill humans?"

"Eve," he says. "You loved me. That's all that matters. Forget what happened before. It's the past. It's gone. You're safe now. I've done things. I've arranged things so that you're safe. No one knows you're here but me. You can start a new life. We can start a new life."

"What was wrong with my old life?"

"You were in danger. It almost killed you."

Finally overwhelmed by it all, I hold my head in my hands. My emotions overcome me and all I know is that I want him to hold me. I want to feel his arms around me, despite the fact I barely know him. I wipe my eyes, and try to get under control. I get up and stand in front of him.

"Can I sit with you?"

He looks up at me.

"Yes." He motions to the couch beside him, but I shake my head and instead, straddle him, one knee on either side of his hips. I don't know why, but I feel such an incredible need to sit with him this way. I put my arms on his shoulders and lean my forehead against his. He exhales heavily, his breath shaky.

"I don't remember your face," I say, looking at him, at his beautiful blue eyes rimmed with thick black lashes, at his strong jaw, the black hair tucked behind his ears. "I don't remember your name." I lean in, my face beside his, my cheek touching his. "But I remember this." I squeeze my arms around his neck and he reciprocates. "My body remembers you."

I kiss him and it feels so right, it feels so familiar, as if finally, I'm where I should be.


I wake and glance around the dim bedroom. Dawn - the faint light from the open sliding glass doors to the deck slowly brightens the room. The king-size bed is covered in white cotton. I'm naked under the covers, and my body feels well-used as I remember the evening and night of tears and pleasure as we made love like first-time lovers, except our bodies felt like they fit perfectly together.

He comes back in through the open patio doors and goes to a closet. He's wearing a pair of boxer briefs and nothing else. My gaze moves over his body greedily as I remember our lovemaking, his arms wrapped around me, him kissing my face, my neck, biting me as we make love and the pleasure was so intense, I can't imagine ever giving it up.

He retrieves a men's dress shirt and comes to the side of the bed.

"Here," he says and holds it out. "Put this on and come out to the deck. You have to see something."

I comply, pulling the shirt on, buttoning it up hastily, following him out the doors and onto the deck. We're high up on the side of a cliff. A new weather system is moving into the region, storm clouds approaching off the ocean. I'll get some respite from the vivid sunlight.

He stands on the deck and looks out at the ocean. I go to the railing in front of him and take in the view. "It's beautiful."

He comes up behind me and wraps his arms around me.

"Watch," he says and points to the ocean with the other hand.

I glance in the direction of his hand and see a bank of clouds along the coast, moving towards us.

"When I bought this place," he says, his lips near my cheek, "the broker told me that sometimes, when the weather is just right, the clouds actually touch the house."

I sigh and lean back against him, my head fitting beneath his chin. I watch as the trees beside us are enveloped in thick white mist. As the cloud bank approaches the house, I hold out my arms. When it surrounds us, I close my eyes.

"I always wanted to feel the clouds," I say, a feeling of such happiness filling me, tears stinging at the corners of my eyes. He buries his face in my neck, kissing the skin beneath my ear.

"How does it feel?"

I sigh and breathe in as the mist falls on my upturned face.

"Perfect."

# EPILOGUE

That night, while Michel sleeps, I sit at his computer and check my webmail, looking for one from the university that I'm expecting about my postponing returning to school until after Christmas due to my injuries. It's then I get an email from one of my other webmail addresses. It's one I don't even remember creating. I click on it and read the message.

*Hello, Me,*

*If you're reading this, it means you haven't made an entry in your journal for two months. This is an automated reminder to keep up your journal. Remember how important you thought it would be to keep a record of everything that's happened since you met Michel.*

*You set this up just in case something happens and you forget your password or worse. You figure mom and dad will have access to your Boston U account and will find this just in case some vampire kills you.*

*You can find all the entries on what's happened since mom's files were released by clicking on the link below. It's all in a web journal and kept secure in the cloud.*

*Love, Me.*

I click on the link and start reading.

MY MOTHER NEVER LIED TO ME about the existence of monsters. When I'd awaken with nightmares, and dreams of shadows that moved in the darkness, she'd stay with me until my terror passed.

"I'm here," she'd say, stroking my hair. "I'm faster than them and I'll protect you. One day, I'll kill the monsters forever."

My great tragedy was that she couldn't protect herself.


Today, I take up the work that ended her life. The floor in my tiny one-bedroom flat is littered with her files finally released a decade after her death and after a long battle with the university archivist. As I sit sifting through the box containing her research, one file in particular draws my attention – an illuminated manuscript written eight hundred years earlier in archaic French, the script ornate, the ink faded.

Inside the file is my mother's typewritten note describing the document:

*By the hand of Julien de Cernay, former Knight, identical twin brother to Michel, former Bishop of Clarmont, bastard sons of Guillaume, Vicomte de Clarmont. Written 1224 - 1229 A.D. Interviewed on 22 December 2004 at Boston University.*

I turn back to the manuscript, but although I've studied French, I can barely read it due to the ancient dialect and difficult script. My mother began to translate but only got so far.

"*A full moon rises*" her hand-written translation starts, "*stained red from fires in the village square where five heretics burn at the stake. The Crusades broke my family, estranged me from my brother and now have killed me. I died, not on the battlefield as befitting a knight protecting my father's estate, but in a bed in an abandoned castle at the hands of an ancient vampire who bewitched me... *"

She stopped there and I realize that I need a translator for her notes were made barely a week before her death. Maybe this manuscript is important and will lead me to the vampire who killed her.

A search online turns up several websites that offer translation services, but I want one in the Boston area. I post a message on a Boston U message board for students of linguistics at my own university as a first start.

*Hello:*

*I have come into possession of an ancient illuminated manuscript and need a translator with knowledge of Old French, 13th. Century. Please respond with fees and availability to haydenea@BU.edu*

*Eve H.*

I don't expect to hear back very quickly – there isn't much activity in the forum and the last comment was months earlier in response to a question about pronunciation.

I go back to my mother's files and sort through them, separating the papers into piles. Some are historical research on the Languedoc region of France, some are more recent studies on blood-borne pathogens and retroviruses. My mother was a hematologist in addition to her work for the Council. Still others are accounts of the Inquisition in medieval France, Italy and Germany and the burning of witches. Finally, I have a pile on the Cathar Crusade in which the Cathars, a heretical Catholic sect, were persecuted in what is now southern France.

The hours pass quickly and I'm absorbed reading about the Cathars when my inbox chimes. I put down the research paper and go over to my desk, sitting on my chair and clicking on the email icon that has popped up on my screen.

It's from a Professor Cormier:

*Eve,*

*I can provide translation services. How old is the manuscript? Do you know which decade of the 13th C? What is its condition? I won't be able to provide you with an estimate of the cost until I see it and can judge the difficulty involved. I'm on sabbatical this semester and have some time. My interest in such manuscripts means I'll be willing to do this for a very reasonable rate. I'm a scholar of that era and have studied the languages of that region. I'm quite familiar with such manuscripts.*

*Yours,*

*Steve Cormier, PhD*

I text back to him, avoiding chatspeak, since he is a professor:

*Thanks Professor Cormier. According to records, written in 1224 and writer from Carcassonne. Eve*

He responds immediately:

*Very likely written in the dialect known as Old Provençal. Do you know who wrote it? S.*

*No. I think it's an old legend or something fictional. E.*

*Most surviving works are religious in nature. There are few works of fiction & most are poems or songs. Will be very interested in reading. S.*

*How do you want to do this? E.*

*You have BU email so student? Will be in office tonight. Bring it over so I can take a look. I'm in Linguistics Building on Commonwealth. Rm 304. 7:30? I have appt with colleague at 8 so it wd be gd for me. S.*

*"Sounds fine. See you then. E.*

I shut my phone off and go back to my desk. I'm so glad I posted that message. The first thing I'll do is get the manuscript translated. I hope Professor Cormier can do it quickly so I can get this whole process started and I can do what my mother failed to do before me – become a vampire hunter and eradicate vampires from the face of the earth.

~

I read for hours, each journal entry making me more and more upset. I stare at the computer screen, my mind numb. My mother was a vampire hunter? I was one as well? I wanted to kill all vampires? I hear something and turn to the bedroom door and see Michel standing there wearing only his boxer briefs.

"What are you doing up so late?" he asks. I click the email closed and turn to him.

"Nothing." I try to keep my face impassive, but I never was a good liar.

*"Eve..."* He comes to me and looks over my shoulder at the computer screen. On it is a picture of a cat with huge eyes, asking for a cheeseburger.

"Just watching funny cat videos."

He brushes the backs of his fingers against my cheek and I hear his indrawn breath.

"Oh, Eve, *no...*"

END OF BOOK TWO

ALSO BY S. E. LUND

PARANORMAL ROMANCE / URBAN FANTASY ROMANCE

THE DOMINION SERIES

Dominion: Book 1 in the Dominion Series

Ascension: Book 2 in the Dominion Series

Retribution: Book 3 in the Dominion Series

Resurrection: Book 4 in the Dominion Series

Redemption: Book 5 in the Dominion Series

**Contemporary Erotic Romance**

THE UNRESTRAINED SERIES

The Agreement: Book 1

The Commitment: Book 2

Unrestrained: Book 3

Unbreakable: Book 4

Forever After: Book 5

Everlasting: Book 6

Drake Forever: Book 7

Endless: Book 8

THE DRAKE SERIES (The Unrestrained Series from Drake's Point of View)

Drake Restrained

Drake Unwound

Drake Unbound

THE MR. BIG SERIES

Mr. Big Shot: Book 1

Mr. Big Love: Book 2

Mr. Big Daddy: Book 3

THE MCINTYRE BROTHERS SERIES

Tempt Me: Book 1

Tease Me: Book 2

Tame Me: Book 3

**Military Romance / Romantic Suspense**

THE BAD BOY SERIES

Bad Boy Saint: Book 1

Bad Boy Sinner: Book 2

Bad Boy Soldier: Book 3

Bad Boy Savior: Book 4

# ABOUT THE AUTHOR

S. E. Lund lives on the side of a mountain in the shadow of an active volcano with her family of humans and pets. Besides writing paranormal romance, urban fantasy and contemporary romance, she dreams of living in a warm climate where snow is just a word in a dictionary.

Sign up for her newsletter and get information on new releases, sales and news. She hates spam and will never share your email!

https://www.subscribepage.com/x8t1t7

www.selundauthor.com

selund2012@gmail.com